No One's Viking

No One's Viking

Megan Formanek was born and raised in Australia on the bright, and sometimes very stormy, Illawarra region. At University she studied History and after graduation worked in Law before moving abroad, first to South Korea, and later to Italy and then England. During this time, she began writing to escape the brutal Korean winters and has continued ever since. She, her partner and their son, now live in the wet tropics of Far North Queensland.

www.meganformanek.com

/meganformanekauthor

NO ONE'S VIKING

VIKING TRADING LANDS BOOK TWO

MEGAN FORMANEK

Published by Life Itinerant Publishing
Cairns, Queensland, Australia

www.meganformanek.com

A catalogue record for this
book is available from the
National Library of Australia

Paperback ISBN: 978-0-6488088-2-4
eBook ISBN: 978-0-6488088-3-1

Cover design, map design and typesetting by Dean Haynes

For Maggie and Katrina
Silent strength often speaks the loudest.

Place Names

The name given to any one place often changes with the passing of time. Just as we do in modern times, we often call a location by a different name depending on the language we speak. This was no different in the Viking Age. In the ninth century, and for a good many centuries after, spelling was inconsistent and largely phonetic. This can be problematic with accents affecting the pronunciation of place names and, thus, the way they are recorded.

Some readers will favour alternative references to those I have selected, but wherever possible, I have adopted the Old Norse designations consistent with the language spoken by the main character. Additionally, the spelling has been adapted, omitting special characters which are especially difficult to pronounce for English speakers, let alone distinguish the sound without reference to an Old Norse dictionary. Further, as more archaeological evidence emerges, and our understanding of all things Viking improves, so does it change our perception of borders and the lands these names may refer to.

Abandoned Paragon — Lyubshanskaya Fortress, Russia.

Aldeigjuborg — Staraya Ladoga, Russia.

Birka — Town on the island of Björkö, Sweden.

Austmarr — Baltic Sea.

Gardarike — Garðaríki in Old Norse, the lands of the Rus' (Rurikid dynasty) now partially in both Ukraine and Russia.

Karlstad — Town in Sweden.

Miklagard — Also know as Constantinople. Now modern day Istanbul in Turkey.

Holmgardr — Novgorod (Veliky), Russia.

Kyiv — City, now capital of Ukraine.

Serkland — Abbasid Caliphate. A land which encompassed much of the Middle East, western Asia and north-eastern Africa. The capital was Baghdad in modern day Iraq.

Svealand — Sweden

Uppsala — Uppsala region, Sweden.

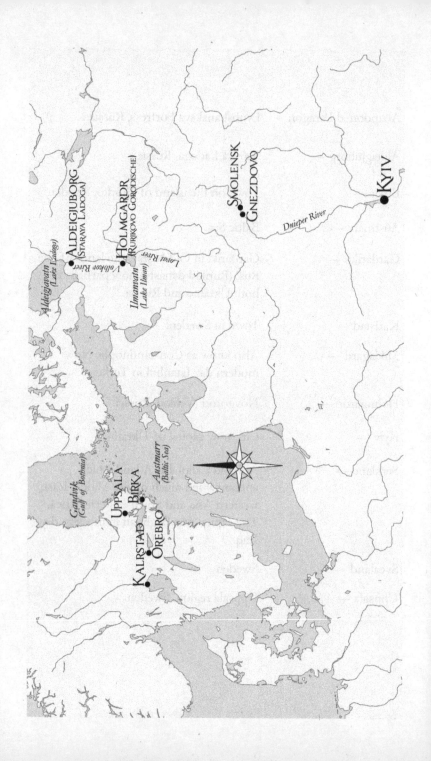

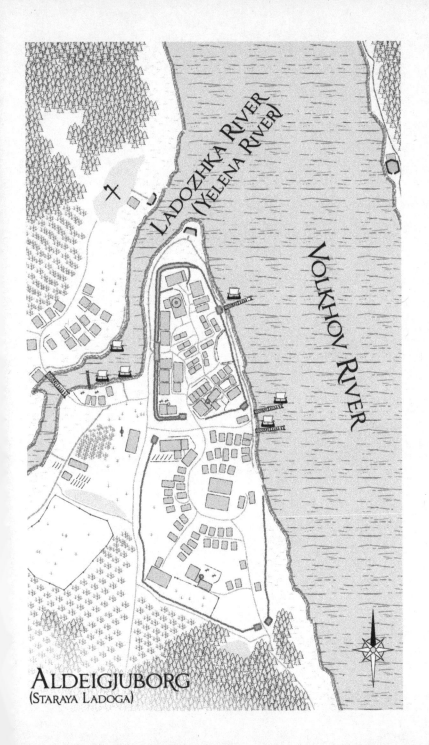

LADOZHKA RIVER
(YELENA RIVER)

VOLKHOV RIVER

ALDEIGJUBORG
(STARAYA LADOGA)

ONE

SPRING 882CE, ALDEIGJUBORG, GARDARIKE

Hands tugged at my clothing, my arm, anything they could reach. The bride's grasp was the most insistent. She pulled me into the circle's centre as women whirled around us in a ring of colourful gowns. Her face was flushed with excitement as the words of the song echoed in neat rounds. 'He will love her forever,' the singing began again as Helga held me tight and whispered in my ear.

'Will Mikel like me?' Her voice caught at the mention of the man she would marry by day's end.

The women were oblivious to her concern. The melody continued without us. 'And bring her flowers every morn and she will take him to their bed and from there, children born.'

'Mikel already loves you.' My voice strained to rise above the gaggle of voices.

The blank look on her face told me my answer had not been response enough to the question that went beyond her asking. She grabbed me by the wrist and broke the circle, dragging me away as far as the confined space would allow. The singing continued and, assured that they would not overhear us, she returned her attention to her previous question.

'Do you think Mikel will *like* me?' she intimated with the arch of her eyebrow.

The meaning was now plain and not a conversation I was keen to traverse. The so-called 'joys' of marriage were unknown to me, and I did not want to add the burden of my own poor experience to her growing concern.

'Shouldn't you discuss this with your mother?' I tried to escape the uncomfortable issue, scanning the room for Helga's mother, Hilde.

The circle was again searching for its centre. 'He found her in a river,' they began but took the hint when I shooed them away. It was not a day to be displeased over spoiled fun, so they encircled someone more willing to enjoy the merrymaking, my daughter Freyja. The infant, content with the attention, thankfully could not understand the words or the song's meaning that was sung.

'Mother has told me what to expect, but I am scared because she had nothing helpful to say about it,' Helga worried.

The poor girl. What was she to look for when those around her had little good to speak of it? I wondered why people bothered with weddings in the first place. 'I am sure Luca has instructed Mikel how to be a good husband to you.'

'And what if he hasn't?'

'Then you must tell him if he does something that displeases you,' I replied.

Unsatisfied with the answer, she proceeded. 'But you did not enjoy being married. What if it's no different for me?'

'That's unlikely. For one, you know and like your husband-to-be.'

A tug at my dress alerted me to Freyja, who pulled herself into my lap. Her tousled curls bounced around with her frantic movements. She was a pretty child, her blue eyes striking and her brown hair tumbled thick just like her mother's had. *How long would it be before someone noticed that similarity?* The thought unsettled me.

'And do not think of using my life as a stick to measure the depth of the river. I was married barely two years, unhappy as it was. Yours will be nothing like it,' I cautioned Helga.

She nodded. Perhaps there was some wisdom in my words.

'More flowers?' I offered, noticing the sprig of lilac blossoms Helga turned over in her hands.

'If you can find room for it.' She turned from me so that I might slot it into place along with the others that adorned her chestnut plaits. With the sprig in place and her hair smoothed after the raucous dancing, she was ready.

4

'The purple suits your hair and will look beautiful in the setting of the forest too. These are in bloom. I saw them just yesterday in the clearing.'

Helga stiffened at the mention of the location of the pagan ceremony.

'I am relieved that Mikel agreed our union would also receive blessing in our church, though how you managed it remains a mystery.'

'It was nothing,' I lied. It had taken many weeks to convince the priest to allow it, and the priest obviously harboured an ill-founded hope of my conversion to his faith, regardless of my insistence that I had no desire to do so. As long as the ceremony happened, the man could believe what he wanted. 'And I am glad you were able to compromise.' Though, she faced no opposition from Mikel, who was keen to give his bride her heart's desires so long as he could be married to her.

'But what will our children be?' she cried, realising that it would conflict any offspring they would have.

'Odin's beard, Helga! Are you only thinking of this now? Try not to worry about it. You will have enough time to talk to Mikel before a *barn* comes along.'

She sighed. 'It is easier for you and Kjarr. You both believe the same thing.'

I shifted. Kjarr and I had never talked about having children. We hadn't spoken at all since we were married. He left the year before on trade to return in the spring, but I had no word of him.

'I'm sorry, I know this is hard for you.' Helga drew me into her embrace. 'He will be home soon.'

'But if he does not reach the Volkhov before the snow, he will need to wait many months for it to thaw. He would have to overwinter in another city, and it could be almost another year before I see him again.' It had plagued my thoughts, and I blamed the boredom of a lengthy winter.

'I will pray that he makes it,' Helga said, clasping her hands together. 'I don't think I could bear it if Mikel was a merchant and had to go away for long periods of time.'

'We should not think about unhappiness today. Not on a day of celebration.' My voice strained with the effort of lifting Freyja onto my

5

hip as I stood. 'Time to go?' I asked Hilde, who had left her appearance until that very moment.

With an efficient nod of her head, she swept the women out of my home and into the street. The procession wove its way toward the church, Freyja bouncing in my arms with every step.

Helga puffed, though the pace was steady, 'I still don't understand how you convinced the priest to marry us.'

'Your man of God knows I have a healthy curiosity in his religion.' The memory of my rapid-fire questioning of the priest creased my mouth in a self-satisfied smirk as we passed the lines of merchant houses.

'Father Niall? He seems quite stern to me. If I ever had questions as a child, he would say, "It is not for you to ask of the Lord",' she remembered with a shudder, her hand reaching to steady the flowers topping her hair.

The holy man had an unsmiling face and encountered no humour in the world. I had talked to him many times about his religion and found he grossly overestimated his ability to bring 'heathens' into the fold.

'He finds me quite persuasive,' I explained to Helga, shifting Freyja's weight to my other hip. 'And, I would wager, your wedding contains the most heathens he has ever had under his holy roof.' My mocking tone evident, I laughed to myself. 'Likely thinks he is going to have some new converts after today.'

As we cleared the open space of the market, she laughed. 'Maybe he will.' The glint in Helga's eye told me she saw past the mockery. 'And you?' She turned to Freyja. 'Will you remain the most adorable heathen I have ever known?' It was her turn to tease now.

'I do hope so, Odin's beard!'

Helga already pined for a child, and once her marriage was completed, I realised, she might have one of her own. Freyja reached up with her pudgy infant hands and, as gently as was possible with her developing coordination, grabbed a tendril of Helga's hair. My friend never tired of my daughter, never spoke harshly, and in return, Freyja loved no one better. An involuntary smile pulled at the corner of my mouth as I thought about how much my life had altered in Aldeigjuborg. My dreams of adventure were not gone but were silently waiting while I was striding toward my current ambitions of enterprise. I found it was not only my mind that had changed, my body, too, had yielded from its hard muscles to one of more feminine softness. My heart, once guarded against love, had also softened, though that was not as visible except when attending a wedding I would have once scorned.

'Go on with you.' I laughed, gently pushing Helga towards the door. 'It's time for you to be married.'

Not wanting to ruin Helga's day with my derision of her faith, I loitered at the entrance to the church with Freyja.

Weddings had always been something for me to endure rather than enjoy. That much I had learned the first time I wed, but this was different, I reminded myself. The bride, Helga, who had been a helper of all sorts to me, had become my dearest friend. And she married for love. This day wouldn't be like my experience. This would be a day of smiles, and yet I found my lips remained a grim line as my mind pulled me back to my first marriage, where I was joined to the ageing Auden. Though I only suffered through two winters of marriage to him, it was enough to deter any further willingness. The Norns, however, had pulled at the strings that bound me to my fate. Though I resisted, I had been handfasted to Kjarr the year before in a strange union in which we shared nothing more than a chaste kiss. It had been an agreement between two friends rather than lovers. Time had kept Kjarr and I separated, during which I longed for something more against all my previous hesitations.

'She needs you,' Helga's mother Hilde whispered in my ear, jolting me from my thoughts.

With all effort, the straight line of my mouth curved upwards into a weak smile. 'Of course.'

'Your mind cannot be elsevere. She needs your strength today. She jitters around like a buzzing insect.' Her voice was heavily accented by the native tongue, but I had long since come to understand her and the dialect. Hilde always looked past what was on the outside. She spoke directly to the core of a person.

I squeezed her hand and, choosing only to respond to the supplication regarding her daughter, I responded, 'She needs you too, as she always will.'

Hilde dismissed the claim with a shake of her head, watching her daughter smooth the front of her new green dress. The colour had been difficult to achieve. Eventually, the right amount of nettle leaves and iron mordant had given us the perfect shade of soft green to complement her similarly coloured eyes and delicate features.

'She looks up to you,' Hilde whispered without a trace of jealousy. There was nothing but recognition of the relationship that had been forged. 'Are you sure you vill not come in?'

With an incline of my head, I answered, 'There are some things that I cannot do, not even for those closest to me.'

She nodded, passing me with a gentle hold on my shoulder as she disappeared into the church. For some time I stared outwards, pointing out things across the square to keep Freyja's interest, but the child was far more enthralled by the happenings inside the religious house. At a distance, I saw Father Niall blessing their union as the couple lit candles, then exchanged vows and rings made from leather. An eruption of cheers told me the matter concluded, and Helga and the Christian world considered the pair married. The couple exited the church to a flurry of exuberant onlookers who decorated the pair with sprigs and blossoms - much to Helga's delight.

Once the party had gathered outside, it was the women who led the way to the forest beyond the city walls for the rituals that would satisfy the old gods. As the couple walked behind the leaders, well-wishers yelled to them their own advice for a long marriage. Flowers, leaves and grass were tossed into the air and fell to the ground as we walked. We made our way through the town, proceeding past the Skogarmaor. Old Ivar, the tavern keeper, leaned out the door, smiling and raising a cup to the couple. Through the gates, the guards yelled bawdy comments that made the younger women blush and the older women wag their fingers as if the soldiers were naughty children. The merchants, their boats in the shallows for repair, banged tools against wood as they cheered our procession filing over the bridge. It gladdened folk to see a joyous moment when so much of the past winter seemed long, dark and dull. Through the outlying homesteads and farms, small children ran alongside, farmers waved and women sang until they lost sight of our group as it faded into the cover of the forest. The mood of the wedding party changed as the journey ended in the clearing. Those who were not of the old faith lingered at the back, their sense of unease palpable. Those who kept with the Aesir were comfortable with the solemnity of the Gothi who stood below the birch trees. The light of the day seeped in between the leafy coverage of branches overhead, giving the impression of a green cavern - the perfect place to call the gods to witness. Mikel led the unsure Helga by the hand to the middle of the gathering, focussing his gaze on his bride, bestowing on her a beaming smile.

'I call on the gods to witness and bless my marriage to Helga,' he spoke clearly amongst the canopy of trees. 'Frigg, goddess of marriage and fertility, bless us. Sif and Freyja, may you bless us with many healthy offspring.' He looked up to the sky, baring his throat. A bulge at his gullet testified he was now a grown man. He bore little resemblance to the thin and gangly child I had known on my journey to Aldeigjuborg. 'Odin, grant me the wisdom to understand my wife, who must have been created with the virtues of Balder himself,' he said with a wink in Helga's direction. 'And I ask you to bless me with the strength to provide for my wife and whatever children we may have,' he finished.

Helga would not summon the gods to witness. Her part was already done. And with Mikel asking for the blessings of the gods, there was but one thing left to do. Behind Mikel, Luca passed him a sword. Traditionally, it would have been a hereditary weapon that was handed from father to son and would be held on trust by Helga for their son to use when he grew old enough. This sword would be mostly symbolic, as neither Mikel nor Luca were warriors, though I had my suspicions that at one time Luca might have been. An auger might have been a better tool upon which to swear, as they were both carpenters, but tradition held fast. Mikel gently removed the leather ring from around Helga's finger. He placed it on the hilt of the sword and passed it back to her, making his vow to protect and provide for her throughout their marriage. Helga did not know what to do, and she looked towards me. I urged her to take the ring from the hilt and place it on her own finger. Once she had done so, the circle cheered, and everyone rushed forward to congratulate Helga and Mikel.

'I did not know what was happening.' Helga laughed when I reached her through the crowd. 'He didn't tell me anything.'

'You did well.'

'I like your traditions.' She smiled. 'It feels like a celebration.'

'You mean, more than a stiff man in a dress giving orders?'

Helga ignored the jibe.

'There is a lot more drinking in our practices,' Luca interjected with a laugh as we followed the procession up to the newlywed's home on the outside of town, close to Helga's mother's home. People gathered about her once more.

'Vell done, daughter,' Hilde said, hugging Helga, a proud smile covering her face.

'Once we go inside your house, there are a few more traditions before we leave you in peace to begin your married life,' I explained.

A becoming blush darkened her cheeks. 'The loving cup? Mikel told me something about that. Drinking from the same cup of mead during our honeymoon seems easy enough.'

I took her by the arm, and we continued on to the house. 'Earlier I stowed the food and drink inside so the guests would not have to wait.'

'And Mikel and I have been working on some furniture. I do hope you like it.' Luca beamed, joining the procession.

'This is like a dream,' Helga said with a wistful smile as the house came into view.

It was a modest abode of one room for sleeping and living. A small landing formed the entrance, and the hearth inside was large enough to keep them both warm without having to fill it with a forest full of firewood.

Mikel, who had freed himself from all the well-wishers, sprung up beside us, seizing the hand of his bride. He spun her about in a circle into his arms, giving her a non-too-innocent kiss.

Waiting for them to break for breath before speaking, I explained to Mikel that we had already set the fare up for the feast. 'After the feasting, tomorrow morning, I can come to help you clean up if you like.'

With a roguish grin echoing the delight of his bride, he answered, 'Thank you for the offer, Signe. But I think we will be too busy for visitors.'

TWO

My head pounded as I woke from a heavy sleep. Certainly, the amount of ale consumed the night before was unhelpful. But celebrations were to be enjoyed, and Helga's wedding had been an event to rouse the town from its long haze. Across the room, a gentle babble alerted me I was not the only one who had ceased my slumber and, as Freyja sat up, I greeted her.

'Good morning, my little love.' My voice was croaky and my movements unsteady as I crossed the floor. 'Seems I might be a little slow this morning,' I groaned, throwing a working dress over the thin *serkr* I had worn to bed.

'Go na, Mama,' Freyja garbled her not yet formed words up at me with a sleepy smile.

'Are you hungry?' I asked, peeling her furs away to free her stretching limbs. She rubbed her eyes and nodded.

'Come on, then.' I held my arms out to her and she climbed into them, allowing me to carry her into the hearth room, where I lowered her onto the floor and set about starting the fire.

Usually, Helga would have the hearth going and, more importantly to my grumbling stomach, breakfast by this time. That I had surfaced so long after sunrise would have met with her playful teasing and stone cold sustenance as punishment. I missed her. She was more than the help. Her cheerful face was one of the first things I saw each morning, and without her, it would be on me to take up all the tasks, unless her husband agreed she could return to her position. Even if she came back, I had no expectation that it would be anytime soon, a thought that sent ripples of vexation through me. I knew I could manage in her absence, but I also knew that I did not want to. Not because of the chores; they would always get done. The part I would miss the most was her friendship.

A fire-steel hung from the hook by the hearth. Taking it down, I struck it with the flint. A couple of attempts resulted in success.

'Aha! There we are.'

Freyja clapped joyfully as the fire took to the kindling, the first flames licking at the larger branches of dry wood. Wasting no time, I fetched the pot and scooped oats liberally to suit my hunger. The milk, I judged with a sniff as I lifted its linen covering, was still alright, and into the vessel it went.

'Some berries too?' I asked Freyja, showing her the foraged fruit that remained from the wedding celebration. 'They are a little soft, but if we put them in with the oats, then they will get jammy,' I said, dropping the dark red fruit into the pot one by one.

Freyja's delighted face erupted with giggles each time she heard the plop of them entering the pot. She looked up with her round eyes and babbled gleefully in a language that only those close to her understood. She said few proper words yet, save for "Mama", "food", "up" and a few other useful ones. I knew the rest would come soon.

'Popo mm,' she jabbered, reaching her hands out to grab the dish.

'Oh yes, I know, it's my favourite too.' I blew on a spoonful of porridge to cool it before giving it to Freyja, who spooned great globules messily into her mouth. I finished my bowl quickly and, taking advantage of Freyja being distracted with her meal, set about cleaning the dishes.

A knock at the door disturbed me from my chores. 'Who would be calling on us today?' I wondered, raising my eyebrows at Freyja, who continued licking her spoon.

'*Hej par,* Signe!' The man in the doorway grinned broadly, showing his missing front teeth. The distinct face belonged to the merchant who had brought me to Aldeigjuborg two summers ago.

'Björn.' I smiled in response. 'Good to see a familiar face. Welcome, come in.' Stepping aside as I greeted him, his eyes darted around the room, widening at the sight of Freyja.

'A child?' His gap-toothed grin shone on my daughter as she bestowed upon him one of her adorable smiles in return.

'Her name is Freyja.'

He crouched to her height and tickled the child under the chin. 'Well, hello there, little Freyja, aren't you just a darlin' little thing?' He beamed. 'Your daughter?'

I nodded.

'Ha, I thought for a moment she was Neflaug's and then, oof, I got concerned she might be mine. Ha!' He breathed a sigh of relief.

'A bit long between visits for that to be possible, no?' I asked, laughing in return.

Björn animated Freyja's stick doll, making it dance in front of her. 'You would be right. And in truth, I cannot tell a child's age rightly well.'

Björn declined my offer of refreshments and, after some friendly banter, asked after his onetime lover and my previous master, Neflaug. 'I do not know where she is.' I shrugged. I had not seen her in a year. Not since she had birthed Freyja on the kitchen table that Björn now sat at. Since then, she had vanished from town, leaving me to raise her child, which had just about forced my marriage to Kjarr. But that was knowledge I was keeping to myself.

'What caused her disappearance?' Björn asked.

Few in the town knew the truth of the matter, and I had long put anything to do with Neflaug behind me. 'Neflaug always has a way of attracting…' I hesitated.

'Adventure?' Björn offered.

It would not have been the word I chose, but it was close enough to the truth, so I nodded. 'She got herself into a whole lot of trouble and had to leave.' That was as far as I was willing to venture, but Björn was a canny creature and did not miss a breath before questioning me further.

'And abandon her business?'

That was an awkward question, and the answer was even more uncomfortable. 'Before she left, everything was transferred to me.' Neflaug had thought, at the time, that she was setting herself up to be a rich mistress without having to do any of the hard work. In the process, she had threatened and coerced her way to exclusion from the Guild, an almost outlaw with little hope of supporting herself in any reputable manner.

I steeled myself for more questioning.

'To you? What luck she had a mind to choose someone so capable. The gods smile on you,' he congratulated me.

'It has not been without trials,' I replied. Neflaug left disaster in her wake, which had fallen to me to clean up.

'And no one has heard from her since?' Björn smiled at Freyja as she showed him her doll again.

'Not a whisper.' And for that, I had been grateful. Since she left, life had been good. Not easy, it could hardly be that, but I had stopped looking over my shoulder in fear of her retribution.

'And now you have a husband and a child? I thought you had sworn off those?' He laughed, remembering our talks during our journey from Svealand to Gardarike.

'Priorities change.'

His eyes wandered about the room, taking in the changes I had made since Neflaug had departed. The room was sparser. I had little taste for finery, preferring practical items to those which only held appeal to the eye.

'Is he a fellow merchant?' Björn asked, and I was sure he was wondering how it was that I still lived in this house and had not moved into the abode of my husband.

'Come now.' I stared at him with a wry smile. 'You would already know that I have married the city's silver merchant, as you might have also known that Neflaug had not been seen for over a year. Is it not your business to know what is going on in every trading town along your route?'

He held his hands up. 'Ah! No fooling you, eh? I thought, as we are old acquaintances, you might have a morsel of knowledge more than the others. And no harm in asking.'

Björn was always a direct but very likeable man. 'No harm at all,' I agreed. 'As you know, I have married Kjarr, who is away on trade.'

He smiled knowingly. 'I saw in you an independent streak. You'll do well, I reckon.'

'And what of you, what news do you bring?'

Björn would have normally called on Neflaug, who gave him great affection when it pleased her and when it provided her with something she wanted. She had a taste for the fineries, such as furs, scents and tapestries. While she enjoyed them, she was not keen on paying with silver.

'Nothing of consequence.' He shrugged. 'Some talk of the raids, though I am more interested in what is happening further down the river here and in seeing what trade opportunities present themselves. I am rather eager on continuing onto the Dnieper River, longer away from home if you get my meaning.'

'How far do you mean to go?' I asked with quick interest.

He stroked his chin thoughtfully. 'I've been down the rapids a few times and wouldn't mind doing so again if I can make my fortune out of it. Looks like I won't be making my wealth today, not with Neflaug gone. She always loved the little trinkets.' He smiled, baring his gums, and rifled in his satchel to produce some pretty baubles.

There were some blue beads that were attractive, melted down from old Roman glass, made new again. Blue was the most difficult and expensive to come across because bead makers could not figure out a way to create the same blue hue as the ancient ones, so they did the next best thing - repurposed a worn out item for maximum gain.

'I have no use for trinkets, no matter how pretty they might be.'

'I thought you might say that.' Björn laughed, putting them away. 'But you might like some fine furs from the north. You'll find nothing as nice here.'

'The best comes from the north. This mink is divine,' I agreed, stroking the luscious pelt. It was hardy and light and, I knew, it would be the perfect combination to combat the harsh Gardarike winters. 'It would make a beautiful addition to my winter cloak.'

His hand dug around inside his satchel. 'And a little taste from home.' He set the jar on the table in front of me, and before he said any more, I could smell the strong acidic scent.

'I have been dreaming of this.' My mouth watered, anticipating the taste of the small fish. 'Freyja has never tried them. Look, you can have some soon.' I waved the pot towards her.

'Go easy on the *barn*.' Björn laughed awkwardly. 'I've not known too many children who enjoy the strong taste so early on. They have to get used to it.'

I recalled my first encounter with it as a girl. The smell was awful and just placing it on the tongue made me gag, but over time I had grown to love the pungent taste.

'I have some *lutefisk* too,' he said, pulling out a small pot of jellied fish.

'Oh, yes please,' I cried, holding the pot with reverence. 'Perhaps there is something I can give you in return for these goods? It won't be the same arrangement you had with Neflaug, but I am sure we can find something that interests you.'

He blushed deeply. 'What do you have to exchange?' There was nothing in view that would warrant a trade of the value needed, but I knew where to find something that would satisfy the merchant's needs.

I carried Freyja to the chamber that was never used, shut up since Neflaug's departure, and pushed the door open. Inside was a cavalcade of fineries, things that my previous master had collected or been gifted by her many admirers attempting to win favour.

'See anything you like?' I asked Björn, his eyes already bulging with disbelief. His gaze darted between tapestries, rugs, glassware, pottery, jewellery and clothing that were left untouched around the room.

It did not take him long to make up his mind. 'That rug there,' he said as pointed to a colourful floor covering. 'That would cover the cost of everything I brought with me today and then some.'

'Then it is yours.'

'Really?' His eyebrows arched in disbelief.

'Take it.'

He stopped, eyeing me. 'Signe, it's worth a fortune.'

'What am I going to do with it? I have no use for it.' I could have demanded a higher bargain for the carpet, but I wanted to erase any sign of Neflaug from the house.

'Well, if you are sure.'

'I am,' I agreed.

Björn stooped to measure the rug with his arm. 'I will need to return with some of my men,' he said, trying to lift it. 'I cannot shift it on my own.'

'Fine, come tomorrow,' I replied with a nod. 'And bring some more of that *lutefisk* if you have it.'

'Are you sure there is nothing more I can trade for it?'

The benefit weighed heavily on his side, and I paused to think. 'There is something more you can do. In the last year my women and I have been making ship sails. What I really need is for someone to spread the word to merchants travelling across the Austmarr and down the Volkhov that they can mend, use or purchase new sails with us.'

'You mean to establish a trade for sails?' He picked up a small jug, brightly coloured with a curving handle. 'So men don't have to repair their own? You mean you're starting a business where they might purchase or borrow for a time a sail so they may continue their journey without delay?'

'Exactly.'

'Interesting,' he mused, turning the jug in his hand. 'My crew don't have need of a sail or repair right now, but I can put the word about.'

'And one more thing, I require a trustworthy man to conduct a trade. If it works, it could be lucrative for both of us.'

He put down the jug he had been admiring. 'I'm listening.'

'We have been buying all the wool we can, but I need someone who can buy wool in bulk and bring it here. My women will sort it for its use, and we will send it along the river to various points where ships put in for repairs and purchases. It could make the merchant who facilitated it quite wealthy.'

I picked up a gold trinket from Neflaug's desk, and I placed it in Björn's hand. His eyes were glazed with far off dreams. 'My husband's wealth and connections, as well as my own, have made such a gamble possible.'

He nodded, too stunned to speak but all-in at the proposition. And when he returned the next day, it was with an armful of pots of my beloved *lutefisk* and a radiant optimism I was glad he shared. We would smooth the details of the trade out before his departure, and we parted with the promise to meet again soon.

As Björn had predicted, Freyja had no taste for the *lutefisk*, and as she spat out a mouthful, I watched with horror as it slid down the wall to fall wasted upon the floor. Some delicacies, I decided, were to be enjoyed by those who had taken their time to grow accustomed to them.

When Helga returned to work a week later, she had a glow about her of a woman who was pleased with her new husband. She studied the contents of the stew that simmered over the hearth, scarcely taking her eyes away from the pot, though I knew her mind was likely elsewhere. The smell of fat and herbs filled the room.

'How do you like your new home?' My voice was soft as I attempted to break her daydreaming.

'Very empty,' she answered.

Her tone alarmed me, and I worried that she regretted her decision to marry. It had been her mother that had broached the marriage, and I, having been convinced of the idea by the two women, had made all the arrangements.

'But you have Mikel. Surely that is all you need?' I asked.

She smiled and nodded.

It was clear at once that her tone was not regret, rather wistfulness. 'Oh, so it's more that you can do whatever you like whenever you like?' I laughed, watching her blush.

Her face turned deep scarlet. 'That's not what I meant. It's just when I was home with my mother there was much to do with the little ones.'

'Ask your younger siblings to stay with you for company,' I suggested, tickling Freyja, who sat upon the hearth room table. She rolled onto her back, swatting my hands away with laughter. 'Careful, my little love, I don't want you to fall off,' I warned, but it was too late for the warning. Still, I caught her mid roll.

Helga laughed and turned to grab two bowls from the wall shelf behind me. 'I think my mother would miss them too much. Now that my father is gone, she hates the quiet times.' She took the ladle from the pot and heaped great spoonfuls of the stew into the bowl, setting them on the table to cool outside Freyja's reach. 'It's just different. Careful, it's hot,' she warned Freyja as the girl climbed onto the bench and pawed at the dish.

I pushed it further along the table and blew on a spoonful as Freyja's mouth dribbled with anticipation of munching on a soft lump of mutton.

'Is it that you already wish for a child of your own?' I asked my friend.

Helga nodded as she took a seat opposite me. 'Of course. I want so many children. Maybe even more than my mother has borne.' She smiled, shoving a mass of stew into her mouth that dribbled down her chin, and then padded the liquid away with the corner of her apron.

'More than nine?' I baulked. Her own mother, Hilde, had a raucous bunch that kept her ever busy, and I could not imagine a willingness to aspire to so many.

'As many as my body can carry.'

Not wanting to betray my own opinions, I stared into my stew but could not help myself. 'You know, in my hometown, couples would have few babies unless they were very wealthy, and even then, it might not be the best of ideas. For one, it is hard work raising children, keeping them in food and clothing, and safe from harm and illness. And two, well, life is tough where I come from; winters were long and cold, food scarce and...' I did not dare mention that, further north, some families would leave their child in the forest rather than suffer the burden of their care. That could have been Freyja's fate. 'Just ponder on it before you rush in,' I suggested.

'Food is plenty here, and life is good to us. I will have as many children as God sends.'

'And Mikel, does he dream of such a brood?'

Helga shrugged. 'He thinks only of the marriage bed. Any suggestion of going to it makes him wild with happiness.'

I covered my eyes. 'Odin's beard! You shouldn't talk like that!'

'The good Lord knows that love between a man and his wife is never wrong. While Mikel dreams of taking me every night, I dream of the day I will be brought to childbed.' The meek and mild Helga was gone, and in her stead was a woman who was not afraid to speak her mind.

'And do you want more children, Signe?' she asked me in return. The question stunned me, and I choked on a lump of meat.

'I have never thought about it.'

Freyja smooshed a soft-cooked carrot onto the wood of the table, making a mess. I passed a square of cloth to her and motioned at the puree, but she ignored the instruction to clean up, tossing the fabric into the air with an amused giggle.

'You are a wonderful mother to Freyja.' A mischievous smile spread across Helga's face. 'When Kjarr returns, you could have more children. They would be the most beautiful offspring, with hair of gold and eyes as pretty as the river.'

'If he ever comes back.'

Helga collected the bowls and set about cleaning. 'He'll return any day now. I will pray on it if you like.'

'You need not pray. I don't think your god would bother with those you call heathen,' I teased, my hand toying with the Valkyrie pendant that hung around my neck.

'He loves all His children...' Helga began, then stopped when she caught sight of the silver token between my fingers. 'He gave you that, didn't he?' she asked, her tone more accusatory than enquiring.

'Kjarr? No, he didn't. You know that.'

'I wasn't talking about him. You know I mean Sven,' she said plainly, her gaze boring into me without reprieve.

I had thought my once best friend left behind in my memories, but seeing Björn had brought thoughts of Sven crashing back. I told myself he did not deserve space in my mind. He had erased that privilege when he tried to corner me into marriage. But I had long considered him a friend before that, and I did not find it so easy to forget him. He had been the reason I had fled my homeland and found passage to Aldeigjuborg, and still I could not bring myself to hate him.

Helga stared. 'Do you love him more than Kjarr?'

'I am not sure I have or ever will love either of them,' I lied, drumming my fingers on the edge of the table. 'And, knowing Sven, he has probably got himself killed by now, so there would be no competition.'

'But you told Kjarr you loved him.'

A billowy breath pushed from my mouth. 'Yes, you're right, I did.'

'Was that a lie?'

'Ahhh, well, it is not easy to explain.'

Helga folded her arms, annoyed with my evasiveness. 'You either love him or you don't. Love is the least complicated thing in life.'

How much Helga had to learn. Love was the most contrary, rebellious thing that was just as likely to get you killed as it was to make you happy. 'At the time I meant it, but I am not sure how I feel now.'

She walked around the table to place her arm around me. 'He has been gone for a long time. It is normal to feel differently. I am sure, when he returns, all those feelings you had when he was here before will come back.' She paused, pulling herself away to look at me. 'But you think of Sven all the time, I can tell.'

'Not all the time,' I protested, standing to remove myself from her unyielding questions. My hand went to the armring, Bjarndýr, under my dress, pushed high up on my arm. 'Of course I think of him. I cannot help that. I wonder if he is well, what trouble he is getting himself into. As much as the oaf angers me, I could not bear to think of him bloodied in some ditch somewhere.'

'You feel no sign he is in this world or the next? My mother always told me that those close to us have a sort of pull on our lives, and when they die, we can feel them leaving. Kind of like a severed tie, it pulls us towards them no longer.'

I shook my head. 'Nothing.'

'When I look for a sign, I pray to God.'

'Not helpful for me. He is not likely to answer the request of someone who does not believe in him,' I brushed off the suggestion. The church was for sheep, people who followed the Christ baby, and though I had visited and spoken with their priest, it was not a place for my worship.

Freyja crawled to the edge of the table, dangling one leg over the side precariously. 'Hep, Mama?' she asked, imploring me with her big blue eyes. I guided her to the floor, and she took two steps before falling.

'She wants to walk.' Helga smiled, watching Freyja's attempt.

'And then she will be running.'

'You can go to your gods? Ask them for a sign?' Helga suggested, still watching Freyja.

It was worth a try, and perhaps it would quieten my mind enough to get some work done. 'I can't take Freyja with me. Will you watch her?'

Helga ran to the warehouse door to bar entry to Freyja, who would no doubt want to cause some sort of chaos. 'Now? Alright, go quickly. There is a lot to do today.'

'I know,' I replied, stopping to kiss her on the cheek, and I stooped low to plant one on Freyja's smooth forehead, 'but I need to take an offering.'

Helga glared at me. 'You mean a sacrifice?'

'A duck will do.' As I quickly ran into the yard, I captured a squawking bird who was less than impressed with my clumsy groping.

Helga was still standing in the hearth room, hands on hips. 'Do you have to?'

'I do, but I promise not to waste her. I'll bring it back for dinner. You can pop it in your pot, and we shall feast on it tonight. Meat twice in one day, what a treat, bye!' I called as I tucked the honking bird under my arm, knife on my belt, and set off down the street to the forest outside the city walls.

'Shh.' The bird squirmed in my tight grasp, attempting to free herself from the crook of my arm as we walked across the bridge.

Animals felt when the weather was changing, but I wondered if they knew when they were about to be dispatched. The duck, I was certain, had sensed there was no use continuing the struggle so had ceased her jerking to lie limp in my arms.

'I will not insult you by saying everything will be alright. But know that your sacrifice is for a worthy cause.' I stroked the soft brown feathers at her neck, but she continued to lay limp as if already dead. 'Almost there.' We walked through the parting in the trees.

The answers I wanted were personal. At home, in Karlstad, I would have worshipped with others, but in Aldeigjuborg, speaking to my gods was a solitary exercise. Not only did I want to know if Sven lived, but I also wanted the gods to bring Kjarr back to me. Most of all, like the years before when I sought a *völva*, I wanted to see where my path was leading.

'I make this offering to you, Týr and Odin.' My voice quivered with uncertainty as I looked up into the sky, clamping my arm around the wriggling bird.

'Show me the answers I seek,' I willed them, kneeling on the ground. The grass was sodden beneath my knees, and I could feel the moisture seeping into the cloth of my dress, likely leaving a green stain on the fine cream fabric. As I reached for the blade attached to the thin leather belt around my waist, the duck hissed and her feet moved urgently, treading imaginary water.

'Show me the way,' I began. 'Bring me a sign of Sven. Lead him to his future and show me, does he live? Help me understand if it is possible to hold both these men in my heart or if I should release the memory of one so that I may be happy with the other.' The blade of my knife, sharp and short, split the bird's neck open with little effort. Her body convulsed with the shock of the motion as the blood spilled from the wound. 'Give me the strength to decide, bring me that which I need so desperately.' My heart was pounding in my chest.

Duck blood ran over my hands, dripping on the ground as I laid the body before me. Death pleased the gods, and without it, their attention could not be assured. Without it, I could not receive the answers I longed for. Tears ran down my cheeks, not for the killing of the animal but for the realisation that I missed him. The tears streamed and my mind was still confused about who I wept for. Kjarr, I missed for his friendly wisdom and absolute belief in my abilities, and Sven I missed for the straightforward part of our friendship; the jokes, the comfort we shared after having known each other since we were children, but it was impossible to long for one without feeling as if I had betrayed the other.

My eyes blinked, flashing images behind their darkness. There was Kjarr as I waved him goodbye when he had sailed away. Then Sven, his startled face as I hurled accusations at him after his stupid proposal. And Torfid, my aunt, her smiling face. Just as she smiled the day I returned to Karlstad after my husband's death. She pointed, but to what, I did not know. Her mouth moved, mumbling, and it took me a moment to understand. 'He is coming,' she whispered, looking straight into my eyes. 'He is coming for you.' Then, I saw ships. Great, tall ships with their sails whipping in the wind. Torfid's voice called out again as the picture faded, 'He is coming for you.' Her tone sounded as if the intention was to be reassuring, but the portend unsettled me.

Still kneeling on the ground, a desperate feeling of impending danger overcame me. I cast a glance behind me. No one. I scanned the trees. There was nothing. Scooping up the limp bird, I scurried back to the house, all the time feeling a dark shadow following me, but every time I turned around, there was nothing there. The eeriness followed me through the streets of the city. The abundance of people did nothing to quell my unease. As I stood before my house, I felt the shadow rush to stand behind me, but as I turned, there was nil but other houses and passing city dwellers.

Calm yourself.

Inside my house was a peaceful picture of happiness. Helga and Freyja played on the floor. I watched for a moment, not wanting to interrupt their time together.

'Mama,' Freyja said as she caught my eye and smiled as I hid the dead duck behind my back.

Helga was sitting on the floor, cross-legged with Freyja's doll in hand. 'It seems you can still play like a child, Helga.' I smiled at her.

She stood, dusting off her apron. 'I've not lost the skill. It helps that I have so many brothers and sisters.' Her eyes darted over me. 'Perhaps you should change your clothes before Freyja sees that blood. I will need to get that stain out.' The blood marked the hem of my sleeve.

'She has to learn of her roots at some point, but I do not want to ruin another dress.' Blood was difficult to remove from clothing. I had learned that much from the night of Freyja's birth. 'Hot water first, then soak it in cold.'

'Did your gods give you answers?' Helga asked as I slipped out of my overdress, taking the duck and placing it out of Freyja's sight.

'It was very odd, Helga. My aunt came to me. "He is coming," she said.'

'Who?' Helga asked, wide-eyed.

'She did not say. Perhaps it was a warning of something darker.'

'Did she show you anything else?'

'Sails, on ships. Sails in the wind,' I muttered.

Her eyes lit up. 'Maybe your gods foretell that your endeavours will be successful?'

Nodding, I wanted to believe that Helga was right. 'On the way home, I felt like someone or something was following me.'

She sat at the table. 'Did you see anyone?'

I shook my head.

'Could it be Neflaug?'

I shrugged, sitting on the bench seat and placing Freyja atop the table. 'I don't know. I am not sure if it was a person or…. This sounds strange but… I felt as though a black cloud was pursuing me.' A shiver ran down my spine.

'It's because you killed the bird,' she teased, covering Freyja's ears.

'No. I did everything my father did when he made a *blót*. When I dispatched the duck, I had a feeling that someone close to me would suffer a terrible tragedy.'

'Us women have feelings when something happens to our kin. Like we are all connected to each other in a way the men are not. Perhaps what you felt was real. Maybe something has happened, and when you asked the gods for a sign, they showed you,' she said, coming close to hold my hand.

'But I have no kin, except for my aunt, but I don't know if she still lives. She is quite old.'

'You may have felt her death.'

It made me sad to think of my aunt Torfid dying without her family to issue her the appropriate send-off. She was well liked in the Karlstad community, so she would not have died alone. I closed my eyes to recite the *bøn* just in case what Helga had suggested had come to pass. 'They bid you to take your place among them in the hallowed halls of Valhalla, where the brave shall live forever.' Then I wondered if saying the words would bring death if it had not yet happened. I shook my head.

'What was that?' Helga stared, eyes wide as I opened my own.

'It is like those prayers you say in your church. We say something to our dead when they leave this world for the next, but we would say it in their presence.'

She laid a comforting hand upon my arm. 'And I am sure it will work even if you are not there for her. If no harm has come to her, then saying a prayer will only do good. Let's hope your aunt was right and that Kjarr is on his way home to you now.'

'Mm-hmm,' I agreed. Whoever was coming for me, I hoped it would be a welcomed reunion.

THREE

As someone who railed against what others decided for me, I found myself ill at ease supplicating myself to the gods. Waiting for an answer felt like relinquishing my fate and, while certain elements remained outside my control, I wrested command of my thoughts. Though, that too proved difficult. After months of waiting, "he", who was meant to come, was yet to arrive. I began to think that the words my aunt had spoken were nothing more than nonsense, and the disquiet that plagued me since my offering did nothing to soothe my concern.

'Will you know when your gods send you a sign?' Helga asked. Every day she would remind me to be alert for a cue.

I picked up wisps of wool and twisted them together to make a strand, before attaching them to the hook of my spindle. 'You will be the first to know.' The spinning whorl gave me the chance to shoot Helga an amused glance. 'You'll likely be standing right next to me and perceive the answer before I do.'

'Because I am always with you?' Helga sat on the floor, pulling tufts of carded wool with Freyja. The two of them were laughing at the cloud-like appearance as it fell.

'Stuck like stubborn mud,' I agreed, returning to spinning my drop spindle. 'Will you have dinner with your mother tonight or will you go home?'

'Mikel is expecting me home, and my brother is coming for dinner. It seems that Mikel and Stanislaus have become friends,' she replied, tickling Freyja with a puff of wool. 'If you wouldn't mind, could I take Freyja with me tonight?'

'Would it bother Mikel?' I asked, sensing it was for Helga's own enjoyment. Mikel would be busy drinking and playing games with her brother.

She shook her head fervently. 'I don't think he would even notice.'

'Is everything alright, Helga?'

'Oh yes, well, no.' She slumped her shoulders.

'Are you already with child?' I guessed.

'Praise God I would be, but no. Mikel cautions me to wait until he has earned enough money to provide. He makes certain that a child cannot happen by chance.'

'Oh, I see.' Mikel had always struck me as rather pragmatic.

She sulked for a moment before shaking it off. 'I will have to content myself with your beautiful daughter until the Lord brings me my own.' She returned to their game, bundling up handfuls of thin wool and piling it upon Freyja's crown. 'Freyja White-Mane,' Helga announced.

I followed the jest, grabbing the tendrils and making them cling to my face. 'Look, a beard!'

Freyja was unsure whether to laugh or cry at my new appearance.

'Oh dear! Freyja, it's only pretend,' I calmed her, removing the fake facial hair. 'She can go with you, but will you bring her back in the morning?'

Helga barely waited for another word, springing to her feet and pulling Freyja into her arms. 'And I will make breakfast too,' she replied.

The sun had just passed its peak when I looked out the warehouse door. 'You will need to leave soon. I don't like the idea of you crossing the bridge in the dark. It's not safe.'

'I would never hurt her.'

'I know.' I squeezed them both. 'It is not you I worry about, but folks who wish to cause harm.'

'I'll be careful,' Helga promised. She wrapped her cloak around both of them and tucked Freyja's doll into the pocket of her apron. 'Say bye-bye to Mama.' Freyja flapped her hand at me in farewell. 'Are you sure you will be alright on your own? I know you are not fond of your meetings with Eryk.'

My relationship with my previous mentor Eryk, who was also Master of the Merchant Guild, had become frosty since Neflaug's departure. I had spent the first months avoiding him under the guise of being a new mother and a successful merchant. But Eryk was the most powerful man in town and continuing to cut myself off from his influence only did harm.

27

'Everything will be fine. Go.' I said my farewells to Helga and my daughter and watched them skip down the path until they were out of view.

My manner had never alluded to my knowledge of his adulterous relationship with Neflaug. If he suspected Freyja was Neflaug's child, let alone his own, Eryk had done nothing to show it.

'A fine child you have created,' he complimented me, not for the first time, when I had greeted him at the Skogarmaor that evening. 'She is a credit to you, Little Bird.'

The pet name still made my skin crawl. 'Do you have to call me that?'

He always acted like it was the first occasion I took issue with it. 'What?' The look of feigned shock wasn't fooling anyone.

'Little Bird.'

'You don't like it?' He gulped from his cup, licking the foam from his top lip, but more remained on his beard.

'I prefer the name my mother gave me, though I did not like her much either.'

He shrugged as if the request meant nothing to him, though I could see it wounded his masculine pride. 'As you wish, Signe.' That was not the name my mother gave me either, but he was near enough. I reserved the use of Astrid, my real name, for the only one who knew it - Kjarr. The tavern always reminded me of him.

At a round table next to me was a group of men playing Hnefatafl. There were two groups of players. The attackers, whose job it was to kill the king in the centre of the board, and the defenders, whose aim was to stop them. The defenders bellowed, attempting to distract the other side with their taunts. It reminded me of watching my father play the game with his friends. "Don't play Hnefatafl," my father would warn me in jest. "It only leads to drunkenness, a feeling of ineptitude and arguments amongst friends." He was right. The men were growing frustrated with each other's strategies. *Best to play a game requiring so much thinking when sober*, I thought.

'Want to play a round?' Eryk proposed, noting my interest in the game next to us.

'No. Our meeting is for Guild business. Do I presume you have granted my application to have Helga's apprenticeship transferred to me?' I asked with unflinching eye contact.

His belly pressed against the table, shuddering as he nodded, shaking our drinks. 'I see no obstacle to your proposal. As Neflaug remains barred from the Guild, Helga cannot continue to apprentice under her.'

'So you will acknowledge her preceding apprenticeship years?'

His hand tapped the table. 'Between the earlier owner of the business and yourself, she has served the relevant time and is now considered a journeywoman.'

'I am pleased you approve.' I took a sip of my ale to mask my relief.

'You are building quite an empire of women over there.' He raised his cup to me, '*Skal*.'

'*Skal*.' I drank in reply. 'But I assure you, it was unplanned.'

'Hmm,' he mumbled. 'And I saw you had erected some large frames in your yard. Would you be branching into seagoing fabrics?'

'Possibly. We have not decided if it is wise to venture into new territories,' I replied, not wanting to give away much before the deals were done.

His head bobbed around in neither a nod nor a disagreeable shake. 'What would your husband say?'

'He isn't here, is he?' Eryk's gaze felt penetrating. 'You disapprove?' I asked.

'I did not say that. Merely wondered what Kjarr would make of his wife spending all his money before he had the chance to do so himself.' He wiped his mouth with his sleeve and belched. 'If you follow the rules, what you do with your business is up to you. You have pained yourself to build an excellent reputation. You should not throw that away.'

The warning was something I had long pondered. 'I do not intend to do that. Whatever move I make will be a considered one.'

He pressed his lips into a tight smile as his eyes fixed on something behind me. The colour in his face drained his ruddy cheeks white. 'The woman over there, no don't turn!' he scolded as I glanced over my shoulder. 'Is that Neflaug?'

The quick glimpse I managed left me in no doubt. 'I believe so.'

'*Haza sayii*,' he grumbled.

'Hardly "bad luck". Her time of exclusion is almost expired. Closer to *mutawaqqa*.'

He chuckled, delighted. 'I see you have kept up with your Arabic.'

'It hasn't proved to be useful to me so far, but you never know.' Local dialects had been far more helpful, but those I learned by exposure, not by lesson.

'You are right. We should have expected her to come back.' His tone was reproachful, though his eyes consumed his previous lover. 'There was no whisper of her return.'

They had excluded Neflaug from the Merchant Guild for a year as punishment for threatening the lives of other members when she had become drunk and deranged. Kjarr and I had been the recipients of her death threats, and Eryk had harshly sentenced Neflaug in what I suspected was a convenient cure for his erstwhile mistress.

'Nothing,' I agreed, wondering why I bothered with a reply. His interest was elsewhere.

He surprised me by flicking me a glance. His face seemed younger, full of hope, and I let out an exasperated sigh. *Lustful, as always.* He stroked his cheek thoughtfully, his eyes appraising the woman behind me.

I shifted my chair to the other side of the table, next to Eryk. If Neflaug was going to approach us, I wanted to see her coming.

Eryk leaned towards me, his voice rancorous. 'What mischief does she brew now? And unburdened by a child. Pah! The lies this woman spun. I can see no bawling infant hanging off her. Perhaps she could borrow your little girl to make the story more convincing.'

I eyed him. *Did he believe his own lies?*

Even now, with her tousled hair and wearing only a simple dress, Neflaug was easily one of the most beautiful women I had ever seen. The grace with which she moved belied a tavern wench. It was a bearing that came with complete self-assurance. Eryk's stare held fast to Neflaug's body. When she noticed, she tossed her hair and sauntered between tables in full possession of the physical attributes that, in part, had lured Eryk into their tryst.

'Such a wicked woman,' he seethed, tearing away from the sight of her.

'Our meeting is now concluded, I trust?' I spoke, seizing my chance.

He nodded. Without so much as a farewell, he rose and departed at speed. He paused before the exit, glancing back as Neflaug flicked him one of her seductive looks across the hall. In a huff, Eryk began walking, without looking, straight into the door frame. Embarrassed, he brushed it off and disappeared into the night as I laughed into the dregs of my cup.

Neflaug had entertained herself, but I saw then she had not lost her charm. She could still beguile a man, even one who hated her. All it took was one look across a room overflowing with distractions.

FOUR

Most mornings as the sun rose, Freyja and I would walk outside the walls of Aldeigjuborg. With my daughter strapped to my back with a wide length of cloth, she would settle. No doubt being so close to me, and the rhythm of my stride, soothed her during her fussy periods.

Sometimes we walked south, through farmlands and outlying houses. The mornings were busy there with families in the field, tilling, planting and harvesting, depending on the season. The pens of livestock were a particular favourite for the children, though its proximity to the midden pit made it one I detested. It was possible to wander through fields for a mile or so before reaching the most southern landmark deemed safe - the spring well. Venturing further was ill advised, only the outlaws and marauders inhabited the forests beyond it.

But today our amble took us north from the Enggatt, the meadow gate, past the farms and houses that were just as common in one direction as the other. The shipyard was not yet busy with repairs. A single vessel lay beached. Often Freyja bawled as we approached, the clang of metal hitting metal and the thud of heavy wood an assault to her ears.

It was the shipyard that inspired my recent venture into sail manufacturing. Merchants had complained over being unable to purchase a new sail along the river and barely being able to find someone to offer repair. It was this gap in service that led to easy access to those in need, and I found no lack of willing participants to test them until we perfected our methods.

More houses and farms followed the shipyard. Further north was a densely forested area that, aside from my private worship of the gods, we mostly avoided. Our favourite location was the practice yard, at the meeting point of the Volkhov and its tributary, the Ladozhka. Here the town's guard would practice their arms. Sword fighting, lance, axe work and archery were drilled on the daily. Freyja never tired of the spectacle and neither did I. Curiously, Freyja never flinched at the clashing metal swords as she did with the iron tools of the shipyard. It seemed some proclivities could be inherited by those who did not share the same blood.

Across the river, overlooking the expanse of the Volkhov, was a tower manned by at least two archers on regular rotation. They saw until the river bent from view in both directions. It wouldn't be possible to pass without someone noticing. Come winter, the water froze completely, making travel by water impossible until the thaw. Then you would have to overwinter wherever you found yourself or brave the journey by horse or sleigh in the snow.

I exhaled sharply. If Kjarr was delayed, he would be far from home again and I might not have word from him for another year.

'Mama,' Freyja cooed from behind me, a gentle hand resting on my cheek.

'I'm alright, just missing your father,' I replied, leaning my face against her soft palm. 'Shall we see who is fighting? What do you think, will it be spears today? Or arrows?' A good fight would have shaken the worries from my head, but I would have to content myself with spectating instead of participating with Freyja in tow.

As we approached the yard, I could see a group of men already gathered. 'Looks like it's arrows,' I mumbled to my daughter. I preferred to watch hand-to-hand fighting. Archery was not as exciting.

Three broad-shouldered men lined up before a row of targets, nocking an arrow and drawing the bowstring. It took great strength to be an archer and years of practice to develop the muscles required to operate the weapon. One after the other, they loosed their arrows, each finding the centre of the target.

'Oooh,' Freyja giggled, impressed by their accuracy.

Again and again they practised, each time the shot becoming more difficult. We stayed to watch until they attached the marks to moving targets. Better to remove Freyja for a nap before she became distressed by the sight.

'Let's get back, little one.'

As we retraced our footsteps home, I watched the water. Any movement on its surface caught my attention, always looking for a sign that Kjarr was on his way to us. Or, at the very least, a ship coming into port that might bring news of my husband's arrival. But today there was none. The chill on the wind whispered that the weather was turning and, in a few weeks, the cold would turn to snow.

'Are you excited to see father when he returns?' I asked Freyja, whose weight had grown suspiciously heavy. 'Are you asleep?'

She didn't answer.

'How could you miss him? You never met him.' She had been mere days old when he departed on trade. 'I can barely remember what he looks like.' My mind clung to the few details I could recall; his smiling face, his fireside wisdom, but lost to me was his smell and voice.

As I neared the Enggatt, the young guard on duty greeted me with a smile. 'You should be careful walking where you can't be seen, Signe,' he cautioned.

'You should have warned me before I left the wall's protection, Laslo.' I laughed carelessly, stopping to talk with him.

He was tall, taller than most men, and lanky. This made his cream tunic appear oversized and ill-fitting as it hung on his stretched frame, falling beneath his knees. 'It's not safe out there.'

I felt Freyja stir behind me. Laslo was one of her favourite people. She never missed the chance to revel in his attention.

'But I feel so protected with you watching us from here.'

His cheeks flushed under his domed helmet.

Folk came and went by the gates, even this one, used only by the locals which Laslo guarded until midday. He knew us by sight even when we were just a speck in the distance. Though he was young, he stood with his hand upon the hilt of his sword, his hood pulled over his head beneath his helmet and his cloak over his left shoulder.

'There's a chill on the wind,' he complained, drawing his cloak closer against his body.

'I feel it too. This winter will be a brutal one.'

'I'd believe it. By the gods, I hope your husband returns soon. Any word?'

I shook my head and stepped through the gate. 'There is still time to hope,' I replied, proceeding through the gate. 'I still have hope.'

With summer's passing, the stink of the city would subside. The warmer months brought with it merchants, livestock sales and odorous crowds. The winter would shake them from our streets, leaving only the residents to overwinter.

Freyja smacked her lips loudly.

'Are you hungry, my little love?'

I felt her nod against my back.

The rest of our route home was short, rounding the wooden fortifications of the town.

'Here we are. What is that?' I stooped to collect the small barge made from sticks resting beneath the door frame.

'Finally.' Helga opened the door. 'What is that?' she asked. 'It wasn't here when I came in this morning.'

I held the vessel before her so we could both examine it. 'A child's toy? Do you think someone left it here by accident?'

She glanced down and back up again, excitement lighting her eyes. 'Is it a sign that Kjarr might return soon? Aren't these the vessels they use for short distances?'

'No, it's far too simple.' We went inside. I stopped to tap the dirt from my shoes and remove my cloak.

'You asked for a sign and now you have it. Are you still looking for more?'

'I'm not sure.' I passed the barge to Freyja, who was delighted at the present.

Helga patted me on the shoulder. 'He will come.' Her hands met her hips and her expression changed. 'I have some news for you.' Her spoon waved about, conjuring the information.

My stomach rumbled. 'Do I have time for some breakfast?'

Helga slopped the morning meal into bowls, plonking them down on the table before me and sliding one leg at a time over the bench. She leaned forward, her eyes wide with excitement. 'It's a scandal!' Her voice was shrill.

'I hope it is nothing about me?'

'No, of course it's not you. No one has dared to wag a tongue in your direction since you're buying up all the wool. They think you are some angelic being dedicated to good business.' She stifled a laugh.

'Thor and his bloody hammer, could you imagine? Me? An angel? Alright, if it's not me, who is it about?'

'It's Neflaug,' she whispered.

'Neflaug?'

'Shh.'

'There is no one here. Why are you whispering?' I asked, shaking my head.

She looked at Freyja. 'Don't say her name in front of the *barn*.'

'Freyja doesn't understand.'

'One day she will.'

Helga was right, one day Freyja might hear what happened. She might discover she was not a child of my blood or body, but that day wasn't today. 'What has *she* done now?' I asked.

'I'm not sure I can say it here.' Helga glanced down at Freyja. But the child was enrapt in her new toy, plonking it into a tub of dirty wool-wash water on the floor and watching it bob around.

I shovelled a spoonful of porridge into my mouth. 'Surely it's not that bad?'

'That woman is not just working as a serving maid at the tavern,' Helga replied, speaking low.

'Mmm-hmm, and?' I answered with a mouthful.

'She is offering *other services,*' Helga intimated, covering Freyja's ears with her hands. It didn't last long. Freyja wriggled free and crawled to the corner of the room, where she had poked some rocks in a crevice in the wall.

'Taking men to bed for money, you mean?'

'It's true.' She nodded.

'How can you be sure? Have you seen this for yourself?' Not one for rumours, I wanted the truth, and Helga's suspicions wouldn't suffice.

'Err, no. In truth, I have not seen it for myself, but I swear that is what I was told,' she confessed.

'Helga, what Neflaug does is none of our business. If what you say is true, it's not for us to judge her or her reasons. I trust you and I trust you believe what you say is true. But we shall not spread vicious rumours nor repeat a word of this with no evidence. Do you swear it?'

'I wanted you to know what was said about her.'

'And now I do, and we do not want to risk bringing Neflaug's wrath upon us. So you must swear.'

Helga cowed her head. 'I swear.' It was a whisper.

'You swear it?' I repeated.

She looked up. 'I swear.'

A moment passed between us. Helga seemed deep in thought, and I wondered what Neflaug was doing back in Aldeigjuborg. She could have gone anywhere, far away, where she could have begun a new life. But I knew Neflaug, and she was not content with the ordinary. She always wanted more. She craved power. I saw the way she tempted Eryk at the tavern. A man with his guard and his trousers down was the best means of getting information.

'I would wager she has set her sights on readmittance to the Guild. She may attempt to take the business back.' Neflaug was a cunning woman.

'She wouldn't,' Helga cried.

'You didn't see how she looked at Eryk. If he backed her application, there could be no opposition. From there, she need only assert her legal rights to the Lawspeaker and she could be reinstated. I don't know who would win.'

'Signe, she gave away her own child.'

'Helga, I asked you never to speak of that! Imagine what would happen if someone discovered what really happened. They may never trust me again.' I did not know if people would care about Freyja's parentage, but I knew they would care that I had lied about my identity.

It had been an innocent mistake at first, being mistaken for Signe when I, Astrid, had escaped Birka. And I had not tried to right the wrong since my arrival. What I was sure of, however, was that if Neflaug discovered my secret, she would somehow weave a web of distrust against me that one lie inevitably led to another and would paint me as a crook. No, a stolen identity, pretend marriage and a child not born of my body were a mix I was not willing to expose. I held my breath, the pressure of the lies smothering the air inside me.

'Do you think her mad?' Helga asked.

'I don't know,' I lied, knowing very well that some sickness blackened Neflaug's mind. I had seen it for myself. She was cheerful and generous, and then there were the times that darkness grew within her to make her destructive. It was as if she could not control those parts of herself. 'Even if she is doing what you say, we do not need to acknowledge her.'

'What if she comes for the baby?'

It was best to ignore someone like Neflaug. To spread rumour, talk about her, was to add fuel to a dangerous and unpredictable flame. 'She won't,' I replied, trying to sound sure, though the dread that possessed me for months continued to beat ominously in my chest.

FIVE

'My mama never taught me how to make this. What did you say it was?' Helga asked, heaping the blanched nettle leaves and wild dill from the pot with a large slotted spoon. The boiling water dripped onto the floor.

'*Kokte örtbullar.*' I looked up from my bowl, wrists sore from kneading the dough.

'I've never eaten it before.' She sat down at the table, chopping the herbaceous mess on the board.

'My mother used to make these when I was a girl.' If there was anything I enjoyed about my mother, it was her cooking.

Since Helga returned, she had adopted the dress of a married woman. Her coiled braids were covered with a white scarf, held in place by a headband embroidered in red, white, and green thread. A snaking line design of her own fashion. Her clothing made her appear older, but her inquisitive face reminded me of the girl she still was.

'Why are you trying to make it now?' she asked.

'Freyja and I were walking through the forest yesterday and I found some wild dill. My mother always used dill and nettle in the stuffing of the buns and, when I smelled the herbs, I had a sudden craving for it. If I can remember how to make it,' I explained, adding some chopped nuts and soft buttermilk cheese to the herbs.

'Can you show me what to do?'

Balls of dough sat on the board. I took one and flattened it to a disc. 'Place a spoonful of the filling in the middle. Then roll the dough back together, but make sure none of it pokes out.'

Her first attempt resulted in a mess, the mixture seeping out of the bun and into her hand. 'I think I used too much.'

'Try again,' I replied encouragingly.

It had been years since I made the dish, but I was able to form the balls without trouble. Wet hands were the trick to avoid the dough sticking. Helga continued to struggle, overstuffing the bun.

'Is your mother proud of your admittance to the Guild?' I asked.

'It shocked Mama when I told her I was your journeywoman,' she replied. This time she could close the dough around the stuffing without it bursting apart.

'Well done. And Mikel? Is he also proud?'

'He wouldn't say it, but I think he is.' Helga placed the last bun on the pile between us, and I covered them with a damp cloth. 'Mama should be here soon with the girls. How should I cook them?'

I stood, removed my apron and hung it on the peg, stifling a laugh. 'Odin's beard, Helga! I don't think you should cook them at all, not when we have these delicious buns to eat. For one, I don't think they would fit in the pot, and secondly…'

'Very funny.' She shook her head, her hair bouncing underneath her headscarf. 'The buns. How should I cook the buns?'

I smoothed out my dress, my favourite light blue but well-worn garment. 'Steam over the stew while I am gone. We will eat when I have returned from my meeting with Eryk. We can dip them in the stew. You will love them.'

'So you don't think you'll be long?' She stood to open the door, hearing the soft voices of the two children.

'I would hope not. But don't wait for me if they are hungry. Go ahead and eat.'

She nodded, opening the door. 'Mama.' She hugged her mother, helping her with a basket covered with a heavy cloth.

'Oh, Hilde, I am just about to leave.' I relieved her of Freyja. 'Hello, my little love.' The kiss I planted on my daughter's rosy cheeks chilled my lips. 'It must be cold outside.'

'Best you be taking your thick cloak,' Hilde ordered.

Following directions, I ran to fetch my fur-trimmed cloak, returning to the hearth room where Hilde had a basket full of woad. 'Why did you bring that?'

'Finally, some luck.' She smiled, handing me two pieces of wool dyed the colour of the summer sky.

'How did you manage it?' I marvelled at the even colour.

From the basket at the door, Hilde gathered the limbs of the woad plant, yellow flowers at its tips. 'I just take the voad leaves like so,' she began demonstrating her hold on the plant, 'remove all the voody bits. They don't give us any colour and are no good except for the garden.' Hilde discarded the stems of the leaves, tossing them into the basket. 'Next, boil it in vater and let it stand for a vhile. Once it cools, squeeze the leaves to take out all the colour and strain the dye through a fine gauze. Ve don't vant any nasty bits. Then ve put the ash in and mix until the foam on top goes blue.' She stopped to take a breath. 'Finally, ve take a square of silk as a filter.'

'Silk?' I exclaimed. The fabric was expensive, and it was better worn on the body of someone paying an exorbitant fee.

'There is nothing better for the job. The fine veave of the silk makes sure only the best strongest dye remains,' she explained. 'Once ve have strained the dye, the stuff that remains on the top of the silk needs to dry, and then ve can use it.'

'Amazing.'

'It helps if ve are using fibres from a vhite beast. The coloured ones are too hard to mask.'

That would not be difficult. We had good connections with local farmers who could provide us with excellent white wool from their flocks. And, I hoped, Björn would source even more.

'You should be proud of yourself, Hilde.'

She smiled. 'I enjoy the vork.' There was a lightness about her I had not seen since her husband had died.

'Your husband would be proud of you too.'

'I'm not sure vhat Andrei vould have thought about all this. He vas a believer in hard vork, and to him, maybe this vould have seemed too uncertain.' She laughed.

Nodding, Helga added, 'Papa needed to know what was going to happen before he tried. But, Signe, we are keeping you from your meeting.'

I stooped low to kiss Freyja goodbye. 'I'd rather stay here with you all, but Eryk promised me an introduction to a spice merchant.'

'A spice merchant?' Helga raised an eyebrow.

'It is possible that he knows someone who trades in powdered dyes.'

She shrugged. 'Let's hope so.'

41

'Before I go, I have some good news to share. We had some success with the sails. Elin has perfected the *priskept* weave, two over and under two threads. It's the strongest we have managed, and I've had good feedback. So, we have a product of extraordinary strength.'

Helga clapped. 'That's such good news.'

'Who knows, perhaps Sigtryggr will have connections that will help us with our sail sales too.' I draped my cloak around my shoulders, steeling myself for the frigid evening air. 'And don't overcook those buns or they'll bounce around the house.'

I walked the short distance to the Skogarmaor, annoyed that I was likely to see Neflaug again that night. There was nowhere better to do her sort of trade. But the real, ever present threat of Neflaug noticing me remained. Eryk had insisted we meet at the tavern. A mere woman would not frighten him, and besides, everyone did their business at the Skogarmaor.

Inside was dark, lit only by the fire, causing raucous shadows to dance along the walls.

I saw her immediately, wearing a new, well-made garment of forest green. *She was back in bed with power.* Walking through the crowd, Neflaug on the far wall, I was careful not to look in her direction. There would be no eye contact, no words exchanged where I could help it. She sauntered around refilling drinks. Up one man's arm she brushed her hand, at another she fluttered her dark eyelashes. Her green eyes flashing their *come hither* look.

The tavern was busy, flush with the last pulse of trade before travelling merchants and itinerant craftsmen departed for other cities. Very few would overwinter in Aldeigjuborg. And tonight Eryk had a constant stream of meetings, of which I was the last.

He was easy to find. Seated at his usual spot in the back, adorned in his finest red cloak and cap, both embroidered with dark blue thread in the local style.

He hovered above his chair as I approached. 'Signe.' He dipped his head.

'Eryk.' I returned the gesture before sitting.

The plate before him was empty, the remnants of which remained in his beard. Next to my one-time mentor was a handsome lank of a man who he nodded to, not bothering to lift his eyes again. 'Signe, Sigtryggr. Sigtryggr, Signe,' Eryk offered as introduction.

Sigtryggr grasped my arm in greeting, his cape over his right arm showing his preference for the use of his left. 'Call me Sihtric.' He smiled, his voice broad and rolling.

'Not Sigtryggr?'

He shook his head as he glanced at Eryk, who was sitting bolt upright with bloodshot eyes. 'Sigtryggr is what my pa named me, but I prefer Sihtric as my ma called me.' He patted Eryk on the back. 'Seems the Guild Master has had more drink than meetings and has found himself witless.'

'Are you alright, Eryk?'

He shook me off. 'Fine, fine. Quite fine! Ah, will you look at that!' he squealed, pointing across the room.

Two men who were in the midst of a disagreement had come to blows. The larger man hit the smaller squarely across the head with a tankard. The crowd broke apart for the action but were disappointed as both men were ejected from the tavern, and once in the bitter night air, their conflict cooled.

'That was a good one.' Eryk laughed as he slurred his words into an incoherent tangle of noises. He rocked in his seat, his body swaying to music that was not playing.

'Perhaps you might wannae go home to your wife, Eryk?' Sihtric suggested.

The Guild Master swatted him away like a fly. 'Never you mind about that. No need, no need.' He was sober in an instant as he locked eyes with Neflaug, who, without so much as a shred of embarrassment, lifted her skirt to expose the outer part of her thigh as she fiddled with her shoe.

Eryk licked his lips. 'Err. You will have to excuse me, Signe, Sigtryggr. I have just seen someone I need to speak with,' he murmured, not caring to see if I heard him or not. He crossed the tavern in two strides, taking her arm and dragging her from the dimly lit hall.

I shook my head. *How could they rehash old ground after everything that had passed between them?* Disgusted though I might be at Eryk's behaviour or Neflaug's attention seeking, I had business to attend to.

'I hope Eryk told you why I requested this meeting?' I asked, turning my attention back to Sihtric.

He nodded. 'I cannae say how much use I'll be to you. As you ken, I trade in spices, not dyes.'

'What are dyes if not ground up things, just as spices are?'

Sihtric laughed, throaty and genuine. 'Aye. If you smear enough about, it's like to end up with a stain. I'll give you that. And someone always kens someone else. I can put it about and see what comes back. That's a good a promise as I can make.'

'I would appreciate it.'

'You two eating?' the server asked in a loud, gruff voice.

Sihtric glanced up. 'Hungry?'

'I can't. I have to get back to my daughter.'

'Alright. One plate of whatever is going, then,' he answered the man.

A plate of stewed meat in a thick sauce appeared soon after. He dabbed a piece of bread in the gravy as I studied him.

'Merchant of spices is an interesting trade. How did you come to it? If you don't mind me asking.'

He raked his auburn hair back with his fingers. 'Suppose you'd say I have eclectic interests. Hmm? I have a taste for exotic flavours, and that leads me to spice. The rest, I suppose, just fell into place.' His reply was enigmatic. A smirk followed. 'Eryk said you're married to Kjarr.'

'That's right,' I answered, flagging down a woman to refill my cup. 'You know him?'

'He's a good friend.' He pushed his sleeves back to avoid brushing his meal, a bracelet of silver bells jingling around his wrist.

My eyebrows rose. 'He never mentioned it. Though, Kjarr has been absent for more than a year and perhaps he never had the chance to mention you.'

Sihtric waited while the serving girl filled his cup, leaving a jug on the table, before answering. 'It's been even longer for me. I went away the year before last but got stranded with a torn sail in Gnezdovo. We missed the season. It delayed us so long we either had the choice of putting in for repairs, which we did, or trying to cart the goods back by sleigh.'

'Oof, that's a long way.'

'And worse, it cost us the trade, not to mention costing our crew their time. Ended up selling for a much lower price that made the journey scarcely worth it at all. But such is life.'

'Such is life,' I repeated. Damaged sails had stranded Sihtric, which surely meant there was some demand for sails along the trade route. 'And if you could have traded your damaged sail for a new one, would you have?'

'Aye. For a pretty *mithqal* of silver too.'

I sipped thoughtfully. Being stranded for a season awaiting repairs was no minor inconvenience. The crew would be without funds, their goods may have perished, and they often found themselves without a market to sell to if their goods remained saleable. 'Is that the first time you've been stranded in such a way?'

'Aye,' he agreed. 'But not the first time I've heard of it. I'd say there's always someone in trouble on the river.'

'You're not wrong there!' Björn's familiar voice sounded through the crowd. 'Someone is always tearing up sails, busting their hull or needing new ship nails. Those rapids can tear a ship apart.'

'Björn, this is Sihtric,' I introduced the men. Björn sat down and pushed his cup forward to be filled.

'What are you still doing here?' I asked, filling his cup from the large jug left in the centre of the table.

'Our last night in Aldeigjuborg before sailing home,' he grumbled, gulping down the liquid. 'But I'll be back with the first favourable weather, armed with your supplies and, hopefully, some connections for you.'

'Busy lass.' Sihtric smirked.

Björn laughed. 'Our Signe is not one to sit idle. She is always busy with something. Oh, and I heard, though I don't rightly know how true it be, that your man put in at Holmgardr.'

'Holmgardr?' I stumbled over the word. It was the nearest Rus' city but still more than a couple of day's ride away, and I wondered why he had not come straight to Aldeigjuborg. 'Do you know about any of this?' I asked Sihtric.

He raised his hands and shook his head. 'Nothing.'

As I returned home, I should have felt elated. My meeting with Sihtric had yielded promise. Björn was going home across the Austmarr to secure trade connections for me, and Kjarr was close to Aldeigjuborg. But I could not shed the dread that had reappeared when Neflaug had. As I approached my door, I could see something resting on the stoop. A horse, carved in beautiful detail. Another 'gift' left without explanation that had me wondering if it was a sign from the gods or an omen from a threat much closer to home.

The next week, the town had almost emptied of its inhabitants. Merchants with families in town or those who did not have far to travel remained, while the merchants in Aldeigjuborg on transitory trade had departed in droves, taking with them the goods that would see them through the winter. The streets were quiet, with most of the revelries concluded save for the last harvest festival - *Álfablót*. Back in Karlstad, the celebration was shrouded in secrecy and confined to one's home. The women would close the house to visitors, but inside, the family would tell tales and eat meat from the fattest beasts to prepare themselves for the harsh winter to come. In Aldeigjuborg, the celebration was marked by a feast which was attended by the notable merchants in residence and anyone else deemed important enough for an invitation.

In the lead-up to the event, the guildhall was decorated, and there was a frenetic buzz in the town. Escaping the walls of the city always brought some relief. Though that morning when I woke, I felt the dark cloud that followed me close upon my doorstep. The gods were warning me to be mindful of where my feet tread.

The leaves littered the ground as Freyja and I took our routine amble along the Volkhov, greeting Laslo as we returned to the city through the Enggatt. We ate breakfast, prepared by Helga. We worked as usual until the midday meal. When my women returned to their families, I ate dinner with Freyja, Hilde, and Helga, and though unusual, Mikel shared in the meal.

Afterwards, I walked to the Skogarmaor for my second meeting with Sihtric. Crossing the square, Father Niall preached about the sin of gluttony, just in time for harvest, and just in time to catch the departing bone craftsman taking apart his stall for the winter.

My business with Sihtric had gone well. He had offered to set up introductions for establishing sail manufacturing and repair along the Volkhov and Dnieper Rivers. Having spent a season in Gnezdovo, he was well acquainted with the merchants that operated there. And for a small cut of the profits, the exchange was promising.

As I left the tavern, I wrapped my cloak around my shivering body and my hair whipped wildly. The wind had kept most people indoors. The Skogarmaor had almost been empty and even Old Ivar, the tavern keeper, had considered shutting early. Houses within the city walls had been battered against the weather, closed shutters and bolted doors.

I had walked ten steps in the darkness when eerily the wind ceased. To my right, I heard a shuffle and a bang in the side street. Likely, lovers stealing kisses. I paid them no notice until I recognised the voice.

'Come to me, my love,' Neflaug cooed.

Her words slipped through me like ice. The night was dark, the moon behind clouds. I could see nothing as I looked toward the couple.

'Err, I am not sure we should,' the deep voice I knew at once to be Eryk's wavered.

Neflaug giggled girlishly. 'We already did, or don't you remember last night?'

'That was a mistake.' He was more forceful this time.

As my eyes adjusted to the darkness, I peered around the tavern and could make out Eryk's outline leaning against the wall. Neflaug draped herself over him, steadying his teetering frame with her hands.

'I will take that,' she planted a kiss on him, 'as a yes.' There was no further argument from Eryk, quieted by wet kissing. She groaned, 'Of course you want me.'

Enough of this! The wind picked up, howling once more, and hid the crunching of my footsteps as I turned to leave. *THUD!* The noise was followed by giggling, and the kissing resumed. Bile rose in my throat as I crept back to the street, pressing my back against the wall of the tavern.

'No!' Eryk protested loudly this time. 'I will have you in my bed, Neflaug, but you cannot be allowed to resume your position in the Guild.'

'And why not?' she asked haughtily.

'You know why! Do we have to go through this again? Stay quietly as my mistress or find yourself another man to fool.'

'How dare you!' she cried. 'I bore your child!'

Stop! I wanted to call out. *Say no more.*

Eryk started laughing. 'My child? Ha! You're a whore. A damn good one but a whore.'

There was no more talking. I thought there would be an argument, but the next sound I heard was a sickening crack. Sure someone had hit someone, I hesitated to leave. I had no notion of who was hitting who, but I knew someone was getting some decent landing punches in. If Neflaug was being beaten, I was unsure what sort of protection she would have, and I would not get involved. If it was Eryk, he was big enough to defend himself.

This is their own mess. Let them deal with it.

A man slunk out of the darkness. 'Get it o'er with,' he whispered across the way, his voice reeking with malice. He walked past without noticing me, and when he reached Neflaug, a torrent of expletives left his mouth. 'You said we would just rob 'im.'

'You didn't hear what he said to me? I... I didn't mean to,' she cried.

'Well, we can't leave 'im like that. He's still moving. Here, give it to me.' An almighty thud followed, then the crack of bone and the squelch of innards being met with force.

'Finally,' the man seethed in the darkness. 'Didn't think that fat lump would die. Grab anything o' worth and get outta 'ere,' he ordered, as Neflaug rifled through Eryk's pockets.

Rooted to the spot with fear, I wanted to call out - scream and rouse attention to their crime, but no sound would come. I cursed myself for leaving Skara at home as I watched them speed out of the lane and up the street before my legs would move. When my senses came back, I tottered up the dark lane like a child learning to walk.

'Eryk?' I called, stumbling as I approached.

He didn't move. I looked over my shoulder. There was no one about, and I was sure the assailants had made haste to leave the city.

'Eryk,' I cried. He was already gone.

They had splayed him out on the ground, his clothes pulled up to extract his belongings, revealing the skin of his belly. They had partially pulled his trousers down, exposing his privates. Beside him, the moonlight showed the damage that had been done. His face smashed of its features, the ground red with blood.

A scream erupted from my lungs without permission, shaking my bones. My legs carried me to Luca's work yard, and my fists pounded on his door. I did not recall reporting the details, but Luca's startled expression told me I must have.

'I'll fetch some men and report it to the Guard. Then we will take him up to the house,' he said to me with a nod. I stood unmoving on his doorstep. 'Are you alright, Signe?' The sound of my name whistled through the gaps in his teeth.

'I must tell his wife,' I replied as I trudged to Eryk's house in a kind of stupor.

Eryk's wife, Alla, opened the door and rubbed her eyes. 'Signe, it's very late and Eryk is not here.' She seemed annoyed by the disruption, and what I was there to deliver would not put her in a better mood.

'He's dead!' The voice that came from within me did not feel like my own. It was not how I wanted to do this. The words sounded harsh, and at once I knew I should have softened the blow.

Alla staggered, her bird-like frame crumbling to the ground. 'Eryk?' But she already knew the answer. 'How?' she asked between sobs, her golden hair falling about her shoulders.

'The men will bring him up at any moment. I warn you, his injuries have made him unrecognisable.' Hesitating to leave, I stopped and my hand awkwardly patted her on the arm. 'If you need anything…' I started, but the offer was empty and she could not hear my words above her wailing.

She didn't ask me any more questions. She couldn't. Her body gave in to the grief as she collapsed further onto the floor, a puddle of mourning. Her children were now around her, holding hands and sharing in her sorrow.

I took my leave as eight men lugged Eryk's enormous body into the house. Hersir Eskil, leader of the town guard, asked me what I remembered and ordered extra guards to duty. And, as my feet took me home, I was thankful that Freyja was with Hilde so she would not see my face or my bloody clothing.

Against the doorframe, again just like the week before, lay a carving. A doll. Stiff and lifeless, a totem of what I had seen earlier that night. It was neither the gods nor the Norns that toyed with me but something far more sinister.

Six

The burial mounds rose out of the green grass north of the town. I stood below them, the solemnity of the occasion crushing my tired self after witnessing the Guild Master's death. The event caused a terror in me that had been difficult to dislodge, and I sent Freyja to live with Hilde until I was sure the danger had passed.

No one had seen Neflaug since that night. She had escaped. Even stranger, no one believed she could murder her lover. Not that people distrusted me. They did not believe that she, as a woman, could kill such a great man. All fury was out for the unknown outlaw who was her accomplice, deemed the murderer, and Neflaug, his unwilling associate. If she knew what was good for her, she would disappear. But something told me it was certain I would see her again.

Men dug the chamber in which Eryk's shrouded remains were placed, surrounded by the things that had brought meaning to his life. Silver coins, carvings, scales and other valuables arranged about him, as were the food and animals he would need wherever he was headed. I wondered if the gods destined him for Hel, that misty grey land filled with those who had failed to prove themselves as heroes, those who would not fill the halls of Valhalla or Sessrúmnir. He was rich and important, so we buried him with the most influential before him and might as likely remain a mound dweller. Who knew the will of the gods?

The frigid wind whipped the mourners' clothing, and leaf debris dusted our hats and hoods as we watched the men who had been Eryk's companions in life come forward to speak and throw fists full of dirt atop his body.

In the end, Eryk and I may not have been friends, but we had found a way to work together. With him gone, there would be a void until a new authority emerged. It was just as possible the next leader would deliver trouble as it would create any sense of harmony. The remaining merchants had already begun the jostling for power, bargaining for support and anticipating the moves of their competition. The Guild would decide upon the Grand Prince's visit come springtime. Until then, Eryk's second-in-command, Gisle, would take the reins.

Eryk's wife, Alla, wailed beside me. 'Remember me!' she cried, huddled with her children.

Gisle stood next to Alla. His greying brown hair was adorned with the ivory beads of his trade, which rattled as he embraced her. Alla had the option of joining her husband. She had not volunteered to do so, and that 'honour' had gone to Eryk's favourite slave, who was laid at his feet to serve him in the afterlife.

The crowd dispersed as I stood watching the ripples on the water, a billowing disturbance on the otherwise calm surface. A small barge moved across the river, not large enough to carry my hope that Kjarr would arrive home that day. My heart sank.

Bjarndýr, my armring, felt cool against my skin, the cold reaching the metal through the sleeve of my dress. My father had always been my champion. If he had been with me today, I knew the words he would speak. "Between each day is darkness." At the time, I thought it was a statement of night between the days. Now I knew he meant there would inevitably be bad times between the good. He would tell me to be patient. How I missed him.

The icy wind nipped at my face as I continued watching the slaves pile earth on the grave. I couldn't stay any longer wondering how long it would be before the frost began icing Aldeigjuborg. No boats would come into the harbour. No ships meant no news and, almost certainly, no chance of my husband's return. Perhaps Björn was wrong.

I shivered against the wind, wrapping my shawl around my shoulders as I walked away from the mounds and into the tree line. By the time I made it to the clearing, the space I found the most calm, I was alone. Everyone else had retired to the walls of the city, and I discovered the peace I needed. My body relaxed, and I breathed a deep breath, contemplating lying down on the grass to nap, but one touch and I knew it was far too sodden.

I leaned against the trunk of a tree, closing my eyes and listening to the sounds of the forest. Animals scurried in the undergrowth, foliage fell to the ground with a gentle gust and a bough above me creaked with the cooling weather. A crunching of heavy footsteps on crisp leaves interrupted my calm.

Was it an animal? I wondered, trying to locate the source of the disruption.

A man emerged from the trees on the other side, fifty paces away. He stepped into the clearing, and just as I recognised him, he saw me. The speed with which he launched himself towards me was rivalled only by the hungriest of predators. His pace slowed as he grew closer, and the smile he gave me lit up his eyes.

'I wasn't sure if I would find you.' Kjarr's voice was deep and unwavering.

My mouth opened and closed, but I could not recover the words.

He stopped, cupping my face in his hands. 'That is not like you.'

'I didn't see your ship.'

He took my hand. 'It's not here.'

'Then how?'

He pulled me into his arms. 'I rode from Holmgardr with a few merchants bound this way. Did you miss me?'

Of course I had missed him. I missed everything about him; his voice and the scent of his skin; amber and moss, with the salt of sweat. Most of all, I missed his counsel and our friendship. Sometimes I replayed our conversations over-and-over, trying to anticipate his advice, and other occasions I wished I had returned his affections when I had the chance.

Kjarr raised my face to his, kissing me hard. 'That was the kiss I imagined so many times,' he confessed when we broke for breath.

'And all you had to do was leave me alone for a year.' I laughed airily.

His face had not changed at all; kind eyes, his playful smile and his tousled brown hair all the same as they ever were, though my memory had failed me in his absence. He pulled my hair out of its binding with his fingers, letting it fall loose over my shoulders.

'Astrid,' he whispered my name. 'I dreamed of you.'

Kjarr bent his head to nuzzle my collar, sweeping my hair to one side and causing my skin to tingle under his lips. Against my back, I met the tree trunk as he urged me backwards.

'It seemed like an eternity being away from you,' he breathed against me.

'I know.'

His mouth moved up my neck, across my chin, and covered my lips as he pushed his body against mine. 'I could not wait another day. I needed to see you.'

'Does that mean you cannot stay?'

'I've left everything in Holmgardr.'

'Everything?'

He held my face so our eyes met. 'Everything,' he repeated.

'You will have to retrieve it before the snow comes.' I tried to be present in the words.

'It might be difficult to find a reason to leave.'

I laughed. 'You're going mad.'

His kiss deepened. 'For you, I would venture anywhere.' He slid my shawl from my shoulders, dropping it onto the damp ground. The neckline of my dress offered little resistance to his prying fingers.

'Kjarr! Don't lose your senses!'

He grazed my shoulder with the coarseness of his beard. 'Not even once?'

'Not here, not now.' Slipping out from his embrace, I scooped my shawl up. 'Please don't leave me with another *barn* to care for alone. This past year has been hard enough.'

This shook him back to reality. 'Freyja! Where is she?'

I pulled him by the hand, and he followed. 'She is with Hilde. The gods sent her, I'm sure of it. I could not have done it without her.'

'And does she hear about me?' His concern was endearing.

'Every day.'

'And you've had no trouble with it all?'

I scoffed. 'About that? It has been the least of my concerns.'

'The least?' he asked, catching his foot on a stone and stumbling.

'A lot has changed in the year you've been gone. *She* was back for a while.'

'Neflaug?' He stopped, mouth agape.

I nodded as we approached the bridge. 'She killed Eryk.'

'No!'

'People find it hard to accept that a woman would do something like that to a great man. They find it easier to blame her accomplice. Either way, she is still about somewhere.'

'I would believe it.'

'Yes, well, I don't have to convince you.' I sighed.

'Do they distrust you?'

I shrugged. 'It's not me. They doubt the circumstances. It was dark and hard to see what was happening. I said there was someone else with her and...'

'You saw it happening?' he asked, stopping by the walls on our way to the Enggatt.

'As best I could in the dark. I did not want to see anything, but I could not move and I didn't have Skara with me.' To be more specific, I felt ashamed about doing nothing, but those words would never leave my mouth.

'Of course.' He squeezed my hand.

'I was the one to raise the alarm. Luca then took care of the rest, and today they buried Eryk.' I pointed to the mounds in the distance.

'Ooof,' he whistled. 'That must have been frightening.'

'You would assume that a trained warrior would not baulk at someone being beaten to death. You would expect that she could defend a person in need.'

Kjarr squinted in the bright sun. 'It's alright. It all would have all happened too fast. If you came to his defence, it would have been too late.'

'Mm-hmm,' I mumbled. 'Most of the town is blaming the accomplice, even saying he stole Neflaug for a slave.'

He shook his head. 'What is this woman's power?'

'I wish I knew,' I replied as the Enggatt appeared.

Laslo waved at us. 'I was getting worried about you when everyone came back and you hadn't.' His eyes were round and his smile spread from ear-to-ear.

'I am alright, Laslo, as you can see.'

Kjarr waved next to me. 'Better than alright, I would say.'

'Welcome back.' Laslo smiled at Kjarr.

'It won't be for long. But I hope it will be a speedy return.'

'You'll have to hurry home,' Laslo chuckled. 'Signe was pining after you every day.'

'Shhhh, don't tell him that.' I rolled my eyes.

'We're glad to have you back.' Laslo stepped aside for us to pass into the city.

We made our way home, walking through the empty streets. Most of the mourners would either be at Eryk's residence feasting in his honour or reliving their memories at the Skogarmaor.

Kjarr hesitated at my door. 'I don't want to open my house up for a visit that will only be a couple of days.'

'No matter.' I stomped the caked dirt from my shoes. 'We are married. I don't think anyone is going to think anything of you being here.'

'But do you mind?'

I pushed the door open and walked into the hearth room. Helga stood gaping at Kjarr's sudden appearance.

'He has returned,' I announced.

'So, he who your gods said would come has finally arrived.' Helga smiled, delighted at her witty wisdom.

'Finally.' Hilde chuckled. She nodded to Kjarr and handed Freyja to me. The child stared with enormous eyes at the father she did not remember.

'This is your father,' I said.

She didn't look away, and Kjarr grasped her chubby hand. 'She is beautiful.'

On the floor, they played together. Freyja took to Kjarr like everyone else, quickly and warmly, but I noticed Kjarr stifling his yawns.

'You must be tired.'

Hilde picked Freyja up. 'Ve vill continue to keep her safe.'

'I know you will.' I kissed my daughter farewell as the girls departed for home.

'Here.' I pushed the door open to Neflaug's room, offering Kjarr her bed.

He seemed disappointed. 'In here?'

'You want to sleep in my bed?'

'We don't have to. But I would prefer not to lie in a bed tainted by a woman who has been out for our blood. Not that I think it will corrupt me. You never know,' he added with his wry smile.

'You're welcome to my room, then,' I agreed. 'Far too tired from your journey to try anything.'

'Not before I wash the road from my bones and my clothing. I'll lie down and not rise for days if no one disturbs me.'

Opening the door to my room, I lingered. 'I will find a basin for you to wash and,' I paused, 'I'll make sure that no one disturbs you, including me.'

Kjarr grabbed my hand as I tried to leave. 'I would never consider your presence any kind of disturbance,' he whispered, pulling me towards him for a kiss.

Tired still he might have been, it pleased him to be home, and that night, after a long time soaking, found the last of his energy reserves, and though sleep evaded him, his desire for me had not.

SEVEN

Dawn had long passed when I woke, Kjarr's arms around my naked body. 'Come on, I need to get up,' I mumbled, trying half-heartedly to free myself.

'Do you?' His voice was husky.

'This house and trade do not run themselves.'

'And yet, I hear pans clanging, women singing, and the ducks quacking without your instruction. It seems both the household and business function just fine when you give yourself the chance to relax.' He ran his nose along the curve of my neck.

I turned around in his arms. 'You want me to believe your aim is to keep me in bed to relax? What would my women say if I stayed here all day with you?'

He propped himself up on his elbow, looking down at me. 'You're not worried about what they will say. No tongues were ever set wagging by congress between a man and his wife.' He stilled me with a kiss. 'You fret too much.'

'Too much? Perhaps you worry too little,' I retorted childishly.

He bristled. 'Usually, I worry the right amount. But, if you are looking for an argument, I shall not detain you any longer.'

Then I saw the concern that marked his face, the tension in his smile. Quick to annoyance and just as speedy to soothe, Kjarr collapsed onto the bed, laying on his back and staring at the roof. 'I'm sorry, I don't want to fight.'

'Me neither.' I snuggled into his arms, my head on his chest. 'Is something wrong?'

He closed his eyes. 'I don't wish to leave you again. Not so soon.'

'But you'll be back.'

'Not soon enough.' He placed a soft kiss on my forehead. 'And perhaps not for long.'

'What do you mean?'

He ran his fingers along the length of my arm, a delicate touch raising skin to gooseflesh. 'The Grand Prince has called some of us to his council. He plans to move the capital, and I hope not to get caught up in it all.'

'Why would you need to be involved?'

'Let me say, I am known to Oleg. And more? I cannot tell, not even you.'

My eyebrows rose. 'And the capital. Will they relocate it here?'

'Not likely. He will want to centralise it, make it bigger and more important. Aldeigjuborg is none of those things.'

'Oh. So they may force you to go?'

His silence was all the confirmation I needed.

'Many merchants would leave if that happened. Money always follows power, and I would be a fool not to do the same.' His fingers combed through my hair. 'I would never ask it of you.'

'Mm, I know.' As I raised my head, his eyes were full of worry.

'If you did, we could build a grand house,' he dreamed. 'Think of the wealth we would leave behind for our offspring. Even greater than what my father left to me, or my grandfather before.'

'Let's not get ahead of ourselves.' I laughed.

He rolled me atop to straddle him. 'I wouldn't want anyone else to have my children.'

'Hmm.' I narrowed my eyes. 'For the sake of continuing our enterprise?'

My hair covered his face. 'Of course,' he mumbled, blowing the strands away.

'You would have to convince me.'

His kiss silenced my challenge, drawing me down with one hand on my lower back, the other on my hipbone. 'I'll do my best.'

When we later emerged, the sun had passed its peak and was sinking below the hills. Both flushed and unrested, we could delay our responsibilities no longer. Kjarr left to meet with Gisle and Sihtric at the Skogarmaor, and I dealt with business at the warehouse.

'Finally risen,' Helga mumbled as I stumbled into the hearth room, 'and ravenous, I would imagine.'

Elin shot a sideways glance at my appearance, followed by a nod and a knowing smile. The others giggled as they headed out the door, making for home.

My stomach grumbled. 'Starving,' I replied.

Helga threw a small loaf of coarse bread at me as I sat on the bench to tie my soft, doeskin shoes.

'Was I missed today?'

She shrugged. 'We managed. You had other things to attend to, more important concerns?'

I blushed, and the involuntary response made Helga's intense gaze cool.

'There is no shame in it, but I'm pleased,' Helga smiled.

'You're pleased?'

'Happy for you, Signe. After everything that has happened, you deserve some happiness. He is a good man. Such fortune is not for everyone.'

I took a bite from the loaf. 'You have it too.'

She nodded. 'I pray to God that it will last for both of us.'

My gods, however, would content themselves with the pulling and cutting of the strings of fate whenever they pleased, and no prayer of Helga's would change that. All the same, I appreciated the sentiment.

'Mama is happy to keep Freyja with her while Kjarr is here too. She left a little while ago.'

'Yes, I said I would call on her today.'

Helga sat down on the bench. 'Freyja is feeling better. Her teeth have been cutting through since yesterday. She cried all night, but Mama knew what to do. She always does.'

'I swear your mother is one of your god's winged things.'

She tore a scant piece off my loaf and stuffed it into her mouth. 'Angels?'

'Yes, those heavenly angels, is that right? She has a care for everyone, and her care for me and Freyja will not be forgotten.'

'You have looked after her well, Signe.' Helga brought a small basin of clean water for my use and set it on the table before me.

I splashed water onto my face hoping it would make me seem more alive. My eyes were heavy, displaying my lack of sleep. As the crisp water hit my skin, I gasped. It was as icy as the wind, but it had the intended effect of waking me up. 'Is it this cold outside?' I asked.

'The weather has turned. You should wear a hood against the breeze and a warm cloak, maybe your thick-soled shoes, the ones with the antler buttons?'

I nodded and slid the soft slippers from my feet. 'The ground will be brisk soon, and I will feel it in my bones. Can you fetch me my fur-lined cloak and I will be off?'

Helga slipped into the hallway and returned with the garment as requested, helping me to secure it around my shoulders.

'Will you be here when I return?' I asked her.

'I hope not.'

I slid the linen hood over my head and tucked it under my cloak. Out of town, I raced, a silent nod to the guard on duty. My feet carried me across the bridge, waving to merchants on my way and farmers in the field. Trees swayed in the gentle breeze that belied the coldness of the air, and by the time I had reached Hilde's home, my fingers were blanched and my nose dripped.

'Some broth?' Hilde asked as she shoved the mug into my hands. The difference between the warmth and my freezing extremities causing pain, I set the mug down on the table and rubbed my palms together.

Around me, children tottered and played. Freyja smiled up at me before returning to her game of sticks. 'It's so cold today,' I complained.

'And it vill be colder still. May be the vorst vinter yet. As I get older, I think my ability to bear it gets less and less. One day I vill freeze in my bed.'

'I will pay for more wood to be brought to your fire. Is there anything else you need?' I asked, searching the faces of her youngsters, some with sniffles that could turn into something without the right care.

'Some meat or some fruit for the little ones. Ve have a little preserved, but it never lasts long,' she admitted.

'I will try my best.'

Hilde picked up a stool. 'Come spin vith me.'

We left the children to play and went into the cold air. Only the stone wall running along the side of Hilde's yard offered us any protection against the chill.

'More broth?' she asked, handing me a refilled mug and then a drop spindle.

I sipped from the mug, and then set it down on the wall. Spinning, spinning. The wool with one hand and spinning the spindle with the other. Down it went until the thread was long, thin and fine. I wrapped the cord around the shaft and started again, continuing until it was too heavy to continue. The work had to be done without mitts or with the fingerless variety. Wearing gloves meant sacrificing dexterity, and a craftswoman would not compromise her craft for comfort. Usually, I could work until I lost all sensation in my fingers, but today I had come with a purpose other than productivity.

'Hilde?'

'Hmm, tell me. You did not come to spin, Signe.'

'You know me well.'

'Vhat troubles you?' she asked, without ceasing her work.

I sat on the stool, leaning against the wall behind. 'It's not a problem, more a proposition.' Hilde remained silent, watching me for a hint of my meaning. 'Recently, I met with a merchant named Sihtric.'

'The spice merchant?'

'Mm-hmm. He has agreed to help us source a connection, but there was a condition.' She looked up from her spinning. 'Someone has to go with him.'

'Vhere?' she asked, setting down her spindle.

'Depends on the contact. Perhaps Kyiv. But he will travel all the way to Miklagard if the trade warrants it.' I swilled my mug of broth, waiting for Hilde to react.

'You vant to go to Miklagard? If you are concerned about Freyja, of course I vill continue to care for her.'

'No, no. I didn't for a moment think I would be going. No, I thought you might want the opportunity.'

'Me?' she asked, dumbfounded. 'Me?'

'Why not?'

She plonked down heavily onto the stool, looking up at me in disbelief. 'Because I am an old voman. Too ancient for such a reckless experience.'

61

'Old?' She had many years ahead of her. 'You're not old, Hilde, and the adventure, there would be some risk.' I had thought about it endlessly since my meeting with Sihtric. 'You have three children that are still small and a daughter pining to care for little ones. She wants to play mother, so why not let her?'

Hilde sat, smiling, her hands clasped in her lap. 'Vhen I vas a girl I dreamed of seeing another city. You know, I have never left Aldeigjuborg. My father always said that everything ve needed vas here. But sometimes I fell God vould have vanted more for me.'

'And now you have that opportunity.'

'I vill consider it.' She sat pensively, staring off into the distance.

'We should go back before the sun sets. It's getting earlier each day. Soon there will be no sunlight.'

'You vant to take Freyja tonight?'

I nodded. 'Kjarr is here. I am safer with his presence, and perhaps we have seen the last of Neflaug.' Behind the thicket, I heard a trio of giggles. 'Freyja?'

'They vould not have gone beyond the tree line, they know the limit. She von't be too far. The little ones cannot carry her for too long. Girls?' Hilde called out.

Two round, ruddy faces popped out from around the bushes. 'Yes?' they responded in unison.

'Is Freyja with you?' I asked.

They nodded. 'It's too cold to go running. We were just playing with dolls. My doll was invited to the harvest celebrations but the others weren't. They're too young!' Hilde's second youngest daughter, Kitka, answered.

'Hmm, vell none of you are invited to the harvest feast. It'll be merchants and the fancy folk only.' Hilde shooed her daughter back into the house.

'But you're invited, aren't you, Signe?' Kitka asked.

'I am.'

'And you vill tell me vhat happens?' Hilde requested, with almost the same impish look as her girl.

'Of course, but I doubt it will be anything scandalous. Nothing like what we have seen earlier this year. I expect the city will be quiet until the Jol festivities. Though, if anything occurs, I will rush the news to your door.'

She nodded, crunching loudly on a stem of wild celery that she plucked from the ground. 'Come, Freyja. Time to go.'

Freya obeyed, letting go of the wall and stepping towards us.

'She's walking!' I exclaimed, crouching down to encourage my daughter to continue.

'Keep going. Vell done!' Hilde beamed. 'There vill be no stopping her now.'

We bid Hilde goodnight. Freyja clung happily to my back, bound with a length of fabric. We made our way across the bridge, through the gates and home again, Freyja wriggling all the while.

'Keep still,' I warned, and she stopped, wrapping her arms around me.

'Cold,' she babbled through the wind.

'I know, I know. But we will be home soon.'

The last stretch felt like the longest. As the sun dipped behind the hills, the warmth disappeared with it. By the time we opened the door, the fire was powerful in the hearth, while my fingers burned from the chill.

Helga stood in front of the blaze, her hands outstretched to its warmth. 'I thought I would warm myself before I go home, and I expected you would be back sooner.' She rushed forward to help Freyja down from my back and quickly put away my outer garments and scooped Freyja up for a cuddle.

'I thought I would have too, but we got talking. Shouldn't you have left for the night?'

She sat down on the floor before the flames. 'I meant to, but Mikel came and, well, now I wanted to stay a little longer.'

'Is everything alright?' I asked, hanging my cloak on a peg.

'Just a quarrel.'

I shrugged, removing my shoes. 'It's normal for there to be some disagreement in a marriage. Unless it's something more serious?'

'I don't know.'

'Helga, you don't have to tell me anything if you do not wish to, but if you need to talk, I am here for you.'

Freyja looked between us, confused. She crawled to the corner of the room where there was a basket of her belongings.

'Signe, we argued over a baby,' Helga whispered.

'Helga, are you?'

'With child? No, no I am not, but that is the problem.'

Filling the cups with hot bone broth, I set them down at the table as Freyja scuttled along the floor to play with her doll. 'Helga, it may take some time before you have a child. For some it takes years, and you said you had agreed to wait.'

'But I want one.'

'Are you saying that Mikel does not?' I asked, blowing on the soup to cool it.

'Not right now.' Her eyebrows knitted together with anxiety. 'He says we must be financially placed to do so. Now is not the right time.'

'I see. But, Helga, sometimes these things are outside of our control.'

She threw her head back and laughed. 'Oh, Signe, let me tell you. Mikel makes sure it is within his control!'

'Oh. Errm.'

'Please, tell me how I can convince him?' she pleaded.

'You can't. I don't know his mind, Helga. But it will not be today, and if you don't let him come to it in his own time, he may end up resenting you.'

'Will I not resent him for delaying?'

'That I do not know. Both of you are working so hard for your future. The rest will follow in time.'

Helga exhaled. 'Am I so impatient?' she asked. 'Oh, I know I am, Signe. But I love him and I want to have his children. It's a feeling inside. Don't you ever feel it?'

'You are asking the wrong woman.' Kjarr and I had discussed that very issue that morning, and I had felt it. The reckless abandonment of sense and an all-consuming desire to have Kjarr and myself create something anew. Like a Berserker in blood lust, hungry for the fight, blind to any consequence.

'So should I wait?'

I looked into her pretty eyes, deep with worry. 'You should keep working towards what you want together.'

Helga tossed her head back in laughter, her plaits loose under her headscarf. 'That is exactly what my mama says!'

'Trust your mother, Helga. She knows a thing or two. Now, go on. Make amends with your husband.' I shooed her towards the door. When she opened it, Mikel stood on the doorstep.

'Um, Helga,' he mumbled, with his arms folded across chest.

'Yes?'

'Won't you come home with me? We can walk together.'

She let him place her cloak over her shoulders. 'Are you sure you don't have anything more important to do?'

Mikel stood tall, unfolding his arms and embracing his wife. 'Nobody is more important than you.' He planted a soft kiss on her cheek.

'Excellent response,' Kjarr congratulated him, walking past the lovers into the house. 'Trouble with the newlyweds?' he asked, as Mikel and Helga left hand-in-hand.

'They will work it out.' I offered him a cup of broth and handed him Freyja's doll. 'Take this. Look, Freyja. Can you walk to your father?'

He held out the doll she so desperately wanted. After a little coaxing, she tottered on unstable legs the short distance to obtain her goal. 'Look at that! Your strong little legs!'

Freyja fell backwards on her bottom, wailing and rubbing her eyes.

'Time to sleep, little love.' It didn't take long to get her to fall asleep. The day and all the playtime had tired her out. When she was soundly sighing, I tip-toed out of the room to sit before the fire with Kjarr.

He paced before the hearth as he did when worries plagued him. 'I'm struggling to organise my affairs before I depart, and finding trustworthy men at the end of the season is like trying to find a fresh fruit after Yule.'

'All the more difficult when the offer does not include certainty of return?'

He nodded and rubbed his temples. 'I thought about pilfering some of the town's guardsmen, but what would that look like?'

'Come, sit.' I dragged him onto the bench next to me, laying his head on my shoulder. 'You have to trust the men you've selected.'

He did not stay there for long, preferring to put his head in his hands. 'I must leave tomorrow if everything is to work out.'

'So urgent?'

'If only I could tell you. Odin! I need a drink.'

I fetched a bottle and uncorked it, filling his cup. 'While you might lack the intention of being in Oleg's court, I sense you don't have the choice.'

He drained the drink in one gulp, gratefully receiving another. 'To avoid his favour would be to our detriment.'

'And your ambition?'

His hair fell over his eyes. 'You know I want to build on all that has come before.'

I nodded. 'And your greatest fear?'

He picked up the bottle and drank directly from it. 'That it might all be lost by my hand.'

'That won't happen.' I grabbed the vessel from his hand and left it on the table. 'You would never let that happen.'

He entwined his fingers with mine, kissing my knuckles. 'But it means leaving you.'

In his eyes, I saw regret. He was in so much deeper than he would ever say. 'It won't be forever.'

EIGHT

'You know I want to stay, but I can't. We will have to live in the memories we have for a while longer.' Kjarr kissed my cheek and pulled me into his arms. Freyja wiggled between us. 'And you,' Kjarr smiled, gathering his daughter up, 'will be running about, causing mischief by the time I return. I have no doubt.'

'Won't you stay just one more day? At least for the harvest feast.'

'And stay for the clawing and positioning the event will bring? I have enough to deal with where I am going,' he complained.

Freyja pulled on his cap, dragging it down over one side of Kjarr's face, resulting in laughter all around.

The morning was early, the air so cold that with every breath small clouds exhaled from our mouths. Down at the livestock stalls, inside the city walls, Kjarr and his companions saddled their mounts. Merchant's horses were often agisted in the field beside the tributary and brought to the stables for departure. Neither Kjarr nor his two associates looked too pleased about their multi-day trek from Aldeigjuborg to Holmgardr.

'We're ready.' The broad man in a dark cloak bowed to Kjarr.

'Thank you, Kani,' he responded. 'Are we sure we have all the supplies, Ingvar?'

Ingvar nodded, his wool-lined hat falling forward.

'Let's not prolong this. The faster you leave, the sooner you'll come back to us.' The lump in my throat made it hard to tease him.

'I'll send word with anyone travelling in your direction whenever I can.' Kjarr leaned forward to kiss me again, covering Freyja's eyes. 'Will you and Freyja wave until I am out the gates?'

Freyja heard the word 'wave' and began flapping her hand around wildly, proud of herself for recognising the concept and offering the action in return. 'I think at least one of us would like that.'

Kjarr hesitated to mount his ride. 'This is so much harder than I thought it would be.'

'You hadn't imagined I would fall for you as quickly as I did.' My response was a whisper.

He blinked, as if replaying the words. 'If anything delays me, even for a day, I'll send word. I promise.' Without caring who observed us, he kissed me. Though our circumstances had been less than ideal, the outcome of our marriage had been surprisingly passionate and coequal.

Freyja played with my hair as Kjarr slotted his foot into the stirrup and pulled himself atop his horse. We watched him, mounted on a dappled grey palfrey next to Kani and Ingvar, amble along the rocky road until it disappeared into fields.

'Frustration? Frustration does not even explain half of it!' I snapped as Helga tried to smooth my hair with a bristle brush. Her touch was gentle, but my hair snagged with every pass. I clutched my smarting scalp.

'Hmm, I wish I could go. Even if I had hair as unruly as yours.' She brushed again, the wayward locks springing back into their rebellious position. 'You know, it wouldn't have been this difficult if you had let me wash it yesterday.'

I felt my face turn crimson. 'Um, well, I was busy with other things,' I mumbled.

'When did he say he would come back?'

'He didn't.' Kjarr could not tell me when he would return for certain. 'There is more than he is telling me. I'm worried he is in trouble.'

Helga smiled, setting the brush on the table. 'He will be rushing to get to you. I saw the way he looked at you.'

My stomach flipped, a sort of giddy feeling I was almost ashamed of having. 'Kjarr is never in a rush.' He was always considered in his decisions, although recently, he had given me reason to believe that his patience had grown thin.

She mumbled to herself, 'If he was in a rush for anything, it would be you!'

Slapping her playfully, I chided her with a glare. 'Yes, we have both become impatient.'

68

'You've changed.'

'Have I?' I asked, surprised by her comment.

Her hands returned to the arrangement of my hair. 'You are more relaxed. I don't know how to say this, but maybe you have more feelings.'

'Perhaps,' I shrugged, 'and I still have a job to do, a business to run, and a feast to attend. Can you help me with this dress?' The garment was slung over the chair in the room's corner.

'What do you call this colour?' Her voice was wistful as she bundled the dress up, hugging it against herself.

'What would you call it?'

'Russet? No, that's not right. Blood?'

My head whipped around, startled. 'Certainly not!'

'Not blood.' She held the dress against her front. 'It's kind of like an apple, darker. More akin to a jewel. A *granat*.'

'A garnet, just the same,' I agreed.

'It's beautiful if not a bit, hmm, provocative?' she ventured.

'I suppose it is, but it has been the most successful colour and I want to show it off. This is a business opportunity. It's not about me.'

Helga scoffed. 'Is that why you had the gown cut so closely to your body?'

One foot after the other, I stepped into the opening at the neck as Helga held it open, 'I would not be promoting our endeavours if I was to wear some drab tent, would I?' We slid the dress to my shoulders, Helga tying the laces at the back until it was firm against my figure.

'Oh, there is no doubt you will draw many eyes.' She smoothed the fabric, letting it hang loose from my waist. 'You look stunning. Kjarr must be boiling with envy.'

'Don't say his name. I can't bear it.'

'You sound like the young maids who fawn over the town boys.' Helga laughed. She brought my lengths of coloured beads and draped them across my front, colours of every variety and shapes of many kinds. My thick, fur-trimmed cloak she draped over my shoulders, securing it with the Celtic brooch Kjarr had gifted me early in our friendship.

'I'm ready.'

Food had not yet been served when I arrived at the guildhall. The air was ripe with smells of roasted meats, stews and sweetly spiced fruits. All the bounty of a profitable harvest. They had transformed the hall into a veritable feast for the eyes; eaves and rafters adorned with greenery from the forest, flowers from gardens and antlers from beasts who succumbed to slaughter during the hunt. Tables were arranged in a squared off horseshoe shape. Three long boards surrounded the raised, shorter trestle on the dais.

Every notable merchant that remained in town was present. In Eryk's stead, Gisle stood at the head of the table, presiding over the feast. He would have the best cuts of meat, the finest dishes, and whatever he refused would be offered to the rest of us in order of descending importance. Rank might have been less important here, but it still existed. Next to him, Alla, Eryk's widow, sat resplendent in a gown of purple and adorned with beads and jewels like she was a foreign princess.

'Word is that Gisle will take Alla as a second wife,' Sihtric whispered, sidling up to me.

'Odin's beard!' My hand shushed my exclamation. 'So soon? That hardly seems decent.'

'I dinnae think she's concerned with the moral high ground,' he replied, swirling his blue cloak behind his shoulder, displaying his colourful brooch. 'You dinnae need to when you've got that much wealth.'

We looked for a place on the lower bench, taking a seat side-by-side. Around, plates were being laid in the middle of the table, and cuts of meat were being skewered with eating knives.

'I feel like I'm not supposed to be here,' I said.

'At least if we are here together, we might have some pleasant conversation, eh, *bhana charaid*?' He smiled jovially. 'You dinnae think that you'd be hiding in the shadows dressed like that, did you?' He ladled a helping of stew onto my trencher.

'I'm starting to think not.'

Sihtric confused me. He was forward, and that usually came with an expectation of something more.

'Why make that face?' he teased me.

I knew my thoughts were written all over my features.

'Just because I think you're bonny does not mean I want to undress you. Kjarr is my friend, and besides…'

My mouth fell open. He did not have to say any more for me to understand. 'Oh, uh.'

70

'I'm guessing he never told you how we met, did he?'

I shook my head.

'Your husband has a penchant for dice, and when we met, he desired my money and I fancied something else he had.'

He reached across me, spearing a sausage on his knife with a smirk. 'Want one?' It fell onto my plate with a thud. 'Neither of us got what we preferred.' Sihtric went for another, biting the end and letting the juice drip down his chin. 'Now you see I'm a heathen and a miscreant.'

I offered him a square of fabric from the table to mop it up. 'No, just a messer, as my mother would say.'

'Mine too.' He smiled. 'Was your ma from Dalriada by any chance?'

'She wasn't. Svealand, born and bred.'

The music commenced. A jaunty tune played on the flute, jaws harp and lyre began. Perfect accompaniment to hide the negotiations for support happening along the tables. Something I was keen to stay well away from.

'My ma was a *braw* woman, but my father... Gods! He was a bastard if there ever was.' Sihtric leaned forward for a piece of duck, tearing the wing from its body with a grisly crack. 'And speaking of bastards, have you heard what that Grand ol' Prince Oleg has been up to?'

'Kjarr didn't mention anything before he left,' I replied as I watched soft slices of stewed celery swim around in the sauce on my plate.

'I ken he would'a been sworn to say nothing, but I'll tell you what I've heard. Oleg sent a messenger asking for certain merchants to attend him in Holmgardr straight away,' he whispered, leaning in close. 'Might have caught Kjarr on the road here.'

'That would explain why he could not stay for long or why he could tell me no more than he did.'

'A few of them, like Gisle and Hakon, will leave tomorrow. Their arses will bounce along on their fast horses, with sore heads.'

Glancing around, I could see many of them had already helped themselves to copious amounts of beer, and come morning, they would be sorry for it.

'Whatever it is, I know Kjarr does not want to be involved,' I mumbled. A plate stacked with roasted vegetables caught my eye. Nestled in the stack, a whole beetroot. Using my knife, I pulled it out and placed it before me.

Sihtric shrugged. 'I dinnae ken he has any say. His pa was part of Rurik's inner circle. His father before him came out with the Prince when he took the throne. When Rurik visited Aldeigjuborg, Kjarr's pa would never leave his side, and they summoned him more than once to Holmgardr.'

'That sounds a little too close for my comfort.' I groaned as I dissected the bleeding vegetable.

'Unlike Kjarr, I will be content to gossip with the others when the jig is done. And speaking of jig, do you care to dance? I ken that dress didne come to sit on a bench all night.'

My head now sufficiently addled for the abandon of dancing, I accepted his offer. We whirled around, arms linked with others, joining the chain to the minstrels' tune. Around us, merchants and their women paired off, dancing to the wild music. When the song changed, the leader called out, 'Ladies only for the lucky dance.'

The men cleared the floor until only the women remained, connecting arms and forming a circle. It was an easy dance and the movements simple. Left foot left, right foot left, keep going, stop, and a little back the other way. We swayed to the music together as one. All good in theory if everyone knows the steps, but still feet were trodden on and obscenities were uttered.

The lucky dance was one of my favourites. The pace was slow and the words interesting; a woman's lover becomes a battle hero, and his exploits provoke unbridled joy until the dancers cheer and dance frantically. It was also a chance for the women to take measure of one another. There was no shortage of appraising eyes for my new gown. Its cut particularly offended Hakon's pretty wife, Gunhild, and she made no effort to hide her disgust. The dress had a modest neckline, the rest of it showing nothing more than the outline of my body. Hardly different to her own, though the colour of her green garment was drowned in the dim light of the guildhall. Gunhild I could ignore, continuing with the dance until I was breathlessly yelping with the others over the lover's triumph. And when the dance was done, Sihtric scooped me into a swinging jig that made my head spin.

My feet ached. I sought the comfort of a seat to relieve the excesses of enjoyment.

'Another drink?' Sihtric handed me a mug.

'What a night. Almost enough to make up for missing Kjarr.'

'He's asked me to look out for you.'

I held my cup out for a refill as a girl thrall passed by. 'I don't need anyone to take care of me.'

'I ken that, as does he.'

Sihtric nodded his head to the stage, where the instruments were being cleared off.

A *skald* took their place on the dais. Tall and wiry, he dragged a stool behind him and sat down, clearing his throat. 'And, now! A tale of long before in prose. I am the *skald* Ivar Ivarson. Sit, take your beer, your ale and lend your ear to me, my friends.'

'Can you believe this shit?' Torketill leaned towards Sihtric, elbowing him in the ribs. 'This *skald* is worthless. Never told a good story in his life.'

'You don't like heroic tales, Torketill?'

'Drivel like this wretch dribbles? No, I don't.' He spat on the ground. Torketill's eyes were red-rimmed, his greying sandy hair lank and dripping with sweat.

Sihtric filled the man's cup and pushed it towards him. 'Drink more and you will forget. Nay, you won't even hear the words anymore.'

He nodded effusively. 'Girl, come here!' he bellowed, dragging the poor slave girl into his lap and fondling her breasts.

'Leave her alone,' I warned.

'She doesn't mind, do you?' Not that it mattered. He didn't need her consent to have her. The girl, young enough to be his granddaughter, received a coin out of Torketill's pouch. She tucked it into her cleavage. 'And one more for you later, if you'll be my wicked little thing.' He laughed as he drove the second coin deeper than the first. She shrugged and took a sip from Torketill's cup.

I turned back to the storyteller, but his words faded as my mind wandered. Sihtric noticed my vacant stare.

'Are ye keen for hearth and home?' he asked.

'Longing to rest my feet. I have not danced like that since I was a girl, and I fear I will be sore tomorrow.'

'All the honest fun is done now. Nothing good happens after the tunes are played. Yet, the night is still young for debauchery and whoresons. I'm not wanting either tonight. Shall I walk you home?'

'Alright,' I nodded.

On the way back, we passed the Skogarmaor. A small group of men were being entertained by something out of our view. 'Next one,' one man shouted. 'Have another. Bet you can't down this one.'

'Grim, you're barely keeping up,' a voice raged that seemed familiar. 'Come on, get it down or she'll have beaten you.'

The group collectively groaned.

'I won,' a woman responded, silky and full of laughter.

Sihtric and I had stopped. 'I know that voice,' I whispered, leaning forward to see. 'My eyes deceive me. Odin's beard! I hope they do.'

It was Neflaug, draining another cup over a table as she bested the fellow opposite her. She laughed as she collected the coins that had been placed for the wager. When she stood, she stumbled, burying herself into the shoulder of a tall man who had spoken earlier.

'Want to win back some of your money?' she asked coyly.

The man turned to walk away, dressed for travel and marked with tattoos that snaked from under his shirt to his hairline. Neflaug fell to the ground with the action. He stopped to help her up.

'Sven,' I murmured. The sound escaped barely escaped my lips, but it was enough to draw attention to myself.

'Are you alright?' Sihtric caught my arm as I stumbled back.

'We have to go now.'

Neflaug sauntered towards me. 'Signe.' My name sounded like poison in her mouth.

I wanted to run from her, but the drink ceased my abilities and rooted me to the spot. 'Neflaug,' I squared off for the confrontation, 'you look a little worse for wear. A lot of wear, it seems.'

She faltered, 'I wanted to introduce you to my new friend.' She didn't miss a thing. 'This is Sven. He tells me he is from your hometown. He is looking for someone, and I thought you might help.' She watched for any recognition between us.

'Karlstad is not a small place.' I fixed my eyes on her. I did not dare look at Sven.

'Not that big,' he interjected. 'It's scarcely more than a few farmsteads.'

Neflaug looked disappointed that she had not stumbled upon anything salacious.

'It's clear we did not live there at the same time,' I lied, making eye contact with Sven.

Neflaug cleared her throat and shrugged. 'Well, Sven. This is Signe. She is married to the silver merchant and has a young child.'

'The Signe who stole your business?' he asked.

'Stole?' I felt the anger rising, and I almost took the bait. 'Hmm, I'm surprised to see you back here, Neflaug. After all, you killed your previous lover.'

'Me?' she asked, full of mock surprise. 'No one would ever believe that.'

'You're walking a thin line,' I cautioned.

'Signe,' Sven repeated. He knew it was me but so far was giving nothing away, so I hoped he would follow along.

Sihtric steadied me.

'Welcome, Sven,' I tried to sound confident. 'Aldeigjuborg's hospitality is well known, but beware of unnecessary misfortune.'

Neflaug glared at me as I retreated home.

'That was uncomfortable,' Sihtric mumbled as he raced to keep up. 'Just as Neflaug likes it.'

He patted my hand, tucked into the crook of his arm. 'And you know the man?'

'Intimately.'

We loitered at the doorstep.

'Perhaps soon we should share our woes over more ale. But for now, we both need sleep. Goodnight, *bhana charaid*.' Sihtric kissed me on the cheek.

'Goodnight, friend.'

As he walked away, I scuffed the street from my shoes and noticed yet another 'gift' left on my doorstep - a pair of tiny bone skates. *Damn you, Neflaug*. Now I knew it was never the gods who left signs at my door. It was her. They had ceased when she left and reappeared as soon as she did. I threw them across the path.

'Keep them! Take it and crawl back to the hole you came from,' I screamed into the blackness.

'Signe, is it?' Sven's voice emerged from the gloom. 'And you're married?' He was drunk and dirty and covered in new ink that marked his journey.

'It's a long story. If you come in, I can tell you.'

'But are you wed to him?' He did not hide the anger in his voice.

'I am.'

He leered over me, pinning me against the wall. 'And Neflaug tells me you have a child.'

'It's true.'

'Then Neflaug tells the truth.' He looked up, taking a deep breath.

'That woman speaks anything but the truth. Sven, let me explain.'

His shoulders slumped, and he pulled back. 'You can't. Nothing you could ever say will make this right. You ran away from me and you told me you didn't wish to marry anyone. And now I find you married and with a child. Exactly the things you told me you did not want.'

'Sven, how can you...' I tried to interject.

'I would have done anything for you! Never did I think I would discover you like this, Astrid. Oh,' he caught himself, 'sorry, I forgot. Signe.'

'If you are finished admonishing me for choosing a life without you, then leave.'

Sven stared in disbelief and, sensing I would not continue the argument, pivoted on his back foot and stormed away. Once the crunching of his footsteps had faded, I collapsed onto the landing, sobbing the cries of a woman betrayed two-fold; by her former friend and onetime mentor. I wept for the mess my husband was in and for the confusion I felt. I opened the door, dragging myself into the hearth room. And then I slept, right there on the floor.

NINE

The Norns have a way of weaving us back into our beginnings. Like a great tapestry, all the threads connected, we cannot escape our past. Even though I had tried to forget it all once I arrived in Aldeigjuborg, nothing was ever truly left behind. My confrontation with Sven had hurt, his accusations stung and his refusal to let me explain vexed me. The only way I found of coping since the collision of our tempers was to avoid him. I did not know where or why he was in the city. Still, giving the Skogarmaor a wide berth seemed appropriate. And sticking with my routine; work, home and the practice yard, it became easier to maintain as the weather worsened.

The dawn air was frosty, the first fall of snow dusting the ground as Freyja and I took our morning walk along the banks of the river. We had woken earlier than usual, packing our breakfast and trudging out of the gates to watch the sun rise. Grey clouds strangled the emerging sunlight, disappointing our hope of an autumnal colour scape.

'It's not much of a sunrise today, hmm?' I complained to Freyja.

She didn't care, too happy munching on the last crop of berries. The blades of grass under us tickled her skin, and she grabbed tufts of it, soil and all, laughing at the mess she made.

'Look at you.' I giggled, lying next to her on my back. We watched the flakes of snow falling, landing on our faces. 'Do you think I can get it with my tongue?' I asked, sticking it out and trying to lick a snowflake from my nose.

Freyja opened her mouth but couldn't catch one. She squirmed around on the grass, rolling in the thin snowfall. Her belly poked out under her cloak and *serkr*.

'A raspberry for my little berry eater.' I laughed as I blew a raspberry on the soft flesh of her tummy. From her mouth came the most beautiful sound of baby giggles, and for a while we forgot about anything else we needed to do and just enjoyed being together. The sun rose as high as was likely for an early winter day, and we could ignore life no longer.

'Freyja, look, the river is beginning to freeze.' I pointed to the Volkhov where a thousand tiny scratches grazed its solid top. 'It will soon be thick enough for ice fishing.'

Men would make holes in the surface so they could fish the water beneath, keeping the town fed with scores of fresh fish even in the depths of winter.

'Come on, it's cold and I want to catch Hilde before she comes to the warehouse.'

We packed up quickly, Skara tied to my belt and a basket for our vittles in my arms. By the time we reached Hilde's house, the sky had barely lightened, but the snow had begun to hammer down. No longer light flakes, it was a deluge that was shaken from our clothing as we stepped into the room. Freyja toddled to the fire and plonked down before its warmth to play with Alva.

'Any vord from Kjarr?' Hilde asked, taking the basket from my hands.

'None.'

'How long has it been? Three veeks?'

'A month,' I lamented. There had been a messenger a week before. All he could tell me was that Kjarr had been delayed; he provided no reason. 'My husband won't return before springtime now.'

'Oh, Signe.' She hugged me.

'I'm alright, just disappointed. Life goes on and we will continue our work until the snow makes things impossible.'

'Merchants still need their sails,' she agreed. 'Shall I bring the girls up vhen ve are ready?'

'If you don't mind.' I smiled, embracing her again before stepping out into the flurry.

Will the guards be practising in this weather? I wondered, walking towards the yard. When I arrived, there were only two figures visible.

'No training today, Signe,' Hersir Eskil called as he packed away weapons. 'This bloody snow has snuck up on us, eh?'

'It's been threatening for weeks, but I didn't expect it to get so heavy so quickly. Looks like it is here to stay now.'

'And freezing, bloody cold. We will be at arms only within the walls.' He shoved a spear shaft into the bag with the others. 'This guy,' Eskil nodded his head towards the dark man sitting on the bench, 'is stranded in Aldeigjuborg. Poor fella.'

At my belt, Skara pleaded for action. The only remaining item in the yard, a practice dummy, receiving her bite. I threw the axe with my right hand, the blade hitting with a thwack right between the eyes.

'Where did a woman like you learn to fight?' the man on the bench asked, his voice soft and foreign. He was unlike me in every way; where I was tall, he was short, my skin fair, and his dark. On his face, a mass of wiry black hair, and on his head, he wore a length of fabric wrapped tightly into a cap. His clothing, more akin to long durable travelling clothes the colour of oak moss, was the same shade as his eyes.

'My father taught me,' I answered.

'With an axe? Not a noble weapon, but a powerful one.' The strong nose, broad cheekbones, and hard lines of his face were intimidating, but his eyes seemed kind.

'I'm a little out of practice, but I used to be quite good.' I smiled, sitting next to him.

Eskil looked in my direction. 'I've got to shift these into storage in the town. Will you be alright here?'

'I think so.' I nodded in reply.

'I'll be back shortly for the rest, so don't get up to any bloody mischief.' He shot a warning glare at the unfamiliar man.

'Where I am from,' the stranger began again, 'women do not take up arms. At least, not with weapons.'

'My mother never wanted me to fight. It was my father who had other ideas.' I laughed, remembering all the arguments my parents had over the matter.

'May I?' He held his hand out for Skara, turning her over in his hands. 'Women from my lands are mothers, wives and daughters. Seldom anything else.'

'Do you have a problem with a woman fighting?' I asked, taking back my weapon.

'No,' he replied. 'Things are different here, and I have grown accustomed to my beliefs being questioned, though the distinction never ceases to amaze me.'

'*Mimaa la shaka fih,*' I responded, reasonably confident of the language he spoke.

He raised his eyebrows, and his mouth twisted into a smile. 'You speak my tongue?'

'And you speak mine,' I quipped in return.

He nodded. 'Indeed. One should learn how to convey meaning to those around them.'

'Even when the differences between our people are so great?' I asked, impressed with his restraint.

'Especially in those circumstances. If we were all alike, we would have little to learn.' He stood to leave. 'And tell me, warrior woman, what is your name?'

For a moment, I was going to answer Astrid. Thankfully, I had enough sense to think before I responded, 'Signe.' He turned to leave. 'And your name?' I asked.

'Ahmed Ibn Rashti,' he replied and dipped his head. '*Wadaean al'ana*, Signe.' He sauntered over the rise, hitching his long garment to traverse the hill. At the top, he met Eskil, who nodded and passed without comment.

'Everything alright, Signe?' the Hersir enquired with a care that was unusual.

'Yes, Eskil. All is fine. Want some help?' I took one strap of the last bag full of untipped spears.

'If you have the time,' he replied, holding the other side. 'What brought you down today, axe in hand, and ready to take your fury out on a wood man?'

'It's a long story.' My breath was quick as we made our way up the hill.

'Not like we'll have much else to talk about.'

I stared straight ahead. 'It's just some trouble I thought was buried; seems it's coming back to the surface.'

He grunted, pulling the strap onto the crook of his elbow. 'Better manage it before it gets out of hand.'

'Oh, I would prefer to deal with it. Perhaps even bury it again.' The walls were in sight now. The bag felt much heavier than when we started out. 'I've got to put this down for a moment.' We stopped and switched sides, the change of arm as good as a rest.

'What kind of trouble could a good girl like you get into?' Eskil asked. 'But good girls aren't skilled with an axe for fighting, so that might say something.' He laughed. 'Do you mind if we go through the Enggatt? I know it's the longer route, but it's closer to the stores.' He heaved the sack in that direction.

The rest of the journey was in silence, save for the grunt of exertion. When the gate came into view, our pace increased notably.

'That was getting heavy,' I puffed as we threw the bag at Laslo's feet.

'A bit of swordplay today, Signe?' Laslo joked, his eyes red-rimmed from night duty.

'You know I would not take up a sword in favour of the axe.'

He stooped to collect the bag, making light work of its contents. 'One day you'll have to give me a go. See if you can overpower me.'

His challenge was ridiculous. Even though he was a guard, by my judgement, he would offer minor comfort as security. 'I think I would have you on your back before you could unsheathe your sword!' I chided in reply.

The boy blushed and the other guard sniggered. The innuendo was not intended.

'Maybe another day.' I winked, stepping past the men.

Inside, my house was busy with the day's activity. Elin was standing before the warp-weighted loom, making quick progress with the two-two twill as she passed the shuttle through the hanging threads weighted with clay discs. Helga and Liv carried a great length of completed cloth into the cold air to be joined with the other two lengths, using a round hem to complete the sail. When it was done, the front side of the fabric would look seamless, completely flat. And, once treated with animal grease, the sail would be hardy and windproof.

Elin stopped her weaving and flagged me over with a flap of her hand. 'David came by some time ago. He said there has been some trouble south of the walls.'

'There has been flooding near the midden pit,' Helga chimed in, herding the small children into the corner of the warehouse where they would play. 'He wanted to send word that the farmers down that way are welcome to graze their sheep on his land until we can be sure there are no ill waters.'

'He could not go himself?' I moaned, having barely been home before I was being charged with another errand.

Helga shrugged. 'It's worth ensuring the message is delivered properly.'

'You're right; we wouldn't want any of the flock dying. Their coats are important. If they don't make it through the winter, it means we have less to work with. I'll go after I've warmed myself and had something to eat.'

I wandered into the hearth area. My backside had not hit the bench before there was a knock at the door.

Behind it was Sihtric. His hooded figure stepped off the street. 'Where did all this snow come from?' he grumbled. 'I've a message from Kjarr.'

'You have?' I wondered why Kjarr had not sent one for me. 'Want something to chase the cold away?' I asked, pouring whatever bubbled in the pot over the hearth in bowls. 'I'm not sure what it is. Helga made it,' I said, handing it to him as he sat. 'So, the report?'

'Nothing much and none too good. He willnae return for some time, if at all.'

'At all?' My eyes widened. 'I know he won't return this year, but he said nothing to me in his last message,' I panicked. Then I thought back to when he told me Grand Prince Oleg planned to move the capital. *I should have seen this coming.*

'He dinnae say any more. I'd wager he cannae,' Sihtric said, taking a gulp of the broth.

'Well, if that is the way of things, I cannot change it right now.' I pretended it did not upset me. 'And I have some news for you. Hilde has agreed to go with you on our trade errand.'

Sihtric untied his cloak and laid it on the seat beside him. 'I mind not the age of the woman, if she's good company. So long as she dinnae complain of discomfort.'

'Do you have much experience with women, Sihtric? Do you know the difference between when a woman is complaining or when she is nagging?' I asked, with wry humour. 'Have you any sisters? Children?'

'Gods no! Not children. But sisters? Maybe. Not of my ma, but my pa spawned many a bastard, and I'm sure some of those would have been lasses, though I dinnae ken for certain.' He reached into the pouch around his waist and drew a small bottle. Not one used for drinking, smaller, and stoppered by a cap crammed into the opening. When he uncorked the thing, a strange scent filled the room, and the contents he sprinkled into his broth. 'Magic,' he smiled, 'and will improve the taste of even the humblest of soups.'

We sat for some time until Sihtric broke the silence. 'Am I right in thinking you were someone else before you came here?' he asked. 'You've got a lady's standing, and my Kjarr thinks highly of you. What were you?'

'Nothing so great as a lady,' I replied.

'Och, there's no shame in it. I just mean that sometimes we can feel trapped by who we were before. But the cage is of our own making.'

'Trapped?' I questioned.

'Aye. See, my ma, she was a lady from where she came from. But my pa stole her from her lands, and then she became nothing more than a slave to his wants. Do you understand?'

'Your mother was a slave?'

'Aye, she was, and my father was an awful arsehole,' he remembered. 'I wasn't a thrall.'

'I'm not saying you were, just that a few weeks ago with that man…' He drummed his fingers on the table.

'Sven?'

'Yes, Sven. You've left something behind with him but…' He hesitated. 'It haunts me.'

'Aye, precisely, it haunts you,' he agreed, clicking his thumb and forefinger.

'And how is it remedied? What did your mother do?' I asked, toying with the hem of my dress.

'She was light and goodness herself, but she never got out, never let go of her past. If she had, perhaps she might have found some happiness.'

I smiled. 'Maybe you're right, Sihtric. Just let everything go, forget about the past and all will work itself out.'

He shrugged. 'What do I know?'

'About as much as I do.' I laughed. 'If he still holds a grudge, that is his problem.' But even as I said the words, I knew they did not sit well. 'Right now, I have an issue that requires my attention. Will you excuse me, Sihtric? Come again soon. This winter is going to be a long one, and I will sorely need company.'

'That is also why I've come,' he began. 'It seems I, too, am called to Holmgardr. A late addition, but I cannae refuse, you ken?' he asked.

'I do.' I nodded.

'Will you be alright? I'll see you when I return, hopefully with a message from your husband,' he replied.

I shrugged. 'You will do what you must.'

'It's with reluctance that I go, *bhana charaid*,' he apologised.

'So everyone keeps telling me.'

He excused himself and left, and I departed for the farms south of the city. Mercifully, this area was protected by the rise to the east, and the forest to the west, which made the wind less brutal. The ground was sodden, not a good start to a winter that had come early and hard. Rain, in the weeks before the snow, had drenched the ground, turning it into the worst kind of *slask*. The overrun midden pit had leaked into the lower part of the Ladozhka. Most of the town pulled their water from either of the wells on the higher ground. But those living south of the walls used the lower well and the tributary river regularly.

'Odin's beard!' I exclaimed as I came close to the midden, wanting to inspect the damage myself. 'There is nothing that smells as bad as this.' I covered my face with my shawl.

A man, digging next to the pit for the overflow, looked up. 'Then why did you come?' Sven's face was splattered with mud. At least, I hoped it was mud.

'What are you doing here?'

'I'm building a house. What does it look like?' he mocked, leaning against his shovel. 'What do you want?'

I had not planned on correcting Sven's misinformed judgement of me, but the opportunity had presented itself and I would not ignore it. 'Can I speak with you?'

The man on the other side of the pit grinned. 'Oooooooh,' he jibed.

'Who was he, then?' Sven launched into the question when we were alone.

'Who?'

He leered forward. 'The baby's father!'

'Freyja,' I corrected him.

'A woman?'

I almost snickered, but he was confused. 'No. The child's name is Freyja.'

'And who is her father?'

'If I tell you, then you mustn't speak to anyone about it,' I forewarned him.

He nodded.

'She is the offspring of a now deceased spice merchant,' I said in a low whisper.

He stumbled backwards. 'She is not the daughter of your husband?'

'No' I said. 'But…'

'Is that how you got all of this?' he asked, splashing my cloak with muck as he gestured with his hands.

'No, I…' I stammered, trying to get the story out.

'You mean to tell me you passed this child off as your husband's even though you were seeing another man?' he accused.

'Do you expect so little of me, Sven? Is your pride hurt so much that you would insult me without listening to what I have to say? Is that the man you are?' The fury boiled, and though I tried, I could muster only mere civility in my tone.

'Pfft,' he dismissed.

'You're so frustrating. You won't even let me explain! Is Neflaug the one putting these ideas in your head, huh?'

'You said yourself, she tells the truth,' he answered condescendingly.

'How dare you accuse me of such things without allowing an explanation. This is just like you to come to your own conclusion, blind to the truth. You never cared about me, not after all the pain you've caused. And here I am, stupidly caring about you still. For what reason? Why should I care?' I turned to leave.

'Pain I caused you?' he asked with a laugh.

My mouth fell open. 'Yes, Sven. The trouble you brought to me. Did you forget about your marriage ultimatum?'

His shoulders slumped. 'It happened so fast, and then you ran away. I thought I would never find you, never see you again. But now you are married and you have an infant. Do you know how much that hurts me to understand that you love someone that is not me?'

We stood in silence. His breath quickened. Taking my opportunity, I grabbed him by the arm and brought him in close. 'The child is not of my body, nor my blood,' I whispered in his ear.

His shoulders stiffened. 'I don't follow.'

'I did not give birth to her.'

'Then how did you come to have a baby?'

'An oath. I did what I promised to do. Do you see? While you may spend all your days drinking and whoring, I am playing mother to a child who is not my own.' I dug the words in deep.

'I, I… I didn't realise,' he stammered.

'Sven, I don't care. You've done what you always have, decided without knowing the truth. Now I have no time for it, so please leave me alone.' I left him standing aghast.

After returning from the southern farms, Helga grabbed me and rushed me to my bedroom. 'Mama is beside herself,' she cried.

'What's wrong? Where is Freyja?'

'Freyja is fine. She is with Elin. It's Mama.' She pulled me by my arm, closing the door behind us. Inside, her mother sat on the edge of my bed, sobbing.

'Hilde, what is the matter?' I asked. She was never like this. Hilde was the most stalwart person I knew.

'Neflaug,' she sobbed.

'Come on, Mama, tell us,' Helga pleaded.

She stilled her breathing and ceased her tears enough to tell us what happened. 'After you left, Signe, Helga came and took the babies away to here. But Neflaug must have seen me. She came not long after. Stinking of drink. She knows. I told her I knew Freyja vas her daughter. I didn't mean to, it just came out. I vas so angry but, vhat if…'

'It's alright, Hilde. We won't let anything happen to Freyja or you,' I tried to comfort her.

'Neflaug accused you of stealing her child,' she sobbed.

'I didn't, I swear,' I answered, shocked.

'We know you would never do such a thing.' Helga squeezed my shoulder.

'Vhen I asked her vhere she had been this past year, if she vanted her daughter so badly, she just laughed at me. She said she vas vaiting for you to return her.' Hilde took a deep breath.

'Neflaug gave up all rights when she left Freyja the day she birthed her. A child is not some whim to be wanted when it suits her,' I cried.

Hilde was shaken. 'Then she asked me to pass this varning to you, Signe. "One day you will get what you are owed. You will know what it is to love and to lose." Do you think she means vhat she says?'

'Freyja must not leave the walls of the city,' Helga declared.

'She will stay here with me. No harm will come to her,' I responded. 'Hilde, do you want to be with the other ladies?'

She nodded. 'I vant to see the little ones.'

Hilde hurried out of the room, leaving Helga and me alone. 'It's not right that Neflaug is still out there without facing the consequences.'

'What can I do? How can I report her without endangering us and exposing the truth?' I asked.

'Perhaps it is time?' Helga suggested, grasping my hand.

'No one believes she is capable of this. That much was proven when Eryk died,' I explained. 'You're right; I need to tell Hersir Eskil. Just to put them on alert in case she tries something.' As I made the decision, I could breathe easier.

Helga glanced up mischievously. 'Why don't you cut her down with your axe? She would fall like a tree, and then we would not have to worry about her. Take her to the forest and she would rot with the leaves that lay there.'

'Helga! Are you promoting violence?'

'I don't mean it! I do, but I would not do that. Surely, Neflaug would never harm the child. Somewhere inside, she loves her and she would have to know that leaving her with you is the best thing for Freyja. Neflaug is lost, that's all. She needs to find something again, and when she does, she will leave you alone.'

I nodded but still worried. Feeling a tug on my sleeve, I looked down. Freyja stumbled into the room, climbed onto my lap, and stroked my face. 'Don't worry, my little love, we will take care of you. See?' I smiled. 'I am not sad now.'

Still, Neflaug's menacing words rattled around in my head, repeating her warning over and over. *Was this what the* völva *foretold?* I worried.

And like a dark cloud threatening a thunderstorm, I could not shake the feeling that my entire world was about to be struck by lightning.

TEN

As if I had prophesied it, the early evening raged with thunder and lightning on the far bank of the Volkhov. Freyja cried in fear when it began, but it didn't last long. The storm had been enough to still the snow, and the powder that dusted the ground did not cover it completely.

'Goodnight, my little love,' I called softly as I settled Freyja back to sleep. Her eyelashes fluttered as she fought the drowsiness.

In my bed, I replayed the conflict with Sven for the umpteenth time. His face contorted with confusion and hurt. *Stop thinking about it.* As much as I willed it, I could not dispel him from my mind. He had been honest for once, and instead of listening, I had done just as he had previously and made my own conclusion. *He isn't blameless.* I tried to remind myself of every misunderstanding he came to, but it didn't work. I closed my eyes, and in the darkness of my thoughts, I saw Neflaug. I was glad to have heeded Helga's warning and reported Neflaug's threats to Hersir Eskil.

She had already attempted to enter the city during that day, when she had set her sights on the young guard on duty. He had been warned well enough to repel her advances and barred her entry. Knowing Neflaug's penchant for persistence, it would not be her last attempt.

BANG!

'Gods! What was that?' I asked, sitting up and looking around. It sounded like the front door swinging on its pivot and slamming against the wall. My eyes blinked against the dark, and I stumbled to my feet.

'Mama?' Freyja murmured.

'Sleep, little one. Everything is alright.' I kissed her cheek softly, patting her on the back until she relaxed.

In the hearth room, I saw the door wide open. 'I thought I bolted this?'

There was no one around. The night was still as I glanced out. After searching the house, I decided that come morning I would ask Luca or Mikel to inspect the pivots and bolt for any faults, but for now, I closed the door and slid the bolt across.

'It must be past *midnott*,' I muttered to myself, climbing beneath the furs and closing my eyes again. I thought it would be a struggle to fall asleep; instead, I succumbed quickly.

Thunder struck. It woke me up.

'Gods! When will this stop?' I wondered aloud, but as my vision adjusted to the darkness, I knew this time was different. The air felt cold and it pricked at my skin.

Another strike. *No, that's not lightning.* I threw back the furs, darting to Freyja's cot.

'No, no, no, no!' I cried, rifling through her blankets. She was not there.

My throat strangled as I tried to scream, but all that came out was a sound that was foreign. From the hearth room, a bang, one that I had earlier mistaken for a thunderbolt. My feet sped through the house, searching, then out the door into the street. There was no doubt who had done this. It was Neflaug, but there was no sign of them.

Quickly, I grabbed the heavy cloak I had hung on a peg in the hearth room, and I ran down the length of houses. In the distance, Freyja cried. I tracked the sound until I saw the dark-robed figure escaping the town walls. She was fast. Try as I might, I could not catch her, my shoeless feet no match for her nimble steps. My soles burned from the cold ground. *Where was everyone?* There were fires lit on the walls but no one to call to.

'Odin's beard!' I cursed. I was on my own.

As I approached the riverbank, I could hear Neflaug singing below the fold in the land where the water had frozen flat. Her song became louder, then softer again. I followed the sound slowly so as not to startle her or to lose my footing. My hand grabbed at tufts of grass below the snow as I descended the bank onto the ice's surface. I trod carefully, for I knew there were holes in the ice used for fishing that may have been left uncovered for the morning. In the centre of the suspended thoroughfare was Neflaug, spinning in graceful circles with Freyja bundled in her arms. The child was dressed only in her *serkr* and a wool sleeping cap, and wrapped in a blanket, vulnerable to the frost of the night air.

I only managed a few steps before Neflaug noticed my presence.

'What are you doing here?' she hissed at me.

'What do you want with her?' I asked, my voice trembling.

'I've come to take back my daughter.'

Disbelievingly, I watched as she continued to dance around, oblivious to the frightened screams of the child.

'Please return to the house, Neflaug,' I pleaded, knowing every moment that passed brought more danger to the situation. 'You can take Freyja home and we can discuss this by the fire.' I had no intention of letting her have Freyja, but I knew I had to bring them both out of the cold.

The change in my tone caught her attention, and she eyed me with a look that seemed evil and deranged in equal measure.

'No,' she shouted. 'You are trying to trick me. I will not come with you, and you cannot make me.' She turned with Freyja in her arms and flitted off in the other direction, disappearing into the darkness.

I worked hard to follow them, clumsy on the ice barefoot compared to Neflaug's speed on bone skates. My feet slid as I tried to keep up. When I found them, Neflaug had Freyja, dangling her legs, imitating a dance. Together they moved from side to side with Neflaug murmuring words of encouragement over Freyja's terrified cries.

'Please stop, Neflaug, you will freeze her,' I implored, desperate.

Freyja screamed loudly, holding her arms out to me, and I scrambled towards her. Each cry sent searing pain through me.

'Neflaug, stop, you're hurting her.' I lunged forward to grab Freyja, Neflaug deftly avoiding my attempt.

'Go away,' she cackled. 'I'm teaching her to ice dance.' Neflaug spun off, skating over the thinnest ice.

A deafening crack echoed off the banks. Both descended into the icy depths, disappearing from view. Without a care for my safety, I spread myself on the ice, screaming for her to take hold of my grip as I manoeuvred to the edge.

'Take my hand!'

My arm sank into the dark water. It was like a hot iron shooting up my arm, and everything inside told me to draw my arm back immediately. I thrashed below the surface, grasping for anything. My fingers entwined with a mass of hair, pulling it upwards. I knew at once it was too heavy to belong to Freyja and as Neflaug's head parted the surface, I realised for certain. She grasped the edge, holding on, too weak to haul herself out. My face, pressed against the ice, burned as my hand groped the wet darkness. Any promise of discovering my child slipped through my fingers, and I gasped cries down like air.

'Get out!' I screamed at Neflaug. 'Get out. Get out of the way so I can find her. Move!' I pulled the woman out of the water, not for her own sake, but for the desire of finding Freyja. Each moment that passed felt like an eternity, and the panic increased. 'Help me, she'll drown,' I cried.

Neflaug just stared at me dumbly without moving, shivering against the chill.

'Where is she?' I yelled over and over, probing the water for my child.

My heart hammered as I prepared to slink below the black water. First my face, then my shoulders. In my throat, rising blood as the cold burned my insides. It felt like my heart stopped. I tried to slither deeper, but two hands grasped my waist and pulled me back into the frigid air. A heavily cloaked figure pushed me against the ice, restraining me despite my screams and clawing hands. It was futile, their strength was too great.

'Stop, you cannot save her,' Sven whispered, holding me against him.

I shoved him away, looking over at Neflaug, who lay sprawled on the frost, panting. 'Where is she?' I yelled, searching her soaked clothing, but her arms were empty. 'Did she fall into the water with you?'

Neflaug nodded and sobbed.

'Did you pull her out?' I raged, shaking her violently. She was so cold.

'Stop,' Sven's deep voice commanded as he shouldered the shivering woman. 'I must take her to get help.'

'Where is my child?' I cried. 'Please, help me.'

He stopped. 'It's too late. She would not have survived the water and neither will Neflaug if I do not take her now.'

'You cannot choose to save her.' I pawed at his legs in desperation.

'I am choosing to help someone live,' he replied bluntly.

My heart lay at the bottom of the river, frozen and cold. Tears poured from my face, freezing as they ran down my cheeks. I wanted to throw myself into the water to be with my child, but Sven was right; Freyja could not be saved now even if I could pull her out.

I crawled on the ice, clambering back to the bank. All I could do was stumble to my house where I slid onto the floor, collapsing into grief. And there I stayed until the sunlight broke through the darkness.

When the first rays of the sun touched my face, I woke feeling the unwelcome warmth. Sprawled in front of the fireplace, my hands hurt, and the skin on my knuckles was split and covered with blood. The ash in the hearth lay undisturbed, I stared into it unable to shed any more tears.

Freyja's loss dawned on me once more. As tearless sobs wrought through me, my breathing was short and difficult. I was drowning, just as my daughter did. Gasping for air in the dark, cold depths of the river. Groping for safety, feeling scared. Searching for… me. *I should have saved her. There had to be more I could have done. Gods be damned! She should have been safe with me.* My heart broke, conjuring images of her tiny body trapped beneath the thick layer of ice.

'You failed her!' I cried, prostrating myself on the cold floor.

All I wanted was to hold her again. Wrap her up and somehow keep her safe, even though it was too late. My innocent 'little love' who knew no evil, did no harm, and brought light into my life had been forever extinguished. Never had I loved anything so completely. She had changed me, and I did not want to go on without her.

On my knees, I rocked back and forward, trying to calm myself enough to stand. My legs buckled, and I grasped the edge of the table as someone came into the house.

'Hush, child,' Hilde's soft voice whispered in my ear as she led me to bed.

She removed the crib and straightened my room, gently cleaned my face and hands with water from the basin sitting by the door. I didn't complain nor speak a word as she discarded my cloak, leaving me only

93

in my *serkr*. She guided me beneath the furs, pulling them up to my chin as I lay my head on my feather pillow.

'Close your eyes now,' she said. 'I vill stay vith you.'

As she instructed, I did. Hilde sat beside me, one hand on mine and the other stroking my hair, continuing as I wailed. Sleep took over then as I cried myself past the point of exhaustion.

'You must eat,' she bid me when I woke sometime later. It was dark. She pulled me up to sit. 'You do not need to do anything else, but you must eat.'

I groaned, wanting to refuse.

'Come now,' she soothed. 'I know this is hard, but you must try.'

Hilde spooned soup into my mouth. I obliged but did nothing to help. I was beyond caring if I lived or died. Helplessly, I looked up at her. Etched on Hilde's face was the pain that mirrored my own. She, too, knew the loss of a child. We held each other and cried until I fell asleep once more.

With no idea how many days had passed, my eyes blinked open into the morning light. As every day before, all the events came flooding back in a nightmare that was real.

Hilde, bustling about with bread and honey for my breakfast, led me to the table in my room and urged me to eat once more. I chewed and swallowed, as ordered, but I did not taste nor enjoy any of it.

'How are you this morning?' she asked.

I grimaced but managed a nod.

'Do you think vorking vill help give you some purpose?'

Tears welled in my eyes anew.

'Perhaps a valk, then?' she suggested.

We donned our winter clothing and walked for a long time without talking. Hilde took me to an area where the town's dead were interred. Seeing the many tiny burials of other small children lost before their third year made me feel less alone.

She led me to a small grave on a grassy outcrop and sank to her knees. 'This is where my Anajya is buried,' she said looking up at me.

I slumped to the ground beside her.

'This vould have been her eleventh vinter, should she have lived this long. Ve lost her five years ago,' she continued, the words choking in her throat. 'She vas an ill child but she always recovered, all but one time.'

We sat there before Anajya's grave, mothers united in loss.

'You never forget them,' Hilde said as if reading my thoughts, 'but you learn to live vith their absence. I am grateful for all the children I have been blessed vith and even those God has seen fit to remove from my care.'

My fingers found my father's armring in its usual position, wishing that he could be with me to bring comfort. 'My father had a favourite tale when I was a girl. It was a story with a simple moral, but one it seems I may have forgotten until now.'

Hilde turned to me. 'How so?'

'I have ignored the warning, my father's teachings.' I remembered the words clearly, as he repeated them often. 'Some cares weigh lightly, while others do not. Think on it before you commit yourself. In the wake of consequence, we are wise. Do not bequeath yourself easily, for the shackles may be unbreakable. In the moment, responsibility is intoxicating. Take a sip before you drink it all, see if it is bitter, for even those burned by flames must continue to endure. And in the morning, pain withal, the sun will rise again.'

'Your father vas a vise man.' Hilde smiled.

'He was superstitious, and I'm not even sure those were his own words. You know, now that I think about it, he probably heard it from someone else.' I almost grinned, but happiness was not something I was entitled to anymore.

'You vill rise again, Signe. The suffering vill dull vith time. I promise you.'

I stifled a cry. 'Grief is all I have of her, and I don't want to let that go.'

'Vhat about Neflaug?' she asked me.

'Neflaug? I care not if she survived the night. She is the cause of it all. The evil thread that has bound this mess together.'

Hilde wrapped her shawl around her shoulders as she slowly got to her feet. 'Perhaps it vill help you find out if she still lives?'

'So I can kill her myself?' I asked, accepting the hand she offered to pull me up.

'She has lost her child too, and God teaches forgiveness.'

'My gods preach vengeance,' I seethed in reply.

ELEVEN

WINTER 882CE

Reluctantly, I resumed my daily existence. There was no joy, and anything I did was done by my hollow shell. My mind alternated between wallowing in grief or the absence of everything. Spoken words entered my ears and fell from my mouth without meaning, but banter never ensued. A smile, a laugh, or any sort of enjoyment felt like a betrayal of Freyja, and I detested anything that would brighten my pit of darkness.

My heart was full of anger. Sven, I hated for his intervention and saving Neflaug. That woman had lost her mind and should never desire another breath. But myself I was repulsed by even more, knowing I had been unable to save my daughter. The worst had happened because I had allowed it to happen. Neflaug had warned me. My guard had been down. I had grown complacent.

As punishment for my lack of strength, every day I walked along the frozen banks of the Volkhov right where Freyja's end had come. The scene of my darkest hour.

The winter air pricked at my cheeks like a face full of tiny painful moments that I tried to ignore. It dried my skin, threatening to crack. My lips formed a grim line, determined to endure the sensation, all the while wanting to scream. But I couldn't tolerate it, pulling my hood up to cover my face for a moment of reprieve. The wind howled as the sun set. I walked on without caring if the setting of the day would bring the dangers of night, for I no longer feared death.

97

The presence of deep snow on the ground slowed my progress. *It's time to turn back.* Even my desire to ignore self-preservation was disobedient. Darkness covered the buildings as I returned to the town, a helmeted guard letting me in through a small door once the main gates were barred for the evening. He had chastised me for my night-time walks at first, telling me it was not safe to wander, and I had ignored him. I always sensed the watch of the guards from the ramparts, observing me until I was a speck on the landscape. Laslo was the worst, with eyes full of indulgent pity. I should have yelled at him, told him to lock me out, but I lacked the will. And so, I continued to walk, and they continued to let me pass as if I was merely a spirit walking along the river.

I was feeling a little more hard-headed than usual as I walked through the empty streets of Aldeigjuborg. If the markets had been on, the tavern might have been overflowing with visitors, and perhaps I might have found a fight. Being pummelled by fists would be a messy way to die, but if it brought the end to my Freyja-less nothing, I would have welcomed it.

As it was, most people sought the comfort of their hearth, leaving their homes only in the sunlight hours for work and play. Very few would stumble in the dark with a belly full of beer, impervious to the cold. Still, there was always one. As I approached the Skogarmaor, illuminated only by soft lantern light, I found Sven slumped over a bench and irretrievably intoxicated.

'*Darae*,' I cursed under my breath. To be there in that state in this weather was indeed foolish. But I was no better.

He was dressed only in dark wool pants and a long tunic, which might have been white at some point. His face and hands were so grimy that he appeared to have swum in brackish water. A deep exhale of annoyance stopped me, considering whether to leave him to the elements or help him.

'Errg,' he mumbled.

'Get up,' I said, jabbing him beneath the ribs with an aggressive finger.

'Ow, ouch!' His body slid off the bench, crumpling onto the earth. He pushed himself to his knees and swung his fists in the air, fighting the wind. He lost his balance and fell prone in the *slask*.

My patience did not last long. 'Sven, it's me,' I huffed. 'Put your fists away and get inside. You have to be in for the night or you may be robbed, or worse!'

His first response was a grunt. 'Perhaps,' he hiccoughed, 'I don't care about…' he continued, slurring his words.

'For some reason, I do.' I crouched next to him. 'I seem to care about you even when I do not for myself or anything else. So, get up!'

He struggled on the ground, unable to coordinate his movements well enough to lift himself to his feet. Covered in mud and snow which had caked to cold brown slush, his clothing was stuck to his body and he shivered.

'We have to go. Come on.' I pulled him up. His arm draped around my shoulder. 'Can you walk?'

He tried, stepping on his left foot, his right foot following along half walking half dragging behind it. His underarm was pressed against my cheek, reeking of sweat, smoke, and uncleanliness. My reward for rendering assistance.

When we had lived in Karlstad together, I had known Sven for his fastidious grooming. I had once joked that he had the most tools for hygiene out of any other member of our crew. That had been incorrect; there had been Erik, who had surpassed Sven in this. It was the first time I had seen Sven since Freyja's death, and the unkemptness of his appearance was nothing short of shocking. In the passing light, I could see his face was smeared with ash. His eyes were red-rimmed, and his skin was covered in a rash. I recoiled from the sight. Sven slid and almost fell.

'Ow!' he exclaimed, groping for my arm.

'Sorry,' I mumbled, helping him to continue. 'What's wrong with you, anyway?' I asked as we passed the carpentry yard.

His foot caught a rock, and we both stumbled forwards as the road sloped downwards. 'Just a littl' round und'r the feet, is all,' he drawled, followed by a loud wet-sounding burp.

'Oh, EW!' The redolence was distinctive of fermented fish and poor quality drink. I waved it away. 'You need to take better care of yourself, rather than spending all your time and money on drink and women.'

He groaned on my shoulder and mumbled some indiscernible words.

'And you stink,' I continued, turning my face away from his wafts of personal odour.

'Pit fire,' he replied, heavily enunciating the 't' with a forceful spit. My head whipped sideways to look at him. 'Down at the midden?' He nodded.

'No wonder you reek as you do.'

'Few people dyin' of sickness and burning them is the only way,' he managed through belches.

'Whatever made you stay in Aldeigjuborg to do that job?'

'You. I need to be here for you.' His mouth curled into something between a grin and a grimace before his head rolled back again with the effort.

Working the midden was hard work. Every manner of waste was hurled into there, which sometimes included the dead who could not be buried or burned properly. Stoking the pit fire was even worse. It was awful, arduous, rancid labour, and only the truly desperate would stoop to it.

The journey home felt inordinately long, dragging the great lump alongside me. And by the time we reached the landing, my body felt like it was being crushed into the earth. When Sven shifted his weight to the railing, it seemed like I was going to rise into the air, free from the encumbrance of his form.

'Come on,' I urged him into the hearth room, where he slumped onto the floor.

I walked to the doorway, obscured by his massive feet, and kicked them out of the way. 'Sven?' My voice roused him from his stupor, his eyes blinking open. 'How are you feeling?'

He smiled stupidly and raised a hand to touch my face. 'Astrid, you are a Val…' he trailed off, turning to his side and vomiting all over my floor. His expulsion of bodily fluids surged a new anger within me, and I shoved a pail under his head. He clung to it, as if it were a matter of life and death, heaving and retching loudly. I left him to it.

'You know, you're lucky I took you in. I didn't have to,' I declared when I returned later.

From the ground, he looked up at me. His bleary eyes betrayed his vulnerability. 'I'm sorry about all that,' he whispered.

I ignored his apology, still appalled at myself for caring. 'You've been throwing up all over my clean floors, but I've managed to get rid of most of it. Are you empty now?' I asked.

He nodded. 'But I feel as if I am caked in filth.'

'That's because you are,' I corrected, handing him a cup of watered ale. 'Fortunately for you, I have a tub and the means of filling it.'

Sven clambered to his feet, stumbling. 'It seems I am still a little unsteady.'

'Really? I was confident you would have shaken it off by now.' I rolled my eyes.

He sat on the bench. 'I'm not sure I can make it on my own.'

'You want me to help you bathe?'

'Please?' he implored, his helplessness quieting my anger.

'Odin's beard! But I am not scrubbing you. I'm not your maid,' I grumbled, shouldering his weight until we reached the tub at the foot of my bed.

It had taken considerable effort to lug it in and fill it with bucket after bucket of water for it to contain just enough to perch in for a shallow bath.

'Get in,' I commanded.

He obeyed, tottering over to the edge of the tub and holding it. He pulled his tunic awkwardly, struggling to get it over his head. 'Help?' a muffled plea emanated from the garment.

With no care, I tugged his tunic off and threw it in the basket. 'I am not helping you with your trousers.'

He fumbled with the knotted cord, squinting one eye as if it would help him see better.

'Urgh! Let me do it, then. How did you get yourself this bad?' I complained as I untied the string, hurrying to exit before he asked for anymore assistance.

He stepped into the tub and gasped. 'It's cold,' he cried.

In fact, it was almost glacial. 'It should refresh you, then.' I laughed. 'And, hopefully, you shall find it sobering.'

Sven squatted in the tub, barely fitting within its confines. On his back, swirling knotwork was inked into his skin. Depictions of the gods; ravens and even a... *Don't you dare think it. Not after everything he has done*, I warned myself. *He does not deserve it.*

'Don't drown yourself.' I left him to scrub while he glared at me over his heavily tattooed shoulder.

In the hearth room, I stoked the fire to roaring. *You laughed.* My heart dropped with the realisation, and at once I wanted to crawl back into the pain that tethered me to my daughter. Hilde had time and time again told me I should not lose myself to grief, but I had been unwilling, finding it a struggle to continue. Helping Sven had reminded me I was not the only one who suffered because of Neflaug's influence. The Norns screamed I was not done with life, no matter how much I might long for its end. They continued to weave until fate was finished with me, and I would have to follow.

From the other room, Sven called. Two oafish feet thudded on the ground as, I assumed, he left the tub.

I did not rise, expecting him to wrap himself and join me before the fire where I had made him a bed on the bench. But no sound followed. After some time, I crept into the dark bedroom that was quiet save for the drunken snoring of a man asleep.

'You're sleeping in here, then?' I whispered, not predicting a reply. To rouse him from slumber, I whipped the furs back. 'Sven! You're naked,' I exclaimed.

Sleepily, he reached out to me, clawing like a creature from the depths of the ocean. Long tentacles drawing its prey down into its lair. 'Stay with me,' he mumbled.

I pushed him away. 'No.'

There was not much resistance, he lacked the strength and resumed his snoring.

Momentarily, I thought about sleeping in Neflaug's chamber, but it was dusty and filled with terrible memories, so I proceeded to the hearth room to sleep on the bed I had made for Sven. It was a lot less comfortable than my sleeping quarters, but it was warm from the fire. With a huff, I covered myself in furs and closed my eyes.

Often when I slept, I had the same nightmare. Each time, I stumbled onto the ice, playing out different scenarios but always yielding the same result. Try as I might, every action led to Freyja perishing below the ice. And each time it left me feeling helpless as I scrambled on the surface, trying to save her from her fate. Sometimes I had a branch, dipping it below the surface for her to grab onto. Once, I crashed into the water and groped around. In one dream, I dove so deep under the water that I could not find the surface when I tried to rise, the cold water enveloping me in its deathly, and somehow comforting, embrace. That was how I hoped Freyja had experienced her end.

Horrifyingly, tonight, instead of the fishing hole, I butted against the unyielding layer of ice. There was no way out, no matter how fast my hands searched, digging my fingers between the fractures and trying to part them. I gasped for air as I woke, startled by the crackling flames.

'I could hear your cries from the room,' Sven said as he stood by the fire, stoking it and adding more wood.

'You don't have to do that,' I mumbled, sitting up and wrapping the furs around me.

'And you didn't have to sleep in here,' he replied over his shoulder.

I rubbed my eyes. 'There was a lout in my bed.'

He placed a log in the flames. 'I would have shared.' He looked inside the pot and, satisfied it contained water, put it on the hearth hook.

'The leaves might be bitter,' I warned. They were the same I had used the night before.

'Do you mind?'

'Not really,' I shrugged. The promise of a warm drink was more inviting than the thought of having to fetch fresh leaves from the stores.

Sven prodded the fire, waiting for the water to boil. 'This is quite some house. Not like the ones back home.'

'Hmm.'

'And not at all like the home we occupied in Karlstad. Well, maybe you lived in something similar when you married Aumund.' He took the pot from the fire, covering his hands with cloth, and looked around the room for mugs.

'Auden,' I answered, pointing at the small shelf on the wall where the earthenware was kept.

'Huh?'

With Sven looking at me, confused, he had neglected his task. I grabbed the mugs down and put them on the table. 'My first husband's name was Auden, as you should remember. And his house was grand, but it was communal. It was nothing like this.'

He poured the green-tinged liquid into the cups and pushed one towards me. 'How did you come to own it, if it is yours?'

'I do,' I nodded. 'A mix of good and bad fortune,' I answered, blowing on the drink to cool it.

'And so many strange baubles that appear to be from another world.'

My eyebrows shot upwards. 'Have you been poking around, Sven?'

He shrugged. 'A little.'

'Well, you are right. These "baubles" as you call them, come from another world.'

'How do you have them, then?' he asked, slurping loudly.

'Now you are willing to listen, eh?' I reclined against the wall, cradling my mug between my hands.

'Don't dig at me. I said I was sorry and I'm listening now.' He sat back in his seat.

'A wealthy woman, who wanted me to be her apprentice of sorts, transferred to me this property but she managed to get herself mixed up in all sorts of trouble. Oh, and I married an incredibly prosperous merchant.' To think back to my arrival in Aldeigjuborg with nothing, it was impressive to see how much wealth I had amassed in such a short time.

'Why did this woman gift you such a valuable property?' He shivered against the cold, bringing his blanket around his bare shoulders.

'Gift might be too generous a term to confer on Neflaug. I'm not sure that woman ever gifted anything freely without some condition. What did she say about me?' I asked.

He scratched his chin. 'At first, she claimed you two were once friends.'

'Mm, I am sure she did.'

'Then she said you contrived to take what was hers.'

'Not exactly the truth,' I scoffed.

'That's what she said, though.' He stopped to sip his tea. 'Then she told me her betrothed was slain.'

'Betrothed? Hah! That is generous. It is true that Eryk was murdered, but I would wager she never revealed that she had a hand in his death and that it forced her to flee the town because of it?' I asked.

'What? No. She never mentioned that,' he replied sheepishly.

'Anything else?' Now that I had him talking, it appeared the lengths Neflaug went to get her claws in was undeniably consistent.

'She said you were not to be trusted.'

'Perhaps she was right,' I agreed. 'She should never have trusted me, but I am glad she did. If she had not, things would have been much worse.'

Sven looked down at his hands. 'She also told me you were married and had a young child.'

I folded my arms. 'That part is true.'

'Is it a genuine marriage or only to cover for your daughter?' he asked.

'Handfasted is real enough. His name is Kjarr, and when he returns, you can meet him if you like.'

'Pah! No thank you,' he exclaimed. 'If he is such a good man, why has he not come back to you yet?' Sven rose and returned to the pot, sprinkling in oats and poking it with a spoon. 'Breakfast?' he asked.

'Yes, honey is in that jar if you're making porridge,' I replied, lifting down two bowls. 'And as for Kjarr, he is presently in Holmgardr. He won't be back until the spring, and that's not his fault. When the Grand Prince calls, you do not ignore his command. One can hardly refuse the ruler of all Gardarike, hmm?'

Sven stirred the pot furiously. 'A man of importance, huh? Oh, now I see why he is a better match than you and I would ever have made.' He glanced over his shoulder. 'He isn't me, and I'm sure he does not make you laugh,' he quipped with a wry grin.

'You are different in almost every aspect.' I had not meant the comment to be scathing, but it seemed Sven took it that way.

His mood darkened until he was mournful, looking at me with sad eyes. A cough to clear his throat and a strangled noise that escaped. 'Does he know yet?'

'Don't look at me like that. I cannot stand the pity I see in everyone's eyes as I pass.' I choked on my tears.

'That night on the ice was awful. I didn't understand what was happening until it was too late,' he began. 'There I was, drinking with some guards outside the walls, and we heard a noise. I was the first one there and… oh gods!' He looked away. 'Astrid, I swear if I could go back, it would be different.'

I bit my lip. 'I know. Every night I dream of it, replay it over and over. It was always going to be like that. Kjarr does not know yet, and I do not know how to tell him.' In truth, I could not bring myself to speak of it aloud or write it down, so I could not send a messenger. That kind of news should be delivered face-to-face. A familiar lump rose in my throat, and I forced it down. 'He was fond of her,' I finished.

Sven busied himself with stirring until the oats became creamy. He ladled it into two bowls, taking the dipper out of the jar to drizzle honey on our breakfast. 'Do you have work to do today?' he asked.

'There is always spinning to do, but I will not expect the ladies today. The snow is too deep to make the journey,' I answered between mouthfuls. 'Do you still believe all the lies Neflaug fed you?'

'Not all of them were lies.'

'And not all of it was the truth. Did you find it easier to swallow when she honeyed the untruths with kisses?' It was a cheap blow but effective.

He went crimson.

'So you?' I pushed the point.

He nodded.

'And I thought my disdain for your actions could fall no lower.'

'You blame me for what happened?' he asked, finding his voice.

'I was angry that you saved Neflaug when she was the one to have caused all of this. Don't you see how she weaved these lies? My life here, though you think it is grand, has not been without a heavy price.' My spoon dropped onto the table.

'What will you do about Neflaug?' As he asked, I knew at once there was a willingness to help me with whatever I decided.

'What is there to be done?'

'You were there when the Lawspeaker decried her, sentencing her to what will be her death.' Sven moved the bowls out of the way and leant both elbows on the table.

'I might have been there, but I was an unhearing, unseeing thing.' Helga had dragged me there, telling me it would help if I heard her punishment. But it did nothing.

Sven recalled the hearing. Most of the town had gathered. 'The Lawspeaker had loudly declared, "The law is clear, the woman Neflaug is guilty of the crime of killing the child Freyja," though he said she had not brought the death to mind so was her intent, or something like that. Then he announced to all, "Still, the child was killed by her own actions," so they found Neflaug liable.'

My eyes blinked heavily as if remembering a dream. 'I think I remember that much. They finally believed what I always knew she was capable of. And then what happened?'

'The Lawspeaker decided on a punishment. "She will not be put to death, though her punishment will almost certainly lead to it. She is to be an outlaw for the term of her life, to live outside the law's protection and to be stripped of all her possessions," then she was tossed outside the gates and she limped away without another word.'

'For once obliging to the fate the gods dealt her.' Though, I doubted it would be the end of her.

Sven drummed his fingers on the table, thinking. 'What revenge will you take on her?'

Grief had consumed me so completely that I had not turned my mind to avenging Freyja. *Could I leave Neflaug to the elements to wither away?* I would sooner cut her down for the satisfaction of watching her bleed before me. Neither would return my daughter to me, but avenge her, I must. The gods required it of me.

'I need to confront her first. It will do me no good until she understands she caused Freyja's death. I want her to have the pain of knowing her havoc on the world. She can wish for death, but it will not come for her until I permit it.' I banged my fists on the table, and Bjarndýr rattled on my wrist.

'Is that?' Sven asked, noticing my armring.

'My father's? Yes.' I nodded. It was a sign, and I knew where the Norns were leading me.

TWELVE

Shin high *slask* hindered our march as Sven and I waded slowly past the lower farms south of Aldeigjuborg. The frigid blast was pushing back, warning us no good would come of this confrontation. Sven had shocked me. First, for knowing that Neflaug was likely huddling in a ramshackle shelter on the edge of the forest, and second, for his insistence on accompanying me there. Neflaug would freeze in that hovel, far from the town walls. *It was the torture she deserved*, I told myself.

I tied Skara to my belt, beneath the folds of fabric, the metal warming under the layers. My cloak was already covered with fresh fallen snow, and the new white flakes fell from the sky and lay upon the brown sludge that slurped under our boots. To the bottom of our shoes, we secured snowshoes. Made from a hoop frame of ash, around which webbing and bindings of animal hide were attached. It made traversing the snowfall possible, but caused our steps to be cumbersome.

Sven's face beside me was obscured by his large woollen hood. Before we departed, he told me the revenge I enacted had to be of my own choosing; he would just act as backup. So, we left in the wicked wind on an errand I had not yet fully fleshed out.

When I saw her, would I beat the door down and confront her? Would I hurt her and flee? It was unlikely that she would be in any condition to offer resistance, whatever I decided.

Last anybody had heard of Neflaug, she had been driven from the town after being declared an outlaw. She seemed to have had enough strength to escape on her own. From then on, anyone could mete out their anger upon her without fear of legal consequence. Most outlaws spent their days hiding or banding with others of the same fate in a type of nomadic existence.

My leg gave way and my shin caught a rock concealed under the snow. 'Gods!' I exclaimed, falling to the ground.

Sven reached out his arm to pull me up. I smiled in thanks, but neither of us could see the other's face except for the eyes, the rest covered by scarves. As we walked on, the sleet eased a little, making conversation possible.

'For a moment there, I thought we might get caught in a snowstorm.' Sven laughed, lowering his hood.

'So did I, and it almost had me thinking this venture was truly foolish. What if we got stuck out here because of my need to confront Neflaug?' I asked.

'You think revenge is stupid?'

I shook my head with great difficulty. The thickness of the two hoods combined made movement of any kind difficult. 'No. And now that we have come so far, we cannot turn back.'

He stared at the pitch of the hill below and sighed. 'It's going to be worse on the way back.'

'It's a slippery slope down. Surely going up will be easier?' I hoped.

The path was mixed up with mud and ice, and bore the markings of those who had attempted the same before us.

'Depends on how wet it gets between now and when we return,' he replied as we both stood contemplating our descent. It was the last hill before crossing the Ladozhka River in her frozen state. Around us, the farms had disappeared, replaced by forest which was outside the view of the guards.

'Come on,' I urged him, plodding down the hill.

My feet slipped more than once, but the rocks underneath provided enough grip to slow my pace. Once we made it to the bottom, the next step was to remove our snowshoes and replace them with bone skates to cross the narrow tributary. Usually, it would have been possible to continue across the frozen waterway without them, but heavy rainfall preceding the winter frost had ensured the river was full and high when it froze. The crossing only took a few steps to reach the other side.

'It feels a waste to have brought them,' Sven grumbled, sitting in the snow to remove his skates and reattach the snowshoes.

'You wouldn't be saying that if you had fallen on your backside a few times. Is that it?' I asked, nodding toward a hut no bigger than my hearth room. It was in bad repair, with a door that hung from its hinges. From the central hole in the roof, I saw a puff of smoke signalling a fire lit inside. Sven strode ahead.

'Wait,' I ordered, stilling him with my hand against his chest. 'I want to go first.'

'Are you sure?' he asked, hesitating. 'What will you do?'

I pulled Skara out from my belt and shrugged. 'I don't know, but I need to go alone.'

There was no landing for the house, no floor inside, and I knew that would permeate the cold through the room with a chilling effect. I knocked, and the door flapped with each rap of knuckles upon it. Over my shoulder shot Sven's impatient fist, banging on what remained of the door.

'Open up, you wicked lying wench,' he bellowed.

A weak voice answered in the distance. 'Go away,' she cried.

'What happened to you waiting for me to do things my own way?' I rolled my eyes at Sven.

'I was just trying to help. Sorry, yes. Go ahead.' He stood back.

I tried again. 'Neflaug, it's me. Open up.'

There was silence, then a slow shuffling until it met the door. Her elegant fingers grasped the edge of the door in the shadows, and she peered around it with her green eyes visible above the rags she wore. Her eyes were devoid of their previous vibrancy. At once I doubted my want of violent revenge.

'Can I come in?' I asked, wondering why I bothered with politeness after everything she had done.

'Why are you asking?' Sven asked, outraged.

I rounded on him. 'Stay here! And don't you dare enter unless I call for you,' I warned.

Neflaug turned, and I followed her inside. It was dark except for the light coming from the small fire in the middle of the room. The smoke made the house dry and filled it with clouds of irritating fumes.

I coughed. 'I'm sure you know why I have come,' I began, gripping Skara's handle.

Neflaug clambered into her cabin bed, barely long enough to accommodate her, and curled into a ball. She hugged her legs, wrapping her arms around them and rocking back and forth. She groaned but spoke no words.

'Are you listening?' I asked.

Still, she rocked, groaning to herself.

'Neflaug?' Annoyed with the one-way conversation, I approached, pulling back the dirty and hole-ridden blankets. 'Neflaug, your face!' I recoiled in disgust, replacing Skara on my belt loop.

There was no need for a weapon, not after seeing Neflaug's frost-ravaged skin. Her hands quickly covered her blackened appearance and cavities that appeared where her once lovely features had been.

'Don't look at me!' she shrieked.

I pulled her hands away to examine her. The tip of her nose was dark and decayed, her fingers were bluish-purple, as were her lips, and some rash that had crusted marked her face and turned to flaking skin.

'Vain, beautiful, Neflaug.' My voice seethed as I stood back, watching her cover her hideous appearance. 'Seems the gods have exacted their own revenge upon you,' I muttered as I walked to Sven.

'What is going on?' he asked. 'I heard her shrieking at you and I thought I should come in, but you told me to stay.'

'Everything is fine. Nothing happened. The ice has bitten Neflaug. Her nose is falling off, her fingers won't be long behind, and her face is burned by the cold. Her toes are probably the same way. It will be a slow and painful decline for her. I've seen it before. Enough to drive the sufferer to madness, and she was already halfway there.' I picked up a stick nearby and prodded it into the depths of the snow.

'What do we do?' Sven asked.

'Give her some food and water. Make her eat, allow her adequate strength to prolong it for as long as possible,' I replied.

'Some revenge,' he scoffed. 'No stabbing, no screaming, no blood. You know, you are entitled to do it however you like,' Sven complained, finding his own stick to draw patterns in the dirt-stained snow.

'Believe me, there will be a good deal of screaming. Just none at the bite of Skara today. It's her own private nightmare, where she has to dwell on the horrors she has created. Who knows, perhaps Loki should whisper some awful things into her ear he thinks she ought to consider.'

Sven rubbed his chin. 'That's cruel.'

'Is it too much?' I thought for a moment. 'You think I should kill her instead?'

He shook his head. 'It's your revenge. Your decision.'

'Neflaug never sought to ease anyone else's suffering, so I will not do her the kindness of ending hers. No, her days will end with her beauty falling away. And then the gods will allow her to breathe her last, knowing she caused it all and no one else.' I threw my stick down. 'Sven, come help me.'

We marched to the well. The water source was fed by a spring nearby and sometimes by the river. I took a small bucket and tied it to the rope, easing it down the narrow shaft.

'Will it be frozen over?' Sven asked, looking into the blackness.

'I hope not,' I replied. 'Down that far, even below the Volkhov, it still flows. As long as it was not stagnant before the chill, we should be able to draw something up.' With some effort, I retrieved the bucket.

'It's full.' Sven grabbed the pail and sniffed. 'Does it smell right to you?' he asked.

'If your nose is as cold as mine, you can't smell a thing. I'm sure it's just fine,' I dismissed, carrying it back towards the hut. 'And anyway, we're not drinking it. Let's give it to her and she can hope she doesn't end up with a bellyache.'

'That's the least of her worries,' Sven mumbled.

Before we went inside, I rifled through Sven's bag. 'What have you got in here that she could eat?'

'Why are you giving away my dinner?' He snatched it back.

'Because you're going to come and live with me,' I replied. 'Don't pretend you have anywhere else to go. I'll feed you, even give you Neflaug's old room, so long as you tidy up and help with whatever I need.'

'Alright,' he acquiesced, handing me the contents. 'There are a couple of oatcakes but not much else.'

'And if you're looking for paid work,' I added, 'Luca and Mikel were needing someone to strip the logs they brought in over the spring.' On the tree line, I spied some bushes. 'You think there would be anything on those that could be eaten?'

'Ha! You can tell you've lived in the city for too long asking questions like that.' Sven laughed. 'There'll be no food out here unless you bring it yourself or you happen upon a sleeping animal with your weapons.'

'Alright, stay here. I'll go in and give this to her, then we can get home and warm up.'

Inside, Neflaug had not moved, but she had ceased her groaning. 'Neflaug? I have some food and water.' I pushed the oatcakes into her black-tinged fingers.

'No,' she squawked, dropping them onto the ground. Her eyes flicked back to the food. I knew she was hungry.

'At least drink,' I offered, reaching for a ladle from the wall and dipping it into the liquid. This time she crept forward, receiving a small sip and then another until she gulped down to sate her thirst. She let me hand her the oatcakes, saying nothing but open to the idea of their consumption. We sat opposite each other without talking. Through the doorway, I could see Sven whittling and whistling to himself as the sun came out.

'Kill me,' Neflaug whispered from her bed.

My eyes narrowed. 'What did you say?'

She sat up, draping her legs over the edge and hunching her shoulders. 'You know I am going to die, so kill me. Take your revenge and do it now.' She held her head up in defiance.

'No, Neflaug, I will not kill you. There will be no easy way out of this,' I replied.

She wheezed, then broke into a coughing fit. Eventually, she composed herself. Her eyes were glazed, and with ragged breath, she continued, 'You can see it. I am dying.'

I had seen men and women die before. Sometimes the process was slow, the sheen of life ebbing away until all that remained was a stiff, pale shell. There was no doubt that would be Neflaug's fate.

'If you believe your end is coming, then use this time to think about what you have done. Are you even capable of such a thing?' I asked, forcing back the tears that welled in my eyes.

She shook her head. 'I do not wish to prolong it, and I know I must pay for all the wrongs. It grieves me that the gods will not welcome me into their hall.' Her tone was reproachful rather than remorseful, and it irked me.

'You killed your own child!' I screamed.

She turned her face to the ground before snapping back to her haughty posture. 'But she was never mine, was she?' She clasped her fingers together and winced from the pain. 'You were right. I abandoned her. You took her in, cared for her and loved her. I didn't want to give her up, Signe.'

'Then why did you?' I asked.

She shrugged and sniffed from the crater that had once been a perfectly formed nose.

'Hilde told me about what happened with your husband,' I probed, wanting answers.

'Which part?' Her eyes flashed with the bright malice they held previously. 'How I poisoned him and took everything he had?'

A deep breath steadied my annoyance at her outburst. 'The years of longing for a baby that went unfulfilled.'

'Oh.' She shrank into herself, creeping back into the bed. 'For a long time, I wanted a child, a daughter.'

'And you had her. You birthed her, you nursed Freyja,' I cried.

'But I could not keep her,' Neflaug answered between sobs.

'Why?'

Neflaug leaned forward. 'Something stopped me.'

'I would have helped you.'

'It's nothing you could have supported me with. No one could remove it,' she seethed. 'I wanted a child so badly, and even when it happened, other things got in the way.'

'Like power?' I assumed.

She pursed her cold lips and looked away. 'Yes, power became my drink, and when I found out I was with child, I could not believe it. That was a cruel tapestry the Norns wove for me.'

'They left other paths open, but this is the one you took.'

'No, Signe,' she yelled with a hint of mockery. 'There were no other paths! I was cursed no matter what I did.'

'What in Midgard are you talking about?' My head hurt from keeping up with Neflaug's nonsense.

'I'm cursed,' she began. 'A long time ago, my great husband had a slave woman he preferred. He made that much clear after I failed to give him an heir. The thrall threw it in my face as often as she could, and when I found out his seed had taken root inside of her, I cast her out. But before I got rid of her, she spoke in strange tongues. I recognised enough to hear the words "your love is death." From then on, whoever I loved met their end and, I knew, the same would happen to the child I had yearned for. So, I had to give her up, and perhaps she would have lived if I could have left her alone. But there was an itch inside me to get her and to plague you.' She scratched her face, flakes of skin floating to the floor. 'I was never fit to be a mother. That is why the gods never allowed it.'

I swatted away tears. 'Until they did.'

She nodded. 'I cried for weeks after I gave her up, knowing it was the worst decision. With no way to take control, I drank. On that night when I took her, my spirit was so tangled I couldn't see straight. There was a voice inside that goaded me, and I listened to it. "Teach her to ice dance," it said, just as my mother had done with me.' She broke down, crying. 'Is there anything I could do to provide her vengeance?'

'Say her name,' I growled.

'What can I do to give Freyja peace, Signe?' she replied.

Her question disgusted me. 'My name is Astrid,' I answered, knowing that revealing my identity to the dying woman bore no consequence.

'I always knew you were hiding something.' She smiled. 'What revenge will you take, Astrid?' She lifted her chin high above the blankets, a proud defiance against her coming demise.

'Your slow and painful disintegration into the earth is retribution enough for me. In the end, you will be of no importance, buried without ceremony. No one will remember your name,' I responded coldly.

Her breath caught, and as I turned away, she wailed. 'Please, don't leave me here. Kill me, kill me! I can't stand the voices.'

When I reached Sven, he waved a whittled horse in my direction. Seeing my face, he stopped and wrapped his arms around me. 'Are you alright?'

'No,' I answered, my voice muffled against his chest. 'As long as she lives, I will have no solace. But my reprieve will come knowing that her evilness will torture her until her final breath.'

115

THIRTEEN

'This blizzard will trap us in,' Sven complained, shutting the door against the wind. He helped himself to a third cup of nettle tea. 'Pah!' He spat a leaf from his mouth with force. 'It's getting weak now. Do we have any more?'

I pushed my mug away, noting its increasing bitterness. The leaves had steeped too long, used over and over, and left a harsh taste. 'I'll have to search the stores after I thaw out my fingers.' *I knew I should have put some gloves on.*

'Is winter always this frigid in Aldeigjuborg?' he asked, waving his hands over the fire. Though it was morning, the sun had not risen. The only warmth we had was by our own creation.

'Never this bad. Odin's beard! My fingers are so cold.' I disappeared to my room to fetch my gloves.

'Bring back some blankets, will you? We might have to huddle by the fire,' his voice carried from the hearth room.

'It'll be out soon, and I can't go out for more firewood. We will have to make do with shelter and clothing until it passes,' I called, throwing Sven a heavy fur. 'There is nothing more we can do.'

He held the furs open, inviting me inside. 'You know, it's not what you want to hear, but we may need to huddle together for warmth once the fire is spent.'

I laughed. 'It's not that bad. Anyway, I've got spinning to do, and I'm sure you can whittle a companion for your horse to pass the time.'

He shifted closer to the dying flames. 'Mm-hmm,' he agreed, taking out the knife and getting to work. With a look of concentration and his tongue out, he chipped fragments off the pine.

My spindle spun around as I paced back and forth. 'We won't be able to travel to Neflaug until this storm passes.' The whorl wobbled, causing a break in the thread.

'You want to return?' Sven glanced up from what looked like a small cat emerging from the wood.

After reattaching the wool together, I resumed my spinning. 'It was my intention, but I doubt she would have survived this snowstorm. Before it came, I would have given her a week, now... It's just... I have more questions.' I paused. 'I have to know if those "gifts" that were left on my landing were from her and why she left them.'

'You might never know, even if she is still breathing,' he warned.

Around the cup of my drop spindle, I wrapped the long thread and set it down. 'Sven?' I looked at him across the table. 'I'm glad you found me.'

'Uh, uh... really? You are?' He stumbled over his words. 'At first, I wasn't sure that you wanted me to look for you. But I had to.' He smiled.

'I don't doubt that for a moment,' I answered, wrapping a fur around my shoulders. For some time, I had wondered if his discovery of me had been by chance or by his will. With curiosity piqued, I looked at him through the veil of furs that obscured my face. 'Was it difficult?'

'It was no easy feat to find you.'

The fire fizzled out, and an acrid cloud floated from the ashes causing us both to cough.

'What made you decide to search for me?' I asked.

He tottered over to the bench, propping himself against the wall. In his hands, he held his carving. 'Besides being in love with you?' he answered with his usual grin.

His candour ripped the floor from beneath me, provoking the sharp intake of my breath and an inability to bring any words to mind. All I found was a deaf nod.

He glanced sideways, his own cheeks flushed. 'It was Erik actually.'

'Erik from Karlstad?' The man was known for his vanity, not his wisdom.

'He convinced me to look for you.'

My eyebrows shot up. 'Why would he do that?'

Sven scratched at the stubble on his cheek. 'Erik recognised what I saw a long time ago. He appreciates beauty, in all its forms.'

'Oh really?' I scoffed, removing a glove and throwing it at his head. 'And when was it that Erik persuaded you to take such a journey?'

From inside his furs, Sven's cat carving emerged. He set it on the table between us. 'Do you want to hear the entire story, then?'

'We have time, don't we?' I shrugged, accepting the open pelts and sitting next to him on the bench. Shoulder-to-shoulder was warmer than on our own.

'So much time,' he agreed.

Sven told me how all the men from our village had been assigned to ships and set off for the summer raids with Jarl Soren. They had met with success off the coast of Irland. Even Sven had been enriched with gold and trinkets, some of which he sold at his earliest opportunity. What remained, he had pocketed, intending to return home to his mother, who had dutifully found a wife for him. And from there, his life would be made.

'It was then I realised what you had been saying all along. A life that was already laid out for you was no life at all. You wanted to be free to choose and so did I. The whole time, I was having this grand adventure, and when I returned was expected to marry some village girl, have some children and grow some vegetables. Maybe I would raid again someday if I was lucky enough. I might even live a good life, but it wasn't the future I saw when I dreamed at night,' he explained.

'You finally understood,' I pushed him gently. 'But it was too late.'

'By then, it was too late,' he agreed. 'Or so I thought at first.' He rubbed his hands together to warm them. 'But I had not returned home. We were on our way back to Birka, and I had not discovered if you had died or fled. The other warriors called me love bound, all except Erik.'

'Erik the beautiful?' I asked, toying with the carved cat.

'Ha! He would like that. Yes. He told me if the Norns destined it, then the thread of our lives would once again intertwine. Don't punch me,' he flinched.

Instead, I elbowed him in the ribs.

'Ouch! But I found you, didn't I? Doesn't that prove the Norns want us together?' he asked, rubbing his side.

'All it proves is that we are in the same place at the same time. What happens with that proximity is still up to us.' I shrugged off the furs and shifted along the bench. 'And when you got to Birka, what happened?'

'When I got there, I thought I might stay for a while or journey back to Karlstad for the winter. Something got inside my head. It might have been the *völva* that prophesied my fate. She told me I was headed for a land ruled by the future. At the time it sounded like nonsense, but she couldn't lie, could she?' he asked, staring at the wall.

I shrugged. 'I don't know.'

'After the seer's words, I asked around. Most people did not know what "a land ruled by the future" could be until I met some merchants. They told me Gardarike was leading its people to a new age. So, I guessed that must have been it, but then I met someone.'

'Oh?'

'Her name was Signe. She told me she had been bound for Gardarike as a spinning woman, but the vessel meant to take her sailed without her on it,' he explained.

'Hmm,' I mumbled, looking at the ground. 'I feel bad about that. But, I swear I did not do it on purpose. Björn mistook me for Signe, and I never corrected him. Was she terribly angry?'

'I was told she wandered around wailing for the first week before acknowledging that no one was coming for her.'

'Urgh.'

'Then things improved. She met Erik.' Sven smiled.

'Your Erik from Karlstad again?' I asked.

He nodded. 'As soon as they saw each other, they were bound. We spent some time in Birka, the three of us, and when I left for Gardarike, they left for Karlstad.'

'So, Signe now lives in Karlstad, and I am here as her?' I laughed, glad that the woman had found happiness and not misfortune as a result of my dishonesty. 'What fate the Norns weave.'

'Once I understood what had happened, I spent a lot of coin securing the passage here. Originally, I was heading to Kyiv, hearing of its size and thinking you would head for the largest town. But on the way, the merchants warned against it because of the conflict between the rulers there and in Holmgardr. So, we went there instead.' He tapped his fingers on the table.

'You sailed right past me,' I chuckled.

He laughed. 'I did, and I might have stayed there too, but I met some, let's call it, misfortune in Holmgardr, which made staying there impossible. By that time, I was losing my resolve and even considered joining the town guard. With no plan of my own, I joined with a band of merchants bound for Aldeigjuborg. Then we got attacked by marauders.'

'Interesting turn,' I replied, my mouth pursed in a bemused smile.

'Hmm, why?'

'Did you not just return from raiding?' I asked.

'Suppose I did,' he agreed, not seeing the irony. 'The attackers killed a man in our group, though we were able to force them back. As you know, I made it to Aldeigjuborg. Then I met that awful woman Neflaug, saw you, misjudged you,' he glanced up, 'spent the rest of my silver on drink and gambling. When it was gone, I worked the pits, made some dreadful mistakes, and now, here I am.'

The cold caused me to shiver, and I sidled up to Sven again. 'You're lucky you were not robbed or killed along the way.'

'Weren't you listening? They robbed us! The marauders took most of what I had, except what was in my boot!' He stamped his foot on the floor.

'A tough lesson to learn,' I mumbled.

'What do you mean?' he asked.

'I've pondered my desire to raid. When I was younger, I thought my father was some sort of brave warrior. He was, but perhaps taking things by force is not the only way to achieve one's wealth,' I explained.

'It's been our way for a long time.' Sven glanced sideways. 'If others are not strong enough to defend what is theirs, then we are free to take it.'

'And were you weak when those marauders killed a man in your travelling party and stole you coin?' I asked.

'Err,' he stammered.

'There are other methods to grow wealthy. And if you are going to steal and fight, then people will not trust your word. It's possible to earn a lot of gold by trade without ever having to raise your sword or axe.'

Sven pressed his fists under his chin. 'More riches than raiding one of those priest islands?'

'In time. The most important difference is that trading is a repeatable activity. When you raid, there is never a guarantee that you'll leave with anything of value,' I continued.

'You'll not always make coin from a trade,' Sven pointed out.

'True. There might be times it does not happen, but if you continue, eventually you'll establish a route and people who will buy from you,' I replied.

Sven continued to stare. 'So, you no longer want to be a warrior?'

'That part of me will never perish, but I am more than that. As I learn, the more I realise there is even more unknown to me.'

'Thank the gods I found you now or I might have had to journey to Miklagard chasing after your trade adventures.' He picked up his carving and continued to finesse the details of the animal. 'It turned out the hard part was not in locating you, but when we saw each other again.'

'You never doubted finding me?' I asked.

'Never.'

'Only you, Sven. Like finding a lone stone amongst the fjords of home.' I complimented his optimism.

'And Erik, he believed it too.'

'Hmm mm,' I agreed, admiring Sven's skill at carving.

'For Freyja,' he whispered with a small smile, taking my hand.

'She would have loved it.' I smiled. 'Some nights I lie awake, wondering if her body is caught somewhere or if she has been carried away.'

'Things will get easier.' Sven squeezed my palm. 'Not easier. I shouldn't say that, but you will go on and you'll not forget her.'

I nodded. In time, the pain would ease.

'Should I find something for us to eat?' Sven asked. 'Are there oats still? How would you like them? Dry or in cold ice water?'

We both laughed.

'Maybe we should sleep the day away, hungry bellies and frozen bodies, and hope tomorrow the storm has passed,' Sven suggested.

The next morning, the worst of the snowstorm had passed, and it was an uncharacteristically warm winter's day. The white that covered everything yielded to the sun's rays, obligingly melting away to expose glimpses of the rock and dying grass beneath it. Sven and I decided the weather had improved enough to attempt a visit to Neflaug. Armed with dried oats, some preserved fruit, and our weapons, we set off. The journey out of the gates was without event. The townspeople loitered in the sunshine, planning work that could be accomplished in the favourable conditions.

Seated on a bench, making the most of the weather and scribbling in his notebook, was the foreign man, Ahmed Ibn Rashti. He looked up from his book as we passed. 'Signe.' He dipped his head.

'You're still here,' I replied.

'My situation worsens. Now, I find myself searching for passage upriver,' he explained.

'You should ask Sihtric when he returns. Our trade takes us in the direction come spring and the crew is yet to be finalised,' I suggested.

'I will do just that. *Shukran*,' he smiled.

Sven's eyes boggled as we continued on our way.

'I told you I'd learned some things since being here.' I laughed.

As we neared the gates, even the guards were smiling, except the two Igors. I wasn't sure they ever did more than sneer.

We took the way down the last hill with care, grabbing tufts of grass to steady our progress as our feet skidded on the moist ground.

'Be careful,' Sven cautioned, as I fell onto my backside, my overdress dampening. He offered his hand.

'I don't need any help.' I swatted him away. Back on my feet, I pulled my dress up to my knees and continued. My shoe slipped on a puddle of mud, and my ankle twisted painfully, making me slide a body length down the rise.

Sven huffed impatiently at my protested independence. 'Just take my hand.'

'Fine,' I agreed, accepting it as we ambled down the slippery slope. 'We should have brought our snowshoes, but I did not think it would be this bad.'

There was no smoke billowing from the roof of the hut when it came into view. The door still hung at a strange angle, and the snow lay undisturbed at the front of the dwelling. I pushed the door open. The smell of defecation was the first to assault my senses before I noticed Neflaug's body on the floor, next to the bed. The rest of the room was unchanged, and in the middle was the bucket with the ladle sticking out as it had been when I was last there.

I covered my mouth and nose with my under hood, drawing closer to inspect the dead woman. She had expired from retching her stomach empty and voiding her bowels until she could no longer. The pail that previously contained water drawn from the spring well was overflowing with Neflaug's repulsed fluid. Bile rose in my throat, and I hurried from the room.

'Don't go in there,' I warned Sven.

'What's wrong?'

'She's dead, but there is... Urgh.' I vomited into the bushes.

Sven, despite my warning, popped his head inside to take a peek. 'Gods!' he exclaimed, running away as fast as I had. 'What a way to die. Promise me you'll never let me perish like that. Cut my throat if you need to.'

Although I rolled my eyes at his dramatic outburst, I fully agreed that it was an undignified end. 'We have to bury her.'

'Or burn her.' Sven doubled over, fanning his face with his hand. 'Just burn the whole house down with her inside.'

'No, it has to be a burial. I don't want the fire smoke to carry her to any sort of afterlife. If the gods want her, they can come and get her.' I searched the yard for a shovel and found one leaning against the back. 'We'll bury her just inside the tree line.'

'I'm not touching her,' Sven managed through dry heaving.

'You dig the hole. I'll bring her out,' I replied.

'Might need your axe to cut through the earth here. It's as hard as ice,' Sven complained through gritted teeth, but continued.

'I wouldn't waste Skara on her. Keep going, I'll be back in a moment.'

Sven stopped, leaning on the shaft of the shovel. 'Are you sure? I don't like this.'

'Stop worrying, it'll be fine.'

She's heavier than she appears, I thought as I lugged her across the dirt on a blanket. I hadn't wanted to touch her, but it was necessary to roll her onto the blanket if I would not carry her out. As I dragged her along the bumpy ground, I almost pitied her, but cradling her in my arms was a step too far.

'That's deep enough,' I managed through ragged breath as I reached Sven. It would be a shallow grave, but I loathed to waste any more time making it deeper.

'Did you touch her?' Sven asked.

'Barely, help me get her in.'

We pushed her into the cavity with our feet and, as she thudded onto the ground, I noticed a distaff clasped in her fingers. I jumped down and prized it from her grasp.

'What are you doing?' Sven asked, looking down.

'Have a look at this,' I grunted, throwing the distaff to him and clambering out. 'There's writing on it. What does it say?'

'How should I know?'

'She's carved something into the shaft. Here, hand it to me,' I asked, standing next to him. 'Listen, "drawn from the sky, I have spun great lengths. This distaff belonged to Neflaug. A woman who lived a life of her own." Sounds like Neflaug,' I derided, throwing the spinning tool back into the dirt with its owner.

As I stood, looking down at Neflaug's lifeless body, I thought about the inscription's meaning. In her last moments, my previous master had clung to the belief that she had done things her way, and maybe she did. Neflaug had the longest, most enchanted thread I had ever known. The Norns had moved her to heights, and she had tumbled. In the end, I knew her thirst for power had driven to her entanglement.

'To the worms you will go,' I spoke, throwing earth upon her. We continued until nothing was visible.

Sven smoothed the top of the burial flat and stood back. 'You know I do not do this for her. There was no connection between us except her desire to use me to get to you.' He threw the shovel down. 'This is only for you.'

'I know,' I answered. After learning of Neflaug's lies, he had a guilty heart and, if time could be reversed, he would have thrown the woman aside for the merest chance of saving Freyja. Though we both knew it would have changed nothing.

'Do you want to say anything?' he asked.

'There is nothing more to say.' At the head of the site, I placed a marking stone. It would bear no inscription, but should I ever want to return, it would help me find the location.

'The Valkyrie will not come for her. She will dwell in the dark corners of Hel, ruled by the same, and never leave. Neflaug was not brave, nor kind, not of any great renown. She is nothing more than rotting flesh in the ground. Food for the creatures of the dirt,' Sven spoke slowly, then turned, picking up his bag and fastening his axe to his belt.

I blinked, surprised at the eloquence of his speech.

'What now?' he asked, ready to leave.

'I still have a business to run, contacts to make. What have you decided?'

'I'm not leaving you again, *minn Svanr*. You said Luca and Mikel might need a strong man, so I will begin there.' He flashed me a wide smile. 'And, if there is anything you require a man for around the warehouse, I can do that too.'

'You can start by forgetting that ridiculous pet name,' I demanded.

We laughed awkwardly, facing each other. He edged closer and took my hand.

'If that's what you want, I will,' he promised.

Without responding, I tucked Skara into my belt and made off in the direction of the hill. About halfway up the rise, we heard a rustle from the tree line and stopped to listen.

'Did you hear anything?' I asked Sven in a whisper.

He nodded, holding his hand up to silence me.

We scrambled, as quietly as possible, to the top. I crested the peak before Sven, just in time to see a couple of skeletal men emerging from the foliage. *One, two, three. There's three of them.* Not daring to move for being noticed, I could not look back at Sven. We were both frozen to the spot.

My foot slipped in the mud, and I crashed to the ground. I cursed. The men turned, having undoubtedly heard my fall.

'Over there,' a man in the dark hood called to his friends in a dialect I had heard before.

'It's a girl,' the lanky one yelled back.

'How can you tell?' Dark Hood asked.

The third member squinted in my direction as I stayed low to the ground, considering my next move. 'Yeah, it's a girl. A nice looking one.'

'How would you even know under all those layers?' Dark Hood teased.

Sven was below their eye-line, still on the hill's ascent. The three men could only see me and, I knew, if I made a run for town, they would easily outstrip me. The guards would be no help. At this distance, we were not on their watch. We were on our own. But we had one advantage; the men had not yet seen Sven.

'Grab the girl,' the tall one with beady eyes goaded his companions. 'I fancy a bit of sport. When was the last time we trussed up a squealing pig, eh?' They laughed menacingly and advanced.

Sven braced, hand on the throat of his axe. 'What are they saying, Astrid?' he whispered. 'I don't like the sounds of them.'

'It's a local dialect. They are not our friends. Be ready,' I warned as I scrambled onto my feet and whipped out Skara, holding her before me.

'Whoa ho! Look, the wench wants to play before she lies at our feet. Alright, then.' Beady Eyes must have been the leader. He grinned as he leapt towards me. 'I like a challenge.'

By now he was three steps from me, and Sven had mounted the rise, standing behind me. His sudden appearance gave me the advantage against Beady Eyes, and I kicked him in the shin.

'Bitch!' Beady Eyes howled, his breath foul on my face.

His two comrades came forward, holding their short blades forth with maniacal eagerness. We faced each other. Sven and I against the three of them, measuring the other's abilities.

Outlaws? I wondered. But none of the men's faces were marked by the type that was burned into the skin. Their clothing was simple, except for their belts, which bore a striking resemblance to the intricately woven colourful designs as familiar as the language they spoke.

Beady Eyes muttered under his breath to Dark Hood, who squared up to me while the other two decided on Sven.

Dark Hood waved his blade in my face. 'Come on, piggy,' he grunted.

The fire rose in me, and I swung Skara to the right. He jumped out of the way. Dark Hood was slow but sure of himself. I swapped hands, landing a strong backswing in the space between his shoulder and neck just as he slipped in the mud. The move caught him off guard, and he fell with a thud, blood spurting from his collarbone. He was done much faster than I had expected, and it had been a lucky swing.

As I tore my axe from his flesh, I ducked, narrowly avoiding the edge of Lanky's short sword. I spat on the ground and readied for the fight.

This man was cannier than the other, and it would take considerable effort to bring him down.

'Sven, a little help?' I called out as the man circled me like a cat.

'Not right now,' Sven cried between clashes of metal upon metal.

Lanky was a rake, with skin darker than my own. His tawny brown hair and eyes the same colour. There was very little contrast to his appearance at all. As he prowled, I realised my face betrayed my fear. And I attempted to fix my expression with an intense stare to fake confidence. Now on my own, Sven had his own battle to win against Beady Eyes.

The man before me was strong, the strength that did well with a bow and arrow. But it was a different power that was required for hand-to-hand fighting, and brute force did not mean agile. A few parries in, I found myself outmanoeuvred. Every step I feinted lured him into taking one of his own until I tired without landing a blow. I stepped to the left just as Sven's axe went hurtling past, straight into Lanky's arm.

He recoiled but did not go down. There was a moment when he stumbled back, and I thought he might yield. Instead, he tossed his head back, face to the sky, and let out a cry of fury as Sven retrieved his weapon.

'Submit to me,' I yelled.

He laughed, bleeding heavily from his forearm as he continued to thrust his short blade towards me. But his time had run out. As his blood pulsed from his body, he slumped to the ground and muttered some indistinguishable words through the groans.

I left Lanky to bleed out on the ground, running to help Sven, who was still fighting with Beady Eyes. Distracted by Sven's axe, the man had no time to defend the kick to the back of his knee. He hit the dirt, dropping his sword.

'Where did you come from?' I asked, speaking the language Hilde had taught me.

'Nowhere. We belong to no one,' he answered through clenched teeth.

'Then why are you here?' I screamed as he capitulated to Sven's axe. He sat back, his mouth full of blood from a well landed punch to the face.

'Easy prey,' he smiled. Blood seeped through his decaying grin.

'Not so easy,' I corrected.

Sven's axe whirled through the air, landing a sickening crack as the metal met sinew. A couple more swings and Sven severed Beady Eyes' head from his body.

My friend dropped to his knees next to me. 'You did well,' he congratulated me as I rested beside him. 'What did they say?'

With a piece of cloth, I wiped away the blood from Skara's bit. 'That they saw an opportunity and acted on it, nothing more.'

'And you believed them?' he asked.

'Should I not?'

Sven pushed himself up against the trunk of a tree. 'When I was with Jarl Soren's men, we always sent a scouting party to see if any dangers lay ahead.'

I stood up, dusting off my skirts and pulling Sven to his feet. 'And you think that's what they were doing?'

He grunted. 'Who knows? But we need to tell Hersir Eskil just in case that was their business. If they were scouts, they weren't very good ones.' He chuckled. 'When men like that see a woman alone, they only have one thing on their mind.' He looked at me with a knowing but sympathetic glance.

'They got more than they wished for, didn't they?'

'Are you alright?' he asked, flicking a stick out of my hair.

'I will be once we get back to the city walls and tell the guards.' No time to spare. I started running toward Aldeigjuborg.

Inside the protection of the town, we notified Eskil and the other guards, who rallied on the walls calling the lur horn for those who sought shelter to come at once. Fortunately, Helga and Mikel returned to the city, but stoic Hilde stood determined against it. The guards remained alert and armed for the fight, but none came. No more bandits that day, nor the next, and we decided it must have truly been a chance attack.

'Nothing is going to get easier when Aldeigjuborg becomes even more isolated from the capital of Gardarike, wherever that will be,' Sven grumbled, as we sat by the hearth fire on another frosty night. 'Do I leave and start somewhere else, or stay here to grind away whilst being attacked by marauders?'

'I think you're making the problem bigger than it is.' I shook my head at Helga, standing over the fire, watching Sven and I argue.

'Bigger than it is? In my short time here, I've been ambushed twice!' Sven yelled. Lowering his voice, he continued. 'It's a difficult decision for you. The business is here. Do you move to build your life with Kjarr, or go adventuring with me?'

'That is not the decision that needs to be made,' I answered with a glare. 'Kjarr will send word, and I have already begun building a network along the Volkhov to ensure trade, even if I were to leave Aldeigjuborg.' My stomach turned and I belched loudly.

'Ooof, still not feeling well?' Sven stood, reaching for a bucket. He shot a worried glance at Helga. 'Was she like this earlier?'

A wave of nausea took me, and I emptied my guts into the vessel.

'It comes and goes,' Helga answered for me. 'This is the second day in a row you've been sick,' she counted, turning to Sven. 'You're not... hmm... she couldn't be with child, could she?'

The cold queasiness battled with the warm flush of my embarrassment.

'Don't look at me. We never. Well, not...' he bumbled, red-cheeked.

'I shouldn't have asked,' Helga replied, kneeling next to me and rubbing my back. 'But you were with Kjarr,' she whispered. 'It's possible.'

It had been three months since Kjarr had left. *Had I missed any courses?* I wondered, shaking my head.

'She just made her first kill,' Sven announced. 'Sometimes that affects the gut of a warrior.'

I blanched, voiding my stomach once more. The last thing I wanted was to have a child in my womb. Even now, the grief of Freyja's loss was a raw wound refusing to heal. As I cradled my sickened middle, I knew whatever was happening did not feel right.

FOURTEEN

Cold water dripped on the bed next to my head. I heard the damp plop as it landed. The cloth draped over my forehead, once wet and cool, had warmed quickly against my fevered skin. Sweat beaded over my flesh, even though the weather was crisp and the snow had returned. Next to me, nervous whispers were indiscernible until they drew nearer. I sensed their presence but could not open my eyes.

'How is she today?' Helga's voice was soft but full of worry.

Sven cleared his throat before speaking. 'She voids her stomach all day and night and keeps nothing down. A few more days like this and I fear she will not have the strength to continue fighting.'

'Some women do have trouble carrying a child. They can be sick all the time, especially in the beginning,' Helga insisted.

My eyes were fused shut by fire. The searing pain in my head prohibited vision of any kind, though I wished to protest on my behalf.

Sven answered for me. 'She is not with child,' he growled at Helga as if he possessed my own voice. 'She is dying, just look at her.'

A tentative hand lifted the rag from my head and in its place lay their palm with a sombre sigh. 'We have time, I believe. But, I don't know what ails her or how to help. I've never seen a woman sick like this from her womb.' Helga doused the cloth in the cool water of the basin and replaced it on my forehead. For a moment I was relieved of the burn, and even the liquid that dribbled into my ears, pooling there, felt pleasant.

'She can't be with child,' Sven insisted.

Helga muttered to herself.

'Did you hear me?' Sven yelled.

'It's possible. I've counted. Kjarr was here. The timing is correct!' Helga replied. Sven's bull-headed protests did not intimidate her.

Heavy footsteps paced about the room, full of frustration and concern. They stopped, and the depths of Sven's chest issued a hearty sigh. 'I think I have seen this before. If I am right, Helga, you cannot stay.'

'I can't go. She is my friend. She is my sister!' Helga said, sniffing back the tears. 'And how do you know you won't get sick?'

'All I know is that I cannot leave her. Besides, I may have encountered this before, and I did not get sick. It may be that somehow I cannot be afflicted with this illness,' he explained, his voice bearing a hint of optimism.

'What is it?' Helga asked. 'Is it a sweating sickness? Aldeigjuborg had something that swept through about seven years ago. They say many people had fevers that raged on like Signe's.'

'Hmm,' Sven considered.

Helga continued, 'I was young then, and I remember little more than it spreading quickly.'

Sven's hand slipped into my open palm laying atop the covers of the bed and squeezed it. His hand was rough and broad. There was no confusing it with the daintily boned fingers of Helga.

'No, it's not a sweating sickness,' he replied. 'That usually has a cough or something with it. This is different. I'm sure this is an illness she got from Neflaug.'

'Not that woman!' Helga complained. 'If that's true then you, too, are at risk. You were there.'

'But it wasn't me who dragged Neflaug out of that wretched hut or who rolled her into the grave. I stood outside, only going in for a moment.' A chair groaned nearby as he sat down.

'And how did Neflaug become ill?' There was no concern in Helga's voice for the deceased woman.

'Hmm…' Sven thought for some time, then a long groan followed. 'Gods! It was that bloody well water Signe insisted on bringing up. There were floods before the winter. I would wager they've infected the well. Something in that water made that woman sick and now she has passed it onto *minn Svanr.*'

'*Minn* what?' Helga asked.

'It means "my sea bird," and Signe hates it when I call her that. Perhaps I should scream it in her ears over and over until she is so mad she wakes up and punches me. Wake up, *minn Svanr*,' he goaded.

'So Neflaug, yet again, is the source of all this trouble? And now, Signe may end up paying with her life?' Helga seethed.

There was silence for a long time. I thought I might have been alone until there were sobs coming from across the room. Heavy, heart wrenching howling from someone that was helpless to do anything and understood they were about to surrender it all.

'Helga,' he cried. 'I can't lose her. Not again.'

Light footsteps raced to his side. 'I know.' Helga's voice was full of care. 'If you worry about my health, I will stay in the hearth room. I can cook and prepare medicines from there, and I shall not enter. We can work together to save her. Mikel will even help me fetch things from the storeroom and bring them here, so you never need to leave her side.'

'But if the risk grows too great, you have to stay away,' Sven spoke through the tears.

'If it comes to that, you have my word,' she promised.

Helga's assurance was the last thing I remembered before succumbing to the bliss of sleep. A moment's reprieve from the pain, where I dived into the waiting arms of Nótt. My body melted until my awareness disappeared. How long I spent in that state, I did not know. But the time between dreams proceeded in an alternating mess of lucidity, shattered by violent vomiting and painful feculence.

At first, Sven and Helga left the room, as I was able to manage on my own. The stench overcame me, and I would have been mortified if I was capable of doing anything other than collapsing on the bed after each episode. When Sven came to empty the buckets without complaint, I did not protest. Nor did I object when he bathed me with such tenderness as he would a child.

Around me, he lay whatever fresh rags he found to keep the furs from soiling. Through my mumbling, I wanted to thank him and tell him to go so he would not suffer the same malady, but as time progressed, I lost my ability to communicate. Days passed, and no longer did I wake, only able to hear the world around me without participating.

Sven sent Helga away on one last errand before he told her to leave, for the risk had grown to great. When she returned, it was with news from Kjarr. Helga implored Sven to deliver it to me, hoping it would break whatever held me. Sven grunted with effort as he sat next to me on the bed.

'Astrid?' he whispered, using my name safe from the ears of others. Exhaustion marked his voice as he cleared his throat to speak. 'I have news of your husband.' That word choked in his throat, and as he pressed his palm to my forehead, he recoiled from the heat. 'Helga,' he screamed. 'Helga! Wait.'

'Have you told her?' Helga spoke through the door.

Sven cursed under his breath. 'She burns worse than yesterday. Helga, that remedy. We have to try it. Please don't die, *minn Svanr*,' he pleaded, hand clasped around mine.

He left my hand, walking away. His voice was gentle as he replied, 'Helga, please. I don't think we have much time. She is so weak.'

'Do you think we can save her?' she asked.

'We have to try. Ask anyone you know, even those you do not. The tisane has to work.'

'I'm scared,' Helga replied, her voice muffled by the dividing wall. 'What if the mushrooms aren't there? I know where to look, and maybe someone may have some dried in their provisions. Perhaps there is a woman with milk thistle too. I'll go now and knock on every door if I need to,' she promised.

'When you return, you should say your goodbyes. You cannot come back, and if you do, she might not…' He sniffled. 'If she dies, you cannot handle her body, not even to prepare her. The sickness may spread from person to person like that.'

She was mute except for muffled weeping. 'I'll return before nightfall,' she swore before leaving.

Alone again, Sven sat by my side, holding my hand. All I knew was his touch, and by it, my pain lessened.

'It will not come to that,' he muttered. 'The Norns aren't done with you yet.'

When the sickness returned, it shook my body and burned my head. Sven could no longer get me out of the bed to rid my bowels of what ravaged it. He kept me as clean as he could, rolling me onto my side

133

and changing the rags he put around me. When he was done, he patted me with a damp fabric and lay fresh linen over my scalp.

'Drink,' he urged, holding a cup.

I tried to obey, but my lips would not part on their own. He pressed a cloth to my mouth and compressed it. The cold tang of salted water seeped in and dribbled over my chin.

'You might have heard Helga before when she said there was news from Kjarr.' His voice was resolute, now was not the time for jealousy. His hand squeezed mine, and I willed with everything I had left to show him the same, but could not. I was so grateful he was there, caring for me in a way that many would not.

'He is no longer in Holmgardr, having been compelled to move south by order of the Grand Prince.' He stopped then to clear his throat. 'The messenger told Helga that Kjarr asks you to come to him when the rivers are ready once more for travel. I assume this means he does not know of your current illness or of Freyja's death.' He coughed this time, a tired rasp. 'I don't think Kjarr has gone to this willingly. He risks much to send you this message, and he warns you to be careful. I wish that were possible.' His voice caught, tinged with regret.

'I've sent no word back with the messenger, but when Helga returns, I will make sure of it. You said before that you prefer him not to know about Freyja until you can tell him yourself. I will respect that. But he needs to hear of your current illness. He may come; I would if I were him.' Sven's fingers danced up my forearm to the place where Bjarndýr hid and traced the metalwork of the armring.

'I'm sorry, Astrid,' he whispered. 'I want you to understand that when I disappeared all those years ago, it wasn't my choice.' He tucked the furs around my waist.

'Your mother was livid when she caught us that time down by the river.' He laughed. 'And I thought my mother would be too, but she surprised me by backing our desire to wed then. When we went to your mother, she denied us. "My daughter will marry for security," she told me. "Passion cannot feed you. Love cannot improve your life." But she was wrong; it can. Even then, I tried to protest, but she threatened me with outlawry for sullying your honour. My mother dragged me away, and your mother, well, we both know what she did to you.

134

'Every day between that day and the one you returned to Karlstad, I regretted my decision. I wish I had stood up to her then, told her it did not matter what she bullied me with. You were all that mattered. You are the only thing that has ever mattered to me.' Sven released my hand, placing it on the bed with a light pat. 'After I've emptied this bucket and brought back fresh water, I'll leave you to sleep. And, I must continue to care for you until you're well enough to annoy me again.' He tried to chuckle.

He laid a gentle kiss on my brow and left the room while fever dragged me into *draumskrok*, the world of spirits. They pulled me to the ground where it was dark and warmer still. Where my eyes fluttered, or just as likely, mischief raged as brightly coloured flashes.

My body shook. It convulsed until all sense was gone. The place ceased to be. I had no awareness of it now, all I knew was the void that removed me deeper. The heat seared like a roaring fire, but I could not get away. It was the fire-side tales that captured my attention, holding me there until the damage was done. Beyond caring and without the capability of helping myself.

I was gone.

The bright light stung through my closed eyes. An intense shining sun, the warmth of which I felt on my skin. My hand moved to touch the rays beaming onto my arm.

My hands move! And my feet! I thought as I wriggled my naked toes.

A tickling sensation brushed along me as I touched down on the mossy hillside. Tufts, warm like the downy fur of a purring kitten. Eyes open, I could see the river before me, a bubbling geyser shooting waters into the air and scaring the birds, who shrieked wildly. My mouth gaped in awe. The birds screeched again, this time the ejection catching one of their flock, launching it and roasting it in the scalding aquatic explosion.

Moving away from the erupting waters, I saw a hill bulge from the landscape. On top, there was a house constructed of wood with a thatched roof. A merchant house. My house. Three rooms, but without the warehouse at the rear. It was unmistakable, with its small landing out the front.

'That's a fine house,' the deep voice boomed next to me. At once I recognised the lilt of my father, my comfort. 'Is that your house?'

Though I could feel his presence, I could not see him. I nodded.

'Are you sick?' he asked. 'You don't look well.'

A laugh caught in my throat. My mother was the one to enquire into her children's health. My father was often leading me into pursuits resulting in injury. 'I think I am going to die. Unless I am dead already.'

He tutted me. 'It is not time to die. The Norns still weave your life line, even if you will it otherwise. You must keep going,' my father instructed. 'Can I walk with you?'

'To the top of the hill?' My hand reflexively moved to my forearm where I wore my father's armring.

'Do you need it while I am with you?'

I shook my head as we walked towards the house. If anyone had been watching, they would have seen a woman walking alone. Inside the building, the walls glittered with gold, and colourful tile fragments covered the floor in tableaus of life.

'This is not my house,' I said, looking around in wonder. 'It's as bejewelled as the stories say Miklagard is.'

'And one day you will see it. Daughter, you will have everything and you will have nothing at the same time,' he portended.

I staggered, grasping for a woven tapestry hanging from the wall.

'You should lie down,' my father suggested. 'Rest a little and regain your strength.'

I'll lie down, just for a moment. The walk to the top of the hill had taken what was left of my energy, and I was tired. My hand groped the nothingness as the shadows returned. 'Please don't go, Father. I need you here.'

'Sleep,' he murmured. 'I'll be right here.'

Obligingly, I closed my eyes. The bed felt like mine, on a hilltop soft as a kitten, next to exploding rivers that sent water that burned like the fires of the funeral pyre high into the cornflower blue sky. My mind was dark again, my eyes hurt, my body ached, but my fingers and toes were capable of slight movement. There was someone in the room with me. Their presence drew closer until their breath raised gooseflesh on my skin.

'Astrid?' Kjarr called my name.

The surprise freed my eyelids that had previously fused shut. 'You came, I knew you would.' My voice cracked, and I smiled weakly, squeezing his hand with all the strength I could muster.

'As soon as I received the message, I came. But I never thought to find you like this. And, Freyja, she has grown so much. I scarcely recognise her,' he said.

'Freyja?' I tried to sit up. 'What do you mean? Where is she?' The movement made me dazed, worsening my confusion.

He gently pushed me back onto the bed. 'Calm yourself, she will be around somewhere, and you need to rest a little more,' he calmed me.

'Such terrible nightmares,' I shook my head. 'You would never believe it.' I lay back, yawning widely.

My mind was dizzy. I screamed, and around me went dark. Kjarr was lost to the shadows, and I felt other presences in the room that were none too friendly. Hands were on me, pressing me down, holding me against the bed. There was pressure on my forehead, on my limbs, bearing down on my body. A dripping on my lips. Water on my face, warming on impact. Salty, earthy liquid filled my mouth until I could not take a breath. *Was I drowning?* I swallowed and gulped until I reached the surface.

Sleep must have come for me then. Time had passed, though I did not know how much when I finally swam into wakefulness, away from the fever that had raged upon my skin and burned my eyes. I blinked my eyelids open, and my eyesight blurred as I searched for my husband. In the corner was a dark figure.

'Kjarr?' I called to him.

As the dark-robed man turned, my vision sharpened, and it brought Sven into focus. 'Astrid, I was so scared. Are you really here?'

'Where is he?' I asked, frantically looking around the room.

'Who?'

'Kjarr. He was here a moment ago.'

Sven shook his head. 'He was never here. Kjarr did not come.' He took no delight in delivering the blow. 'I am sure he would have returned if the Prince released him.'

'I thought he was here just now,' I rambled, growing distressed. 'We were talking. He was here.'

Sven looked at me with pity. 'It was the fever dreams. You raved, but it has broken. I managed to get that tisane into you a few days ago and it helped. Thank the gods. You've not had any convulsions or vomiting for two days, though it's likely there is nothing inside you to come up. You're skin and bone.' He picked up my thin wrist.

My face felt sunken, and my body was weak. 'How long?' I asked.

'Weeks,' he replied. 'Are you hungry?'

I shook my head as I tried to sit up, a great dizziness overcoming me. 'A drink?'

He brought the cup to my lips, and I sipped slowly.

'I thought I was going to lose you. And I swear, I almost did,' Sven said as he put the mug down. 'Helga will be overjoyed when she hears you are awake. She has been at prayer for days, her knees will be hardened. In the end, I was determined to take whatever help was offered, no matter which gods they appealed to. More water?' he asked, pressing the vessel against my mouth.

This time I took a deeper drink, my stomach turned, and I eased it away, not wanting to tempt further illness.

'I've washed you the best I could these past days. As you were stirring just now, I brought in the tub, filled it with piping hot water from the fire. It should be nice now, but I'll bring more to top it up.'

My head bobbed in agreement, thinking how nice a soak sounded. My body felt abused, sore, and undoubtedly bearing the marks of a long illness. I watched Sven as he set about his work, sweat beading on his brow as he waddled with buckets laden with steaming water. When he was done, he came to me, slipping his hands under my body and lifting me from the bed.

'I'll have to stay with you to make sure you don't drown yourself. But I promise I won't look,' he assured me as he lowered me into the tub.

The water was delightfully warm as it rose around my torso. My hands dipped below the surface, scooping handfuls up to drip over my shoulders. I only managed a limp hand flapping and even that wore me out.

'Sven?' I called.

He turned around from his position at the door. 'Are you alright?'

My face reddened, anticipating the request I was about to make. 'Can you wash me? I don't have the strength.'

138

He nodded, and without another word, washed me carefully. When he was finished, he turned his back once more to give me the privacy to relax without being watched.

'Did you have to do that when I was unwell?' I asked, sensing embarrassment would follow his answer.

'If you were going to improve, I had to keep you clean,' he responded. 'We never have to speak of what was done.'

'Even so, you stayed when you could have left. There was great danger in looking after me. So, thank you.' For all the time I had spent hating Sven, I had never seen him so dependable.

He grunted and chuckled. 'It gave me a chance to think about everything I have done in my life.'

The water trickled from my hands down the back of the tub. 'Oh? And what is it you have learned?' I asked.

He glanced over his shoulder, towards me, a small, relieved smile on his lips. 'A man does not always need to look abroad to find his greatest adventure.'

'Is that right?' I leaned my head back against the wood.

He turned away. 'Now, I am sure this is where I need to be.'

FIFTEEN

JOL 882CE

By the time I was well enough to leave my bed, it was Jol. My recovery had been slow and, though I could walk without pain, I still had not left the house. With the town continually iced, the paths were made slippery. For me, walking outside was ill-advised. Sven had set a chair by the door for me to sit. Wrapped in my furs, I watched Aldeigjuborg's inhabitants as they prepared for the celebrations. All day I sat or paced in the hearth room until Sven returned from his work stripping wood for Mikel and Luca.

The first days of quiet observance bore little action. The sky was dark, and the days were filled with heavy snowfall. Then the decorating began. People emerged from their houses, armed with wreaths, carvings and runes bound for the evergreen trees that grew outside the city walls. Though I might have liked to follow them, I lacked the strength. But Sven reported the ornaments were hung on the fir boughs in such a manner that would have pleased Odin.

'You should see it,' he beamed, after returning from the spectacle.

'Tell me, you'll need to describe it,' I commanded, scooting my chair closer to the fire.

He sat on the floor next to me. 'There were so many carvings I did not think mine would find a place. And runes! Everywhere, the tree was so full.'

'You spent so long on those figures,' I smiled.

Sven had chipped away at the twin forms of Thor's goats; Tanngrisnir and Tanngnjostr, for three days. He had perfected their shaggy coats and horned heads until they bore so much vigour that I thought they would leap from their place and join the wild hunt led by Odin on his eight-legged horse, Sleipnir.

'Gisle chose them for the front of the tree.' Sven radiated with pride.

'The prize position,' I congratulated him, but I had not missed the vital information. 'So Gisle is back from Holmgardr? Did the others return also?'

Sven nodded. 'Most of the merchants called to attend the Grand Prince have returned. They arrived in a sleigh. You would have thought...' he trailed off.

I wrapped the furs around me tighter. 'I'm sure it would have been quite a sight.' Sven did not have to report anything. I knew Kjarr would not be with them. He had gone onto Kyiv with Oleg. There would be no return. 'Was there any message? Did they say anything?'

Sven shrugged. 'Only what you were already told. The capital is to be moved to Kyiv, and someone from Oleg's retinue will come in the spring to appoint Gisle to the position he assumed after Eryk's death.'

'We knew it would happen,' I agreed.

Sven nodded. 'Do you want to get out to see the rolling of the Sun Wheel? Alla and Gunhild worked on the wreath this past week. It's so huge it remains outside, propped up against the guildhall.'

'When will they set it alight?' I asked.

'Tomorrow. Then they'll roll it down that big hill at the bottom of David's farm.'

'I don't think I can make it that far, not yet,' I groaned.

'Do you want me to carry you?'

'No! When I leave this house, it will be walking on my own, not being carried like some poor crippled woman,' I replied obstinately. Though seeing it in flames barrelling down the slope, wishing for the return of the sun, would have set anyone's spirits higher.

'More like an angry Old *Amma*!' he chided, squeezing my foot.

I stood up, the light-headed sensation returning. 'All I do is pace back and forward in this room,' I grumbled, doing exactly that. 'Or sit by the door, in my Old *Amma* chair. They all stare at me as they walk by. I hear them talk.'

'Gods! Astrid. Listen to yourself.' Sven rose, hands akimbo.

'Struck down by their god, so the Christians claim. A curse for letting my child die, retribution for my part in it all.' I held back the tears.

'You don't believe in their god! Whatever "retribution", or so they call it, matters not to us. Our gods don't curse you for this,' he replied.

'It feels as if they do. All I want is to leave this house but be strong enough to do it on my own.'

'And you will, just not now,' he tried to comfort me. 'And don't plan on sneaking out to do something stupid. You'll not get past me.'

'Even at full strength, I couldn't overpower you,' I huffed, sitting down again. 'Are you sure the gods haven't cursed me?'

'They have not. In time, this will pass and people will forget,' he promised. 'Will you be alright by yourself? I told Luca I would strip one more log before nightfall. Now that the merchants are back, the commissions are flooding in.'

'I'll be fine. Go,' I grumbled, leaning back into the chair. 'Hopefully, I can leave the house by the time the bonfire is lit.'

'Before then,' he smiled. 'You will see the trees decorated with my goat carvings, even if I have to transport you there myself.'

When Sven closed the door, my eyes shut and sleep was upon me. It was easy to tire when one had nothing to do and no energy with which to complete the task. No matter if it was night or day, nightmares plagued my slumbers. Screams filling the darkness, spirits dragging me down, laughing at my ignorance of the signs shown to me by the gods. My father's words rang in my mind each occasion I woke. 'You will have everything and you will have nothing at the same time,' he had told me.

My father was telling me to listen, just like the *völva* had years before. I questioned every decision now before I made it, thinking I was wrong and right in equal measure. My mind was a mess of confusion, and each time, Bjarndýr burned on my arm as a warning.

I cannot ignore what they have shown to me.

'Astrid? The fire is out,' Sven worried, dusting the snow off his cloak as he stepped over the threshold, the sky dark behind him.

'I'm sorry. I must have fallen asleep. Had you put the Jol log on?' I asked, trying to strike a spark from the flint into the fireplace.

'Not yet,' he replied. He took the poker from the hook on the wall and sat by me in front of the hearth.

'Thank the gods. I'm not sure my luck could get any worse.'

'I was going to ask you to carve the runes into it. If you're feeling up to the task.' He blew on the small flames as they took to the kindling. 'Now that you are a learned woman,' he added with a smile.

Flattery was a welcome reprieve from the ineptitude of my physical incapacity. 'Yes, I think I could do that.' I took a log from the floor and placed it into the fire. 'But only if you fetch some hay to make goats for the landing. I can't be inside all day with no markers for celebration. It hardly seems like Jol.'

'Sit down. I'll do that.'

'I can do it. Am I not well enough to put a log onto the fire?'

He motioned with the poker to the bench. 'What if you had one of your dizzy spells and fell into the flames? It would burn your face off! I swear to the gods, Astrid, you need to rest a while longer.'

Sven was right. Several times, blurred vision had caused the room to spin, and darkness had overcome me. He had to usher me to a seat because of my stubbornness to attend to things that were beyond my current capabilities. I did not care for my helplessness one bit.

'When I am mended, you cannot boss me around. I'll be down with the guards with Skara and my shield.' I glowered with defiance.

'When you are mended,' he agreed. 'Practice is a good plan. You need it. When we fought those marauders, you were brilliant. The way you tore through them as if you had no fear.'

'I'm no *berserker*.'

He scoffed. 'I never said you were rabid. You defended well and with skill, just like your father,' he answered with a sentimental smile.

The compliment had been my greatest desire since I could remember. 'When I am well, I will be even stronger than before. Not that it will do me much good as a merchant,' I complained, tracing the wood grain of the table with my finger.

'Fighting skills would do no harm…' He stopped himself. 'Well, knowing them is useful,' he added, with a hint of mischief. Sven stood by the fire, scooping some herbs and mushrooms into a pot of water to make soup. 'That night, when you raved, you thought you saw Kjarr?'

'But he wasn't there. It was a load of nonsense. Nothing was clear,' I replied. 'There was even a point I heard you speaking.'

'Oh?' He looked up from the vessel. 'And what did I say in that rambling head of yours?'

'That you left Karlstad because my mother threatened you with outlawry.'

Colour crept up from his collar to his hairline, shading the skin behind the blue-green ink of his skin drawings. 'Do you recall why?'

'Because you asked for my hand and my mother denied you, even though we were as good as wed in the eyes of the gods.' Now it was my turn to experience my cheeks burning. 'For years, I have blamed you for deserting me, thinking that you got what you wanted and left. I thought I was the only one who paid the price for it.'

'You carried the heavier burden,' he mumbled, his back still to me.

'And you without a word.'

'I made a promise,' he confessed. 'And as hard as it was to keep, I'm glad you never knew. Thinking about what could have been was a torture I would not wish upon you. I'd rather you hated me than long for something you could not have.' Sven prodded the contents of the pot, stirring with an intensity that belied its importance. 'And what else did you dream of during your days of slumber?' he asked, avoiding delving deeper into the past.

'Strange things that mean nothing,' I replied.

He swivelled around, looking at me with wide eyes. 'Nótt is unlikely to show you idle imaginings.'

'Do you promise you won't laugh?' I asked.

Sven cocked his head. 'Never,' he promised, though the eager light in his eyes indicated it was not in his power to swear.

'Odin's beard! Fine. I will tell you, even if you cackle.'

Sven listened as I explained being pulled into *draumskrok* and what I thought was random nothingness. He remained silent as I described the mossy hill and the house that looked like mine from the outside, though different in its interior.

He sat thoughtfully, tapping his chin. 'And were you alone there?'

'No, there were birds in the sky and...' I hesitated.

'And someone else? If it's Kjarr, don't think you need to exclude anything just because it might make me jealous.'

'It wasn't Kjarr. It was my father,' I answered.

'Your father? Then that is no nonsense dream. The gods are trying to tell you something.' He filled two bowls with ladles of soup and set them down on the bench.

'He wasn't there exactly. Not like you are sitting here now. It was more a shadow of him, yet he cast no dark figure on the ground,' I struggled to explain. 'It felt no different from my father's presence when I speak to him through Bjarndýr. I know he is not there, though somehow I feel him.'

Sven leaned forward, not finding anything strange in my explanation, and I couldn't help the feeling that he understood me more than I cared to admit. 'Your father,' he stopped for a breath, 'was telling you or showing you something. What else do you remember?'

'Nothing that was coherent.' I squinted, remembering the words that replayed each time I dreamed. 'He spoke strangely when we walked into the house. There was some kind of warning.'

'What did the place look like?' Sven asked, motioning around to the walls. 'Was it like this?'

'Not at all. Sven, inside it shone akin to a gilded Christian relic,' I began. 'The whole chamber glittered. On the floor, shattered fragments of tile, each one coloured, and together they formed a large scene. The walls, wrapped in detailed tapestries as I've never seen them. Almost as if I had walked into what I can only imagine is…'

'Like Miklagard?' he finished.

'Exactly.' My eyes lit up. 'Precisely what I see when that great city is described to me. My father declared that one day I will see it. Stranger still, he said, "You will have everything and you will have nothing at the same time." Then I felt dizzy, and he told me to lie down and go to sleep.'

'Ha!' Sven guffawed. 'That sounds like your father. It's clear, then.'

'Hardly.' But I stared at him, waiting for an explanation anyway.

Sven dipped his spoon into the broth. 'Your father meant you to leave this place and travel to Miklagard,' he said with a mouthful.

'I don't think he meant for me to quit my business, my husband and my life for some golden city. And even if I left, what would I do when I got there?' I asked.

Sven shrugged. 'Why would you stay here?'

'Staying here is no longer an option. It's already been decided that I will move to Kyiv to be with Kjarr. My trade from Aldeigjuborg will continue, with Hilde and Helga's help, and expand along the Volkhov.

But the only person travelling to Miklagard is Hilde when she leaves with Sihtric,' I clarified.

'Why don't you leave Hilde and Helga in charge and go with Sihtric yourself? I'm sure he would have a place for me. I've heard journeying past the rapids comes with a great deal of danger,' Sven explained, slotting himself into the expedition. 'He will need as many armed men as he has room for.'

Even if I decided to depart, there was more to consider. 'Hilde seemed to want the opportunity. I wouldn't want to take that away from her.'

'The both of you could go.' Sven nodded.

'You cannot promise any of this' I answered, through a laugh. 'After all, it's Sihtric's ship. But it's something I need to think about because I am not about to leave just because a dream told me to. Despite what you say, it all could mean nothing.'

Sven shook his head. 'Maybe it means everything.'

I rolled my eyes. He was incorrigible.

He continued to eat until his bowl was empty, then he stopped. 'What will you do now?' Sven asked, his gaze serious.

'Right now, I intend to eat this soup,' I replied.

'Not the soup, you know I don't mean that. You cannot tell me you are willing to pack up and journey to Kyiv to be a wife and nothing more. You are a Viking's daughter, proud and ambitious. What do you dream of, without the help of fevers?' The look he gave me brokered no jesting. He demanded the truth.

'I am still the same.' I smiled in return. 'Always my father's daughter, even though he has gone to the great hall.'

Sven inclined his head, a mark of deference to my father, whom he had respected.

'But now?' I resumed. 'I am broken, nothing. Not a *Skjaldmaer*, not a Viking myself.'

He watched me, eyes narrowed until a grin changed his face. 'Astrid, daughter of Tarben. You are a *Drengr*.' He leant across the table and took my hand. 'You have more courage running through your blood than many of the men I raided with. You were never going to be Viking or *Skjaldmaer*, for they lack the valour of discipline. Unlike me, you do not need to belong to anyone to make it so.' He sat back, releasing my hand. 'I crave attachment to someone exceptional, a person who will order me to do their bidding. You are the greater, and I am sorry it took me so long to realise it.' Sven picked up a mushroom between his finger and thumb and threw it into his mouth. 'It is a bad time for you. We know it. But all matters pass, and you will find your place again.'

I stared at Sven, his accolade rendering me unable to reply.

'Astrid, you know I would follow you. I will swear to you if you command it,' he said.

'Is that your Jol oath?' I joked.

'It could be. Would you have me swear it as we drink?'

A deep breath steadied me, and I replied, 'Sven, I don't need your oath. But when we do leave…'

He looked up, astonished.

'If we journey to Miklagard, it will be on my terms,' I explained.

'And Kjarr?'

'He knows me well enough not to stop me. Perhaps he can join us,' I hoped. But as I formed the words, I knew they did not echo the truth. He was bound by something far greater than I understood.

That night as I nestled into my bed, I was hopeful for the first time in months. In the warmth of the furs, sleep did not seem to be a thing to fear any longer. Years before, when I had encountered the *völva* in the groves of Uppsala, she had looked into my future. She said the signs were right in front of me, and I would remain blind to them unless I learned to see. And I hadn't. In my complacency, I had failed to look deeper, to question people's motives. I gave away too much and had been too generous with oaths. Maybe my dream had been more than the ramblings of an addled mind. It could have been the foreshadowing of the path I needed to take.

But how could I know for sure? I asked myself as my body grew heavy.

So far, I had doubted, and all that brought me was loss and confusion. If only I learned to see the truth, only then would it be plain which course was correct. But that was the will of the gods. Thor guided me to strength, Freyja to love, and Loki, as always, who toyed with me, showing a path that led in the wrong direction.

Perhaps I just needed to leap, holding the thread that the Norns were weaving, and hope that wherever they were taking me, my landing would be true.

SIXTEEN

An urgent knock on the door woke me in the early morning. Each bang took me back to those nights that Neflaug came home in a drunken stupor. The times she was manic about Eryk's dismissal of her as his mistress.

It's not her, I reminded myself. *She is dead, Eryk is dead. You're safe.*

The frantic rapping increased in intensity as I hurried to drape my cloak over my *serkr*. There was no time to dress. By the time I unbolted the lock, the person was hitting the door with such force that demanded answering.

'Sven?' I called, as I passed Neflaug's old room.

No response. Sven was likely down at the training yards with the Guard's men, as he often was at the start of each day for the last two weeks. Since I was well enough to be left unattended, he had taken the opportunity to hone his skills with bow and arrow that he had neglected in the year prior.

'Who is it?' I shouted, approaching the door, too wary to open it without warning.

'It's Hilde. Open the door!' the woman's voice called back. Rage replaced all kindness present in her tone.

Without further hesitation, I opened the door. Hilde pushed past and rounded on me.

'She is sick,' she cried, her eyes wild with fear.

'Who?' I asked. 'Hilde. Who is sick?' I urged her to sit, but she shrugged me off.

'Helga!' she answered, curling her lip. 'She must have vhat ailed you for so long.' Hilde paced the room, muttering. She stopped and looked up at me. 'I cannot lose another daughter. I varned her not to come here, not to go near you vith you being so ill. But she vould not listen. She loves you too greatly.'

'I know she does,' I agreed, worried about my friend's health.

'You should have sent her away,' she demanded, wagging her pointed finger.

'I can assure you, if I was capable of speaking, I would have done so,' I replied.

Hilde was not usually given to blame nor outbursts of anger. Wrath turned to weeping and, I realised, she had come searching for help in her own way.

I laid my hand on her shoulder. This time she did not shrug me off. 'What can I do?'

Hilde looked at me through eyelashes clumped together with salty tears. 'I don't know if anything can be done. I am helpless.'

'The least I can do is give what we have left of the tisane she made for me. If she suffers the same affliction I had, then it will help her greatly. I think it saved my life,' I said, wrapping the dried mushroom and milk thistle in some gauze and handing it to her. 'Has anyone in the neighbouring farms taken ill?'

She shook her head. 'No one north of the tributary,' she advised. 'There vere some outlaws that emerged from the forests seeking medicines for the illness, some survived and others did not. One farmer south of the city valls fell ill but recovered.'

'It could have been much worse,' I mumbled. 'Helga will be alright,' I promised. 'She is a strong girl. Tell her I will come to see her as soon as I am able.'

Hilde sat down at the bench, sniffling into a square of cloth. She nodded. 'Helga vould like that. She has missed you these past veeks.'

'We were very careful. She never came into the room. Sven saw to that. How long has she been ill?' I asked.

'She said she felt off for over a veek, but the vomiting began two days ago. Since then, I've not let her go home,' she answered.

'We have time, then. If we get this into her now, she may escape the worst,' I suggested.

Hilde shook her head. 'She keeps nothing down. Helga has taken to her bed, but thank the Lord, she does not fever.'

'Tomorrow, I will come to visit. I've not ventured that far on my own yet, so I might need Sven's help. Do you want to wait for him to return to walk you home?' I asked.

'No, I'll be alright.' She stood, walking towards the door. 'Mikel is vith her but he does not know vhat to do, and he does not appreciate the seriousness of it.'

Young men were quick to dismiss illness, often leaving it much later than they ought to seek help. I walked Hilde to the door, and as she passed the threshold, she paused.

'Signe? Forgive me, I should not blame you. It's just…' She lingered on the word.

'You are worried for your daughter. I understand.' I hugged her. 'Do not trouble yourself. All is right between us.'

Hilde squeezed her fingers around the tisane ingredients. 'I'll make sure she drinks this. But I am sorry.'

'You have more important things to worry about than my feelings. Go, I'll see you tomorrow.' I waved as she plodded down the path.

Sven, however, did not feel the same way. When he returned later that evening, he was indignant on my behalf after I told him about the confrontation between Hilde and myself.

'How could she speak to you like that?' he glowered. 'Why would she imagine you would endanger Helga? We did all we could to keep her away, but the girl kept coming back.' He paced before the hearth fire as I cooked the evening meal.

'Oh, Sven. Please! I've told you everything is resolved. Hilde was upset because Helga has taken ill. It might not even be the same sickness. She doesn't have a fever,' I replied.

'Then why does she blame you?' he asked, sitting down.

'A mother worries about her child, that is all. She knows what Helga is like, and once the girl has set her mind to something, there is no talking her out of it. Sometimes the grief can be ill placed, other times it's levied exactly where it needs to be. I am not about to hold a grudge for an outburst from a woman who has been my greatest support each time I have needed it.'

He leaned forward on his elbows. 'But to be so angry with you makes no sense.'

'It seldom does. That's what happens between families,' I added, trying to cool his temper.

'They're not your family.'

I stirred the pot of bubbling broth faster as my irritation grew. 'As close as I have here. I consider them as such, and there are times when coarse words can be ignored. Tomorrow we will go to them and you will see, everything will be fine.'

Sven crept closer, belly grumbling, and spooned soup into our bowls. 'If you say so,' he responded with a shrug. 'Though, if the girl is worse tomorrow, her mother's mood will not be improved.'

'The anger won't linger. I know Hilde,' I promised.

'Are you well enough to travel there?' Sven asked between mouthfuls.

'If I'm not, you'll be there to carry me,' I answered, shooting him a mischievous smile.

'Ha! You'd never let me do that. You would sooner limp along, declaring there was nothing wrong,' he said, 'I know you.'

I sipped my soup, pretending my provocation was made unwittingly. 'And so you do.'

The next morning, Sven and I set out on our visit to Helga, who was being cared for at her mother's house. I had been eager to go, not having left the city walls for more than a month. As soon as the sun's first rays woke me, I was knocking on Sven's door to depart. Our progress was slow, and even before we passed the gate, I had to stop to catch my breath.

'Are you sure you should be leaving, Signe?' Hersir Eskil enquired as he stood on guard duty.

'My stamina is less than usual, I'll admit. But, I can do it. Anyway, it's not your job to harass townsfolk. Where is Laslo?' I asked between laboured breaths.

'Poor boy has taken ill,' he replied.

Sven and I glanced at each other.

'Ah, don't look like that! It's not the bloody sickness you had. I assure you!' he croaked. 'I brought in a cook special for them so that there could be no contamination.'

151

'Still, there are other ways of getting it,' Sven intimated. There was no denying that military men had a particular penchant for romantic services.

'Ha!' he guffawed. 'I made them swear off the bloody whores too.'

'You think they would listen?' Sven laughed at the suggestion.

'You would if it was by pain of death,' he addressed Sven. 'You're lucky to have survived it, Signe. Most who are infected do not.' The captain nodded at me. 'It was pretty bloody easy to convince the men that paying for their own painful expiry was not a good use of coin.'

'Ooof,' Sven groaned. 'I wonder how long it will last?'

'Them or the illness?' Eskil chuckled. 'When the danger has passed, there will be a surge in the price, I'd wager. Until then, I'll put them to rigorous practice in the yard to make sure they have a way to get all that energy out…' he was about to continue.

'Well, we could stand here all day discussing a substitute for a woman's touch, but we have somewhere to be, Hersir.' I dipped my head as we passed.

'I thought it was a neat solution,' Sven mumbled as I trudged off ahead of him.

'If it works,' I replied. 'If the town's guard were to fall ill, there would be no protection.' My foot twisted on the path and I staggered.

'You can take my arm if you want to,' Sven suggested. And, not wanting to turn back from tiredness, I accepted.

'It might be that on the return journey, you'll have to carry me, Sven,' I panted half-jokingly as we crossed the bridge.

He looked at me with mild shock. 'Are you struggling that much? Do you really need me to?' he asked.

'It seems I have weakened more than even I believed possible. I'll need to rest awhile at Hilde's before returning,' I replied, leaning heavily on his arm.

He nodded but said nothing. He understood it took me a lot to admit when I was faltering. 'It's not too far now,' he encouraged me.

'Urgh,' I groaned. 'It feels so much longer than it did when I was at full health.'

'Speaking of full health. When you are well, Eskil has agreed to let you train with his men.'

'What?' I gasped.

'I talked to the captain yesterday, and he was eager to have found a new opponent for them, especially one so skilled with an axe,' he explained.

'Hmm, I hope you did not exaggerate my competences, Sven.' My eyes narrowed.

'You are a better fighter than at least a quarter of his force. The other lot you can learn from,' Sven suggested.

'Alright,' I accepted. 'But they realise it is me, right? You've told them expressly who it is that possesses these "skills" as you call them?'

'Yes, they know I'll be bringing you, Signe. It seems you've got an admirer in the ranks,' Sven teased.

'Who?'

He raised his eyebrows. 'Your friend, Laslo.'

'Very funny. He is a nice boy, and trust me, there is no admiration past friendly banter. Every morning I talked to him when I returned from my walk with Freyja,' I trailed off into a whisper.

Sven gripped my arm a little tighter. 'I'm sorry. I meant nothing by it. Laslo vouched for you, that's all. So, now you are in!'

Still distracted by the thought of my deceased daughter and absent husband, my enthusiasm did not match Sven's own.

'Astrid?' he called. '*Hej?* Astrid?'

'Shh,' I hushed, throwing a glance over my shoulder to ensure no one heard him addressing me by another name.

'You really should let me call you *minn Svanr*. It would make things easier.' He winked down at me. 'Then I would have no cause to address you by any other name, and we could avoid this secrecy.'

I rolled my eyes. 'If you must.'

'Even when your husband is around?' he asked, grinning like a cat cornering its prey.

'Odin's beard! Sven, stop. You are getting too familiar.' I pushed his hand away, walking on my own. 'Thank the gods we are near now.'

'*Minn Svanr*, you need to tell them you are going,' he called after me.

'And, I will. When the time is right,' I wheezed as I limped towards Hilde's home. 'Sihtric came to visit yesterday when you were out.'

'Bearing a message from Kjarr?' Sven asked with a hint of concern.

'Not so much, but he told me more than I knew. Apparently, after journeying to Holmgardr, many of the merchants were notified about the moving capital. Some have decided to move their business whilst others, including Sihtric, will continue to live in Aldeigjuborg for as long as possible,' I explained.

'What did he say?'

'I believe his exact words were, "I have become accustomed to living at arm's length to high authority and wish to continue that." He will maintain a residence in Kyiv, as will the other merchants wealthy enough to do so. But he has no intention of relocating there permanently. He said, "Fortunately, the frequency of my trade adventures makes it likely that no one will notice my absence." Trade routes will remain unchanged. They all still have to pass through here if they want to trade with the north. Unless merchants suddenly change their preference for the Volga route from Miklagard, the town will keep some importance. But, Sihtric told me something concerning,' I lowered my voice.

'About Kjarr?' Sven asked.

'Hmm. He said, "Owing to Kjarr's connection to the Prince," his star is on the rise whether or not he wants it to,' I growled.

'You suspected as much,' Sven pointed out.

I nodded.

Sven elbowed me, trying to lighten the mood. 'You know, Sihtric sounds nothing like that,' he joked.

'It's the accent. I can't do it!' I tried to forget about Sihtric's warning.

'Need me to push you up this rise?' Sven asked as we approached Hilde's house at the top of a small hill.

'I'll manage,' I grumbled. 'And I don't want anyone to see me this weak.' I pushed his offered hand away, huffing the last few paces to the door.

'As you wish, *minn Svanr*.' He bowed.

'Use it sparingly or I'll walk home on my own,' I threatened.

Sven laughed, knocking on the door. 'I would be more afraid if it were a credible threat.'

Hilde opened the door, her countenance much changed since the day before. She no longer seemed at her wit's end, no more overcome by concern.

'Come in,' she whispered, her head low and without meeting my eyes.

'Is everything alright?' I asked, concerned about her stark change in tone. 'Where is Helga?'

'Through there,' she replied, pointing through the doorway into the hearth room, where I could see Helga bundled before the fire. 'I'll let her explain. I need to vatch the children.' Hilde grasped Sven's muscular forearm. 'You,' she commanded, her manner changing to that of a matron who demanded compliance. 'Come vith me. I need a powerful man to help me vith these little ones.' Hilde dragged Sven away, leaving me alone to enter the room.

'Helga?' I called. Even in the dim light, I could tell she was pale and unwell. 'I did not expect to see you out of bed, especially after your mother told me you were so sick.'

The young girl coughed and reached for a bowl, into which she vomited loudly. She set it down, turning back to me, and giggled. Not exactly the reaction I had expected.

'Oh, Mama was worried.' She laughed airily. 'I instructed her not to go, but she wouldn't listen, and now she is quite embarrassed.'

'She does not need to be, all is forgiven.' I smiled, reaching out to touch her hand. 'I'm glad to see that you do not have a fever. Did the tisane help?' I asked, pulling a stool to sit alongside her.

Helga shrugged the blankets off her shoulder, tucking them in neatly around her waist. 'We did not need it after all.'

'But I thought your mother said you caught ill from me?'

Helga twirled the end of her braid. 'Oh, I am certain this ailment did not come from you.'

I furrowed my brow. 'I'm not sure I understand.'

'Really?' she teased. 'I am not sick at all. I am with child,' she announced, reclining in her chair.

'What? How?' I stammered.

'Now, Signe, I would have thought you knew how these things were done,' she mocked.

I caught my surprise and glared at her. 'Of course I know. I only meant that you had said Mikel was careful not to cause such a thing to happen.'

'And he was, but his momentary carelessness seems to be my gain.' She placed a gentle hand on her still flat belly.

Every part of my body had been tense until that moment, and I willed it to relax. 'I am so happy for you.' I beamed, taking her hands in mine.

'There were some days that my mother thought my upset stomach resulted from illness until I told her yesterday that I had not bled in two months. She was quite mad at me for allowing her to believe…' she mumbled.

'It will pass. Is she pleased for you?'

Helga stroked her plaited hair. 'She will be once she is over the shock.'

'And Mikel?' I asked.

'He is happy I'm not dying.' She rolled her eyes, flicking the braid back over her shoulder. 'As for the baby, he has a few months more to grow accustomed to the idea.'

Mikel had not been keen to start a family until he could provide for them. But knowing Mikel, I suspected he would not believe he was in that position for many years to come. Helga had been impatient for offspring, and now it seemed Mikel had found his own moment of urgency. Once the time arrived, I was sure Mikel would find joy in the birth of his child.

'I should confess that I have not been very patient. Don't worry, there have been a lot of confessions! But none of that matters anymore. Come early summer, I will start my labours and a baby will lie in the cradle. Oh, who knows? Maybe there is more than one in there,' she rambled, eyes wide at the possibility. She stopped, glancing sideways. 'Here I am going on about the life inside me when Freyja is gone and you must still mourn her. I'm sorry, Signe. It was thoughtless of me.'

'I miss her, but I can be delighted for you at the same time,' I replied, trying to smile. Will it as I might, life did not stand still. 'And while we are on the subject of cheerful news, I bring some of my own.'

Helga clapped her hands. 'Oooh, you do?'

'More good for me than good for you.' I squinted, anticipating the impact of my words.

Helga eyed me suspiciously. 'Does this have anything to do with this trading mission of yours? Mother has been talking about it endlessly.'

I looked to the ceiling, scrunching my face with displeasure. 'That is what I am worried about.'

'I don't think she wants to go. Please don't ever say I told you so, but,' she lowered her voice as I returned my eyes to hers, 'she thinks you are the greatest woman she has ever met. You are so brave, and she would never choose to disappoint you. Not to mention that she would worry about her children, and what would we do without her?' she added with a shrug of nonchalance.

'Particularly now that you are expecting a child of your own.'

'She would not wish to miss that! And who will you send in her place?' Helga asked.

I kept her questioning gaze, holding it, not daring to look away. 'I will go.'

Helga's eyes widened for a moment before she calmed. 'I suppose it makes sense. I suspect you will need to meet with Kjarr, if he is not back before then.'

'He won't be,' I grumbled.

Helga tilted her head questioningly to one side. 'What do you mean?'

'He won't be returning to Aldeigjuborg.'

Her mind was working to keep up with the revelations. 'Has something happened?'

'Many things and none of which I can speak of,' I replied enigmatically.

'Is everything right between the two of you?'

'How would I know? I've seen him for three days in almost two years. Much has changed in his absence, and I have questioned all things. And, now I know, if I want to see him I must go to Kyiv,' I explained.

'Why Kyiv?'

I shrugged. 'He is not in a position to leave, so it is I who must travel.'

'What a mystery.' Helga paused, placing her hands together in her lap. 'When will you depart?'

'As soon as the ice has melted and it is safe to go. The details are not yet organised.'

'And, how long will you be gone?' she asked. 'You'll return in time for the birth?' She patted her stomach again.

'Helga, I may not come back for a while. Maybe residing in Aldeigjuborg is no longer an option for me.'

'What will you do?'

'Exactly what we already planned, except instead of someone else acting as our agent in Kyiv, it will be me. You and your mother will be in charge of the shipments from the north, as we arranged. Our plan continues.'

Her eyes were brimming with tears. 'You don't have to go to your husband,' she cried.

'It is time,' I whispered, holding back tears of my own. 'Kjarr is not coming back, and there is nothing else here for me anymore. No, don't look at me like that. I'm alright, I promise you. Now I must find my way. Sven helped me realise that, but don't tell him,' I added with an attempted grin.

'I understand why you could never forget him,' Helga whispered.

'Sven?'

'You do not even need to speak words to him for there to be understanding between the two of you. It is as if you are of one mind and possibly of one heart.' She nudged me. 'I've seen similar closeness of spirit before, and it is clear that you and Sven are meant to be near one another. I believe you would say "fated by the gods"?' She sighed.

'Pfft,' I discouraged the comment.

'If there is nothing between you, then tell me so.' She eyed me, daring to speak.

I couldn't. I knew that Sven and I would not be together in the manner he wanted, but I could not deny that fate had connected us. The Norns had tethered us together as Sven said so long ago. There was no way that he would have been able to find me in all the seas, all the land masses, if it were not so. 'Helga, I am married.'

'That was an arrangement borne out of the circumstances,' she responded.

'For one of us,' I agreed.

'He would release you if you asked him.'

Her brazenness shocked me. 'Helga!'

'It was a handfast union, easily undone with divorce. My church is against it, but it's not the same for you, no? There was no official ceremony, nothing to tie Kjarr to you,' she continued.

'Helga. I couldn't. I don't want to,' I protested.

'It is your marriage that created the separation from Sven you require.'

It was a realisation that Helga and I came to at the same time. 'Because Sven respects I am another man's wife. He would never betray that.'

She nodded. 'I'm sorry, I only meant to…'

'It will never happen. Sven and I may be fated, and as much as he may wish we were lovers, it can never be.'

'Why?'

'If you weren't my best friend, my sister, I would call you impertinent.' I laughed.

She giggled. 'And I might mention that you were stubborn.'

'I couldn't, not again. When we were younger, we loved each other,' I began.

Helga sat up, latching onto the words. 'Loved? And how far did that love go?'

I shot her a reproving glare. 'I should have said nothing, and I will speak nothing more. Helga, I want to be myself. Kjarr knows he should never expect more than what I would freely give. Sven does not possess that same comprehension.'

'Does Kjarr know Sven has found you?' she questioned, none too innocently.

'No. I think that is a discussion best had when we are together,' I responded.

'But when he does, he may see what I see,' Helga warned. 'And does Sven realise you will never be his?'

I looked away, heart hammering in my chest. 'I have told him as much, but I know he still holds hope. It would be simpler if he finds someone else.'

'Would that make it easier for you?'

'As he has, in time I will bear it,' I replied. Having had enough talk of men and the tender nature of relationships, I stood. 'Where is your mother, I wonder?'

'You will come to say goodbye before you leave, won't you?' Helga asked.

'Of course,' I answered, wrapping my arms around her. 'And when you are feeling better, please visit the house. I have many things to arrange with you.'

It did not take me long to locate Hilde. She was in the field, trying to wrangle her young brood from their merrymaking.

'We need to talk,' I began.

She looked at me sheepishly from under her hood. 'Oh, Signe, I am very sorry. I should not have blamed you. You did nothing, and now you know about Helga's situation. I feel awful.'

I embraced her. 'Don't think about it for another moment. We are *fostra*, but, I suppose, this changes some things.'

She nodded. 'I have thought about it, and I cannot go in search of this new dye. Not vith Helga needing me. You understand, don't you?' she asked.

'Of course.' I smiled. The relief was now mine, not having to disappoint another person. 'And I will go in your place. Hilde, I must tell you, as I have told Helga, I may not come back to Aldeigjuborg at all.'

Her look was just as her daughter's had been, wide eyes surprised with a touch of sadness. 'But ve vill miss you.'

'And I will miss you, but Kjarr cannot return to Aldeigjuborg, so I have to be with my husband in Kyiv,' I explained.

Hilde nodded. My explanation had been an oversimplification of the matter; however, she understood being at one's husband's bidding. 'Kjarr vill need you there, vhatever he is up to.'

'That remains to be seen,' I agreed. 'There are arrangements to be made, but when I leave, you and Helga will be in charge of the northern operations. Do you think you can manage it all?'

'Us?' She gaped, grasping her shawl.

'Of course. Who else would I trust?'

'Ve vould be honoured. On Christ himself, ve vill take the best care ve can,' she vowed.

'Thank you,' I replied, hoping their god would be more interested in mercantile dealings than my own. 'Hilde, what have you done with Sven?' I asked, looking around for my friend.

'Catching children.' She laughed, pointing to the tree line. 'Vatch out!' she cried, ducking before a well-formed snowball thudded into my chest.

'Ooof.' I crouched before the next one landed and threw two back in defence. 'Come out, you beasties!' I called.

Sven emerged with three youths dangling off him. Hilde's youngest sons, Boris and Dimitri, were hanging from each arm, and her youngest daughter, Alva, was swinging from his neck and whooping loudly.

'Faster, horsey,' she squealed with delight as she hit him with a stick, 'run!'

Sven obliged, trotting up the hill towards us, the two boys in his arms encouraging their sister to beat the 'horse' with more vigour. Sven flopped onto the ground at our feet, and the boys scarpered away whilst Alva stayed mounted, her little knees squeezing Sven's shoulders.

'Mama, my horsey is sleeping. Wake up, horsey,' she commanded as she continued to whip the grown man.

He groaned, prone in the snow.

'I expect,' Hilde began, 'your horse requires a rest. He has done an excellent job of bringing you in for your breakfast, but I think he needs to return to the stables.'

'Oh, alright,' Alva grumbled as she clambered off Sven's inert mass.

Boris and Dimitri had already sped away without so much as a word, in search of food. After embracing Hilde in farewell, she took Alva inside, running after the boys. I turned to Sven, offering my hand to help him to his feet.

'Is that offer of being carried home still standing?' I joked.

He groaned. 'I don't even know if I'm still standing after all that.' Sven rubbed his shoulders.

'It's alright, I can manage.' I grinned to myself as we walked at a speed we could both maintain to the town I would soon be leaving.

SEVENTEEN

'Parry an axe like that and your opponent will take more than just your sword!' I shouted at Laslo, after I had hooked him for the third time with my axe.

Even though the repetition of his error had irked me, there was a part of me that took pleasure in each win despite my challenger not matching my abilities. The young man was willing but grossly under-skilled, and it made me shudder with horror to think of each morning as I passed him as a guard of Aldeigjuborg, protector of the town.

'All I need to do is this,' I bellowed, pulling his sword that had once again caught on the heel of my axe. 'And now,' I grunted as I jerked the sword free from his hands, 'I can gut you at close range.' I pointed the blade at the flesh of his stomach. 'With your own weapon no less.'

He furrowed his brow, his mop of curling brown hair falling over his eyes. 'But you won't,' he replied. The upward inflection at the end of the word made it sound more like a question.

'Not today. However, if you were not my friend, I would not give it a second thought, and the contents of your innards would lie approximately...' I lingered, searching for the spot. 'Here.' I stamped my foot in front of his toes.

Laslo chuckled uneasily, glancing down at the ground. He gulped. 'Lucky for me, then, you are friend and not foe.' He dodged a jab from my finger, recoiling in time to put a protective hand over the imaginary gutting wound.

'Good thing I know how to control my weapon and my anger. Today I was not intent on killing, but, you...' I pointed the eye of Skara towards him, '...need to practice more if you ever hope to survive against someone willing to end you with one of these,' I warned, shaking the axe menacingly.

'You were easier to beat when you were newly emerged from your sickbed,' Laslo grumbled, stooping to pick up his sword.

'Easy prey is not worth having.'

Laslo loitered by the side of the practice yard, cleaning his weapons. 'You're very good, Signe. If we were on opposite sides of the fight, I would fear you.'

'But country boys don't know their faces from their arse, so who are you to say what is skilled or not?' Two men on the sidelines laughed together at the jibe. The burly one sat lazily on the bench with his companion.

They were both dressed for fighting in their leather jerkins and domed helmets, difficult to manoeuvre in without practice but providing significant protection. To wear such garb at training told me the friends were inexperienced. I preferred a simple, longer quilted shirt belted around the middle. It would not save me from a mortal blow, but it would protect me against a nick or poorly timed slash, perfect for the practice yard inside the town's defences.

The men stared at me, and even when I spat on the ground, they maintained their attempt at intimidation. 'Easily beaten,' the smaller Igor mumbled to the burly one as Laslo left the yard, returning to duty.

'Something you would like to say, Igor or Igor?' I demanded, arms akimbo.

They bore the same name and had garnered the moniker "the Skulking Shadows" for their fondness for dwelling in the fortress' corners, in addition to their ostensible dislike for productive work.

'Would one of you prefer to remove your backsides from that seat and have a go?' I asked.

Burly Igor glanced at his friend, raising his eyebrows. 'Oh yeah, I'd like that. But how about you take that horse blanket off and we can go for a tumble instead?' he guffawed.

'Perhaps the two of you are tied at the hip?' I pointed Skara at them in challenge. 'If you don't want to be separated, I'll take you both on,' I dared.

They stood. 'And what do we get if we win?' Small Igor asked.

Tossing my head back, it was my turn to guffaw. 'Pah! You think you might beat me? I think not, though you are welcome to try.'

'We will take you if we win,' Burly Igor declared, as if it were his right to name whatever prize he desired.

Their misdeeds were well known in the town, trying to woo the daughters of merchants indiscreetly. Hersir Eskil, Captain of the Guard, had a job of keeping them in line and took them to task for any offence they had created. Still, Aldeigjuborg's forces were lean enough to need every man they were sent. So, despite their regular reprimands, the only way of ensuring their compliance was sending them to guard the walls, far away from the honourable women of Aldeigjuborg.

'What do you say? Are you game for the wager?' Small Igor leaned forward, taunting me.

'Personal services are not on offer, Shadows,' I replied. 'Make it money and you'll have a deal, or an ale, that's a wager appealing to everyone's tastes,' I suggested, motioning for them to arm themselves.

'Three,' Burly Igor demanded, hunching his broad shoulders.

'Agreed,' I answered, shaking my head at his arrogance. 'Until first blood?'

They nodded.

'To weapons, then,' I commanded, and they obliged, each arming themselves with their preferred sword, while I kept Skara in my hand.

Even before we began, I knew inexperience would be their folly, and I intended to use it to my advantage. Instead of attacking them outright, I waited, rocking on my back foot and setting Skara in front of me to the right. In their arrogant assumption of superiority, they were oblivious to the gestures that gave them away. A small glance here, a twitching hand there, each time betraying their move before they made it. Burly Igor slashed; I blocked. Small Igor darted closer with a feinted jab. I pounced, driving to close the gap with Skara to block his next attempt. A careless whirl from one, and a careful hook of Skara upon their blade, stole the weapon from their grasp and another sword into my own.

'Shall I cut you to make it seem more defeating?' I asked Small Igor as I taunted him with his own blade, dodging the advances of his friend.

He slunk off to the bench without a word, skulking as only a Skulking Shadow could.

'A bit of a sore loser, eh?' I laughed at the remaining Igor.

'Not much of a fair fight,' Burly Igor complained.

'No, you're right. It's two against one,' I replied, pushing his sword away with Skara's blade.

He screwed his face up in a childish tantrum. 'You've had more years to practice.'

'Oh, so now you admit I'm not so easily beaten?' I scoffed.

'Not saying that, just, if I had a shield, I would make easy work of you,' he grumbled indignantly as he slashed the air.

'That's not what we agreed to. If you wanted a shield, you should have mentioned it at the beginning,' I shouted, struggling to form the words with strained breath and a hammering heart. 'And even if you had one, I would remain unmatched.'

He thrust his blade at my stomach as I stepped back to my left. With the speed of a cat, I spun around, taking him from the back in time to restrict his movements. His friend's sword, still in my left hand, ran along his throat that was covered in downy hairs not fit to be called a beard.

'I doubt if you had two swords, a dagger, and a shield, you would win. Even if I was asleep and completely unarmed,' I whispered in his ear.

He struggled against the embrace, trying to overthrow me.

I jabbed Skara into his ribs on my right. 'Odin's beard! I almost forgot, I promised you first blood,' I recalled, running the sharp toe of Skara's head against his cheek, making a shallow cut. A trickle of blood ran down his face, dripping onto his leather jerkin as a whimper escaped his lips.

'Three ales, that was the agreement. Make sure Ivar knows to put it on my account,' I instructed.

Burly Igor nodded and ceased to struggle.

'And you would be wise to stop tormenting the girls, including the ones that aren't free,' I warned. 'It will come back to...' I pushed him away and wiped Skara's blade, 'bite you!'

He limped over to his friend.

'If, for some reason, Ivar has barred either of you from the Skogarmaor,' I barked, 'then find someone else to inform him of my win. Be decent for once.'

He nodded, turning on his heel, and both scarpered.

'Hey, you two!' a deep resonating voice called from the stairs leading to the wall.

They skidded to a stop.

'Get back to work! You're supposed to be on watch,' he growled at the Sulking Shadows. 'If I have to bloody warn you again…'

They disappeared before the Hersir could finish his threat.

'Always doing whatever they want instead of their duty. They would be more useful to me as fodder for the horses than bodies on the wall.' Eskil shrugged.

'Hersir.' I inclined my head as he descended the last two stairs into the yard.

'And you,' he stopped to speak, 'put the wastrels through their paces, as they deserved. I hope a bloody good trouncing will straighten them out.' He shook his head, knowing, as I did, nothing would dissuade them from mischief. 'If you were a man, I would ask you to join my Guard.' He paused. 'But as you're a woman… Ah, gods! I'll ask anyway. So will you?' His blue-eyed gaze was completely serious.

'Uhhh,' I stammered, intimidated by not only his frame, which was as wide as it was towering, but also the boom of his voice, which shook my insides. 'I can't,' I managed.

'Bloody shame,' he complained. 'These farm boys they send me are all talk and no action. If I wanted to train weaklings, I would have remained at home to teach my children.' He kicked the loose dirt with his foot. 'Your friend Sven said the same thing. It would have been welcome to have two from the north I could count on, especially two that can fight.' He scratched his head under the domed helmet. 'You know what I mean. Might not be a man, but you are bloody good with that axe.'

'So Sven declined your offer too?' I asked, polishing my weapon.

Eskil removed his helmet and smoothed the mess of tawny hair beneath. 'He did. Said something about the two of you setting off for a slice of adventure. I envy you. If only they would send a bloody replacement, I would join you. Wouldn't mind a bit of raid and trade myself.' He laughed.

I shook my head. 'No forays will be happening, Hersir. Strictly business.' Old habits were hard to replace. 'Our intention is to travel to Kyiv as soon as the waters run. In fact, we have not yet settled all the details, and Sihtric may be looking for another man for defence.' I pondered,. 'But why would you want to leave? You have a position here. What would you do in Kyiv when we got there?'

He shrugged. 'Honest to the gods, I have thought about leaving this town every day since I arrived. I'd not desert, but I know being Hersir of Aldeigjuborg is not for me. Perhaps I'll find employment as a mercenary, part of a free company seeking coin. That would have to be better than this bloody provincial work! At least more money and excitement, eh?' He chuckled, stopping to clear his throat. 'As you say, nothing is for certain, and I have to await relief from the command of this cesspit first,' he grumbled.

'They will send someone from Holmgardr soon to appoint Gisle to Guild Master. Perhaps a new commander could be found then?'

Eskil slammed his helmet over his shock of hair, coughing again. 'We can only hope the gods agree! Still, you and Sven are welcome to the yard, and when we open up the area across the bridge, there too. Practice with the men as much as you can, even if you refused my offer!' he added with a wink. 'And now I have boys to supervise.' He gritted his teeth, marching away without further comment. As Eskil disappeared into one of the log cells in the wall's supports, Sven passed him in the opposite direction.

'Nice guy, huh?' Sven grinned. 'Asked me to stay and join the Guard.' He sat down on the bench next to me.

'Eskil is direct, I'll give him that,' I agreed, 'and also asked me the same question.'

Sven glanced sideways. 'He did? Must be desperate, then.'

I shot him a reproving glare. 'Especially desperate if he wanted you.'

'I'm not surprised,' Sven continued, ignoring my jab. 'You're almost back to full strength. A few more weeks and you might be able to beat me,' he teased. 'How hard did you pummel those Igors?'

'Not as much as I would have liked to,' I replied.

'I'd wager you scared them enough for them to give you a wide berth from now on,' he predicted, unstringing his bow. 'I only caught the end of it. The boy almost crapped himself when you had Skara at his neck.'

'I might have enjoyed that part a little too much,' I confessed, leaning back.

He nudged me with his knee. 'Are you tired now?'

'Always trying to protect me,' I grumbled in between deep breaths. 'There have been times I've struggled to catch my breath, but I'm alright. Just need more practice and, eventually, the endurance will return. Their hubris made it an easier win. What I really require is more time and opponents who have seen battle.'

'More?' he gasped. 'You are here every day, sometimes for far too long, and still you have your work at the warehouse.'

'My women don't need me for much. I do my spinning, just as they did all winter. Elin and her daughters weaved so much cloth through the cold months that we have another sail to stitch together.' I stamped my foot on the ground, freeing it from a cramp. 'Before I forget, I'll need you to help with transporting the bolts to the warehouse so we can lay it on the frame.'

He nodded.

'When I am there, in the warehouse,' I continued, 'I feel like I am in the way. Much better for me to be here.'

'Some days, you surprise me you're still standing,' Sven worried.

'Don't worry for me now. You've had months at that task. Before, when I could only leave my bed for short periods, you treated me like one of the ancients when all I wanted to do was to get back here,' I grumbled.

Sven elbowed me. 'All I did was to suggest gentle tapping practice, seeing as you were so keen for Skara to get out.'

'And by "gentle tapping practice" you meant sitting me in a chair while you held a shield, allowing me to hit my axe at various places on the wood,' I replied, shaking my head.

'To strengthen you!' Sven insisted. 'We did the same with Ancient Olaf.'

'When you were a child!'

'There was this time when Olaf gave me such a flogging. He had this moment of madness when he thought he was young once more. Ivar and Igban had to come and pull him off me. He said he was fighting the Saxons again.' Sven chuckled at the memory. 'I must have been no older than eight. Most of the time, he could do no more than swing his sword around a bit, tap the shield a few times, and dwell in his former glory. For us young boys, that was a good introduction. Holding the shield up at that age was hard enough work. But it built up strength and gave the Ancients something to do.' He smiled.

When I was recovering, I had given in out of boredom and let him treat me like Ancient Olaf, and it had worked. With regular practice, I grew stronger, could hold Skara for longer periods, and my aim improved. Having something to work at allowed me a place to fix my focus. From there, I progressed to standing and tapping, except by that time the hits were not so gentle. Sven would goad me and push me to advance. Though he stopped when he realised I was working harder than I ought to. We continued in that manner until Hersir Eskil had agreed to Sven's request for training with the Guards. Both of us were pleased with the challenge, and it had benefited our abilities.

'Maybe you could replace that handle,' Sven suggested, running a finger along the wood connecting Skara's blade.

'I like it this way,' I retorted obstinately. The wood could be refinished so long as it remained functional. It was the head that was useful, but even that survived unembellished. 'I could,' I agreed. 'I have the funds to do so.'

'Something nice, like this?' he proposed, slipping his shirt over his shoulder to show his inked skin. 'I had it done in Birka when I returned from raiding.' He pointed to the knotwork that swirled over his back. 'Do you see what it is?'

'Muninn?' I asked, pointing at the head of a bird.

'No, it's not Odin's raven. You know what it is,' he replied, covering his shoulder again.

'I saw it the night you were so drunk you almost killed yourself,' I admitted. 'So, you got a bird drawn on yourself to remind you of me?'

'To remind me not to make the same mistakes. And the rest of them are markers of the journey,' he continued. 'This one,' he pointed to the space behind his ear, 'looks like the serpent at the prow of the warship I was on.' Sven pushed his head before me for my inspection.

'I have no need for anything like that on Skara. She works fine as is, but I do plan on painting my shield.'

Sven returned to his seat. 'What symbol will you use?'

'I'm undecided about the design,' I responded without looking up.

'You should make up your mind. The market will return shortly. I saw the bone craftsman come into town this morning, and the rest will soon follow,' he explained. 'Which means we should depart in a matter of weeks.'

'I know. Sihtric is finding the last of our crew, and then the final arrangements will be made. It's not long away,' I groaned, thinking about a life at Oleg's court in a role that I could not fully comprehend.

'And Eskil? Do you think he was serious?' Sven queried.

'How could he be?'

'That man gets drunk on opportunity, but he would make a useful addition. He knows how to fight, and we may have need for that along the river.' Sven tucked his bow string into its leather pouch and stood up. 'No one wants to linger here, not once the town becomes nothing more than an outpost. Talk is that there might not even be a market.'

I rolled my eyes. 'There will always be a market, just as there will be rumours. And, plenty of people want to stay here, just not you, I, or Eskil.'

'Tell Sihtric I vouch for him.'

'But he couldn't explain to me what he wanted to do once he left Aldeigjuborg,' I tried to argue.

'And you can?'

I had to laugh. 'No,' I agreed, 'but I am not the leader of Aldeigjuborg's forces.'

Unperturbed by my logic, Sven continued. 'He has given me reason to believe he is seeking a position as a commander.'

'He already is... and he plans to leave that post.'

'Not for Oleg's Gardarike, he wishes to make money. His dream is the same as ours, to journey to Miklagard. Instead, he wants to offer his services to the ruler who pays the most.'

'And become what they call *Varjazi*?' I asked.

'That's what he said. Maybe I will join him.' Sven's eyes glazed over as he wistfully stared into the distance, no doubt conjuring images of gold and glory.

'So changeable, Sven. A few months ago you were willing to swear yourself to me,' I derided. 'While you think of riches, I have work to do.' I elbowed Sven roughly as I stood up as punishment for making me late.

'Even if you're in the way of your women?'

'Won't be for much longer, and then they'll miss me,' I replied as I started walking.

'Always in a hurry,' he grumbled. 'You have enough to do. Slow down and make sure you don't hurt yourself,' he shouted as the distance between us widened.

'I'm no longer unwell,' I called, racing away and sticking my tongue out in response to his rebuke. 'You can't boss me around anymore!'

EIGHTEEN

SPRING 883CE

White winter thawed, yielding to the burgeoning freshness of spring's arrival. Released into the air was the clean fragrance of grass, its blades reaching skyward in search of the sun. I marvelled at the meadow soaked with colourful blossoms as I bustled back from my early morning practice at the training yard outside the walls. The blooms announced the season that would wipe away the darkness that had preceded it.

The downside of the snow's disappearance was the reappearance of scents which assaulted, as well as those that delighted. Pungent odours associated with the keeping of animals and the town's waste, which had been subdued by the frost, lay in wait for the melting of the ice. Now that it was gone, the aroma's intensity seemed tenfold. The rivers flowed once more, and the harbour was crammed hull to hull with trading vessels after Aldeigjuborg's moorings had been vacant for far too long. Inevitably, with the return of ships came an influx of people to market, and, more importantly, news that could not make it across the distance during the colder months. I had hoped to get back to the walls before the flood of temporary residents began, but drawing nearer to the Enggatt, I found the gates flung open and the line long.

'Good morning, Hersir,' I greeted the town's captain.

'Signe.' He nodded, holding his hand out to collect the trading fee from a merchant as they passed. 'How was Laslo at arms today?' he enquired.

'Stronger,' I replied. 'His stance is good and he can push back with his shield as good as any brute. You should pit him against one of the Igors. I expect he is ready for a real fight.'

'Hmm,' he mumbled. 'You think all of this will be gone when news gets out about the capture of Kyiv?'

'Shhhh! I'm sure the word will soon be out, but let's not stoke that fire,' I cautioned.

'If I know, everyone knows,' he replied, shaking his head. 'The question still stands. What is going to happen when the capital is even further away than it is now?' he probed.

'You think people will just sail past without so much as a wave in our direction?'

'There'll be no money to be made selling wares to soldiers,' he grumbled. 'It'll be a big bloody barrack.'

'It won't be that bad,' I replied. 'There will always be a market here for those who do not wish to travel further down the Volkhov.'

Rarely, did a single merchant travelled the length of the trade route; they met with others along the way, bartering their goods for mutual benefit. And, I knew, marketplaces at the mouth of important rivers would always be popular.

'When I first took this position,' he began, lowering his voice, 'I thought building a guard was strange. Most of my experience was fighting as I willed it, taking what I wanted, and having some fun while I was doing it. Now, it seems the Grand Ol' Prince is obsessed with centralising his rule. How he expects to do that while we are all the way out here… is beyond my understanding,' he rued.

'That is how things are done here. It's what the tribes knew before and they expect it to continue like that,' I explained, worrying Eskil had a sudden sickening of melancholy.

He shook off his misery and stood tall. 'At least there are always whores and the tavern.'

'And what else could a man want?' I quipped.

'True. We have no need for trifles. But, I know the proper merchants, the ones with all the wealth, will move to Kyiv.' He eyed me knowingly.

'Fighting men have no funds for rich pickings, else they would not have to work for their coin.'

'Right enough,' he chuckled.

The line had not moved the entire time we had been talking, having been stilled by Hersir Eskil's raised hand.

'What do you trade?' Eskil asked a man dressed in a long light-coloured tunic with embellished trims of red at the cuffs and collar. His group were all men except for a lone woman dressed in white, her head covered with cloth and her arms holding a basket. Behind them, they dragged a small cart laden with their wares.

'Tablet woven bands,' they responded, bearing a sample for inspection.

'Enter.' He nodded, holding his gloved hand out for their offering. 'And Dimitri?' Eskil returned to his questioning of his troops. 'What about the others?'

'They all need more practice,' I replied. 'You know, Eskil, if you wanted me to do your job for you...'

'Pah!' he spat. 'You should have taken my offer to join my guard then!'

'At least I would be paid for the work I am now doing for free.' I laughed, cutting through the front of the line and proceeding inside.

'*Hej*, Signe,' a familiar voice called as I walked clear of the gate.

'Björn, you're back.' We shook arms in greeting. 'How was your journey?'

'Lengthy,' he complained. 'We are later than usual. The river took a long time to thaw, eh?'

I nodded.

'But I have news for you. Lots of wool. My friend, Asmund, will arrive in a month's time with the shipment.' He beamed.

'I'll look forward to hearing the details soon. How long are you here?'

He shrugged. 'Nothing is for certain.'

'Hiding something, Björn?' I questioned the old sailor. 'Is there a reason you are not keen on the return journey?'

'My wife,' he answered sheepishly.

'Don't tell me. With child again?'

'Seems now I only have to look at her for a *barn* to take root,' he replied. 'More mouths to feed, more wealth is needed.'

'And the longer you are gone, the better rest she might have,' I joked.

'As she said,' he chortled. 'I've just seen Ingvar, but I'll see you at the Skogarmaor soon,' he called as he ran after his friend.

For a while, I sat and watched the ruckus in the marketplace as people carried various sacks of goods and pulled carts loaded with wares to be sold or traded. For the inhabitants of Aldeigjuborg, the opening of the town's market meant the austerity of winter was over and held the promise of a prosperous trade to come, and plenty of opportunity to spend. There was an energy of excitement. Children ran through the legs of the crowd, playing games and singing songs. Stalls were set up in whatever available space there was, and voices filled the air, trying to entice would-be clients to inspect their offerings.

Not one to miss an opportunity, Father Niall was on his dais preaching a sermon on recognising the dangers of greed. In his resounding voice, he began. 'Thou shall not gain wealth by false pretence. Do not be tempted when the Devil says unto you, "I shall show you the path to riches," for it is a falsity.'

A small group had gathered before his platform in front of his Church of Saint George, enrapt in the discourse. Others ignored the words and proceeded with their business.

'Be honest how ye comes to all ye own and use your wealth to serve the Almighty Father,' he boomed.

On the fringe of the congregation was the group who had been earlier admitted by Eskil. Their long tunics bore similarity to Father Niall's garb but, from their disgruntled faces, I could tell that was where the similitude ended. As Niall spoke, they shook their heads, muttering to one another. Alongside them, some traders dressed in the Northern style also voiced their disagreement at the oration.

'Shut up, priest man!' a bearded man called.

Father Niall continued undaunted. 'You shall not covet what the next man has! Do not covet his icons covered in gold.'

'Oh, I see,' the bearded man shouted, 'all those relics you have in there, eh? I suppose your god just created them out of nothing, did he?'

Father Niall ignored the derision, lifting his chin and fixing his stare on the receptive. I was sure he would direct his next sermon at the worship of false gods. It was one of his favourite issues. The crowd tittered and dispersed, though a fevered temperament ran through the place that was just as likely to give way to brawling and enmity as it could cause celebration. But I had work to do and could not sit around waiting for the frenzy to begin.

Since the icy winds had blown over, shepherds were preparing their flocks for shearing. Soon, the warehouse would come alive with the clap of shuttles passing from side-to-side on the loom, the gentle hum of wool being spun on the spindle and the excitable chatter of my women. There was much to organise. Hilde and Helga would manage all facets of the business in my absence. Hilde would persevere with our dyeing endeavours, hoping that the wealthy wives of the Holmgardr elite would grace us with their patronage once they realised the quality of our work. Helga would oversee the accounts, divide the wool based on condition, and see to its processing. It was a lot of responsibility, but together, I knew, it could work. It was everything else I doubted.

The plans for leaving Aldeigjuborg were skeletal. Our first significant stop was Kyiv to deliver Kjarr's belongings, as he had requested in his last message. We all assumed we would have a brief stay there before continuing on for the last leg of the passage to Miklagard. But that would depend on the water levels. As the weather warmed, the rivers would become shallower, making journeying by them more difficult. A successful voyage relied on a well-timed departure.

'Spare a morsel for your less fortunate, lady?' an old woman asked, proffering her hand. Her grin was emptied of a few teeth, and the clothes she wore were of good quality but ill fitting.

'I've nothing on me, Old *Amma*,' I replied truthfully.

She spat on the ground. 'Ungenerous when you have so much. God smite you where you stand,' she cried, crossing herself.

'Odin will protect me.'

My opposing faith only outraged her further.

'Heathen! You will be smited by the one true God,' she rambled, crouching low to the ground. 'Forsake your false gods and come into His light, woman, and you will learn grace.' She waggled her finger.

As she moved, I glimpsed a string of beads around her neck. 'I have no need for your god's light,' I responded, leaning in close. 'And know this, whilst asking for help may not be strictly illegal in Aldeigjuborg, vagrancy absolutely is.'

'Huh?' The woman looked up with her brow furrowed.

'Be on your way, Old *Amma*, with your fancy beads. If you beg for fun, that's your business, but don't try to curse me or I'll report you to the Hersir. Do you understand me?'

She nodded curtly and ambled away.

'The gates are open to everyone and with it always came a few who meant to cause trouble,' I muttered to myself.

No wonder Eskil was in a foul mood. As Captain of the Guard, he bore responsibility for keeping the peace and making certain any disobedience was punished. If he had reliable Guardsmen, it would be more tolerable. But with the likes of the Skulking Shadows, he could expect them to pocket a bribe over enforcement of retribution. Thankfully, the way home was uncrowded, and once I was in my hearth room, the noise of the street was forgotten.

Helga was bent over a pot simmering over low flames. She wore a smile as she sang to herself and the slight bump that protruded from her stomach.

'I hope there is a bowl for me,' I said.

She swatted me away with her spoon. 'You'll have to wait. It's not ready yet,' she replied, generously sprinkling some dried herbs into the broth.

'Dill?' I asked, the aroma unmistakable.

She nodded.

When fresh, the dill's scent was akin to the sweetness of a fruit and the crisp grassiness of spring meadows. It always reminded me of the abundance that came with *Nóttleysa*, the time when the days were at their longest and the fields were fragrant and green. Unless it was in stores for months on end to dull its potency, it inevitably overpowered every dish. Helga was likely masking the fact that our provisions had not yet recovered from what was a difficult winter.

There was always bread to soak up the broth and worse things to eat, I reminded myself. At least we had food.

'What is it about the first market day that attracts those intent on mischief?' I complained to Helga as I gathered up bowls ready to be filled.

'You too?' she asked, eyebrows raised as she began filling bowls with soup.

'An Old *Amma* begging and hexing people. But she had a string of glass beads around her neck as fine as any woman would want.'

She glanced at me as she passed another steaming bowl to me to put on the table. 'You think it was stolen?'

I thought for a moment. 'Or maybe she was set on a swindle for a bit of fun, but I sent her on her way. What trouble have you had?'

'Oh, just the usual wandering hands and promises of marriage. No serious harm, I swear. No one touched me except for the man with wandering hands, and trust me when I tell you, he won't be putting his paws anywhere unwanted for a while,' she answered with a wink. 'Why are they always emboldened by market day?'

I shrugged. It was a common complaint of the womenfolk when visiting men would try their wiles. 'People are bored after such a long winter.'

'It seems worse this year,' she replied, setting down the last bowl.

'An omen of things to come,' I scoffed. The peace of winter and an empty city had been enjoyable, but it did not produce money. 'If we hope to make our fortunes, we should welcome people to town.'

Helga stood, hands on hips. 'There is a limit to my welcoming.'

'And Father Niall was preaching from his church door again, inciting conflict,' I grumbled.

'He believes he is doing God's work.'

'If God's work is to annoy the heathens with his belligerence, then he is succeeding.'

'Want me to fill your ears with wool so you can pass through the marketplace without having to hear it?' she asked, grabbing spoons for the meal.

I chuckled. 'It wouldn't hurt.'

The women were called to share in the food, eating in companionable chatter until everyone was done. When the room had emptied, Helga sat against the wall with her feet up.

'That's not like you, Helga. You're usually bustling about with no time to stop. Are you alright?' I asked.

'It's my head. My body. Urgh, everything really,' she groaned, closing her eyes.

'Should I fetch your mother?'

'No. Please don't. Nothing is wrong,' she promised, opening her eyes. 'Mother says carrying a child is not so burdensome on the body, but for me it is so weary making.'

'Every woman carries differently,' I explained, sitting at her feet. 'I recall a woman in my longhouse that was so ill and tired right to the very end. When the baby was born, the sickness was gone.'

She looked at me wide-eyed. 'So I may have to endure this until the baby is out?'

I tried to stifle my laugh. 'It will end. I promise you that. Whether the sickness stops at the first flutter or right to birth, it will end.'

'Urgh,' she moaned, setting her feet in my lap.

'Did the dill help a little?' I asked as I massaged her feet and ankles.

'I can't bear the smell or the taste,' she wailed.

'Oh. You're off your food, then? That's also common. For now, just ale and bread?' I offered the small loaf from the table that had been picked at. 'You have to eat something.'

She nodded, tearing a small piece and nibbling it. 'It will end, it will end,' she repeated.

'Do you think it will be a boy or a girl?' I wondered, trying to distract her from the discomfort.

She laughed giddily. 'I had a dream last night that it was a girl.'

My heart sank as I remembered Neflaug telling me she had the same expectation. That daughter had become my Freyja. I swallowed hard, masking my pain.

'Really? A little girl? I'm sure she will be just as strong and lovely as her mother.' I managed a smile.

'And if she is the girl I have dreamed of,' she began, 'then I would like to name her after the strongest and most beautiful woman I have ever known. I'll call her Signe. A name of honesty,' she dreamed.

'If it is honesty you seek, then you might want to choose a different name,' I mumbled. 'You know, I have not always acted truthfully.' Helga had never known my true identity, with Neflaug gone, there was no one left to use it against me.

'It doesn't matter what you have done in your past, Signe. You have always been constant in your support of me and my family. Sincere in your affections and helpful to all those who need you. It will not be forgotten.' She smiled.

I swallowed hard, about to admit what I had only told Kjarr before this moment. 'If you wish to name your child after me,' I started, 'then perhaps you might choose Astrid. It is a name far more truthful to the person I am.'

She sat back and closed her eyes, a peaceful smile on her lips. 'Astrid,' she mused, looking at me once more. 'Yes. That is a name that suits her, and you, much better. I cannot believe I didn't see it until now.'

I held my breath.

'It matters not what you call yourself. What you have done or have not done proves who you are. No matter how you happened to be here,' she whispered. Her hands found the curve of her belly and came to rest there.

Discreetly, I wiped a tear from my eye. 'And what if it is a boy? What then, Helga?'

'Mikel the younger, or something similar,' she dismissed with a wave of her hand. 'The father names the boys. If she is a girl, then she will be mine to name and free to be whatever she wishes to become, just like her namesake.'

NINETEEN

'The boy is back asking questions again,' Sven called through the door. 'He wants to know where all of *his* things are to go.'

I drummed my fingers on my knees. 'Kjarr's things,' I replied with an exasperated breath. 'As we discussed the day before yesterday, they are to be packed into chests. The rest is to be sold, as I detailed.'

'He was unsure what you meant when you said "use your judgement," and your husband's house-help was none the wiser,' Sven advised.

With a steady exhale, I opened the door. Sven must have been leaning against it and lost his balance as I flung it open, stumbling forward.

'I've tried my best with him but there are just so many questions. Thought you would know better,' Sven grumbled, getting to his feet.

'You should not have to deal with it at all. It's not your problem.'

'Nor yours,' he responded.

'Ha!' I scoffed. 'I wish that was true, but this is exactly the sort of role a woman is expected to fulfil for her husband.'

'Tell me, what needs to go?'

'Not the furniture. Kjarr will have already commissioned what he requires to furnish our new accommodations,' I advised.

Sven bristled at the sentiment.

'His belongings,' I continued, 'any clothes, tapestries and the like are to be packed into chests. My instructions were that the rest of the possessions are to be sold.'

'So, empty the house of personal effects and the rest is to be traded?' he clarified.

'Please make sure nothing is forgotten,' I urged.

He scratched his head. 'I'll try. Um, wouldn't it be easier if you tell him yourself? I'm not sure I can explain the difference between what stays and what goes.'

'You could if you tried,' I replied. 'No? I suppose I'll have to go there myself. Just order the boy to do as he has been told, and I will come after midday to check. If I have to prepare two piles, one to take and one to sell, I will.'

Sven nodded as I turned to retrieve my soft leather slippers from the floor.

'And don't forget, we are meeting with Sihtric at the Skogarmaor tonight,' he reminded me.

I sat on the edge of my bed to put on my shoes. 'I've not forgotten, but I have a lot of work to get through before then.'

Sven chewed his bottom lip. 'Have you decided what you will do once you arrive in Kyiv?' he asked.

'No, and I would prefer not to. Not until I cannot delay it any longer.' I strained through the words as I forced the second shoe on.

'Is that really for the best?' he began.

'Sven, stop,' I cautioned him with a glare, standing up. 'It is my way of doing things and you cannot talk me out of it.'

'I just meant...'

'Sven. Everything will be done,' I promised, laying a hand on his shoulder, 'but my present concern is the warehouse.'

'You spoke to the women this morning. I heard you,' he mumbled.

'A mere formality, everyone knew what was coming, but I wanted to ensure they all learned it from me. I will have none of these rumours and certainly no confusion over who I was leaving in charge. But, as I expected, they've all been supportive,' I explained as we walked into the room under discussion. 'It feels so quiet in here.'

Spindles lay on the bench alongside tables of shorn wool to be carded. On the walls, hanging skeins of spun fleece waited for Elin to use her skill to weave them into fine cloth. Without them, it seemed massive and soulless, but if I closed my eyes, I could almost hear the singing that often occurred there.

'Will you miss it?' Sven asked beside me.

I nodded. 'It was a life I never expected to know and, while there have been some terrible things that have happened, there has also been great joy.'

He ran his fingers through the hair on his jaw, hesitating to speak. 'You could have sold all of this and taken the money.'

'That was never my intention,' I replied. 'The women will continue to spin and weave and will need these tools to make sure our business grows.'

'And none accepted your offer of passage to Kyiv?' he asked.

'None.' I shook my head. 'Hardly surprising. Most of them enjoy their life here. They have homes outside the walls and do not wish to uproot their families to live in a crowded city they have no connection to.'

Sven clicked his tongue. 'Doesn't sound like you want to go either.'

'It's complicated.'

'How will you feel once the final plans are laid and everything you worked for here shall be gone to you?' he asked.

'Sven,' I groaned. 'It's not gone to me. Urgh, you're set on frustrating me today, aren't you?'

He laughed. 'And every day after.'

'I will not sail into Kyiv and cease to be me.'

'You don't know what you will be going into,' he pointed out.

'Just as I didn't when I arrived in Aldeigjuborg, and if you remember correctly, I took that leap just as I will this time.' With a deep breath, I calmed my pounding heart. 'All that kept me here is no more, and every step is leading me towards something greater.'

'I know,' he agreed.

'Like you said, Sven. The Norns weave what we cannot see.'

He stood in front of me, laying his broad hands on my shoulders, and looked down. 'Let us hope the fate they have chosen for us leads to a successful journey,' he replied

'If I have grasped anything in Aldeigjuborg,' I began, 'it is that there will always be a way. You just have to find the right people to support you.'

'I've learned a thing or two here as well.' Sven grinned.

'Oh, yes?'

He hugged me tight against his chest. 'If you shovel crap for long enough, the woman you love might take pity on you and forgive your wrongdoings.'

I pushed him away. 'Not that I've forgotten, more that I found a way to make you useful.'

He roared a deep belly laugh.

'Don't laugh like that. I mean it! Odin's beard, Sven! You know that when you meet Kjarr…' I started.

'Who says I want to meet him?' Sven asked petulantly.

'You think you'll be able to avoid him?' I questioned as I wandered over to the skeins on the wall. 'If you want to be near me, it will be impossible.' I ran my hands along the fine threads of wool. 'When you do meet Kjarr, who you know is my husband…'

'Pfft,' he derided, rolling his eyes. 'Your husband for now.'

'You cannot say things like that,' I snapped, turning on him. 'Especially not in front of Kjarr. And you cannot look at me like that.'

'Why?' he pouted. 'Don't you like it?'

'It's not fair to me or Kjarr.'

'Would he not be flattered by someone else wanting his wife? Does it not make him prideful to know he has what others want?' Sven asked, tilting his head to one side.

Many men I had known in Karlstad would raise their woman in esteem if she was desired.

I studied his face as he finished speaking. 'He is not you and would not be flattered. That notion is in such stark contrast to Kjarr's own mind that you couldn't be less alike.'

Sven stood stiffly by the wall, refusing to look at me. 'I'll be in the hearth room if I'm needed,' he mumbled, walking out of the warehouse.

It had not been a calculated comment, and his reaction left me feeling guilty. Knowing I had hurt him was not the same as inflicting pain, and his harboured hope to change the nature of our relationship vexed me. Now that Sven had returned to my life, I did not want him, or Kjarr, to leave. And, as departure drew closer, it was a situation I knew I would soon have to confront.

'You ready?' I asked, walking into the room when I had finished recording all the tools and stock.

Sven sat at the table, deep in thought.

'*Hej*, Sven!' I called again, waving my hands in front of his face.

This time there was some recognition and his mouth curved. 'Yes, yes,' he mumbled, smoothing the edge of his smile. In his hand, he had both of our cloaks.

'Are you still upset with me?'

Sven whirled his cloak over his left side, leaving his right arm free of the garment. 'Why would you think I am troubled?'

The tediousness of his childish irritability irked me. 'Was it my comment that you and Kjarr are so different? Or is it the reminder that you and I will never be?'

'Never is a little too sure,' he joked. 'I wouldn't say never.'

'You wouldn't?'

He draped my cloak over my shoulders and fastened it with the brooch Kjarr had given me. His fingers fumbled with the fastening as he pinned the two sides together.

'No, I wouldn't,' he said, and as he spoke his voice became solemn and serious. 'To me, everything else is a minor departure from the true course that has been set for us.' He smoothed the fabric across my back and looked down.

I raised my head, not wanting to look away but refusing to find the truth in his statement. 'And yet, some, like the shape of this brooch…' I held it forward to show the broken ring, 'will never touch. They will never meet nor ever become one.' My voice shook as I spoke. 'I am married to Kjarr.'

'Do you love him?'

'Yes,' I replied stoically.

Sven seemed undaunted by the declaration. 'I respect that, Astrid, as I respect you. I've not always shown it and, if what you say gives you the space you need between us, then so be it. My feelings for you will never go away. No amount of time or distance can change it. So, if you decide we can never be, I have to accept that. But I will never leave you. All you have to do is tell me you do not feel the same way,' he challenged.

My mouth was dry. 'There will be time enough to talk when we are stuck on a ship together,' I said, drawing my cloak around me. 'Now, we have work to do.' I ignored his longing gaze as I walked out the door, Sven trailing behind. 'This way,' I announced, pulling Sven's arm down a side street to Kjarr's home. 'This is it.'

'I'm not going in,' Sven grumbled with folded arms and screwed up his face.

'Don't be a child, Sven,' I goaded him, pushing open the unlocked door. 'Come in.'

From behind, I shoved him towards the house, but his enormous frame barely shifted. Eventually, he gave in, curious to see the inside.

'It's grander than my house,' I commented, noting Sven's raised eyebrows and pursed lips. 'And it was nicer when it was filled with all his beautiful things and lit by the fire. We used to sit here, two seats side-by-side.'

'I don't want to know,' he mumbled.

'It's just fond memories. Anyway, we are here for other reasons. It looks like the boy has done his job. The small furniture is gone,' I muttered as I walked around the house. 'Of course, the larger items will remain to be sold with the house. These three chests are all we take to Kyiv.' I peeked into the box. 'Oh, yes. He will want this.' Inside, his trinkets, combs and clothing lay neatly arranged.

As I wandered through the home, it felt strange to see it so empty, just as it had with the warehouse. No servants fussing about with food or fire, no Kjarr pacing the room as we discussed business or scandal. The hearth had been my solace, speaking to Kjarr before it had made me feel valued for the first time in my life. Now, everything had changed, and life had moved on.

'I will send for these when the ship and Sihtric are ready,' I decided, shutting the lid on each of the chests, having concluded my inspection.

Sven stood awkwardly in the dark room. 'Can we leave now?'

'The house or Aldeigjuborg?' I asked, dragging the last stool to join the other items to be sold.

'Both,' Sven mumbled.

'Soon enough,' I replied. *The next adventure*, I told myself as I shut the door behind us. All it entailed was closing off one life and opening another. I had done it before and I could do it again. But the volume of the unknown threatened to overwhelm me, so I ordered myself, *one step at a time*.

'Do you think Sihtric will be waiting for us?' Sven wondered as we meandered towards the tavern.

'If by waiting you mean greeting people and enjoying the chaotic air, then yes.' I laughed, but the sound was hollow.

The meeting tonight would finalise our plans and determine how many days remained until I was reunited with my husband. My mind spun, trying to remember Kjarr's steady voice that always filled me with calm and certainty.

Would it be the same this time?

In Kjarr's absence, I had lost Freyja, waded through the depths of Neflaug's deceit, and had been close to death, saved only by the meticulous care Sven provided. None of which had reached Kjarr's ears because I could not find the words to do so. I had told myself it needed to be delivered in person, but now, I was unsure.

Then there was Sven, whose sudden appearance was sure to throw fat onto the fire. Kjarr knew the stories. He understood Sven had tried to entrap me with marriage, offering me adventure in exchange for my vow that had ended with my escape to Aldeigjuborg. *How would he react when they met?* The thought filled me with agony for reasons I was not willing to give words to.

'It feels like trouble is in the air,' I whispered, taking Sven's arm as we rounded the corner. 'With so many people together after a long winter, there is sure to be disquiet.'

'Don't you remember wintertime at home?' Sven asked as we pushed through the throng. 'Someone always ended up with an injury after doing something stupid, or getting a woman with child. And worse, when parents discovered their not yet married children at the work of creating one, probably in the stables.' He laughed, eyes alight with mischief.

'Hmm, I remember well enough,' I replied, breaking free of his grasp. 'Can you see him?' I asked as we entered the tavern.

Sven craned above the crowd to find our companions. 'He's here. Down the back,' he shouted, leading the course.

As we made our way, the throng thinned. Those who could find a spot before the tables sat in groups, drinking together. Some were engaged in games where the stakes rose with each mug of ale. And some were trying in vain to conduct business, their voices straining against the ruckus. The poor female thralls serving the patrons had their backsides pinched until their rumps were numb, and the tavern keeper

Ivar was run off his feet selling plates of food from the kitchen. But, with trade so good, it was no wonder his wrinkled face was grinning from ear to ear.

'I've not seen this place so full since... oh, I don't even remember,' I gasped, as we managed our way to the back.

'The rivers flow to Kyiv!' Sihtric cheered, raising his cup. It was apparent that he had begun his celebrations long before we arrived. 'Two jugs of ale for the table, lass,' Sihtric ordered with a wink at the serving girl. 'Sit, *bhana charaid*,' he directed me, 'we are waiting on one more.'

'Who?' I asked, glancing around. Before me sat Sihtric, Björn, and three men I did not recognise.

'I believe you already know Björn?' Sihtric asked.

'Signe.' Björn nodded, creating room for me at the bench.

'Hmm, I do,' I replied, 'but I thought you were supposed to be making connections in the north for me?' I grumbled.

'Already done.' Björn smiled his gap-toothed grin as Sven and I took our place between the others.

'Björn's shipmate, Frodi,' Sihtric returned to the introductions. 'They will both be lending their considerable experience with portaging. And Thorsten here is a craftsman of bone and antler, seeking passage to Kyiv, as is Gunnarr,' he paused, nodding at the tall man with sandy hair. 'Gunnarr is returning from Svealand to his home in Kyiv.'

'I believe there has been a change in leadership there?' Gunnarr winked.

'How many do we need?' I enquired, ignoring Gunnarr's probe for information.

'Five at the least, but for an easier journey, ten or more,' Sihtric replied.

'So, all us here tonight, does that complete our numbers?' I asked.

'We are eleven in total. You,' Sihtric began, 'Sven, myself, and my man Kari, Frodi, Björn, Thorsten, Gunnarr and his thrall, and Ahmed Ibn Rashti, who you ken already, and one more who is currently keeping us waiting.' He stood to cast his eye around the room. 'Here he is,' Sihtric beamed.

I turned to see the final addition to our crew. Hersir Eskil pushed his way through the crowd, barging a wiry man out of his path, and plonked himself down at the end of the bench.

'Hersir.' Sihtric nodded.

'Not any more, now you call me by the name my own bloody mother gave me,' the captain grumbled.

Sven and I exchanged a quick look, then I turned to Eskil. 'They've sent a replacement for you, then?'

He shook his head. 'Not so much. I have installed a temporary hersir until they can send a more experienced man to take the command.' Eskil leaned forwards, taking a cup from the centre of the table and filling it from the jug of ale. 'So, Laslo will probably only have the position for a month or two, but it has to be done. He is the best of the lot, though it's slim pickings.'

'Odin's beard!' I cursed. 'What have you done?'

Eskil gulped down his drink, refilling it immediately. 'The boy'll be alright. He's not stupid, and there has been no trouble since that run-in you and Sven had during winter.'

'The men don't respect him like that. He is yet to prove himself,' I explained. 'Did he accept the assignment willingly?'

'He didn't have much of a bloody choice. I've decided I'm going and I need a bloody replacement, that's it!' he roared. 'Who else could I have chosen? I could not have given the post to one of those bloody Skulking Shadows, could I? Look at them over there.' He gestured to the corner where the two Igors stood observing the room. 'One of those cretins would have been more than eager for the job, but Laslo is a better man.'

'What about one of the older men?' I pushed.

'No one knows the land like Laslo. What he lacks in battle experience he makes up for in intellect. Stop bloody pestering me, it's done!' Eskil growled.

'Gods protect him,' Sihtric interjected.

I downed my own cup to stop any further remarks I would have liked to make.

'You better hope there is no trouble until your replacement comes. Laslo is a good boy and leading the men is a big responsibility,' Sven warned.

'I told him you and Signe will come to make sure he is up to the task before we go,' Eskil commanded, brokering no argument.

'Me?' I gasped.

'My suggestion was Sven. Laslo insisted you would be the best to judge his readiness,' Eskil answered, reaching for his third ale.

'He isn't ready,' I mumbled, shaking my head in exasperation.

Eskil banged the table. 'He will be alright. Laslo is clever. He will find a way to win the respect of his men,' he detailed, his tone suggesting he observed some ability that I was yet to witness.

The rest of our party merely shrugged despite the fact that Aldeigjuborg was being left in the charge of an untested captain that could not be expected to repel marauders let alone a serious attack.

'That takes us to eleven,' Sihtric confirmed.

'Twelve,' Eskil threw in. 'Got myself a thrall at the market. Wasn't much left, but he was the best of the bloody dregs. I'm calling him Toki.'

I closed my eyes against the pejorative comment. My place in this journey was already difficult enough without upsetting the man even further.

'To Kyiv,' Eskil raised his cup, 'then, for some of us, to Miklagard!' he roared.

Björn followed. '*Skal.*'

'*Skal,*' our group repeated, thrusting their cups together.

Next to me, three men played a game of Taflkast, their wager a drink on the loser. I watched them to distract from my anger. Each man had their own set of dice, rolling their hand in turn to throw the highest number.

Under the table, Sven squeezed my fist in support. 'Just worry about yourself and not them,' he whispered.

'How many days will we stop in Holmgardr?' asked Thorsten, his fire-blonde hair sticking out from under the simple cap on his head.

'Depends on the weather,' Sihtric answered. 'We need to travel quickly to Kyiv to deliver Kjarr's belongings.' He sipped from his cup, watching me over its rim. 'Keen to see your husband, Signe?'

Mouth full of ale, I did not have a chance to react before Sven butted in with his own retort.

'She can think of little else.' The derision in his voice was unmistakable.

'Shut up, Sven,' I growled, spitting the ale out into my cup.

'Kjarr was so generous with his payment that we barely needed paying passengers. I cannae help but ken his cargo is precious.' Sihtric smiled deviantly.

Sven was quick to insert his sharp wit while I chose my words. 'He does not even know the value of what he has,' Sven replied, maintaining eye contact with Sihtric while the surrounding men conversed.

'Shut up, Sven,' I snarled, this time louder.

Sihtric's eyes widened, enjoying the spectacle. And the rest of our group remained oblivious, distracted by food delivered by the pretty thrall.

'Does Kjarr ken you dinnae intend on remaining in Kyiv?' Sihtric asked.

'Yes, Signe,' Sven began. 'Does your husband know what is coming for him?' he teased.

Under the table, I drove my heel into Sven's toes. His eyes did not show pain, if there were any. 'Shut up, Sven. No,' I replied, turning to Sihtric. 'I have not sent word of my intention, but I am sure he will not begrudge my wanting to travel to Miklagard, just as he has.'

'Won't he be concerned that you may not come back to him?' This time it was Sven asking the questions.

'I never said I wouldn't return,' I explained.

'You dinnae say you would,' Sihtric pointed out.

'I haven't even seen the man in almost a year, and before that, only for a few days since we were married. It is difficult to make a decision before I know what I am walking into,' I barked at my interrogators.

Sihtric raised a mollifying hand. 'I'll return to Kyiv once business is done in Miklagard. You're welcome to journey back with me.'

I folded my arms across my chest. 'Just leave me alone, will you? The both of you!' I snipped at Sven and Sihtric.

The rest of our party, catching the drift of the conversation, hooted at my outburst, and I glimpsed the tour ahead where I may be prodded like a baited animal for their fun.

Sihtric steepled his hands in front of his face, resting his chin on his fingertips. 'I ken Kjarr,' he spoke in a hushed voice, 'and he willnae be pleased if you keep this from him.' He leaned forward until he was speaking to only me. 'Nor will he enjoy the thought his trust has been betrayed, *bhana charaid*,' he intimated, eyes darting to Sven.

'I am not keeping anything of significance from him. When I arrive in Kyiv, everything that has occurred this past year will be spoken of, and I would never lie to him. He trusts me,' I insisted.

Sihtric sat back, narrowing his eyes. 'I ken he does, but even that trust has a limit.'

'Let me worry about Kjarr, and you worry about our crew!' I responded. 'I've dismantled my husband's house and packed his belongings. Is everything arranged for the ship?' I asked, smoothing the harshness in my voice to shatter the tension.

Sihtric took the peace offering, breaking from his seriousness. 'We have enough men to fight and row, we ken our route,' he said, sliding a crudely drawn map across the table.

'Is this Lake Ilmen?' I queried, pointing at the basin below the point marked "Holmgardr".

He nodded. 'From there we follow the Lovat until we near Gnezdovo, then into the Dnieper all the way to Kyiv,' he said, tracing the way with his finger.

'That sounds straightforward,' Sven spoke up.

Björn and his friend Frodi guffawed. 'And between Holmgardr and Gnezdovo there are rapids and overland sections, eh?' he explained through the laughter. 'It'll be hard going with some of the narrower parts of the rivers.'

The table next to us emptied of half its players, replaced by the long cream tunic-wearing tablet weavers that I had seen toting their wares at the first market day. This time, their woman was absent. Each member retrieved their dice and challenged the remaining competitors to a game.

'When do we leave?' Sven asked, pulling my attention back to our plans.

Sihtric put his cup down on the table. 'In two days' time. The water should be its highest.'

'Making the progress faster than later in the season,' Björn interjected.

'Not long then, thank the bloody gods,' Eskil mumbled.

Thorsten leaned his elbows on the bench, tearing at a piece of meat from the trencher before him. 'What's this I heard about Oleg taking Kyiv?'

'Thought it was common knowledge by now,' Gunnarr replied, keen to rehash his earlier attempt to garner intelligence.

'Aye, but some of the local folk don't think it's correct,' Björn grumbled. 'Some are still insisting Oleg has no right to hold the seat as it is.'

'By rights it should go to Rurik's son, Igor,' Frodi insisted, 'so a farmer was telling me the other day.'

'Pah!' spat Eskil. 'They have some notion of it passing down from father to son, but that's not the way of things.'

The group next to us paused their game.

'Aye, Eskil,' Sihtric agreed. 'The position passes then to a brother or a man of appropriate age with the ability to fight to keep it, not some lad a few years weaned from his wet-nurse.'

'And what does Oleg want now he has the throne?' the leader of the tablet weavers questioned in a voice full of foreign inflection.

Eskil turned to face them. 'Expand the Gardarike lands is my guess.'

They shook their heads, one of their numbers spat in disgust.

'Not pleasing to you?' probed Gunnarr. 'Perhaps, then, this is not a conversation you should listen to.'

I stared at the interjector who bore some kind of flower insignia. He narrowed his eyes but said nothing, returning to his game.

'Seems you're not the only one intent on mischief tonight,' Eskil commented.

'Me?' Sihtric pretended to be surprised, though everyone had witnessed him provoking my temper earlier. 'I dinnae ken your meaning. Who else is…?'

Eskil rolled his eyes. 'Loaded dice,' he grumbled, tossing his head sideways, 'it's always bloody loaded dice.'

Before we had time to comprehend his meaning, stools crashed onto the floor next to us.

'You're cheating!' the man in a red cap roared, throwing a cup against the wall as he scooped up his dice.

'What?' the leader of the opposing side asked in reply. 'We have done no such thing. If you cannot take part honourably, why play at all?'

'I saw you changing out the piece!' Red Cap claimed.

The tunic-wearing tablet weavers did not wait for any further disagreement. They scooped up their winnings and made for the door before Red Cap and his friends could get out from behind the table, drunk as they were.

'Let's go and tear some petals off, boys,' Red Cap bellowed to his companions.

'I need a new peg for my collection.' His friend chuckled as they stumbled out of the tavern.

'What are you going to do about it?' Sven elbowed Eskil.

'Do? Nothing. Let them settle this matter themselves. If they were stupid enough to play at a game of dice and get swindled, then they can get themselves out of a brawl,' Eskil bellowed.

Men, with nothing better to do, followed the fight outside. While our group concluded our conversation, no one saw the two Igors sliding up to Eskil before their usually sullen voices spoke.

'Hersir?' the burly Igor declared clearly.

'Not anymore,' Eskil replied.

'Hersir, a word?' The burly one was doing all the talking and, I noticed, that was for good reason. The wiry Igor swayed on the spot, leaning against his friend.

'What in this stinking crap hole do you two have to say to me that cannot wait?' Their previous captain did not even bother turning to address them.

Burly Igor cleared his throat and straightened up. 'The man with the loaded dice, Hersir. We overheard him talking.'

'And?'

'They said something about causing trouble in town. I think they need to be watched,' he mumbled awkwardly.

'Then watch them, boy!' Eskil commanded gruffly. 'They've already caused unrest at dice, and if that is what they meant, it's nothing we cannot handle. But, if they so much as put one bloody foot wrong, go straight to Hersir Laslo.'

The sober Igor nodded, then dragged his friend from the emptying Skogarmaor tavern.

'And I thought I was done with Aldeigjuborg,' Eskil complained.

'Has anyone noticed how empty it is in here now?' Sven asked, looking around our table. The hall, full only moments before, was devoid of patrons. Just a few locals remained.

'It smells like inconvenience,' Eskil slammed his cup on the table, 'and I don't appreciate it one bloody bit. You two,' Eskil pointed at Sven and I, 'get up, I need you to come with me.'

'Where?' I asked.

'To see what's going on!' he barked.

Eskil might not have been in command of Aldeigjuborg any longer, but he knew the business of conflict, and we recognised the need to obey.

TWENTY

'What are we going to do?' I asked through laboured breath, trying to keep pace with Eskil and Sven as we ran into the night.

Eskil looked back at me. 'First, we need to find out where everyone has gone, and after that...' He trailed off as we approached the open space where market stalls were still erected.

'Oi, flower men!' Red Cap yelled, sauntering through the marketplace.

The tablet weavers stood next to a shut up stall, hands clasped together in a circle. Their woman was in the centre, chanting some words we could not hear.

'I said, oi, flower men!' Red Cap bellowed again. This time, when the group did not answer his call, a member of his own, who was dressed in a brown shirt, slung mud at the clean garment of the leader. 'Give us back our silver!'

'Why does he keep calling them "flower men"?' I asked, leaning into Sven's shoulder as we loitered near the houses that fronted onto the area.

He shrugged. 'Don't know.'

'You should not have done that,' the tall leader seethed, turning around.

A shorter man lay his hand on the tall man's arm. 'Don't respond, Svatopluk,' he cautioned.

'You cheated yourself,' Svatopluk spoke slowly. 'If you play drunk, you play to lose. Don't lay blame elsewhere when it ends poorly.'

Red Cap's friend stepped forward. 'Give us our silver back or I'll smash your face in,' he scowled.

'You're welcome to try,' Svatopluk replied defiantly, flicking the lump of mud off his clothing. 'But I would suggest that you do not.'

In the gatehouse's torchlight, Red Cap and his three friends fronted the tablet weavers. 'And why would that be?' asked the man with a serpent tattoo curling around his skull.

Red Cap pulled him back. 'I don't like it, Ingvar.'

'We can't let them take our coin and forget about it, Odholf,' Ingvar replied as he turned and grabbed the front of Svatopluk's tunic.

The leader tilted his face down to Odholf, standing head and shoulders above the shorter man.

'We should do something,' I whispered to Eskil, 'or it may come to blows.'

'I'm sure Laslo will be in earshot. He'll be out here shortly. But, oh bloody gods!' He squinted into the dim light. 'Looks like the priest has arrived to preach to the rowdy,' he replied, motioning to the door of the church.

From behind, Father Niall strode out, lighting the ensconced lamps on the church's external walls. Once the front of the building was illuminated, he stepped onto the elevated platform and held his hands out to his sides and raised his head to the sky. 'Turn not to violence,' Father Niall began, his voice carrying across the marketplace, and the crowd that had gathered to witness the conflict turned towards him.

Both the tablet weavers and the group led by Red Cap let go of each other's clothing.

'Keep them in your sights, Ingvar. They'll not be getting away again,' Odholf instructed.

'Your differences can be settled by seeking the one true God,' Father Niall declared, addressing the men who had been in conflict moments earlier.

I elbowed Sven. 'Just the other day, I was thinking his next sermon would be on false gods. Looks like I was right,' I whispered.

'Children of God, do not be led to worship those idols made from craftsmen's hands,' he began, 'for it is the work of the Devil.'

'Is the Devil bad?' Sven wondered, leaning close to my ear.

'Apparently. See the silversmith over there?' I said, gesturing to the man. 'He doesn't look too pleased.'

'And neither do that lot,' Eskil interjected, throwing a glance towards Svatopluk and his followers. 'Not sure this approach is going to settle their bloody dispute,' he grumbled.

'Would have thought they were Christians,' Sven commented.

'The Lord said, "You shall have no other gods before me." Do you see?' Father Niall beseeched the crowd.

Some were amenable to his pleas, nodding with reverence. Most of the others, though, had taken offence to the sentiment.

'Why would he choose tonight to preach such a thing?' Sven questioned.

'Because he is an idiot,' Eskil replied, cursing under his breath. 'Alright! Enough,' Eskil bellowed over the priest's decrying, stepping up to confront him. 'You,' he pointed at Niall, 'are allowed to be here by Grand Prince Oleg's tolerance of the religion, but do not overstep your mark,' he warned. 'Take it inside. Those who wish to listen can follow.'

'Even you, Hersir, might realise the true faith if you opened yourself to God's light,' the priest replied.

'I'm not opening myself to any bloody thing. I've got my gods and you have yours,' Eskil grumbled.

A woman from the congregation stepped forward, grabbing Eskil by the sleeve. 'Father Niall has helped me understand that our gods can be seen as part of the Lord's creation,' she smiled.

'What?' Eskil looked down at her and blinked in disbelief. 'What a load of…'

'But their God is also false,' Svatopluk spoke out. 'Before Him came Deivos, who created all things.'

'What is going on?' Sven whispered as we stood on the fringes of the conflict. 'I can't understand. Are they talking about more gods?'

I nodded.

'Deivos?' Father Niall scoffed. 'Is a belief only held in the farmsteads.'

'Ooof,' I groaned, speaking to Sven, 'he will not win favour with an approach like that. I'm sure when he was sent here, it was not with the agenda to malign Aldeigjuborg's inhabitants.'

'And before him was Odin!' screamed Ingvar.

Father Niall shook his head. 'That's not true.'

Eskil waved off the Christian woman's grasp. 'Who gives a festering sheep's carcass about who came first?' he bellowed over the rabble.

The crowd broke into factions. Christians around the church, their head, Father Niall, and believers of the old gods gathered near Red Cap and his men. Whatever the tablet weavers were, they had collected only a few more additions, and they stood defiantly behind their leader, the man named Svatopluk. The woman that had been with their group had broken away. I glimpsed her long gown trailing in the mud as she ethereally wandered from the mire.

'You heathens have no soul,' one of the Christian crowd yelled.

'And you're all weak, thinking your god will save you in some glowing afterlife if you behave like meek little sheep in the fields,' Ingvar shouted back, his allies tittering behind him.

A rock was hurled, hitting Ingvar squarely in the chest. 'Bastards,' he cried, launching himself at the Christians.

It was all they needed to ignite the conflict, as all three factions ran towards each other, slinging mud and throwing punches. In the centre, Ingvar grabbed a man by the front of his shirt and shook him violently before head-butting him. Svatopluk threw a woman backward into the sludge, and Odholf received a solid punch to the jaw.

'Stop, all of you!' Laslo's voice roared from the ramparts. 'I have archers on the wall, and I will use them if necessary,' he warned.

Heads shot up, searching the *tyn* construction for the bows drawn against them. Seeing four men, elbows back with their hands to their cheeks, the fighting ceased, knowing that a few carefully aimed arrows would stop their brawl if it continued.

'They started it,' a woman yelled from the mob, pointing towards Odholf, Ingvar, and their men.

Laslo peered down. 'I know very well who began this conflict,' he spoke with authority, 'and it is not these merchants who were swindled of their winnings.'

A ripple of disquiet ran through the herd.

In his hand, Laslo held a length of red and white woven band. 'You men there,' he addressed them in the dialect of the old Eastern language, 'give them back their silver.'

Svatopluk stepped forward. 'We won that fairly, Hersir,' he declared, arms akimbo.

'You did not,' Laslo replied, preferring to continue the conversation in the Norse tongue. 'Empty your pouches now or I shall set the arrows to rain down on you.'

They did as they were instructed, throwing the coins in the mud as Ingvar and Odholf stooped to gather them up.

'And now, you will leave.' Laslo nodded to the guards, who opened the gate and stood by them. 'You are barred from trade here or entry to Aldeigjuborg for a period of two years for inciting violence.'

'Hersir, I implore you,' Svatopluk began.

Laslo stilled him with a raised hand. 'No. Withdraw and not return, else your punishment may be graver still,' he warned.

Knowing they were bested, the tablet weavers inclined their heads to Lalso's authority and marched out of the exit. The crowd hooted and hollered until the gates were closed again, then they were ordered to disperse. Svatopluk's men disappeared from the town's fringes but to where was unknown.

'We need to speak with Laslo,' Eskil grumbled, tugging Sven and me roughly towards the walls. 'In here,' he directed, pausing by a door that led to one of the larger cells.

'Do you mind if I go in first?' I ventured, placing my hand on Eskil's muscular forearm.

He squinted down at me. 'For what?' he asked. 'We just avoided some sort of rebellion and we don't have time for some matronly benevolence you wish to bestow on the green blood.'

'He didn't seem so green up there,' I responded.

'Humph,' Eskil grunted.

'And besides, you're not the hersir anymore, so you can't order me around,' I retorted, pushing him aside. 'Wait until I call you.'

Inside, Laslo was bent over his desk with his back to the door.

'Laslo?' I called. 'We don't have much time. I wanted to see how you are. I know you may be swimming out of your depths, and if you ask, we will help.'

'Right now, I'm trying to keep everyone alive,' he grumbled. Laslo stood to his full height. 'You are right, Signe. It was a position thrust on me and well beyond my abilities,' he worried. His curls tumbled from one side to the other as he roughed his unhelmeted head with his hand. 'My mother always said I was destined for more, but I never thought it would be this much and never so quickly.'

It struck me, in the low light, how young he was. His lanky frame was yet to fill out, and his face had retained its soft features that would harden as the years passed. In age, he would have been close to the year of my birth, but to have command of Aldeigjuborg was unusual.

'You did well out there.'

His head shot up, a flicker of hope in his eyes. 'Do you think so?'

I nodded. 'The men obeyed, and that's the first test, isn't it?'

'But was it the right thing to do?' he wondered. 'What would Eskil do?'

'You can ask him yourself. He is waiting outside.'

Laslo stood taller, puffing out his chest. 'Bring him in, send someone to find Sihtric and anyone else that might be useful,' he instructed. 'We will need to conference before I make any final decisions.'

They needed no further direction. One by one they filed in; Eskil, Sven and Sihtric who arrived shortly after we did.

'Tell me. What do you know? What have you seen?' he prompted, standing behind the table with an air of confidence that was new to him.

Surprisingly, it was Sihtric that delivered most of the information we had garnered, in a voice that bore more formality than I had ever heard from his mouth. He detailed how the offenders had posed as merchants, selling tablet woven bands.

'I admitted them myself,' Eskil contributed, recalling the first market day. 'And, if they are intent on getting back in, we have to do something.'

'Then we need to fortify the rear of the town,' Laslo said, looking down at the desk before him. 'Have the carpenters…' he hesitated.

'Mikel and Luca,' I offered.

'Mikel and Luca prepare any logs as palisades to protect the lower edges of Aldeigjuborg.'

Sven leaned back against the wall. 'You think there might be a more concerted attack?' he asked.

'Yes, and for that reason, we must shut out all those who seek to harm the city,' Hersir Laslo responded.

'But what is their bloody motive?' Eskil pondered from the stool in the room's corner. 'They were a bunch of flower-loving weavers that live in the forest,' he derided.

'Eskil,' Laslo breathed, 'do you understand the significance of this flower?' He held the band before the previous captain's eyes. 'This is a six-petalled rose inside a circle. A symbol of their divine god, Deivos. These men might be farmers now, but they were not always,' he explained. 'You may not recall this, seeing as you are a Northerner,' he began with none of his usual kindness. 'It has only been twenty years since the tribes of the Volkhov invited Rurik to rule their lands. I was a baby then, but I remember the request being born from the desire for protection from raiders.'

Eskil cocked his head sideways. 'I'm not following.'

'Some were content with the relatively peaceful life that Rurik's authority brought to the land, some were not. However, to most, it was the only choice available to stop the persistent attacks by the very sort of man who came to lead here. And with the change in leadership…' He paced in front of the desk.

'Rurik perished three years ago,' Sihtric spoke again.

'And his brother has taken the throne,' I contributed.

'He did,' Laslo agreed. 'It was assumed that Rurik's son, Igor, would succeed to the position. In these parts, they held the passing of a title from father to son as law.'

'They believe Igor is the true heir to Gardarike,' I whispered.

'And so, they see Oleg as a usurper,' Laslo continued.

'If Rurik died three years ago, why is it an issue now?' Sven asked.

'Word's spread of Kyiv coming under Oleg's control,' Sihtric replied, 'and that he holds the lad.'

All heads swivelled to look at Sihtric.

'He has Rurik's son in his hands,' Sihtric confirmed.

'It is one thing to invite an overlord for protection. It is a very different situation to be approaching the edge of a war between two branches of that same family. There are tribesmen who may think that capturing a fortress town such as Aldeigjuborg could re-establish the rule of the eastern tribes.' Laslo drummed his fingers on the table loudly.

'Why pose as traders?' I asked. 'What were they hoping to achieve?'

Laslo ran the tablet woven band through his hands. 'To gather supporters,' he mused. 'They posed as itinerant merchants so they could distribute these.' He held up the band. 'We should question anyone found wearing one. Make sure no one leaves the town until everyone is dealt with,' he ordered.

Sven stroked his chin. 'Do you think these people could have had any connection to the ones that attacked Signe and I in the winter?'

'If they do, it indicates a bigger issue. Captain?' He looked towards Eskil, still seated.

'The command is yours, Laslo.'

'I would have your counsel,' he deferred to the older man.

Eskil stood and approached Laslo, towering over him, though Laslo did not appear in the slightest bit intimidated. 'You have shown a far better grasp on the politics of the region than I ever managed. But there are two things that should have been done.'

'Tell me,' Laslo ordered.

'First, we send a messenger for Holmgardr. We may require reinforcements,' Eskil detailed. 'To go any further would take too bloody long. We need a small contingency to support us from outside the walls. And if further enemy was to bloody approach, well…' he trailed off.

'I understand. Our fastest rider will be sent at once. Sihtric, can I entrust that to you?' The young Hersir nodded at Sihtric, who disappeared at once on the errand. 'And the second thing?'

'I would not have driven them all away. We could have used the information, better still, if Signe and Sven had not butchered those marauders in the winter, we may have seen this coming. But there is nothing to be done about that now,' Eskil complained.

'Eskil,' I interjected, ignoring his disdain for my earlier self-defence. 'When they were admitted, there was a woman with them,' I remembered.

'Where is she? Did she take off with them?' Laslo barked.

'I don't bloody know,' Eskil grumbled. 'Did anyone see her leave?'

'She wandered away before the fighting began,' I responded. 'I'm sure she is still here.'

'You and Sven find her,' Laslo ordered. 'We need to learn their plans. Eskil, you tell Varr, Dimitri and Bonde, once they have determined if there are any traitors in our walls, they are to arm the merchants and have them join in the defence of Aldeigjuborg.'

He stopped suddenly as two dark figures slipped into the room.

'What do you want?' he glowered, full of contempt for the Skulking Shadows. As soldiers, they had undermined him, and he expected nothing different as captain.

'You almost have the measure of it all,' tall Igor spoke slowly. 'We heard 'em planning to take the town. Might be Kryvichs or the Ilmen Slovenes, but I couldn't say which one.'

'I don't think they're from either,' the shorter Igor interrupted. 'Both tribes have aligned themselves with Oleg. It's more likely they are disaffected stragglers.'

They stopped to look at one another. 'We came to warn you,' they said in unison.

All the mouths in the room were agape.

'You?' Eskil gasped in disbelief. 'So you're not useless bloody good-for-nothing wastrels?'

They both shrugged, unbothered by the insult. 'Not today.'

'And how would you know all this?' It was Laslo who addressed them.

'We weren't all born of raiders,' the shorter Igor answered. 'Know a tribesman when see 'em. Doesn't mean we agree with 'em, oh no!' At the same time, they leaned back on opposite sides of the door and folded their arms.

Laslo sent a fist down onto the table. 'You're right, it doesn't matter where they are from, only that they may represent a greater risk to Oleg's rule and to the safety of our town. You two,' he gestured to the Skulking Shadows, 'find out what you can, watch the townspeople, and come to me with anything you gather. And you.' It was my turn to be addressed. 'Take Sven and find that girl. I will be on the walls if anyone requires me.'

'That was interesting,' Sven murmured as we walked into the passageway. 'Laslo surprised us all.'

'Hmm, but why send us to get the woman?' I wondered.

'Not to try. He needs us to bring her back.'

'So, no pressure, then?' I scoffed, avoiding the guards that passed us in the opposite direction.

'He trusts you, and perhaps he thinks it will be easier for a woman to capture another woman?'

'Women always know more than they let on. Hopefully, it's true of this one. But what happens when we do? Is this leading to war? I've only just made my first kill,' I protested over my shoulder.

'Those men were starving, skeletal and desperate. What we face now will be a more pointed attack. It's different,' Sven uttered the words as we pressed on to the foot of the steps.

I rounded on him. 'Are you saying I can't handle it?'

'Astrid,' he groaned, grabbing my elbow and pushing me against the wall. 'We did what we had to do before, but you could get yourself killed going into battle.'

I pushed him away, mounting the stairs to the ramparts. 'A *drengr* does not fear Valhalla.'

'You do not have to seek it either,' he warned, following me. 'Just promise me, if the time comes, you will not rush to your death.'

I rolled my eyes.

He reached out for my hand. '*Minn Svanr*?'

'I promise,' I swore, placing my hand on his chest as we made it to the wall walk, heading south. 'Where do you think this woman of theirs will be?'

'You said you saw her wander off from the marketplace?' Sven responded, covering his head as it began to rain.

'Back towards the tavern,' I replied. 'I'd wager we'll find her in the stables. Perfect place to hide.'

'If that's what she is doing. What is our plan?' Sven asked, looking out over the spiked defences, the approach to the town swathed in darkness.

'I'll go to her, asking if she has lost a trinket,' I suggested, holding forth the brooch that fastened my cloak, unclipping it and laying it in Sven's arms.

'What if you lose it? Didn't Kjarr give it to you?'

I shrugged. 'We will get it back when we capture her. I need a way to gain her attention without scaring her.'

'Alright. And what am I supposed to do?'

'You stay hidden until I have spoken with her. See, there she is.' I pointed down to the stables directly below us. From the vantage point on the wall, we could see the girl huddled under the roof less than a stone's throw away.

'She doesn't look like she's hiding,' Sven mumbled, carrying my cloak as he peered over the side.

The woman was young, perhaps Helga's age, dressed in a long flowing gown of cream, now sullied by the muck. Just as she had been before, her eyes were glazed and she was deep in chanting unfamiliar words.

'Quick, let's go before she moves. Not that way.' I grabbed Sven by the arm. 'Down here,' I gestured to the stairs, 'this way leads directly to the stables.' We came to the entrance. 'You wait here until you have the opportunity to grab her.'

'How will I know?'

'You will.' At least I hoped he would.

My plan was only half hatched as I walked towards the stalls. 'Excuse me,' I started, approaching the woman. 'Did you drop this?' I asked, speaking in the tongue of the river lands. The brooch I held out glittered in the moonlight.

She looked up and shook her head. 'Where is Svatopluk?' she demanded. 'Dalibor? Or Bela?' Her brow furrowed.

The horses in their pens whinnied at the sight of me, hoping to be taken to the field.

'Who?' I tried to mirror her demeanour. 'I'm not sure who you speak of,' I responded, stopping to stroke the muzzle of a pretty brown mare.

She tilted her head to the side and squinted. 'The men I arrived with.'

'We could look for them,' I suggested. 'What is your name?'

'Mokosh,' she replied, standing up. 'But I can't go with you, Northerner,' she hissed. In her eyes danced entities beyond this world. 'I won't be contaminated by those who do not worship Deivos. He has promised, when the land returns to the blood of our forebears, those who stole it from us will be scorched with the earth.'

'Odin's beard,' I cursed. 'Do you have a weapon?' I asked, unphased by her premonitions.

Mokosh blinked her eyes. 'No. I don't need a blade when I can bring the wrath of Deivos and Perkunan with just one word.'

I stepped closer. 'Good,' I answered, stuffing a fistful of hay into her mouth. 'I didn't want to get stabbed, and I've really heard enough furore over faith for one night.'

She screamed through the mouthful.

'We should take her to Laslo,' I yelled to Sven, pushing Mokosh towards him. 'Back up the way we came down.'

'You didn't call for me,' Sven whined, holding the woman's hands and directing her up the stairs.

'I didn't need to. See, I can handle myself,' I responded, reaching the top of the stairs and pulling the woman along the ramparts. 'We've got her,' I announced. 'She's a woman of words, not of fighting.'

'You made quick work of it,' Hersir Laslo congratulated. 'Now, let's see what we can extract from this one. Eskil, keep guard in case her men decide to come back.'

'Yes, Hersir,' Eskil answered.

'I commend you on your first success, Laslo,' I whispered.

A smile broke over his face, returning the boy I had come to know during my lonely walks in Kjarr's absence. 'Has she said anything?'

'Only her name, Hersir. Mokosh,' I answered.

Laslo turned and vomited over the ramparts. 'Gods!' he exclaimed. 'Get her into the lock up. Now,' he commanded, wiping his mouth with his sleeve.

Together we dragged the girl away, and when she was secured inside, Laslo took two deep breaths and ran his hand through his curls. 'If she is the embodiment of their god Mokosh, then she is more important than we realised. They will come back for her.'

He reached across and pulled the stuffing from the girl's mouth. 'Will you speak, woman? If not, we have ways of tempting you to words.' He spoke in the Norse tongue, and when she looked away defiantly, he repeated the same in the dialect he was born to. Seeing that Laslo understood the circumstances perfectly, she whimpered and nodded.

'Good,' he smiled, grabbing her by the arm, 'then you may keep most of your fingernails.'

TWENTY-ONE

Two days were all that stood in the way of our departure for Kyiv. But that was before the group of rebel Slav Deivos worshippers had disrupted everything. They lingered in plain sight, even though they had been ejected from the town. They had set up their camp on the opposite bank of the Volkhov. For the first night, we had thought ourselves rid of them when they left as Laslo commanded. The next day, however, they emerged from the forest in the east, parading back and forth, taunting us with their defiance. Laslo had forbidden retaliation until a war council could be called to decide the course forward.

We had sent our fastest rider to Holmgardr, and if Svatopluk had also dispatched a messenger, we were unsure to where and to whom he would appeal and even more unsure what aid they might receive. Our rider, sent by Sihtric, would travel speedily, but even he would take two days to reach the previous capital. Once our man reached Holmgardr, and if the forces could be mustered immediately, it might be another week for a contingency of men to be quick marched north to us. We could hope for a mounted advance guard; however, for the moment, we were on our own.

'Five days?' Sven asked, making the same estimations I had.

My knife whittled away at the end of the stick I had been holding. 'At the fastest. That would depend entirely on what forces they have to spare and how quickly they will urge them here.' My eyes strained against the dark, stinging from the smoke.

'Surely Grand Prince Oleg will want to send men to bolster his most northern town, the choke point to the Austmarr and the trade route to the north?' he asked, stroking his beard.

I shoved the pointed end of the stick into the soft ground. 'He would if he were there, but he has moved the capital to Kyiv, remember?'

I huffed. 'If we had to go so far south for support, we would be in serious trouble.'

'Gods,' Sven cursed, as the fire crackled. It was the only light against the evening as we sat waiting for a report of Mokosh's questioning. 'How long would that take?' he asked.

'Weeks. Much longer than we have.'

'Oleg wouldn't leave the town undefended. He could not afford to lose Aldeigjuborg,' a guard named Knudd replied. In the dim light, he removed his helmet and roughed his birch-coloured hair.

'He won't likely hear anything until the battle is done, if it comes to that,' I mumbled. No ruler would allow themselves to be cut off from valuable trade partners, none would risk losing a profitable port. Once, Aldeigjuborg had been the very heart of the Rurikid dynasty, the first town established when the Rus' came to rule the land they called Gardarike, and now it seemed it was destined to be on the periphery.

'Whatever happens,' Sven spoke with determination, 'we have to hope Thor is with us.'

'And, if the Slavs have also sent a rider...' Knudd began, 'that their journey is longer.'

'And their own gods forsake them,' I agreed, throwing my stick into the flames. It sizzled and popped, too green to burn properly. 'Laslo?' I wheezed through the smoke as the commander emerged from the guardhouse. His red-rimmed eyes were hidden beneath the mop of dark hair that fell over his forehead. Laslo stroked the wisp of a beard that lined his chin as he stared at the fire.

'Did the woman scream when you pulled the nails from her fingers?' Knudd asked.

The Hersir looked up, trying to connect the voice to the face. 'No, Knudd. She did not because I did not need to do it.'

'She told you everything?' Sven wondered.

Laslo flopped onto the bench beside me. 'Once she realised her menfolk had left her, she dropped the veil.'

I found another stick to prod the earth with. 'So, she isn't really the embodiment of their god Mokosh?' I asked.

'She has been raised to believe so, but she is also a scared young woman. And frightened people answer questions to save their skins,' he replied ruefully.

'What did she tell you?' the Skulking Shadows asked as they sat by the fire. All heads turned in their direction.

'I'd never want to be snuck up on by you two,' Sven chuckled. 'Wouldn't see it coming.'

'Igor and Igor, meet me in my room after you've eaten. I have a use for your skills,' Laslo ordered, and the two Igors slinked away without another word.

Once they were gone, I leaned in close and asked the same question. 'What did she say?'

'Much of what I expected; they came to garner support,' he grumbled.

Sven moved to join us, sitting on the opposite side of Laslo. 'Why now?'

'Because Oleg is distracted in Kyiv,' Laslo explained. 'They saw a means to take something from, as she called him, "the usurper." But their plan was never to keep Aldeigjuborg but to rebuild the old ruins to the north.'

'The Abandoned Paragon?' I asked.

He nodded. 'Before it was a heap of crumbling walls, it was the seat of the voivodes, the strongest warriors of the Slavs. As you know, they loved fighting so much they turned to killing each other.'

'And then Rurik came to cease the tribal feuds,' I added.

'This isn't a small band of rebels, then?' Sven asked. 'Are there more of them?'

'That's what we have to find out. Presently, Svatopluk and his band occupy the eastern bank of the Volkhov, near the archer's tower. What if they have more men at the Abandoned Paragon?' Laslo contemplated. 'The Igors will go north through the forest and spy what they can across the river. Then we offer to the gods whatever they need to make sure their rage does not rain upon us.'

Sven drummed on his knees. 'Did the woman not tell you their plans?'

'She couldn't,' Laslo answered. 'She doesn't know them.'

'And you believe her?' Sven asked, eyebrows raised.

'You may think that women in our town are confined to their duties and kept out of the workings of men, but for them it is worse,' Laslo explained, 'especially for a *vedunya*.'

'*Vedunya*?' I stumbled over the word.

'Like one of your seeresses,' Laslo answered.

Sven nodded. 'A *völva*.'

'Yes. A *vedunya* is alike to your *völvas*, though Svatopluk and his men likely believe she is the vessel of their god Mokosh,' the Hersir continued. 'They would have cloistered her since infancy. Fed her nonsense until she believed it herself and kept away from anything that would have led to her questioning what she was told.'

'So, they'll be back for her?' I asked, understanding her significance.

'They'll want her back,' Laslo agreed.

Sven leaned forward, studying the young man's face. 'Hersir, how is it you know all of this when Eskil did not?'

'I listen and I watch. Ever since I was little, I have. People will speak especially when they think you are not paying attention, and it helps that folk trust a youthful appearance.'

'Why didn't you mention this to Eskil?' I asked.

'And explain what? The politics of the land long before he arrived. Let me ask you both this. Do you think he would be interested or give me the time to explain myself?'

I shook my head. 'No. He is not one to hear something he does not believe is important.'

Laslo ran his hand through his tumble of hair. 'I could have tried harder to teach him... But for now, my concern is the men on the other side of the river. We posted two archers there, as usual, before the insurgence,' Laslo explained.

'Has anyone heard from Gamal and Karse?' Sven enquired after the men.

Laslo shook his head. 'Nothing. They may have locked themselves in or, if they had any sense, could have pretended they were not there. I expect we will know soon.' He looked at the ground.

'You couldn't do anything about it.' I tried to comfort him.

'My first days as a hersir and already I have had an uprising, and our sentries have seen nothing of the archers across the water,' he spoke, his voice hoarse and deepened.

'They might survive...' I trailed off, seeing Sven warning me off continuing.

'What do you need us to do, Hersir?' Sven asked tactfully.

'Make sure those logs get sharpened to spears and have someone dig them into the ground at the rear of the town's fortifications. We desperately need barricades there.'

'I've already spoken with Luca and Mikel,' Sven confirmed. 'When the lur horn sounded, most of the farmers and their families streamed in through the gates. More hands to do the work.'

'Kjarr's house is full. Mikel, Helga, Hilde, and her children are in there,' I responded.

'Good,' Laslo commented absently, 'at least they shall remain safe for now. Gods protect their lands, and let's hope our enemy does not decide to pilfer or burn all their hard work or it'll be another lean winter. Until the farmers can return to their farms, we shall set them to useful tasks making arrow shafts. The smith will be busy forging arrowheads and pike tips, and we require more eyes on the wall,' he detailed.

I squeezed him on the shoulder. 'Make use of Eskil, he might not have command any longer, but he cannot leave the town and will be restless.'

He smiled. 'And the ale is being rationed too, so perhaps he'll be less bull-headed,' Laslo added, running his fingernails over his chin.

'I wouldn't count on it,' I replied.

'I can't help thinking, if only they built the fortress of Aldeigjuborg in stone,' he mused.

If I ever get to Kyiv, I told myself, *I would ask Kjarr to take that suggestion straight to Oleg.* 'Build a stone fortress at the mouth of your empire to keep it safe,' I mumbled.

'So, what do we do?' Sven asked what we had all long been pondering.

Laslo resumed dragging his nails through the short hair on his neck and chin. 'We wait. Wait to see whose reinforcements arrive first. In the meantime, we all try to get some sleep. We will rotate on watch and hopefully nothing happens.' He stood to leave, arching his back in a stretch that clicked the parts of his body together. 'Thank you. Without you both, this would have been much harder than it has been.'

'There will be time to thank us when it's over,' Sven grumbled, rubbing his eyes, red with weariness or fire smoke. I could not tell. When Laslo left, Sven turned to me and pulled me to my feet. 'Come, *minn Svanr*. We need to rest.'

I pushed his hand away. 'I thought you were going to drop the *minn* part of that name?'

'And just call you *Svanr*?'

'Mm-hmm.' I nodded.

Sven's mouth curved into a smile. 'Alright, *Svanr*.'

I let him take my arm again as we walked towards my home. 'And why do you say "we need to rest"?' I asked.

'I assumed you were as tired as I feel.'

'Ha! Are you admitting you are capable of feeling tiredness?' I joked, pulling on his arm.

'There is nothing weak about needing to sleep, but if I am honest, I think my eyes will close as soon as I lay flat on my back,' he answered, his eyes blinking sleepily.

Sven was right. After we said goodnight, he proceeded to his room, where he fell asleep fully clothed and snored loud as a dog's growl. When I peered in on him, he was not asleep on his back but face down and sprawled upon his bed with his feet, still in their shoes, dangling over the edge. It was there that I left him and made my way to my own bed. Sleep was calling. It swallowed me, dragging me into nightmares, and I found myself trapped within the walls of Aldeigjuborg for eternity, screaming for release. When sunlight finally stole the night's grasp of me, I awoke sweat soaked and disorientated.

'Did I call out in my sleep?' I asked Sven as we broke our fast together.

'I didn't hear a thing. Slept like a man without a care in the world,' he mumbled between mouthfuls. 'Was it a bad dream? What did you see?'

'Just the inside of the walls. I was trapped.'

'We've only been trapped here for a few days,' he replied, pulling a chunk off the round of bread on the table.

'And we were meant to be leaving for Kyiv,' I complained. 'That won't be happening.'

'You need a distraction.'

'In normal circumstances, I would have worked, but manning the walls and preparing to fight is more pressing.'

Sven tutted me. 'Then prepare.'

'What? Braid my hair and paint my face?'

Sven shrugged. 'Why not?'

Why not indeed?

'Now is not the time, but I've wanted to paint my shield,' I replied.

I knew I desired something meaningful and had settled on the scene that had been carved into my daughter's cradle as a newborn, the goddess Freyja's cats Bygul and Trjegul, who pulled her chariot. If I was ever going to leave this town, I knew I would want her with me.

Two more days passed with nothing but insults waved across the waterway that left us all feeling infuriated at the inaction. The Skulking Shadows had been sent north on a two-fold errand. First, to spy what they could and discover if the Abandoned Paragon played a greater part in the Slav's plans. Second, to intercept a merchant's ship bound for our town.

Björn had told Laslo of his associate travelling to Aldeigjuborg, laden with wool, which was destined for my warehouse. His friend, Asmund, was due to leave Birka a month after Björn's departure. If they reckoned the dates correctly, and Asmund left on time, we expected him any day. His ship might give us the advantage we required, if the two Igors could stop Asmund and his crew before they made it down the Volkhov. To miss contact with Asmund's ship meant the merchants would sail directly past the Abandoned Paragon, and if they were captured, silver, supplies and a ship would fall into the Slav's hands. If we could intercept Asmund, he could warn other merchants, and we could ensure the rebels were not enriched by capturing an unsuspecting trading vessel.

'Asmund has agreed to tether his vessel at the mouth of the river and wait,' burly Igor reported.

'Do we trust his word?' Laslo asked, directing the question at Björn, who shrugged.

'He is a fickle man for certain! He might wait or maybe turn his ship 'round and head home. Only thing I would say weighs in our favour is the coin he expects in exchange for the goods.' He tried to sound optimistic.

'No bloody guarantee, then?' Eskil grumbled from the corner of the room.

'All I know is,' Björn whistled through his teeth, 'if there's a danger, he might not make it down. He won't tempt the gods!'

'But will he let our men use his ship to cross north of the Paragon?' Eskil demanded.

Björn frowned and scratched his scalp. 'If you pay him, he'll comply,' he reckoned.

'Thank you, Björn.' Laslo nodded as the older man left. 'And, what else? How many are there?' he asked the Igors.

'Forty, perhaps fifty, Hersir,' they replied in unison.

'They looked like they were having some sort of council,' burly Igor added.

Laslo swore and glanced at Eskil. 'Let's hope they begin with fighting amongst themselves.'

'Any reinforcements spotted?' Eskil probed.

'Nothing in the forest, the lowlands or the rivers,' the second Igor confirmed.

Laslo paced behind his desk, stroking the hair on his chin. 'What about the rear fortifications of Aldeigjuborg?'

'Complete, Hersir,' Eskil responded. 'Spears and pikes are prepared, and the smith has been at the forge night and day to provide arrow tips. Ditches have been dug at the narrow points of the wall. When the time comes, we will be ready for the bloody bastards.'

'And the barges?' Laslo questioned.

Eskil spat on the ground. 'A terrible bloody idea,' he mumbled. 'Too much noise in the forest to bring the trees down, and once we are spotted, and we will be, it'll give the plan away.'

'We need to have something in the woodland, north of the Abandoned Paragon, in case Asmund flees,' Laslo worried. 'Protect the ship builders but get the job done as quickly as possible.'

'Yes,' Eskil agreed, but obviously still thought the idea was bad.

'Signe, Sven? Keep a watch across the river. We are yet to have word of Gamal and Karse, and I observed Svatopluk and his men by the banks in the evening, noting the water levels. I suspect they will soon attempt something, but if they do, Signe, I do not want you on the walls,' he ordered. 'Is that understood?'

I inhaled an annoyed breath. 'Yes, Hersir,' I promised, though I knew when the time came, I would have to busy myself with something.

That night, the sunset splashed the sky with hues of purple and orange. Almost beautiful enough to forget about the danger that lurked east of its colour show. Once the sun had disappeared behind the forest to the west, Sven crept up next to me.

'Go to bed,' he urged as we looked across the water from our post on top of the River Gate, the Slav's campfire visible. 'If anything happens tonight, you'll hear the blow of the lur,' he reminded me.

'I'm not ready for bed,' I protested, 'but I am in need of company that does not consist of men who think the height of conversation is how much ale they will drink or women they will swive when this is over.'

'Save me some of Hilde's delicious cooking?' he asked as I began the descent from the walls.

I stopped at the bottom of the steps. 'Of course.'

It was a short walk between the River Gate and Kjarr's home, where I would find my friends and, despite the brief distance, I had to endure the belligerent preaching of Father Niall.

'Find solace in His light,' he announced to his growing flock.

I rolled my eyes. In the absence of anything else to do, people had remained to listen to his sermons, whatever their beliefs. 'Give it a rest,' I shouted across the marketplace.

'When the troops come, you shall ask me to bless your efforts!' he cried back. 'You are practical, Signe. Ensure you know the true God before He calls you home.'

'I doubt that will ever happen.'

He smiled as if our banter entertained him, and I sensed a softening in him since the tri-religion confrontation days earlier. 'Brothers, sisters,' he resumed, 'we are not so different. In your gods, you can find the miracle of God's creation,' he boomed to the crowd.

A novel tact, I laughed to myself. Incorporating Odin, Thor, Frigg and the rest of our gods into the Christian church was an interesting approach. But I doubted it would work.

'Signe?' Helga's voice cried as she opened the door I hadn't realised I had knocked on. 'You look different.' She smiled, noting the change of an apron dress in favour of breeches and tunic, the latter being much easier to move in.

'So do you,' I replied, stepping inside.

She placed her hand on the bulge around her middle. 'It grows, and they squirm,' she grinned. 'Come in. Mother is about to serve the evening meal.'

It was strange being in Kjarr's house without him. The women had turned it into a home bustling with children and filled with inviting smells.

'It's so dark tonight,' Mikel mentioned after he greeted me. 'Luca and I have been working from sunup to sun down for the last two days,' he grumbled. 'My back hurts and my eyes no longer want to be open.'

'It won't be for long,' I responded, taking my place at the table.

'Ve just vant to go back to our lands,' Hilde complained.

'Being here is better than being killed out there,' I replied, setting my spoon down. 'What was that?' I asked as the sound became louder.

'The horn,' Mikel groaned. 'Looks like there will be no rest for us tonight.'

'Don't go,' Helga pleaded, grabbing at her husband's arm.

He hugged her tight, kissing her forehead below her headscarf. 'You know I have to. Signe? You too?'

I nodded. 'Laslo has prohibited me from the walls, but that won't stop me fighting on the ground.'

Mikel, Hilde's two oldest sons, Stanislaus and Andrei, and I ran to the gathering point, armed with our weapons.

'Who is on the River Gate?' Mikel asked when we were told an assault had been attempted there.

'Sven,' I answered, my voice trembling.

'Nock!' I heard Eskil bellow from above. Looking up, I could see nothing but the former commander's frame. 'Fire,' he roared. 'Light them with bloody flames, boys!'

'I'm going up,' I whispered to Mikel, but before I could take another step, Laslo's steady hand stopped me.

'I expressly told you not to, Signe,' Laslo said. 'You're no good to me up there. Sven knows how to use a bow, and he is not alone. If you need to be useful, take Mikel and make sure the Enggatt is secure, while I make certain this is not a distraction from something greater.'

Mikel and I sprinted to the rear of the town. 'I hate this,' I seethed, slowing our pace as we neared our destination.

217

He inspected the stakes on the perimeter. 'Do you think you will go to Valhalla or Sessrúmnir when the time comes?' he asked.

While Mikel checked the defences, I strained my eyes into the darkness for any movement. 'I'd let the Valkyries decide.'

'No you wouldn't.' He laughed. 'You would tell the Valkyrie where to take you.'

'Valhalla,' I replied, grinning. 'I want to see my father again.'

'Freyja's Sessrúmnir has always sounded better to me,' Mikel spoke, sitting in the dirt behind the sharpened poles. 'There is something about the green meadows of Fólkvangr, the open space, the clean sky that I like more than a noisy drinking hall.'

'Hmm,' I mused, touching my armring, 'the Valkyries will come for neither of us if we waste away in the dark instead of fighting.'

'This is important work too, and besides, Helga would kill me if I let you run into the fray,' he replied.

We both laughed at that. Helga was a formidable woman.

'Soon you will be a father.' I smiled. 'It was not long ago you were the boy that arrived with me to Aldeigjuborg. Now look at you.'

'Look at both of us.' His voice was soft in the night air, not loud enough to drown out the screaming of commands and furore of the men who fought to the north.

Mikel and I sat in the darkness for what felt like aeons until relieved by Knudd and Varr. The two guards approached, the ground crunching under their shoes.

'Signe, Sven is looking for you,' Knudd said.

'Is he alright?' I asked.

He nodded.

Mikel rubbed his eyes and looked between the men. 'What's happened?'

It was Varr who answered. 'Seems the Slavs attempted to rescue their woman. They chanced a river crossing in the darkness but misjudged the current and found themselves unprotected when Sven and Bonde set their arrows loose,' he explained.

'They're all dead?' Mikel asked.

Knudd shook his head. 'Not all. It was only three who perished.'

'Odin's beard,' I cursed. 'Why try it at all?'

'Eskil said it looked like they were trying to find a ford in the river further north of Aldeigjuborg but were carried away by the flow. They 'ended up right in front of the River Gate, and I'd wager that was not where they intended,' Knudd explained with a snort. 'The gods favoured us tonight.'

'A ford? Up there?' I blinked in disbelief.

'Perhaps there was at one time. Rivers change, narrow, and become shallower or deeper at times,' Knudd said. 'We've killed three of them, but they have slaughtered two of ours.'

'Who?' Mikel asked.

'Gamal and Karse,' Varr responded. 'After Svatopluk's men were shot in the water, he and his three remaining men ran from the tree line to the archer's tower, dragging our archers into the firelight. The Slavs slit their throats and threw them into the marsh.'

'Our men will be caught in the reeds, but with the flow of the river being what it is now, their dead ended up in the docks south of the gate. That's where we found them and...' Knudd hesitated.

'And what?' I asked, searching their faces for answers.

'We shouldn't say,' Varr replied, looking down.

Knudd did not look away. His eyes held fast on my own but were full of pity. 'Something of your daughter's. They've taken it to the River Gate.'

If they said anything more, I did not hear it. My feet carried me to the River Gate in time with my heart's heavy pounding. Around me, people's mouths moved, but all I saw was a small wool sleeping cap with tiny yellow flowers stitched upon its rim, clasped in Sven's hands.

'It's hers,' I said in a foreign voice.

Sven placed the sodden fabric in my palm and closed my fingers around it. 'Home' was the only word I recognised as he spoke to me, guiding me towards my house. 'Are you alright?' he asked, placing our shields against the table as he sat next to me on the floor.

'You're covered in sweat,' I mumbled, wanting to think about anything other than grief.

'It was hard work,' he replied, removing his helmet and laying it down, 'but there is no denying we are now at war. Svatopluk's actions are as good as a declaration.'

I gazed across the room, my eyes fixed on my shield. Planks of stained linden wood butted against each other, making it strong enough to avoid fracture with impact. On the front, a domed iron boss to fend off swords and protect the hand behind which grasped at the handle that was secured into the wood with several iron nails. It had also been a gift from my father, just as Bjarndýr and Skara had been, but it had remained unpainted. As I stared, an image burned so brightly in my mind that I could not ignore it.

'Where are you going?' Sven asked as I sprung from the ground and opened the door.

'Wait here,' I said. My destination was the guildhall, which had been undergoing some repairs. The exterior was being lime-washed once more, after years of use and fading. In the absence of anymore meaningful work to be done, white lead paint was being used on the trims of the building to accentuate its importance. *Taking a little would go unnoticed*, I told myself, *and it was for Freyja. No one would begrudge me that.*

As I walked back into the hearth room of my house, Sven had fetched our last remaining sealed flagon of mead and removed the stopper. He poured the liquid carefully into two short wooden cups that we used for only drinking the strong fermented drink. This particular batch I could smell as soon as I entered, smooth with only the faintest hint of sweetness.

Sven glanced at the small bucket I carried containing the white lead pigment. 'Hardly the time for painting, the sun is almost gone and…' He didn't get to finish as I cut him off.

'I want to paint my shield.'

'White?' he asked. His own shield was painted the customary red in alternation with the natural hue of the wood to form a pattern. 'Entirely white?'

'I want to paint something that means more to me than any fealty,' I replied.

With the idea seared into my mind, I formed the lines with a small brush, taking great care not to blur the brushstrokes together. The profile of the figure emerged with ease, the curling stroke of the ear, the mane, and the wide eyes shaped like the pit of a fruit until the image was recognisable. Sven watched silently, sipping his mead as I started on the second head, a mirror of the first. Around the entire design, I finished with a stroke that encircled the twin profiles. When I was done, I sat back on my heels and assessed my work.

'You always stick your tongue out a little when you concentrate.' He chuckled but ceased when he saw the tears in my eyes.

I grabbed my cup of mead and gulped it down. 'Now my shield is adorned with Freyja's cats, a gift from Thor,' I said softly.

'A worthy dedication to your daughter,' Sven said with uncharacteristic sageness as he placed the refilled mug into my fist and kissed me on the forehead with such tenderness that I almost faltered.

I held his hand against my shoulder and looked up at him. 'You think I do her justice?' I asked, laying Freyja's cap on the shield rim.

He crouched next to me so he could better view my work. 'How could you do anything less? She will be with you wherever you go now.'

My stomach grumbled.

'Hungry?' Sven asked, moving my shield against the door to allow the paint to dry.

I nodded as I untied my unruly hair and snagged through the knots with my bone comb. Another task to take my mind off my grief. 'But I don't want to eat.'

'You need to eat something. And, anyway, I'm ravenous,' he said as he nibbled on a round of bread, throwing me one that landed on the table with a stale thwack.

I tried to bite through it, but it was too hard. 'How about a broth to soften this?' I asked.

'Wouldn't say no,' Sven replied with a smile. 'We have some shrivelled meat remaining in the stores. I saw them when I fetched the mead. You start the flames and I'll get it. Perhaps there are some wilting roots we can throw in?'

The fire was lit by the time he returned but was not yet hot enough for cooking. To prepare our meal, we threw in pieces of preserved meat and gnarled vegetables into the pot as Sven grumbled that they both appeared well past their best eating. To complete the dish, a sprinkle of the ubiquitous dill, and we hung the vessel over the hearth to boil away until the contents were soft and the soup flavourful.

My fingers wove through my hair, attempting the neat braids of a warrior woman. It frustrated me that I could not get the first braid to sit right. It bent unnaturally around my ear, pressing it forward at an uncomfortable angle. Sven watched me with a bemused grin. I combed the braid out and tried again, but my fingers cramped awfully and I gave up.

'Would you like me to try?' Sven asked.

'Is that a jest? Since when have you had any competency with braiding women's hair, or should I not like to know?'

He motioned for me to come around to sit before him on the floor between his knees. 'Why would it bother you how I came to have such knowledge?' The curve of his smile showed he was pleased to have riled me. He turned away from the table, and I lowered myself to the floor, sitting between his open legs, draping an arm over each knee and leaning back against the bench. 'And if you must know, it was my mother who turned her reluctant son into somewhat of a capable hair weaver.'

Sven was not a man to deny his mother anything in his power, so it was not difficult for me to imagine her teaching him to braid.

'Alright,' I agreed, 'but try not to pull as hard as Torfid would. She always left my braids so tight that I felt I was pulling a ship with my scalp.'

My aunt was many things but she would not broker an argument when she thought she was right. And, despite my protestations, she would shrug and tell me the braids would last longer if they were tighter.

Sven began by lightly combing his fingers through my hair, sectioning it into the parts he would braid together. Then with agility wove the strands so fast that I could feel the path his fingertips carved from my forehead to the base of my neck. With a gentle pat on the middle of my back, he released the braid, turning his attention to the next one until he had completed half.

I downed another cup of mead. My eyes wandered about the room, not wanting to disturb the silence between us. While I knew Sven was doing nothing more than touching my hair, it felt intimate, a closeness we had not shared since our youth. My gaze fell on my painted shield drying against the wall. *Freyja*, my heart called, but it took a moment for sorrow to steal my breath with painful memories.

'What is it?' Sven's voice was full of concern as he stopped his work, placing his hands on my shoulders for comfort.

I tried to say "nothing" but the words would not come because it was not nothing, it was everything. So I cried. I sobbed with my body hunched forward, remembering the night my daughter was taken from me. There was another feeling too. Guilt. A sense that I had caused it all.

Sven's hands remained where they were, and his presence brought me some solace, but I was confused. I had drunk too much mead and my head spun. I cried, but I wanted to forget. Not to forget, I craved a reprieve from the overwhelming pain and a way to bury it. Sven refilled my empty cup as I held it forward, and I swallowed it down two more times until the flagon was drained and there would be no more unless one of us rose to get it.

My hands moved much faster than my thoughts could follow. I reached for Sven, pulling him down as we clumsily tumbled onto the warm ground before the hearth. His lips were on mine with urgency, and his hand slid behind my head, tangling his fingers through my half braided hair as he lay me down, his body above mine. We kicked our shoes off without separating our mouths. My fingers fumbled with the laces at the side of his jerkin, tugging the garment over his head and broad shoulders. His tunic gave lesser resistance, and I tossed it on the floor along with my own jerkin. Sven's rough hands traced the length of my body, feeling what lay beneath the protections of clothing. He tugged at my shirt, freeing it to allow his hands to explore underneath.

I gasped. My head arched back, exposing my neck to his fevered kiss that moved up to my ear.

'*Minn Svanr*,' he whispered against my skin.

For the first time, the thump I felt inside was not of disappointment at the pet name but desire, unbiddable, intense want. He pulled my shirt up, pressing his skin to mine, and my hands raked the expanse of his back.

Sizzle. Crack.

I closed my eyes to shut out the intrusion, surrendering to Sven's demanding touch. He heard it too. I could tell by the way his body tensed the next time the sound came, and we both looked towards the flames to see the pot over boiling. For a moment, neither of us knew what to do, too unwilling to sever the entanglement, but that lasted only as long as it took for a small log to roll free of the hearth straight for my head. Sven blocked it with his bare hand, a painful expression with the impact. We moved quickly then. I fetched a cloth to protect my hands and removed the pot that ceased boiling almost immediately, and Sven banked up the fire. The interruption had broken the trance. The impulse still surged in my blood, but with the urgency gone, I could steady myself, understanding that my grief had opened me up to seek something else.

'Are you alright?' Sven asked, standing behind me. He wrapped his arms around my waist.

I mumbled in reply, stiffening at his touch. 'Will you fetch two bowls? I am starving.'

He understood that whatever had occurred had now ended and did as I asked, setting them on the table, ladling the over boiled soup into them. 'Is that enough for you?'

I nodded, dipping the hard bread into the liquid. 'Sven, I'm sorry.'

'For what?'

'Letting my grief overrun me. I should not have used you like that.'

He watched me, brow creased. 'I did not feel used,' he replied. Behind him lay the clothes we had hastily discarded and, though I was still clothed in my shirt, Sven was undressed to the waist. 'I would have you use me a hundred times over if it went any way to lessen the pain you have.'

His gaze did not falter with my discomfort, and when I had finished what little food I could manage, I reached for his hand from across the table.

'Will you stay with me tonight?' I asked. 'I don't want to be alone.'

He didn't answer with words, he just led me to my room. On the bed he lay me down, getting in beside me and holding me against his bare chest. I buried my face into that safe place and sobbed. Sven said nothing, and even though my grief once again threatened to yield to longing, he told me it would not happen unless I freely sought it. Now was not the time, and sorrow would not be the catalyst. So, we slept in a tight embrace and no more occurred between us, no matter how much we each desired it.

TWENTY-TWO

Sven sighed as I disentangled myself from his arms but did not wake. The night before had left my eyes puffy and my spirit bruised, and thankfully, I had checked myself before things went too far. Quietly, I walked to the table where I washed myself with the small basin of water and dressed in my trousers, tunic and jerkin. Into my belt loop, I slotted Skara and walked from the room to collect my shield that was now adorned with the dual cat heads. I scooped it up by the handgrip, placing Freyja's cap into a pouch tied to my belt, and held my shield in my left hand. If I had been walking a great distance, I would have attached it to a leather sling across my chest so I could wear it on my back. But my destination was the gatehouse, and I was in a hurry to leave.

'Up early this morning, Signe,' Laslo greeted me as I neared. His eyes were bloodshot and lined with dark shadows.

'Nowhere better to be,' I replied. 'Nothing better to do.'

Laslo nodded. 'I am about to meet with Eskil, after our night watch. Would you join us?'

'Of course,' I agreed, falling into step as he made his way to the area beneath the gatehouse. The wall walk was dim and cramped. I grabbed Laslo by the arm. 'Why me? Why is it you want me there? And, please don't tell me it's because I remind you of your mother.'

'My older sister, actually,' he replied as we reached the room.

'Is she just as wilful as I am?'

'She was,' he agreed, holding the door open for me. 'Her name was Yelena, and she was just as stubborn as you are, and just like you, I found her presence somehow calming, despite that.'

'Oh, Laslo,' I sighed, not knowing what to say, but the conversation was over because we were no longer alone.

'Today marks seven bloody days since we sent word to Holmgardr,' Eskil began. 'Are we assuming we are on our own?'

'It would have taken our rider two days to reach the city, five to march their forces here. Do you suggest we wait no more?' Laslo asked the older man.

Eskil had stopped protesting that he was not the captain, and the two of them had adopted a quasi-ruling partnership. Laslo dealt with the politics, and Eskil managed the martial machinations. The men in their co-command respected the arrangement.

'We can't bloody out-and-out kill them. That's too risky when we do not fully understand their plans and have heard nothing from our messenger,' Eskil grumbled, taking his seat in the dark recess of the room.

'There has been no word,' Laslo confirmed. 'At this stage, we cannot even assume the rider reached his destination.'

Eskil coughed and spat on the ground. 'Have the Igors returned from their second scouting mission?' he asked.

'Not yet,' Laslo responded. 'They were last ensuring the barges were hidden in the woodlands to the north. But near enough to the banks of the river to be useful if we plan to cross above the Abandoned Paragon.'

'Hersir,' Knudd spoke through the other side of the door, knocking twice.

We all turned, awaiting the man's entrance.

'Enter,' both Eskil and Laslo replied.

Knudd proceeded into the room and stood erect before the table. 'Hersir, uhhh…' he hesitated, not knowing to whom he should turn, Laslo behind the table, or Eskil sitting in his seat in the corner.

'Yes, Knudd, what is it?' Laslo commanded.

'A rider, Hersir. Says he is from Svatopluk's men and he wants to talk.'

'Gods!' Eskil cursed. 'That's a start, at least. Now we need to send someone to speak with them.'

'I'll go,' Laslo decided, pacing behind his desk, as had become his routine.

'You will not!' Eskil bellowed, stopping the younger man. 'You're too important. You know more than anyone here about the tribal conflicts.'

'That's precisely why I should,' Laslo argued. 'You can't go, Eskil. You don't have the manner required.'

226

'Send Signe, then,' Eskil suggested with a careless wave.

'Uh,' I hesitated, not knowing where to look.

'Absolutely not!' Laslo protested. 'I may trust Signe, but they will not, purely because she is a woman.'

'Send me.' His voice was steady as he walked through the door, and as Sven passed me, I felt the brush of his fingers against my hand.

'How did you get in here?' Eskil bristled.

'I followed Knudd, and I heard you talking, Eskil. If you don't wish the entire town to hear your plans, you should learn to speak in a quieter voice,' Sven teased.

Eskil chuckled. 'Not bloody likely.'

'They want their woman, right?' he asked.

We all nodded. Their *vedunya*, their Mokosh, must have been part of the reason they were yet to launch a full-scale attack. The other half of their reluctance had to be numbers. With the estimates the Igors gave, forty to fifty men, they could not hope to take a fortified place like Aldeigjuborg without a protracted siege.

'Are you sure?' Laslo asked.

'They will not harm me if they expect to bargain for their woman,' Sven confirmed.

'But keep at a distance from their rider, stay away from anywhere there could be archers,' Eskil warned.

My heart hammered in my chest. I wanted to scream at Sven and tell him I would not permit him to endanger himself, but he had decided, so I swallowed my discomfort and said nothing.

'They declared we were to send out only one, just as they will,' Knudd explained.

'So it shall be an equal risk for them,' Laslo mused.

'Not if they are in sight of the wall. They'll be in range of our arrows,' Knudd interjected.

Laslo scoffed at the suggestion. 'We will honour their request for negotiations and their safety, so long as they do the same. Sven shall be protected. Thank you, Knudd,' he said, dismissing the man. 'Now, everyone else, please leave us. Sven and I will discuss what compromises we can make before he rides out.'

Onto the ramparts, I followed Eskil to watch the scene below. The Slav representative stood alone on the bridge that straddled the

Ladozhka River. The distance was too great to make out any more detail than the clothing he wore, dark billowing breeches and a long, even darker coat. He had no headwear and carried no shield. If he bore arms, there was no glint of metal in the sunlight to warn us. By comparison, Sven cut an impressive figure. On his head was a borrowed iron helm with a nose plate, under which he wore a hat of sheep's wool. Sven was dressed in his padded practice jerkin, long dark wool trousers with contrasting leg wraps, and a cloak over his left shoulder. On his back, his shield was slung and, I hoped, somewhere under his cloak he had hidden an axe.

The uneasiness inside me grew to more than discomfort as the gap closed between the men, and I held my breath. Laslo appeared up the ladder, straining his eyes for any detail that might give away the success of the parlay.

'Close enough to be heard but not to cause harm,' Laslo muttered next to me.

'Nothing spotted in the tree line,' I confirmed.

The pair in the distance moved very little, remaining erect and serious until what needed to be said had been. Then they separated, returning to their commanders. It seemed like an eternity waiting for Sven to be back within the protection of the walls and, as soon as he was, we met again in Laslo's rooms.

'They want their *vedunya*,' Sven confirmed, removing the shield from his back. 'They seek your mercy in returning her.'

'There was no mercy when they slaughtered Gamal and Karse,' Laslo argued. 'What will they give us in exchange for their woman?' he asked.

Sven shook his head. 'They will allow those who reside in Aldeigjuborg to live when they dismantle the town.'

'Nothing else?' Eskil demanded.

'Nothing. It was the only concession Bela was instructed to make,' Sven replied.

'They are rather sure of themselves,' I muttered from the back of the room.

Eskil threw his helmet on the ground. 'Well, they shouldn't bloody be! Give us nothing yet release a god unto them?' he scoffed.

'I did not agree,' Sven clarified.

Laslo paced behind the desk. 'Of course not. But if they left, and we delivered their Mokosh, then…' He leaned over the table without finishing the thought.

Eskil slammed down his fist before the boy. 'Do not even think about it! It would be better if we killed her!' he seethed.

'No,' I protested. 'If you kill her, we would have nothing to ensure their compliance.'

'There is no compliance,' he roared, spit catching in his beard. 'We have to be rid of them.'

'Wait, Eskil, wait.' Laslo stopped the older man's fury, thinking. 'What if we make a feint?' he suggested. 'We tell them we agree to hand Mokosh back to Svatopluk.'

'What?' Eskil asked disbelievingly.

'We're not really going to. So, we say we will return her. Buy us some more time, but if no one comes from Holmgardr… we need to draw them out,' he explained.

'But I already told them no,' Sven complained.

'No matter. I'm sure they would be willing to renegotiate if we agree to their terms,' Laslo dismissed.

'If we are going to pretend to hand her back, someone will have to dress as the woman. It'd only be possible at night,' Sven proffered. 'But it could work.'

Eskil stroked his beard, his mind working through plans. 'It could work,' he agreed.

The ploy seemed questionable, but Laslo believed in it. And, though his acceptance had been initially begrudging, Eskil had eventually become enthusiastic about it too. Sven and I were not privy to the further arrangements, as we both had our sentry duties dragging into the early afternoon. We were posted to the rear of the town, where Mikel and I had been the night of the River Gate attack.

'I didn't enjoy watching you ride out this morning,' I said as I pulled blades of grass from the earth and stripped them with my fingernail.

The smile was present in his voice. 'I knew you wouldn't, but I thought if I died, at least it would be with glory and with you observing me. The *skalds* would sing of my bravery,' he responded with a chuckle, enjoying my discomfort far too much.

'Just a few days ago you told me not to rush to my death and now...' I stopped. Beyond the farms was a flash of light. 'Did you see that, Sven?' I asked, pointing.

He squinted into the distance, following my finger. 'I can't see anything.'

I kept watching, waiting to catch it again. 'There,' I replied, dragging him before me. 'Odin's beard! I think it's a rider.'

'I see it,' he confirmed, turning to call to Varr, who was pacing the ground behind us. 'Fetch Eskil and Laslo to the ramparts. There is a rider coming for Aldeigjuborg. Quick, run!' he commanded, grabbing my hand. 'If it comes to a fight, promise me you will get away.'

Even as he said it, I knew he did not believe I would agree to it. 'Never!'

He shook his head but had no time to begin an argument as we mounted the ladder to the top of the walls and heard Eskil cursing. 'God's bloody vengeance,' the previous commander swore.

Laslo was not far behind, and as he raced to the ramparts, his eyes darted over the area indicated. 'What did you see?' he asked Sven and I.

'A glint of metal, there.' I pointed toward the first sighting.

'Anything else?' Laslo demanded. 'Do you see any tamgas?'

I shook my head. 'I can't see well enough to recognise any banners or symbols,' I confirmed.

'Does anyone see the rider's tamga?' Laslo called out as men clambered onto the walls, arming themselves and donning any protection they might own. After so long waiting, they were all hungry for the fight to come.

All on the walls strained their eyes in hope of seeing the red banners that would represent the forces of Holmgardr. The distinct image of a white bear, rearing on his hind legs, against the red was associated with the Gardarike lands, something of a derivation from their northern origins. Just as likely was the banner of Grand Prince Oleg himself, a bident of white with one prong straight and the other leaning back like the sails of a warship filled with wind, also on the red background.

'Bring me a man with good eyes,' Eskil boomed.

A young boy was brought forward and propped up on Eskil's shoulders until the child was satisfied he could see as far as possible. 'There are men in the distance, Hersir, behind the rider. Maybe forty,' he spoke in a squeaky voice.

'What do you see?' Eskil asked as he held fast to the boy's legs draped over his chest.

My hand touched Bjarndýr, searching for my father's strength, and then I checked for Skara, understanding, too, that I would soon have need of her.

Moments later, the boy wriggled around on Eskil's shoulders. 'Red, the tamga is red, Hersir. I can't quite see what the…' He didn't finish.

Eskil dumped the child on the floor and pushed him towards a guard. 'Get him down now, return him to his mother. The riders are from Holmgardr. First we plan, and then we call a council for the town,' he instructed.

Laslo nodded, also making his way down the ladder.

'What do you know of war, boy?' Hersir Hemingr of Holmgardr asked Laslo.

Laslo's face reddened. 'Nothing, but…' he blabbered.

The commander cut him off with a glare. 'Then you have nothing to contribute.'

'Hersir,' Eskil began with an attempt at being conciliatory, 'the fellow knows what he is talking about.'

'And you!' Hemingr turned on Eskil. 'Call yourself Hersir when you command a force of less than thirty men? You're laughable! Not to mention putting this child in your place. You're scarcely better than a deserter, and I have a mind to drag you back to Holmgardr for punishment,' he threatened. 'Lucky for you, we have bigger concerns.' Hemingr faced Laslo, staring him down with an intimidating glare. 'You've got about as long as it'll take for someone to fetch me an ale and for me to down it.'

They sent a boy to find the commander a drink, and Laslo straightened himself up and took a deep breath.

He explained what he knew about the conflicts between the tribes, the discord that occurred in Aldeigjuborg, and the subsequent confrontations. 'I know if we commit ourselves to battle, one of two things will happen,' Laslo went on. 'If we overcome these Slavs, it will strike fear into those who seek to rebel against Rus' leadership. Instead of continuing their tributary to the Khazars, they may capitulate to Oleg.'

'Ah, look. My drink.' Hemingr grinned, raising an eyebrow. 'And the second?'

'If we fail here, the tribes will be emboldened and they will come again and again until we fall,' he replied. 'Hersir. These men may have Slav blood but they do not represent the tribes, that much is evident. In seven days we have sighted no reinforcements for them. They are rebels.'

'So we can kill them with impunity,' Hemingr responded cheerfully.

Laslo drew a breath. 'They threatened to destroy Aldeigjuborg,' he thundered.

The commander drained his cup and smiled wryly at the young Hersir's outburst. 'We have no choice then but to meet their opposition with force. You know the land?' he asked Laslo.

He nodded. 'I can tell you where it floods, where the densest forest is and where it is safe to ford the river,' Laslo detailed to prove his worth.

'Tell me, then,' Hemingr hissed, 'where will we find them, and which location will give us the advantage?'

The rabble filled the space of the guildhall, from its rafters to its long tables lined with senior guild members and ship owners. All had been called to meet with Eskil, Laslo and Hemingr. Everyone knew by now that Aldeigjuborg had received the aid she required but were craning their necks to discover the finer details.

'If you have weapons, I urge you to join us,' Laslo began, addressing the crowd. 'Merchants with whatever arms you carry on trade or a boat hook if you have nothing better, farmers be it with scythe or pickaxe.'

'But you cannot compel us to give you our ships,' a trader with a long white beard complained loudly. 'What if one was destroyed…'

Hemingr stilled the man with his raised hand. 'And you cannot expect us to protect your ships in Aldeigjuborg's harbour if you will not allow us to use them in defence of it!' the commander roared.

White beard swallowed audibly and resumed his seat.

'We only need one ship,' Hemingr clarified. 'Surely, one of you is braver than a squealing pig?' He cast his eye around the room.

Only one man stood, Sihtric. His usual ostentatious garments he had exchanged for something more practical and the colours far more subdued. 'You may have the *Bhobain*, Hersir. Then she may cause as much havoc as her namesake.'

'Good man!' Hemingr bellowed. 'The gods will favour this fellow! Eskil will lead Aldeigjuborg's forces across the water south of the city. A rope will be your way to silently cross there. So, all of you who denied the use of your ships, we will need your ropes.'

The crowd grumbled. Ropes were expensive and took a long time to make, pulling and strengthening the fibres took a whole day at least and the manufacturing of ship ropes even longer.

'And what if we say no?' one travelling merchant braved the question.

Hemingr narrowed his eyes. 'Then I may find a thinner cord to wrap around your neck. I might dangle you from it for a bit until you realise the benefits of assisting in the defence of this town.'

The man did not reply.

So, Hemingr continued. 'My men will be with me and cross to the north making use of a vessel I understand has been moored south of the basin.'

'What about the merchants?' old Torketill called out from the back of the hall.

'What about them?' Hemingr shrugged.

'We have no one to speak for us. Our Guild Master was killed last year, and we are still waiting for the appointment of a replacement,' Torketill explained.

Hemingr sighed. 'Who do you want?'

A few names were bandied about, but in the majority, Gisle was recommended, as I had expected.

'Then Gisle shall be the new Guild Master,' Hemingr agreed.

'With the same privileges as Eryk had?' Gisle asked.

Hemingr rubbed his head and closed his eyes. 'We are in the middle of a war!' he shouted. 'You should be more concerned about an axe cleaving through your skull than a discussion regarding powers available to you. If you are still alive tomorrow, we can resume this conversation.'

The room was quiet after that as they listened to Hemingr lay out the deception that Eskil and Laslo had planned. They would launch a boat containing Mokosh from the River Gate, across to the other side of the river, where Svatopluk would place a couple of men to ensure her collection. Only, there would be no Mokosh in the boat, just an archer disguised as the *vedunya*. There was no shortage of volunteers for the role.

'I would welcome the chance to prove my bravery,' an archer from Holmgardr named Othere spoke. 'The gods would greet me in Valhalla if I fall, but I won't,' he said, beating his fist against his chest twice.

'But how is your aim?' Eskil growled.

'My last target got a piercing through the ear for fun before I shot him through the eye.' Othere laughed, sculling his drink.

'It's true, I saw it,' guffawed the archer beside him.

'Othere is my best archer,' Hemingr agreed. 'The rest of you, enjoy living while you can. My men, we leave at sundown for the north.'

Eskil stood next to Laslo. 'And my men, eh, our men,' he corrected himself. 'We need eyes on the River Gate at every moment. You may not even shut your eyes to blink.'

'We need to know how many men are on the other side at all times,' Laslo explained.

'And when Othere has met his mark,' Eskil began, 'we steal across the Volkhov like the Wild Hunt, stalk like the wild bears of the mountains, and kill like the bloody spirits that claim infants in the forest.'

TWENTY-THREE

THE ABANDONED PARAGON
SPRING 883CE

Aldeigjavatn
(Lake Ladoga)

VOLKHOV RIVER

ALDEIGJUBORG

ABANDONED PARAGON
(LYUBSHANSKAYA FORTRESS)

Deep in the hours that belonged to the owls, the knock on the door came and we were ready. It was the call to gather ahead of Othere's departure across the water. I was already dressed in my dark wool breeches with brown leg wraps wound around my calf and ankle to protect them from the forest undergrowth. On my feet, I wore my sturdiest leather boots with a thick sole. My tunic was hemmed at the top of my thighs, and over that, a close-fitting leather jerkin I had commissioned from the leathersmith for our journey to Kyiv. My head would don no helmet, no mail, for that was the garb of the wealthy warrior. What I could manage were leather forearm guards and my shield, which would have to do the job that my axe could not. On my belt, my last weapon was a sax, just as useful for eating dinner as it was for stabbing, if it came to that.

Sven was dressed almost identical to me, save for his jerkin, which was a little looser, not having been fitted for him. It was one he had taken during his season at raiding. On our backs, we slung our shields. In my hand, Skara sang, and for Sven, he was armed with his bow and a quiver of arrows, an axe and a sax at his belt.

'Do you think this will work?' I asked Sven as we stepped out of my house.

'Othere is clever with an arrow, even better than me. This afternoon, I saw him hit a mushroom from four hundred paces away.'

'You did not,' I gasped.

'I swear I did. Maybe it wasn't exactly four hundred, but it was a great distance. Anyway, if he can shoot down the men before any of them raise the alarm, we'll have a good chance of surprising them with an attack before dawn.'

'Do we know how many there are across the river near the tower?' I asked.

'Last count was three, but we'll have guards up on the walls confirming no one else is in sight. Three, Othere can manage. I'm sure of that.'

We turned left, heading up the path to the marketplace that had been cleared of stalls and now acted as grounds for farewelling loved ones as they set out for war. I had seen it before. Vividly, I recalled the time we departed for the raid I never participated in. Women clung to their men then too, for they knew it was an adventure, but defending one's home was a valorous deed, and the cries were greater because the risk was as well.

I saw Hilde, her soft features scrunched and pained, and her eyes beading with tears as she embraced her sons, Stanislaus and her eldest Andrei, named for his father. Her younger boys, Boris and Dimitri, were still too young to take up arms, though, if they were allowed to, would have followed the brothers they admired into the fray.

Helga clung to her husband, Mikel, as if her life depended on it. 'I don't want you to go,' she whimpered.

He held her tight, her burgeoning belly containing their unborn children between them. 'Everything will be alright,' he lied, stroking her hair. 'I'll return to you, I promise,' he spoke. As much as he was unable to promise such a thing, the same was whispered over and over throughout the marketplace.

When the women saw Sven and me, they rushed towards us.

'You make those forest dwellers run away, alright?' Helga smiled through her tears.

'We won't be letting them escape,' Sven glowered. 'It will be them dying or all of us.'

I cringed. 'It won't be us,' I promised. 'We have the numbers. With Hemingr's men, we are almost double theirs, and if everything happens according to plan, they will be gone from this area and no one shall come for Aldeigjuborg for a long time.'

Eskil and Laslo commanded the preparations to be conducted in silence, as much as that was possible. Women of the town farewelled their menfolk, and their excitable offspring delighted in their father's appearance, trying on various pieces of armament before they, too, scuttled out of the way.

Father Niall offered blessings for the Christian folk, and looking up at me, he smiled. 'I'll say a prayer for you too, warrior woman.'

'I thought your god did not bother himself with heathens like me,' I replied.

In the days since the initial confrontation with the Deivos worshippers, Father Niall had smoothed his coarse approach to converting Aldeigjuborg to Jesus. He now preached harmony. He claimed the gods could all be one, that our gods are part of the majesty of the Christian god's creation. It was a creative method, and though I did not believe it would work, I had to admire his resourcefulness.

'We are all God's children,' he answered, hands out with palms to the sky. 'Tonight we will be victorious, and as the sun rises, Aldeigjuborg shall be free of those who seek to harm us.'

Eskil and Laslo led the way, quietly calling and waving the men to gather, Othere front of the pack with the hersirs.

The guards still patrolled atop the walls to create a facade of normality. If we were about to hand over Mokosh, who remained in the lockup under close watch, we should not look like we were gathered to launch an attack.

Earlier, as darkness cloaked the hills, Hemingr led his men through the Enggatt. Unlike our own forces, the Holmgardr force was dressed in an issued uniform of red breeches, brown leg wraps and earthy-coloured tunic. Over their left side, each wore a bright red cloak fastened around their necks. Some had mail. Hemingr was the only one to have a full shirt of mail from neck to waist. Those who had this additional protection had only a hood or a curtain that protected the neck and upper back. Each man had on top of his head a domed helmet with a broad nose plate. On their arms they had leather arm guards, just as I did. On their backs, their shields were painted in red and white, bearing the Holmgardr tamga of a rearing bear. All possessed at least one decent weapon, a mix of axes, swords and spears. Some of the more senior rank, and therefore better paid, had the addition of a short sword or sax. In neat formation, they quick marched across the bridge straddling the Ladozhka River and into the dense forest, out of sight.

Now, as we stood, waiting for the command to leave, I saw Ahmed Ibn Rashti standing by the walls.

'Will you not fight?' I asked him.

He shrugged. 'This is not my war, but I will stay to defend the town just like Sihtric and the others,' he said. 'It serves no one here if Aldeigjuborg falls.'

'And you will not have passage to Kyiv if it does,' I jested.

He tipped his cloth wrapped head and smiled. '*Hazun saeid*, Signe,' he whispered.

But, I hoped instead of his hope for good luck, the gods would lead us to a fight we would win. Ahmed was not the only man remaining to defend Aldeigjuborg. The Skulking Shadows were left in charge of Mokosh, the seeress of the rebels, after they had successfully captured a spy who had fled the walls to warn our opposition. It had come as a great surprise that Toki, Eskil's thrall, had escaped into the forest north. However, the two Igors made quick work of finding the slave's trail and bringing him back to the town. A frame was brought to the centre of the marketplace, and despite Father Niall's protests, Toki was gruesomely bled to death in front of the Church of Saint George as part of the offerings to Thor and Odin. And, though he might have been vexed at the sight, the priest threw his hands up, turned, and set about preaching a private service to those more committed to the Christian faith.

After the rituals, people had smeared their face with the blood of man and animal, and ash from the fire. I, too, had smudged the coal over my eyelids, down my cheeks and on my chin. In the dark, it would help disguise my fair skin, and it had the added advantage of making me feel like a different person, a hardened warrior without fear. As I looked around the gathering, I wondered if anyone felt dread as I did. Perhaps they didn't. We were raised on the stories of killing for sport and wealth, never questioning the right or wrong of it.

Sven squeezed my arm.

Fighting against someone who wanted to kill you was one thing. I had done that in the winter, when Sven and I had returned from Neflaug's hut after she died. But heading into a pitched battle where the enemy was largely unknown was another thing entirely. How would they be armed? Would they be better or worse equipped than our forces? Were they all trained men without fear of death? Overcome with questions and queasiness as the sick burned in my stomach, I turned to the side and retched.

'Just wipe your mouth and stand up,' Sven whispered. 'You're not the only one feeling this way.'

To me, it seemed as if the entire force was aching for the fight.

'Most have been drinking since the Holmgardr forces arrived. It's their manner of preparing. Personally, I like to be a little less addled,' he spoke, helping me to my feet.

Some might harden themselves with drink, but for me it was jarring that two weeks before I had been more concerned with making sails than killing a man. I hadn't sought it, and the thought that I had previously desired the raid made me uncomfortable with the reality of fighting. It was necessary; I knew Aldeigjuborg had to be defended, but standing there, in line, looking at the intoxicated faces smeared with Toki's lifeblood, I knew that unlike those who thirsted for battle, I would never ache for it. The murderous members of our group were locked in a trance that only slaughter could slake. For them, this was not about trade, not about life, not about freedom. It was entirely for the joy of killing, and I hoped to never be on the receiving end of their furore.

As I glanced behind, I could see some who were feeling uneasy at the prospect of going against an enemy in the dark. The men at the back of the forces were the least armoured, the least armed. They were the farmers. Each of them wore their usual clothing and bore only a simple weapon, such as a scythe or a pitchfork. In front of them were the merchants and guild members. Their garb generally comprised better clothing, some light armament such as leather cuffs, and a better weapon. Some had a shield, but none wore a helmet or mail, just like Sven and I. And then there were Aldeigjuborg's guardsmen who were the best armoured of the lot but still a great deal less than Hemingr's men. Just like the Holmgardr men, they wore a cloak of red over their trousers and tunics, the quality of which depended on what the wearer could obtain or afford. Every guard had a helm, shield and one weapon. Eskil bore two visible weapons, a sword and an axe. I assumed he had likely hidden a sax somewhere on himself as well.

Sven and I stood ahead of the merchants, at the back of the town's guards. As an archer, Sven was valuable. And Laslo had given me the task of being Sven's protection, which made me laugh because Sven had always assumed he would be my protector, not the other way around.

'Is everything bloody clear?' Eskil hissed down the line. 'No one is to move until Othere pulls on the rope. His job is to row across and shoot those men down, and your job, when the time comes, is to pull that ship across the river like your woman's pleasure relies on your every haul.'

There was a ripple of hushed laughter at that.

'Get that ship across, then the core crew back again. Three times should get every man to the other side, then we make our way through the forest and up to the Abandoned Paragon. We shall be the rear attack to Hemingr's frontal ambush,' he finished.

'They won't see us coming,' Knudd called a little louder than he ought to.

'That's the bloody idea,' Eskil replied.

'Shhhh,' Laslo warned. 'Stay in formation and do not break. Above all, do not move until Eskil tells you to.'

There was a quick flash of light from the ramparts, signalling the scouts on the other side had gone on their rounds, leaving the banks of the Volkhov. It was time to get into position.

'Go now,' Eskil ordered, sending twenty men to the *Bhobain*.

They stepped quickly, streaming down onto the decking like ghouls. The men slithered into the ship, lying down inside the hull, completely out of sight. There they were directed to remain until Othere had completed his task and the rope was pulled. The *Bhobain* would traverse the breadth of the waterway as the men silently heaved the vessel along the length of the line. First, all depended on Othere.

While the ship held a third of our crew, the rest of us remained in the wall's shadows, straining to see through the night. Othere donned a long white robe, covering his head with the hood. In the dark, he glowed, the garment seemingly illuminated from within. He lowered himself into a small rowing boat that contained his bow and arrow, combat clothing and shield, and began to row. Behind him trailed a long rope, secured to the mooring of the docks, and would serve as the signal to begin our crossing.

'That man has a desire for renown,' Laslo spoke next to me.

'The *skalds* will sing his name,' Torketill, the aged senior guild member, replied admiringly.

It did not take long for him to near the opposite bank of the Volkhov. Above the water, three men approached, hoping to have their goddess back in hand. Two of the guards bore bow and arrow, the other seemed to be armed only with a spear.

I held my breath. Othere was now close enough to shoot his bow accurately, but any movement might give him away. His oars dipped again, propelling him further towards the enemy, then, quick as a flash of *elding* from the sky, he nocked an arrow, loosing it into the chest of the broadest looking archer. Before the first had fallen, the second

242

arrow whistled through the air, finding its target in a smaller archer's eye. The final man sprinted from the banks with the speed of a frightened rabbit. Othere, knowing he could allow no survivors, rowed hard to the shallows, beaching his boat and scrambling from it. The other man was headed for the tree line when Othere threw his axe through the night, slicing through the man's helmet with a hideous crunch.

Othere wasted no time getting back to his vessel and rowing south to the point opposite the docks. He disembarked to secure the rope to a thick trunked tree, and he jerked the great line made from at least ten ropes joined by weaver's knots, long enough to cover the expanse of water.

The men inside the *Bhobain*, seeing the jolt in the rope, sat up and grasped the line and pulled. With twenty men's strength, it took very little time for the first crossing to be done. However, on the return with only five, it took much longer. The next time the ship crossed that narrow point, the tired men got out along with half of the new crew, and the *Bhobain* again returned to the other side. On the last journey, Sven, Laslo and I were among their members. We untied the rope from the moorings and secured it to the prow. The men on the other side heaved us towards them like a great game of *toga honk*, a tug of war. When we were across, we set down the anchor and there we left the *Bhobain* to be returned in the morning, if we survived until then.

With our entire force successfully across the river, and Othere dressed for battle instead of a Deivos ceremony, we crept into the forest. If we thought the night was dark, under the canopy was pitch. No stars seeped through, and the moonlight's brightness was only glimpsed in gaps between the foliage. To keep from separating, we kept hold of the person in front or beside us. We walked slowly to avoid making noise. Still, the cracking of twigs underfoot, the scurrying of woodland creatures and the hooting night birds might have given us away. And, in that space between victory and vanquishment, my mind played tricks on my eyes.

As a child, the dark frightened me. When my mother prepared the evening meal, she would often send me to fetch things she needed from the unlit stores. Sometimes I felt an evilness following me, causing me to sprint towards the comfort of the fireplace, and other times I would silently weep for the fear of enduring it. As a woman grown, facing the dark was terrifying for a different reason. When there was no light, the mind wandered to the depths of fear. A noise ahead became the enemy. *Were we surrounded?* No, it was just one of our numbers making their way through the undergrowth, just as I was.

'Breathe, your eyes will soon adjust,' Sven murmured beside me, holding my hand.

'It's just...' I began.

'Everyone feels it. Some are better at pretending they don't,' he replied.

We continued, and my eyes adjusted to the darkness. I could make out the tree trunks as they passed, avoid low-hanging branches, and step over rocks and roots that snagged toes in the night. Above our heads, the sky was visible in a large opening to the forest canopy. The twinkling lights of Karlsvagn, the grouping of stars shaped like a cooking pot with a long handle which signified the chariot of Thor. Though we often saw it at this time of year, it comforted me to know the gods were watching us.

'Slodi and Dimitri,' we heard Eskil command in the darkness. 'It's your turn to scout. Remember, only go as far as you can retrace and come straight back if you see anything.'

All the men of Aldeigjuborg's forces would take turns, in pairs, cycling through a shift at spying. They stepped ahead, creeping through the branches to the edge of the tree line to ensure the rebel scouts were not on the verge of discovering us. Each time a pair returned, they could not report anything. There were no enemy scouts at the fringes of the forest, no one on patrol.

'Strange,' Eskil grumbled as we pushed on. 'You're telling me there is no one patrolling the perimeter of the bloody Paragon?' Eskil asked.

'None we could see, Hersir,' Dimitri replied.

'Go again,' he ordered, 'this time further. See if there is anyone inside. Keep your distance and don't give us away.'

Slodi and Dimitri vanished into the sheet of black while the rest of us continued to the edge of the woodlands where the trees grew sparser. Our group stopped and crouched low, hiding behind the evergreens. A whisper rippled through the ranks.

'It's up ahead,' they were saying. 'And soon the sun will rise. We need to ambush them now before the light gives us away.'

Knudd and Varr had been sent to the west of the Abandoned Paragon, while Slodi and Karse were yet to return from their explorations to the east. It was the western party that was the first to come back.

'Two men inside the Paragon, Hersir,' Knudd mumbled.

'Two?' Laslo confirmed. 'Only two?'

'All we could see,' Varr replied.

As the dawn approached, the sky brightened from black to grey with the promise of a sunrise on the hills to the east. In the low light, the men were disappointed. They were ready for the battle, but with no foe in sight, their hunger would dissipate to restlessness. Disappointed men would likely find some way of filling that void, and some were already discussing marauding in the forest if our battle came to nought.

Away from the group, Eskil and Laslo spoke rapidly in hushed voices before returning to address their army.

'If there is no one at the Abandoned Paragon, our situation has changed,' Laslo began.

'We will break into two groups. Hersir Laslo will take the archers, merchants and farmers directly ahead to the southern side of the fortress to assess the area. And I will take Aldeigjuborg's guardsmen to the east, approaching from the rear. Varr says the stone fortifications have crumbled there, so we will be able to see if anyone remains inside. It is also where we expect the rebel forces to be if they have seen us coming,' Eskil detailed as the groups separated as directed.

'And if we find their forces, what then?' Othere asked, stepping forward. He, too, wanted a kill. His earlier triumph was enough to win him accolades, but the thrill had worn off.

Eskil shrugged. 'We engage them. Our command is to bloody destroy them, and that is what we will do! Right, see you inside the fortifications, then,' he farewelled Laslo and his group.

Laslo stilled our departure until Eskil had passed around the bend in the forest. Then we walked arm's length from the man next to us. Below the walls of the Abandoned Paragon was a clearing of twenty paces to the tree line. For a force wanting to bring fury upon the inhabitants of the fortress, the distance between the tree's coverage and the stone seemed great. I stepped forward, holding my breath and thinking with each movement we could be discovered.

'There's no one here,' Sven whispered as we tightened ranks.

To the left, where once there might have been a tower, the stone was gone, but otherwise, this section of the wall was intact. The door that would have limited entry was gaping open, devoid of its wooden gate.

'These walls are even taller than Aldeigjuborg's,' I spoke to Sven, 'the height of four men end to end.'

'You've got to wonder why they abandoned such a place,' he replied.

Knudd pushed between us. 'They say the ground moved so much it made the walls sink until parts just tumbled down,' he interjected. 'Then the river pushed the bank back, and it was unsafe to stay.'

'The river moved the bank? What nonsense,' Varr complained as we came within touching distance of the wall.

'It's not nonsense,' complained Knudd. 'The water washed away the earth, and the bank started crumbling.'

'Silence,' Laslo hissed. 'It's not time for a lesson in history. Anyway, Knudd, that's not the only reason. The voivodes fought so much and the place changed hands so frequently that it could not be held by one leader. Without the stability of leadership, there was no one to maintain it, so it fell into disrepair. Now you have your answer. Shhhh.'

A brave few, of which Othere was the first to volunteer, passed through the opening in the stone fortifications to scout the inside of the Paragon while the rest of us remained on the outside. When we were signalled through the door, we found that it was indeed abandoned.

The space within the Paragon was as big as Aldeigjuborg's inner fortifications. The wall on the western bank was about five hundred paces long, and the same along the southern portion. It tapered to around one hundred paces where the fortress fronted onto the narrow tributary and where we knew an earthen rampart existed. Along the eastern side was a wall that undulated for a distance of seven hundred paces, or it would have when it was newly built. But, in its current state, the wall was barely fit to be called as such, with large portions that had crumbled away, leaving the fortress open to attack. The Slavs had constructed temporary wooden fortifications to fill the gaps in the stone, but the job was incomplete. There were no rooms in the walls and no residences within. So, the rebels had set up their tents in the spacious green interior of the Abandoned Paragon, surrounding a central fire pit.

'Still warm,' Torketill murmured as he knelt and waved his hand over the charred wood. The old guild member had wanted to join Hemingr's men for a "real adventure" but, from the look on his face, he was enjoying the current investigation. 'Didn't Knudd say there were two guards here?' he asked, looking around.

There was a scuttle in the shadows, and I saw someone move. 'Over there,' I called.

With our group desperate for a show, they quickly captured the guard. He was younger than Laslo, small and wiry, with eyes full of fear as he shrank back from his assailants. Othere drew his sax and held it to the guard's throat as piss ran down the younger's leg.

'Where have they gone?' Othere asked, digging the weapon into the gooseflesh of his quarry's neck.

The man shook his head.

Laslo repeated the question in the native tongue.

'They didn't say. Only that I must remain here,' the guard replied to Laslo.

'You should have some idea,' Laslo prompted, but if the boy knew anything, he was not about to proffer it. 'What about the other man here with you? We know there were two.'

'When he saw you, he ran into the forest to hide like I should have done,' he responded.

'Which way?' Laslo asked.

By this point, the young guard was shaking so hard he could barely hold his arm straight as he pointed south of the fortress. Then Laslo nodded at Othere, who dragged his blade along the guard's smooth throat and stepped back as a gush of blood fell from the wound.

'None of it makes sense,' Othere complained as he cleaned his weapon.

After concluding our search of every tent and remaining nook, Eskil and his men entered through the crumbling stonework to the east with similarly disparaged looks on their faces.

'Bloody nothing,' Eskil grunted. 'Not in the forest and none outside the walls.'

'We've searched all the tents. Othere found and dispatched one of the two guards that Knudd spotted earlier,' Laslo relayed.

'Tell me they blabbered? Otherwise, why'd you kill him before I got here?' Eskil asked.

Laslo cleared his throat. 'He could only tell us the other one ran away to the south, and he did not know where the entire force of Slavs went.'

Just as Eskil was about to lose his temper, a man sprinted through a gap in the broken wall. Behind him, the sun rose above the forest, painting the grey sky in vivid reds and purples.

'Hersir,' the man panted but could say no more. From his clothing, I knew him to be a Holmgardr soldier. His red cloak and bear painted shield was all that was required to identify him.

'I know this messenger.' Varr stepped towards the Holmgardr man, offering him a skin of mead. 'He is Ingevald, one of Hemingr's messengers.'

Ingevald nodded as he collapsed onto the floor. 'I had to run,' he managed through ragged breath. 'Hemingr missed the drop-off point. They…' He gasped, unable to continue.

'What is bloody happening?' Eskil demanded.

As he regained his breath, Ingevald got to his feet. 'Hersir, Hemingr overshot the beaching point. He sailed too far. I do not know why.'

'Were you in the first boat?' Laslo asked.

Ingevald nodded. 'We disembarked further north, near the waterfall, and were meant to meet them in the forest. We saw them sail straight into the reaches of Svatopluk. There would have been nowhere else to land.'

In the distance, we heard battle cries. The great bellow of a leader, rallying forces, calling to them to find their courage and attack without fear of death.

'Knudd, Varr, go north now,' Laslo ordered, sending the two men towards the wall that was known to lead to the ramparts and from there steeply declining to the shore where it was possible to bring boats onto the land.

Eskil huffed. 'What happened then?'

'I don't know. I sprinted directly here, knowing we would need reinforcements,' Ingevald said. Then the shortness returned, and he doubled over trying to get air in.

'This is not what we bloody planned,' Eskil complained.

We did not have to wait long before Knudd and Varr came back, also breathless and gesturing wildly to the sound of the fray. 'Svatopluk and his men have descended on the Hemingr's ship mid-water. By my reckoning, a third are down,' Knudd replied.

'The first half of the Holmgardr men has reached the tributary, but they are matched for numbers and both sides are putting up a fight,' Varr added.

'We go now,' Eskil commanded. 'Archers and your support to the ramparts. The rest of you form up. You say that Svatopluk's men are on the shore?' Eskil asked Knudd, who nodded. 'Then we will swing east and come up behind them on the flat ground. You all know what to do. Let's go bloody crush some rebel skulls,' he cried.

Most of Aldeigjuborg's forces left to cover the seven hundred paces between us and the rebels. The archers, Sven, Othere and Bonde were ordered to take their place on the ramparts, as their guards, Slodi, Hilde's son, Andrei, and I, followed them. Our position was atop the slope that rose high above the shore below, on top of the earthen ramparts. Stone slabs had been laid, and a small defensive mound had been constructed to hide from rebel arrows. It was not as protective as Aldeigjuborg's wooden walls. There were no spiked palisades to duck behind. When you were up there, you were exposed, unless you could move faster than your enemy.

Luckily, no one had noticed our appearance; they were too busy exchanging blows with each other on the rocky shoreline, half in the water near the intersection of the Volkhov and its small tributary. All that separated us and the enemy was one hundred paces and a steep decline to the fighting grounds. Sven, Othere and Bonde smiled, nocking their bows, knowing their weapons would be accurate and deadly at this range.

'Don't give us away until Eskil and Laslo appear,' Othere directed. 'We'll be able to pick a few off while they are distracted, and we don't want to risk hitting any of our own men.'

Andrei, Slodi and I crouched before the archers, holding our shields together to form a small wall we all stood behind. It was our job to protect them so they might concentrate on finding a target below,

'I'd prefer to be down in the fighting,' Slodi grumbled next to me.

'When our job is done, we can run down and get the stragglers,' Othere replied.

Andrei pointed. 'Here comes Eskil.'

On the shore behind the Slavs, Hemingr's men howled, seeing their reinforcements had finally arrived. Their dead lay in the shallows, and the rest of them had hardly made it out of the boats before being harried. The other half of the Holmgardr men, the ones who had disembarked near the waterfall, were still fording the shallow tributary in shin-deep water and were also engaged in the fighting.

Aldeigjuborg's forces, numbering over fifty, stepped out of the forest and screamed in unison. Eskil roared before his men, like a bear full of fury. He cut an intimidating figure dressed in his battle gear and standing a head above the others. Behind Eskil's guards were the merchants who yelled insults, and behind them were the farmers who waved their long weapons above the ones in front and made as much noise as they could. It was a terrifying sight, and, I thought, if they had not been on my side, I may not have acted with bravery.

Battle ceased for a moment as a ripple of panic ran through the rebel men who now understood how severely outnumbered they were. Some turned, looking to flee. Between the Volkhov to the west, Hemingr's men behind them on the northern shore and Eskil to the east, they realised they were penned in. A few scrambled up the southern slope, trying to use the ramparts we stood on as an escape.

Bonde drew back his bowstring, aiming it at one rebel climbing the hill. As soon as the man looked up and saw the archers, he knew he was done. Bonde loosed his arrow, sending it through the air, straight through the man's face.

'And that's why she's called Skull-Piercer,' he announced as he took another arrow from his quiver.

Sven, Othere and Bonde released three arrows apiece onto the enemy. The Slavs were executing their parries with increasing desperation, trying to draw back from one-on-one combat to form some kind of shield wall.

Eskil and Laslo's forces crashed into them like a wave, forcing the rebels backwards. The likelihood of the arrowhead finding an unintended target increased as the two sides pushed against the other.

A core of fifteen Slavs had managed to withdraw, including three men dressed more impressively than the others. One I recognised as Svatopluk and the other two must have been voivodes from other tribes that supported the rebellion. Two other leaders, who by the screams of their group were named Volodimiru and Igori, stepped back into the shield wall. The shields they held differed from the round ones used in Gardarike. Theirs were longer than they were wide, and when locked together and overlapped gave the appearance of shingles. The rebels boxed themselves in on the side, and the second line held their shields high to form a flat roof, keeping out the arrows.

Outside of the rebel shield wall remained ten men. One pressed Olaf of Aldeigjuborg back, hoping to have a moment to retreat to Svatopluk's group. The feint did not work. Olaf stepped back on his right foot and hooked the blade of his axe on his enemy's shield and yanked it out of the man's hands. Without a shield, the Slav tried to defend the blows, but Olaf was ruthless. Faking a right-handed blow to his opponent's left, the rebel shifted his stance, blocking with his left arm, while Olaf quickly changed grips and shoved his opponent onto the ground with the eye of the weapon. Once floored, Olaf stood on the man and, with an almighty arc, cleaved the centre of the rebel's body open.

Hemingr's forces harried the Slav shield wall, slashing below the blockade at ankles and toes. The rebel men that remained outside of the defences cried for help, but no one was willing to break from the group to rescue them. They were picked off, run through with saxes and spears without mercy.

With nothing more to do than kill whoever remained behind the shields, the entirety of Hemingr's remaining men, and Aldeigjuborg's combined forces, turned towards them.

'Odin's beard!' I cursed. 'We're useless up here if they have those shields up.' With the field so close quartered, we could shoot no arrows.

'Look!' Sven shouted.

The roof of the shield wall slid open. Eskil, Laslo and Hemingr drew back. Our men crowded the foreground, looking confused. Next, the shield wall loosened enough to allow the man in the centre to launch a half-sized javelin towards us. It went soaring through the air.

'Nock,' Othere urged. 'Loose, men. As fast as you can!'

Our arrows found a target within the gap in the shingles, taking down two men inside the wall before it closed up, but no one could hit the javelin thrower.

'Move,' Eskil roared, as the javelin curved back to the ground, short of the ramparts but headed for a group of merchants in the heart of the pack. Men jostled, and some on the periphery ran, but for those in the middle, it was too late. The tip of the javelin pierced Torketill straight through the head, skewering him to the ground.

'Aw, not Torketill. He was a lively bastard,' Slodi grumbled, watching the old merchant twitch on the shaft.

'I'm going to be sick,' Andrei groaned beside me.

I grabbed him by the arm. 'Keep doing what you're doing, watch and move quickly.'

The javelin thrower was unmistakably targeting the archers, but his range was just about equal to the distance between us, the accuracy of that estimate I was not willing to test.

Below, Eskil and Hemingr returned to hacking at the Slav's shields, the edging of some splintering. With great strength, the rebels pushed back the front line of our forces and the roof opened once more.

'Sven, you focus on that cursed javelin thrower,' Othere directed. 'Bonde and I will aim for the leaders. If we get them, their men won't keep fighting.'

Looking up behind me, I saw my friend place a new arrow on the front of his bow, drawing the bowstring back between the fore and the middle finger of his other hand. Inside the wall, as I looked towards the fight once more, the javelin thrower prepared, his right arm angled to give power to his launch. Sven released his arrow, and it whistled through the sky above our men's heads and arced down perfectly to penetrate the javelin thrower in the neck before he had a chance to release the weapon.

'May Odin feed you to the crows,' Sven bellowed in triumph. 'Did you see that?' he asked, kneeing me gently in the back as I remained crouching before him.

With the javelin thrower dispatched, our forces were crazed for the final slaughter. Swords jabbed the gaps between the enemy shields, axes hacked the shields to shreds. Longer weapons, such as pickaxes and spears, were raised overhead to harass the rebels who, our men screamed, were not brave enough to leave their defences to fight.

'We're not needed up here anymore,' Othere said. 'There are only twelve of them left, maybe less, and I want one. Signe and Sven, stay up here and get any of the weasels that try to flee. The rest of you follow me if you desire glory.' He nodded to Slodi and Bonde, who were only too eager to follow. 'For Valhalla!' he roared, leading the way down the slope. Andrei went down after them but did not run into the fray.

Inside the enemy shield wall, the men were growing tired. Their shields slumped lower to the ground, gaps widened and the rebels slipped on the boggy ground. Eskil had forced the group back onto the shore where the ground was marshy and unstable. Hemingr's men opened their lines, permitting the Slavs to move further back until they were at the water's edge. Our forces continued to hack at their shields until they had nothing left. The rebels broke apart and prepared for the final fight. Scenting blood, our men pushed harder, dividing the remaining men until three or four of our fighters encircled each one of theirs. Some of the combined Aldeigjuborg and Holmgardr men teamed up and toyed with their rival until they had tired of the sport.

The first of the leaders to fall was Igori, his brilliantly coloured cloak splashed with his own blood, as a group of Aldeigjuborg's resident merchants hacked into his shoulder. Distracted by the melee, I did not see another spear thrower who sprinted for the hill until he was at the base of the ramparts, defended by three farmers. Andrei, David and Stanislaus had stood away from the fighting, having no desire to kill when so many others fought for the opportunity. The Slav launched upon the men, thrusting his iron-tipped weapon towards them.

'No!' I screamed, watching the scene twenty paces away.

It was too late. The spearhead punctured Andrei's chest, stopping at the wings of the weapon. The rebel could not have hoped to survive. Once David and Stanislaus ripped the spear from his hands, they pushed him to the ground and ran him through with his own weapon. Stanislaus knelt beside his older brother, cradling Andrei's head as blood bubbled from the dying man's wound.

Rooted to the spot, I watched Knudd and Dimitri goad Volodimiru with their axes in the shallow water on the shore, prodding and nicking him. The voivode shrieked as Dimitri hacked his arm, almost severing it. The limb remained attached by sinew, and as Volodimiru cowered, hugging his dangling stump to his chest, the Aldeigjuborg men laughed at his defect. Knudd pushed the leader to the ground, dunking his head into the river.

'This is horrific,' I cried to Sven.

Knudd knelt on Volodimiru's body below the surface, cackling to the crowd gathered behind him. The Slav leader's hand, grasping a small dagger, rose from under the water, and he plunged it into Knudd's chest. Knudd keeled over, his blood running into the river, and Volodimiru struggled to his feet, standing proud as ten of Hemingr's men, and Knudd's friend Varr descended upon him.

I turned away.

'This is war, Astrid,' Sven spoke softly, with his hand on my shoulder.

'Then I vow I will never be part of it again.'

He tutted. 'That's not a vow you can keep. There might be a time when you have to fight for what is yours, defend your life and that of others.'

From the shore, there was cheering, and I looked down to see what horrors would occur next.

'What are they doing?' Sven asked.

The group of men blocking our view stepped back as Eskil pulled the last remaining rebel to his feet by his long brown hair. Svatopluk, the man who had entered Aldeigjuborg and tried to garner support, the one who thought he could overthrow the northern land for those who had failed to keep it before. The man who started this all.

'I'll be taking your pretty little *vedunya* back to Holmgardr with me,' Hemingr promised, forcing Svatopluk onto his knees as Eskil unsheathed his sword.

The defeated leader looked up at Hemingr in terror.

Eskil sauntered forwards. He raised his blade before bringing it down into the space between Svatopluk's head and his neck, trying to sever it from his body, but it took three attempts. All the while, Svatopluk's lower half thrashed against the violence.

'For Odin!' Eskil roared, holding the Slav leader's head aloft by its shaggy hair. All the men banged their weapons on their shields and cried to the gods of their victory.

'Your head will adorn the gates of Aldeigjuborg!' Hemingr bellowed, and he kicked Svatopluk's headless form on the ground.

Bodies lay everywhere, some on the earth, some floating in the water. The work of picking over the dead had begun, and men were already bickering over the best finds, claiming they had delivered the death blow.

I closed my eyes and exhaled the intensity that had gripped me since the moment we left the walls. When I opened them again, I caught a glimpse of dull metal in the corner of my vision, then my head met the ground with a thunk and all the world went black.

EPILOGUE

ALDEIGJUBORG, GARDARIKE, LATE SPRING 883CE

They say, one day the end of everything will come. When that happens, there will be no light, no warmth, no food. Man will become so desperate to feed himself that he will kill his kin to fill his belly. Then the fighting will begin, and each will slay the other until nobody remains. Not the gods, not the stars, perhaps not even the Norns who weave each man and woman's fate. In the end, there will be nothing but darkness.

As I lay on the ground, the day of the battle with the world was black to me, I could have sworn it was the end of days. But it wasn't. The world had not sunk into the sea. It still existed, and when Sven pulled me to my feet after the battle's conclusion, I knew that I, too, had escaped the abyss and would live. It was not my time to die.

The injury to my right eye had stolen my sight from that side. When I was brought to the healer, she had mumbled that I was lucky the blow had missed the socket and cracked my brow bone instead. Pain and swelling did not leave me feeling fortunate, but I had only been robbed of one eye. I could thank Odin for that. Though a week had passed, it remained unclear if my vision would return in time or if I was blinded permanently. Still, it left me with a grisly appearance, and I was told one half of my face was black and blue.

Curiously, when your eyes cannot assess a person's body, their words become clearer. Your mind does not fool you with the actions others want you to see while they hide their true intentions. A waver in the voice betrays lies, deceit by forcefulness, and love with a presence that lingers well after a person leaves your side.

Hilde sobbed beside me, knelt on the ground over the mound that contained her eldest son Andrei's remains. As she keened, I felt the deep love turned to grief.

'Stanislaus will be the eldest of our family now,' Helga whispered next to me. Her brother, Stanislaus, behind us hunched his shoulders forward and was murmuring a prayer for the older brother he had lost in the battle against the rebels.

'He vill vatch over his sister, Alva,' Hilde managed between the cries. 'I pray God vill take them into his paradise.'

Helga clasped my forearm, leading me to kneel next to her mother, away from her husband, Mikel. 'Though she was not of our faith, we will keep Freyja in our hearts and our prayers also,' she sniffled.

Where children went after death was as uncertain for us who worshipped the old gods as it was for the Christians. Some say they have nowhere to go, or that they dwell in the light-drenched plains of Hel, far from the dark corners in which they would trap people like Neflaug. Others, however, claimed their family took the innocent to the feasting halls of Valhalla to keep them company. It heartened me to think of Freyja meeting my father, Tarben. Him, taking her to his knee and telling her stories as he did when I was a girl.

I squeezed Helga's arm as a familiar lump in my throat stole my words. My daughter's tiny sleeping cap had not left the pouch that was tied to my belt since the day it was discovered. I kept it with me always, a talisman just as Bjarndýr had become.

'In the spring, we'll lay blossoms here for her too,' Helga whispered.

Sometimes it worried me that Freyja's remains were never found. I wondered where she was and hoped that she had not drifted far from the only home she had known. But then I reminded myself, if she had gone to Valhalla with my father, the gods would fetch her and she would have all she might ever need.

'Are you sure you are well enough to travel?' Helga asked as we walked to the banks of the Volkhov.

'I'm alright, I still have one good eye,' I joked. 'Besides, I won't be alone.'

'Yes, Sven will be there,' she replied, looking at Sven as he comforted Stanislaus and Hilde's younger children.

'I owe him my life,' I said, recalling the moment awareness left me at the mercy of my attacker.

'And he owes you his,' she responded. 'The only reason they ambushed you were because you were protecting him.'

'Then the debt is equal.'

'You can't delay a few more days to recover? To know if your eyesight will return?' she pleaded.

'It's time, Helga. I need to be with Kjarr and tell him everything.'

'What will he think when you turn up looking like this?' she asked, stroking the unbruised part of my face with a gentle hand.

'That I got hit in the face defending Aldeigjuborg. My husband and the Grand Prince should be thankful,' I replied curtly.

'Oooh,' she exclaimed, clutching my shoulder with one hand, the other at her round belly. 'They kick me constantly. I cannot believe you're leaving me before the *barns* come.'

'Are you still convinced there is more than one in there?'

'She says there are two,' Hilde answered, walking in between us.

Sven and Mikel also joined us on the bluff. 'How do you feel about two coming at once?' Sven asked Mikel.

'One or two, it's all a surprise to me,' Mikel shrugged.

We laughed. It was nice to have something to look forward to and to lighten the clouds that had hung over our lives the past year.

'This is what I will miss the most,' I said, 'being with all of you.'

'Promise us you will be careful and not forget us,' Helga urged.

'And if you can, come back to us,' Hilde wished aloud.

'Of course. I have to make sure our business is going well,' I replied. 'And, of course, I would not miss the chance to see you all again.'

'It's time to go,' Sven said, looking towards the docks. He smiled, but I could tell it was hard even for him. 'Thank you for taking care of us,' he said as he hugged Hilde and Helga.

'Will you come down to the river to wave us around the bend?' I asked.

'Even better than that,' Mikel beamed. 'Laslo said we can go up on the walls to watch until you are out of sight.' His excitement at being closer to the sky outweighed any sadness over our departure.

Hilde shifted on the spot. 'I don't know if I vill be able to see over the valls.'

'I'll find you a step,' Mikel offered, taking his mother by marriage by the arm towards the town for their vantage point.

'Come on, Astrid, we should go,' Sven urged.

Helga clung to me like a child. 'I promise I'll wave until you are gone,' she mumbled into my shoulder.

'Oh, Helga.' My voice caught as I spoke. 'I will miss you.'

She kissed my cheeks and pushed me away. 'Go now or I might just hold you so tightly that you can't leave.'

Sven dragged me by the hand.

'Take care of those babies. I'll want to see them when I am here next,' I yelled over my shoulder as she swatted away tears with the back of her hand.

There was a light wind that whipped through the cornflower blue sky, perfect conditions for a river journey, and even more ideal for drying tearful eyes. The breeze caught my hair and sent tendrils over my face, obscuring what remained of my vision. I followed Sven across the bridge, through the Enggatt that led to the place where I had lived these past years. Within its fortifications had been so much happiness, but also fear and sorrow.

'Will you miss it?' Sven asked, not for the first time.

'I know it's time to go, but I will remember Aldeigjuborg fondly,' I replied as we continued through the town.

We strode down the embankment, to the docks, where our crew had completed loading Kjarr's belongings into Sihtric's ship. Most men named their vessels something fearsome, like *Dragon-Fire*, or *Beast-Wing*, or a merchant vessel, *Gold-Bringer*, as an encouragement for their success. But Sihtric had named his ship the *Bhobain*, which he told me meant "my darling little rascal" in some foreign tongue. Apparently, it was the name his mother always called him, and he styled the ship in her memory.

Our shipmates were elated. Our success against the Slavs had increased the excitement of the journey. And, Eskil had been positively jubilant every time he passed Svatopluk's gruesome head skewered on a pike near the main gate. Though he was much happier to forget the fact that his newly purchased slave, Toki, had been the one to attempt to warn the rebels. Now, Eskil was without a thrall, although he declared he would purchase another from the markets in Kyiv. Thorsten, Gunnar, Frodi, Eskil and Sihtric's slave, Kari, were already perched at the oars on-board the *Bhobain*, while Sihtric stood at the fore and Björn at the steering oar. The remaining passengers, Ahmed Ibn Rashti and Gunnar's female thrall, Odrun, were seated at the aft. When we joined them on-board, we took our place on the benches to relieve the others when the time came.

As we cast off, I found my feelings mixed, anticipating my reunion with Kjarr but dreading having to leave everything familiar to me. Time would fade that reluctance, and I would come to look forward to the adventure ahead. The oars dipped below the surface, increasing our speed with each stroke.

People gathered on the docks and on the banks. Even the guards had turned out to see off their previous captain. And, as we looked up at the towering walls above us, there they were. Hilde, Helga and Mikel were flapping their hands in the air and singing their farewells into the wind.

'Goodbye, friends,' I whispered. 'Wherever I go, this shall have been my beginning.'

AUTHOR'S NOTE

The Viking Age has been a great fascination of mine for many years. Initially, I stumbled upon the Vikings on my morning commute when I lived in the outer suburbs of the Mornington Peninsula and worked in the inner city of Melbourne. Back then, I had a two-hour commute both ways, and I became a prolific reader of just about anything historical. It was the archaeological evidence that reignited my interest in history after years spent studying it at University. The gravesite discoveries I read about conjured the lives that accompanied the objects. From there, I fell into the deep rabbit hole of researching this time period and learning about Norse mythology, language, culture, and customs. I was hooked. Once the characters were on paper, they had lives of their own. I simply recorded it for them.

As I delved into researching back in 2015, I realised that the people known as Vikings were not a homogenous group that dreamed only of raiding and killing. It became clear they were a variety of communities that also traded and peacefully settled throughout the lands we now know as England and Europe. Now, of course, I am not saying that all of their exploits were conducted with a friendly hand. However, what we usually read about the Vikings omits their trading voyages and assimilation into faraway lands.

My hope in writing the Viking Trading Lands Series, though fiction-alised, is to show the multi-faceted impact the Scandinavians had on the wider world. A person could be a farmer, a raider, and a trader at the same time or at different points in their lives. Though, for the moment, the modern depiction is the sensational image of a warrior intent on wealth and renown - one who delights in rape, pillage, and murder. In reality, we do not know to what extent this is factual.

With any merging of people, there will be tensions. Just as there are today, those living in the ninth century might have found individuals different from themselves, dangerously 'other'. We have many records of armies fighting over religion, ideological and cultural differences. Even the tribal groups that occupied the land, referred to as Gardarike in this novel, fought. The terms used, and the discord between the cultural groups in this book reflect the tensions of the time and in no way reflect the author's sentiments.

Most of what we know about the Vikings comes from works written either well after the time they described, or recorded by outsiders to the cultures of the north. A large part of Rus' Viking knowledge comes from The Primary Chronicle, thought to have been written by a Christian monk named Nestor the Chronicler. Composed around 1113 CE, we must view this through the lens of legitimising rule as was often the catalyst for beginning these expansive works. Other texts which record the events of the Viking Age include Mission to the Volga by Ahmad ibn Fadlan, an Arabic diplomat, written in the tenth century. This is widely considered the best depiction of Viking funeral rites and is reported with as much objectivity as one can expect from the time. Christian monk Alcuin in the eighth century wrote of the pagans that descended upon the monastery at Lindisfarne and spilled blood there. Alcuin is often cited as being one of the most important writers during this time because of his later position in the Carolingian court, thus taking his knowledge of the Viking impact across to the continent. Such recordings are not without the skew of their writer's beliefs and are written from the perspective of the victims. As we know, the Scandinavians of this time period had not begun recording their own chronicles. There would be a prolific explosion of sagas in Iceland in the thirteenth century, but even these texts tell us little of daily life.

For evidence of the past, we must turn to archaeological digs, and study the way things work in practice. However, even these are not above dissent. The different methodologies employed can cause varied conclusions. Even so, when researching this period, there is a lack of contemporaneous reports. The rest is filled in with what we deem possible until proof reveals itself.

A few notes on the content of this novel. While I have detailed above that this work is one of fiction, some will question the basis of some elements. Below, I have drawn out some of these to explain my position.

Some readers might be quick to find the houses in Aldeigjuborg inconsistent with descriptions of the dwellings we know as part of a Viking community. In the archaeological evidence found in this settlement, there is an absence of longhouses and a prevalence of what is referred to as 'big houses'. These types of structures have been, thus far, only identified in Aldeigjuborg, and whilst they may not be entirely identical to those described in this novel, they differ from those held in our minds.

The current fortress at Staraya Ladoga was built in the sixteenth century. Some glimpses of a previous tenth-century structure remain, but nothing from its earlier wooden fortifications. A lot of the descriptions of the town are educated guesswork based on the natural attributes of the land, hills, marshes, and so on, and what is currently built on that land. Excavations have found evidence of all manner of artisanal enterprise, including glass, bronze, and fabric, and interestingly, a smithy which was deduced by the discovery of a hearth and anvil.

In addition to the settlement, the last battle scene in *No One's Viking* takes place in what I have named the Abandoned Paragon. Whilst this location exists, it is now known by the name Lubshanskaya Fortress. Nowadays, it is little more than an overgrown area with some hints of stone walls hidden among the foliage. It is thought to have been built in the seventh century by a Slavic group in their efforts to defend the strategic position overlooking the Volkhov River. The location was a mere two kilometres away from Aldeigjuborg, though there was little overlap between the habitation of both locations.

There are contrasting opinions on the significance of the structure and its subsequent abandonment. One thought is that the location was abandoned when the Rurikid dynasty was established. Another is that it was abandoned because of fighting between the tribes and lack of maintenance. Finally, another hypothesis suggests the disuse was due to changes in the terrain because of erosion, which saw the transfer of importance to the nearby post of Aldeigjuborg. My preference is for a combination of the above effects, though changes to the topography of the land are particularly evident in this area. Either way, the location was certainly abandoned sometime in the ninth century. The fortress itself may have been impressive, with walls almost 12 metres high, the size of the fortification estimated to be up to one and a half kilometres squared. Work is still needed to ascertain the size, importance, and use of the location, and I am sure we will learn more about this site in time. The Abandoned Paragon certainly made for an interesting setting for the final chapter.

The establishment of the Rurikid dynasty, named after the initial ruler of Gardarike, Rurik, is shrouded in a fog of mystery. Again, we face multiple theories surrounding the origin of the founder. Rurik is cited as having been a Danish Prince, a pirate, and a warrior, depending on the source material. His ethnicity is also unclear. In some authorities, he is a Dane, others a Swede, or even a Slav. As if his descent was uncertain enough, his rise to power was also ambiguous. He was either called to rule by the warring tribes and provide stability, or took the region by force. What is clear, though, is by the end of the ninth century and well into the tenth, the Rus' territories drew in wealth. We could say this was the golden age of Gardarike lands.

Hierarchy during the Viking Age was divided into four classes; the ruler and his family, well-to-do households, including wealthy merchants and well-regarded warriors, everyone else, and slaves. During this period, the mobility between the middle two ranks was greater. The opportunity to make one's fortune by exploiting the growing empire was obtainable owing to rapid expansion and the need for skilled men.

Readers might be surprised to discover warriors in the top ranks of society, but in the Viking Age, land was held by might. Those who had the force to repel would-be invaders remained kings, and those strong enough to take it could become one. Of course, this is an oversimplification. But, what we find in the early days of the Rurikid dynasty is the Grand Prince surrounding himself with the strongest warriors to ensure their continuation of rule. The enigmatic character known to history as Oleg the Prophet will be explored further in the next book of the Viking Trading Lands Series.

During the initial years of the Rus', towns were not garrisoned, or at least, we have no evidence this was the case. This is consistent with what we know of Norse Viking settlements, which were defended by the people who lived within them. On the whole, there were no standing armies. Raiding parties and defending forces comprised men who owed allegiance to their Jarl, King, or overlord. When they were called to do their duty, they would gather to fight against their foe from their far-flung farms and settlements.

The Vikings were masters of the small group attack, using surprise to their advantage. They had, what appears to us with the lacking written evidence, an uncanny knack for happening upon undefended lands with rich pickings. But a lack of documentation is not proof of reality, and, I am convinced, they did not turn up to these lands without doing reconnaissance first. It is reasonable to suppose that for years before the raid on Lindisfarne, Scandinavians were trading and observing before making their move.

Around the tenth century, coastal areas of the British Isles and Europe wised up to the threat of Viking raids, and it was about this time guerrilla warfare was exchanged for military strategy. Now that the Vikings had secured lands in England, Eastern Europe, and Frankia, they would have to learn to defend them. Smash and grab strategies were no longer effective. So, it stands to reason that a guard would emerge to protect its citizens. Though I admit, the guard of Aldeigjuborg is fictionalised, we have evidence of such armies later, and disciplined warriors serving the Byzantine emperors of Constantinople. But that is a story for another book.

Finally, my sincerest thanks to my supportive family, beta, and ARC readers, editor, and writing communities, without whom this process would have been more difficult. All the assertions of the historical environment in this book are my own and any mistakes or misinterpretations of the sources are also mine.

If you enjoyed this book, I'd appreciate a short review. Sharing your thoughts can really help new readers find this book, and make a big difference. Want to get in touch?

Connect with the Viking Merchant newsletter and be the first to know about upcoming releases, Viking Trading Land's promotions, and even some freebies by signing up at: www.meganformanek.com/free

9 780648 808824